Resounding Praise for

TANYA ANNE CROSBY

VIKING'S PRIZE

"A TANTALIZING TALE
that will hold you in thrall."
Romantic Times

"ABSOLUTELY ENDEARING . . .
Tanya Anne Crosby at her best!"
The Medieval Chronicle

SAGEBRUSH BRIDE

"Never has a tale so captured my
imagination and heart"
Affaire de Coeur

ANGEL OF FIRE

"SUPERB . . .
You won't be able to put it down."
Rendezvous

TANYA ANNE CROSBY

ONCE UPON A KISS

An Avon Romantic Treasure

AVON BOOKS ◆ NEW YORK

ONCE UPON A KISS is an original publication of Avon Books. This work has never before appeared in book form. This work is a novel. Any similarity to actual persons or events is purely coincidental.

AVON BOOKS
A division of
The Hearst Corporation
1350 Avenue of the Americas
New York, New York 10019

Copyright © 1995 by Tanya Anne Crosby
Inside cover author photo by Gary Eaton Studios
Published by arrangement with the author
Library of Congress Catalog Card Number: 94-96261
ISBN: 0-380-77680-4

First Avon Books Printing: February 1995

AVON TRADEMARK REG. U.S. PAT. OFF. AND IN OTHER COUNTRIES, MARCA REGISTRADA, HECHO EN U.S.A.

Printed in the U.S.A.

RA   10   9   8   7   6   5   4   3   2

To sweet, sizzling, unforgettable first kisses

So help me God, I am astonished that this worthy man decided to inform my husband of his shame and dishonour, that his wife has had two sons. They have both incurred shame because of it, for we know what is at issue here: It has never occurred that a woman gave birth to two sons at once, nor ever will, unless two men are the cause of it.

—MARIE D' FRANCE, LE FRESNE

Chapter 1

England
The Reign of Stephen

'Twas a mortal sin.

To lust after one's brother's wife.

Not that they were wed as yet . . . but soon enough they would be, and he had no license to burn as he did.

It was the crimson she wore, he told himself, that set him afire. Dominique Beauchamp was ablaze as she rode within the bailey atop her small palfrey. Her gown was rich crimson; her cloak, crimson; her lips, as sumptuous a shade as the ruby jewel she wore at her breast. And her hair . . . it burned a shimmering copper beneath the late afternoon sun, a glorious mass of ringlets that defied rule. Like some enchanted faerie creature, all of her seemed to glimmer with each stride of her horse . . .

Against his will, his body quickened at the sight of her.

She was bold, he decided with a shudder. Perchance too bold. Why else would she ride so fearlessly into their dominion? *What did she*

1

hope to gain? Whatever it was, it was other than she claimed, he was certain.

She was dangerous, he sensed.

Still he craved her . . . craved as never before . . . and for an instant . . . for the first time in his life . . . he coveted his brother's place—though only for an instant, and then he cast the unforgivable sin away, to that black hollow deep within his soul.

Hardening his heart against her, Blaec d'Lucy cast a glance at his brother, scrutinizing Graeham's reaction to the woman who had elicited such a profound response in himself. Graeham stood impassive, seemingly unaffected by the creature riding so proudly into their midst, looking every bit a pagan sacrifice of old.

Did she feel herself a sacrifice?

He wondered, wishing he knew precisely what was in his brother's mind. Graeham's face revealed, if aught, a slight uneasiness, though little else. For his part, Blaec only wished he were so undisturbed, and he couldn't keep himself from wondering how else he might respond were he the one receiving this barter-bride today.

Impatient? Doubtful? Mistrusting?

Not indifferent, he was certain.

Never indifferent—and he couldn't help but consider, too, that had he been given his rightful place as heir . . . she would have, in truth, been his.

Aye, he knew.

He'd known for long, for confidences were rarely private with so many ears about. Yet it mattered not, for he was firstborn merely by a matter of moments, and if aught wounded him more, it was the simple fact that his father had all but disowned him. The truth was that he'd sworn to serve his brother, and serve him he would until his last waking breath.

If he felt aught of anger, it was for the simple fact that their father had done Graeham an injustice, consigning him as leader, for either his brother knew naught of warfare, despite his years of battle training, or he held himself a death wish. Which of the two, Blaec knew not. Only one thing was certain: Graeham *needed* him. God's truth, but the fool battled with one leg e'er in the grave. Of a certain his younger twin brother would never have survived this long without him, and Blaec had long made it his life's purpose to protect Graeham at any cost.

Straightening to his full height, he turned to find her riding toward them still, her shoulders back, her posture erect, her eyes—she was near enough now that he could spy their color— deepest blue.

And brilliant . . . as though with unshed tears.

Reluctant, was the thought that first came to mind. His gaze shifted to the man riding beside her upon his own steed, his dress as lavish as her own, and then back.

Aye, he decided, 'twas reluctantly she'd come to do her brother's bidding.

Nevertheless . . . she'd come, and with that knowledge came a surge of rancor.

For in truth, he did not trust her.

Most assuredly, he did not trust her treacherous brother.

Like his father before him, William Beauchamp was to be suspected—despite that he offered peace between them. Most especially not when he offered his exquisite young sister in the bargain. Graeham was unwise to think it would end so simply. These two were involved in some intrigue, and whatever they were after, he would discover it, by God.

That, he vowed as vehemently as he did that he would not—he refused to—covet his brother's bride.

This, then, was to be her prison?

A quiver raced down Dominique's spine at the sight of the stronghold that loomed before her.

It appeared so.

Upon their approach, Drakewich had appeared animated with preparations for their arrival—a flurry of movement upon the castle walls—yet now that they were within the bailey, it seemed more forbidding a place than London had surely been to the Empress Matilda—and she had been driven from the city by an angry horde! Not a soul stirred, neither to greet them nor to spurn them, yet for the latter, at least, she was grateful. Even the donjon itself seemed a formidable thing, with its dark, high tower windows. From such a great height, a body could spy from the shadows and never be seen. 'Twas no wonder William had sought this alliance; never in her life had she seen the likes of Drakewich, so vast and so impenetrable did the stone fortress appear from within.

Had she truly thought it modest from without? Had she dared deem Arndel its equal? Leaning discreetly toward her brother, she murmured beneath her breath, "They seem so . . . so inhospitable . . ."

"Do they?" William answered noncommittally.

She looked at him incredulously. Sweet Mary, but how could he not have noted the overly cool reception? Even beyond the curtain walls, the villeins kept their silent vigils from the portals of their scanty wattle-and-daub homes.

Frowning, William berated her. "You fret overmuch, Dominique," he said.

"Nay, William," she denied at once, "'tis but that . . ." She cast him a despairing glance. "What if they will not accept me?"

He considered her at last, though the look upon his handsome face was that of amusement rather than concern. "Come now, Dominique, you cannot have expected they would receive you with open arms?"

"Nay, but—"

"Hush. I promise 'twill change with time," he heartened, terminating her protest once and for all. He gave her a conspiratorial wink. "Cease your brooding, sister mine."

Dominique nodded dejectedly, catching her lip between her teeth, recognizing his tone. Lest she incur his anger, she left off at once. Alas, but she could only hope he was right. She sighed, and her gaze strayed toward the area before the donjon, caught by the figure of a man, his stance proud, his countenance dark. She swallowed convulsively. Blessed Mary, but she knew him at once—the Black Dragon. He was unmistakable dressed in Danish black. God's truth, but she'd tried not to imagine him when considering this union, tried not to think of him at all, but seeing him now, she could well believe every tale she'd ever heard recounted of his battle fury.

And more.

Though he appeared to be weaponless, he wore hauberk and chausses, and to her mind no one had ever appeared more prepared for battle. She tried in vain not to gape, but standing there, scrutinizing their approach, he reminded her of the barbarian Viking invaders of legend, his stance threatening even in his unaffected stillness.

Fraught with anxiety, she cast a glance at her brother and found him watching her prudently. Though William smiled in encouragement, panic burst through her at once. There would be no deliverance this day, she knew. *He coveted this too much.*

With all her heart, she wanted to reel her mount about and flee before they chanced to lower the portcullis, entrapping her for always, yet she merely returned William's smile, reminding herself that she did this for him. Still, her heart raced so that it ached. *For him and for peace*, she told herself, trying desperately to calm the ruthless beating within her breast. God's truth, but she thought she would die here where she sat!

Nay, but how long had it been since last William had smiled so? she chided herself. The truth was that he rarely smiled at all, and now . . . now that he found cause to do so— well, she could not fail him. She observed him an instant longer and knew without question that it was the right thing to do.

She would not fail him.

Resolutely she turned toward her future, advising herself that she wanted this, too. It had been far too long, after all—too many battles fought, too much death, and too much enmity. She, too, needed it all to end at long last—for William's sake, for the sake of his soul, as well as her own. And if William was willing to call a truce, so, too, was she. Too long had this vendetta consumed her brother.

Still she shuddered . . . for how could there ever be peace in the Dragon's very den? The thought plagued her.

"Smile, Dominique," William commanded her through clenched teeth, startling her out of her musing. She turned abruptly to find him leaning toward her discreetly. "Smile," he bade her once more. "You look as though you ride to your death."

Mayhap 'twas because she felt so. Still, she made a better effort for William's sake. "I . . . I was searching for my lord, Graeham," she improvised, trying to sound eager. "Perchance do you spy him yet?"

William gave her a sidewise glance. His blue eyes, so like her own, scrutinized her an instant, and then his brows knit as he indicated, with a discreet nod, the very place Dominique had been staring so long. "There," he stated, lifting his chin slightly and glancing in the vicinity in which the infamous Black Dragon stood so ominously. "Standing aside his blackhearted brother."

Dominique's eyes widened, though not at William's epithet, for he used it so oft, it seemed almost an affection. With a stifled gasp, she turned her gaze toward the man standing directly at the Dragon's side.

Sweet Mary, but how could she have missed him? Though as soon as she wondered, she knew. Standing aside the infamous Dragon, her newly betrothed, Graeham d'Lucy, second Earl of Drakewich, was all but indiscernible. In contrast to his brother's darkness, he was colorless: Though his hair, as fair as sun-bleached flax, was the shade so many coveted, it did not stand apart. And his skin, though swarthier than most of his coloring, was merely pale in comparison. Though comely, his features alongside those of his ruthless brother called to mind those of a youth and not a man, for the Dragon's in contrast were harsh, with his black shoulder-length hair and towering height.

At her side, William's voice was soft, thoughtful, as he remarked, "I thought you'd spied him already? Of a certain, you gaped long enough."

His remark seemed to convict her somehow, and her cheeks heated fiercely. Averting her gaze, she drew at her gold-threaded gown with suddenly tremulous hands, straightening the crimson folds. To her immense relief, she was saved from replying, for Graeham d'Lucy started forward to greet them in that instant. The Dragon, on the other hand, stood his mark. His expression, she noted, was as grave as those of Drakewich's tenants, who were observing from their safe perches. A terrible sense of foreboding swept over her suddenly, but she inhaled deeply, bolstered herself, and tore her gaze away to meet that of her betrothed.

"A hearty welcome!" Graeham exclaimed as he sauntered forward. Her mount shied a little at his approach, but she quickly soothed it, returning Graeham's greeting with a wan smile. His pale hair tousled softly in the breeze as he smiled up at her. His brother, on the other hand—well, she refused to look at him again, refused to even think of him. Lifting her chin slightly, she continued to smile serenely down at Graeham. Though, truth to tell, she'd never in her life felt more ill at ease.

"My lord," she said softly, with a gracious tilt of her head. Discreetly, she wiped her palms upon her gown.

He reciprocated her nod and turned to address William. "Welcome, Beauchamp," he exclaimed once more. "Though I fear we did not quite expect you as yet."

There seemed to be a question in his declaration, and William's face fell into a frown. "What say you, Graeham? Did my messenger not reach you?"

There was a moment of taut silence as Graeham glanced briefly toward his brother—

the Dragon shook his head, almost undiscernibly—and then Graeham replied with concern. "Nay... nay... most assuredly he did not. Perchance when did you dispatch this man of yours?"

William at once dismounted, his expression grave as he came to stand before Graeham d'Lucy. "'Tis been overlong now. Surely..." He glanced up at Dominique. "No later than midmorn, I wouldst say?" Dominique thought he might wish an affirmation, yet the instant her lips parted to speak, his brows drew together in condemnation, and he averted his face. "Mayhap he was laid upon by brigands?" he reckoned, with growing distress. "I've heard tell you've been troubled with them of late?"

Dominique's brows knit as she glanced about, wondering who it was that her brother had sent ahead to announce their arrival. She knew all of his men, few enough that there were, and none were unaccounted for this day that she could recall. Nevertheless, if William claimed that he'd dispatched a messenger, he'd dispatched a messenger, for certain. Never had he lied to her. Whatever else she might say of him, he'd never forsworn himself.

"But, William," she ventured, hoping to set him at ease, "we saw no signs of struggle. Were the herald laid upon by brigands, wouldst there not have been evidence *somewhere* along the course? We saw none, did we not?"

Like blue fire, William's gaze snapped up to meet hers, his eyes bright with ire—at what, she knew not. Mayhap he feared to have lost another man when Arndel could little spare them. Yet to her bewilderment, he simply glared at her an interminable moment, as though cautioning her to remain silent. She tilted her head, silently questioning what it was she'd said to anger him so easily, but he said naught, only glared at her.

The silence between them lengthened.

"Perchance he took another route?" a deep voice interjected.

A shuddering raced down Dominique's spine at the intense, slightly mocking sound of it. Without being told, she knew at once who had spoken, and her face flushed as she met *his* gaze. For the boldest instant he held her eyes fast, as though he were appraising her. God's mercy, but she had the perception of being seduced into their clear green depths— and did she not break free, she would be eternally lost. And then abruptly he glanced away, and his release of her was as physical as though he'd thrust her bodily aside. Shaken by his perusal, Dominique averted her gaze to her brother, and at once heard the Dragon call for one of his men to come forward.

"Aye . . . of a certain 'tis so," William agreed, eyeing her wrathfully still. "Mayhap he took another route . . ."

Unnerved, though not by her brother's glare— she'd weathered them afore—but by the Dragon's very presence, Dominique ran her fingers along the length of her mare's reins while attending their discourse. She dared not glance up again for dread of meeting *his* eyes.

"I'd have you search every route betwixt Drakewich and Arndel," she heard him command his man. Like a terrible blade, the sound of his voice sliced through the air, prickling the tiny hairs of her nape.

"Take as many men as you should require and search *every* last route," he reiterated without the slightest pretense at civility. 'Twas evident to Dominique that he cared not a whit whether he offended them.

"Search them thoroughly," he charged the man, "and then report to me at once."

Dominique could scarcely imagine why he'd mistrust such a simple tale. Of course, it made sense that her brother would send a man to herald their arrival. Why would William bear false witness about something so pointless?

"By chance did he reach our borders," Graeham was quick to point out, "and he lived . . . I'd not have it remarked upon that we left a man—a guest at that—to die unshriven upon our lands. You understand, I am certain, Beauchamp," he appealed. "Perchance you might even wish to send along some of your own men to aid in the search?"

Once again William glared up at her, though Dominique kept her gaze averted, watching in her peripheral. She still could not conceive what she might have said.

"Of course," William replied tightly, his gaze reverting to Graeham. "How very obliging of you." And then he turned to the Dragon. "You *serve* your brother well, d'Lucy," he yielded, stressing the word "serve," and leaving Dominique to wonder whether her brother was baiting him. Yet surely not? Not when he'd striven so long for this truce? Still, this was a bitter pill for him to swallow, she knew, and her heart ached for him.

The Dragon said naught, simply stood, and when she ventured a glance, she saw that his eyes were steely, no longer so bright a green, but darkened to gray. Blessed Mary, by the sight of him, the size of him, she thought it unwise for William to rouse him so recklessly: Judging by the feral look in his eyes, she thought he might pounce at William's throat any second. She wanted to speak up, to warn William, but dared say naught more, lest she anger him further.

To her relief, it was Graeham who spoke at last to ease the discord between them. "Perchance he serves me too well," he agreed with a modest smile, and his eyes were momentarily sad with the admission. He placed a hand upon William's shoulder. "Come now, Beauchamp," he bade William. "You and I have much to speak of." He glanced up at her, his dark eyes kind. "Lady Dominique," he bade her, "by your leave?"

It was only then that Dominique realized she'd been holding her breath, for she could only nod at his request. Words would not come. Nevertheless, she was pleased there seemed to be some accord betwixt her brother and Graeham, despite that she felt it rather indelicate to be dismissed so easily—and so directly!

"Certainly, my lord," she managed. "I assure you I would be content to simply take my respite before the evening meal." *And even more elated to remove myself at last from the Dragon's presence*, she added silently. "If you would only be so kind as to direct me along my way?"

Graeham nodded empathetically. "Certainly. The ride from Arndel must have been wearisome," he acknowledged. "Blaec would be pleased to see you to your bower, m'lady." He gave her a smile, one with such sincerity that it took her an instant too long to realize to *whom* it was that Graeham referred, and then her heart leapt into her throat. And yet she had no chance to protest, for with that, her betrothed turned to go and William followed, leaving her entirely alone at the Dragon's mercy.

She swallowed convulsively as she turned to face him, for she'd already determined that in Drakewich's Black Dragon, there was no mercy to be found.

Chapter 2

Every terrifying tale Dominique had ever heard whispered of him sped through her mind in that instant as she stared down into his piercing eyes. Like a blessed half-wit, she sat unmoving upon her mount, her heart racing wildly, and she feared that he might have guessed her thoughts, for his lips curved contemptuously.

"Contrary to what is recounted," he told her, "I do *not* spew flames." His eyes mocked her as he came forward, offering his arms in aid. "Most particularly not to *innocent* maids."

He'd emphasized the word "innocent" as though it were a gauntlet he'd pitched at her feet. And still Dominique sat, staring at his extended arms with something akin to horror, her mind racing at his insinuation. She had no notion what he'd meant by the taunt, nor did she perceive how to respond—nor did she wish for him to touch her. Of a certain she was innocent!

"Demoiselle?" he prompted. One dark brow lifted diabolically. "Have you plans to dismount some hour this day, or did you plan to take that

15

respite you so crave upon that feeble mount of yours?"

Dominique bristled at his arrogance. Forgetting her dread of him for the moment, she pitched aside the reins and asked pointedly, "Are you ever so ill mannered, my lord?"

"Without exception," he answered unremorsefully, and his lips curved yet a fraction more.

Truth to tell, Dominique thought he might even have been grinning save for the wintry chill that remained in those disquieting, scathing eyes of his. She wanted to smite the condescension from his face.

"Demoiselle," he said impatiently, "would you have me assist you, or nay?"

Dominique cursed him beneath her breath, knowing it was within his power to *assist* in making this difficult passage more facile for all. But nay! She had the feeling that he would make it infinitely more difficult were the choice his own.

He advanced upon her abruptly.

Dominique's heart vaulted into her throat. "I can manage well enough of my own, thank you!" Goaded into motion by the merest threat of his touching her—his hands upon her waist—she promptly dismounted, slipping to the ground. In her haste, the hem of her bliaut caught upon the pommel. One foot in the stirrup, the other midway to the ground, she froze the instant she felt the breeze upon her stockinged legs. Her gaze flew to his at once, and her eyes widened in horror at the look upon his face. He shuddered—in revulsion, she thought—and her heart skipped a beat.

"Oh!" she cried.

He moved swiftly to aid her, as though he could not abide the sight of her an instant longer—why his reaction should prick at her, she knew not, though oddly, it did. It wrenched at her heart. It mattered not, she told herself. She'd endured worse in her life, and all that truly signified was that Graeham d'Lucy should find her pleasing. His wrathful brother could fling himself from the highest tower window for all that concerned her! Yet despite her doughty words, her breath remained stilled, wedged painfully within her breast, as she watched his fingers work quickly to liberate her gown. Only when it was free did she dare breathe again.

Though to her dismay, once he'd freed her gown, he merely held it instead of releasing it, snatching it nearer as though to study it closer. Dominique gave a startled shriek as her hem rose higher whilst he tested the material between his fingertips, examining it, his countenance darkening.

"My lord, please!" she exclaimed, struggling with his unrelenting grip to lower her gown. "Please!"

As though recalling himself suddenly, he crushed it violently within his fist and flung it down wrathfully at her feet. It swished about her ankles as his gaze pierced her once more. Gooseflesh erupted upon her skin as she slid the rest of the way to the ground under his critical regard.

"'Tis as fine a cloth as ever I've seen," he yielded tautly, his eyes locking with hers. Sweet Mary, but they were so deep and dark a green—made to look all the darker by the sinister shadows that rimmed them. Yet they suited him, she decided, for they were the eyes of a man who never rested, never trusted. They were the eyes of a dragon, she determined, and he'd lied when he'd claimed he did not spew flames. *He did, though not from his mouth.* His eyes burned her, consumed her—and still she could not break free. 'Twas as though she recognized the menace in him, yet still she allowed him to hold her mesmerized, riveted. She shivered, noting the telltale muscle that ticked at his jaw, and then abruptly he turned from her, releasing her at last. Dominique inhaled a breath, for his dismissal left her reeling.

"This way, if you please, demoiselle."

For an instant Dominique stood, stupefied, watching him go, before she understood that he meant for her to follow. And once again she bristled. Arrogant cur! And more, why she suddenly felt compelled to defend her gown, she knew not, but something in his tone had accused her, she was certain. "My brother wouldst have me at my best," she informed him haughtily, barely keeping pace with his long strides. "After all, 'tis not every day a woman celebrates her marriage *and* peace for her people!"

"I see," he mocked her, turning those sinister eyes upon her. "Then you rejoice in this union with my brother?"

She lifted her chin. "Of course!" she answered. But he didn't reply, merely turned from her and continued toward the donjon. She practically stumbled over her gown in an attempt to keep pace, wishing fervently she were a man so she could challenge him properly. Dearly would she love to wipe the ill-begotten smirk from his face—from his very eyes!

"For the sake of peace, I presume?"

This time he didn't bother even to glance back at her to acknowledge her response, nor even to be certain she followed—curse his hide! "Aye!" she snapped. "Certainly! And why else, my lord?"

"Perchance," he countered, still without turning to acknowledge her, "that is something about which you would care to enlighten us, demoiselle?"

"You do not trust us!" she accused him.

He halted abruptly before the stone steps that led into the great hall, and Dominique nearly collided with his mail clad chest as he turned to face her. Stifling a gasp, she peered up at him, unnerved by his remarkable height. God's love, but she was tall for a woman, taller than some men even, yet still her head scarcely reached his shoulders.

"Let us simply say that I do not convince so easily as my brother," he told her. "Tell me, Lady Dominique . . ."

A quiver sped through her at the way he spoke her name, deeply, sensuously, intimately, as though it were something to be savored and ravished at the same time, yet she perceived it had naught to do with her at all—proof was in the way he'd glared at her only moments before. Nay, she sensed he spoke so always, for the man before her would be passionate in all he did; in battle, peace . . . love . . .

Would he be a passionate lover?

Her heart lurched at the private fancy. Sweet Mary, but what ailed her? Was she no better than her brother's lecherous warriors? *It appeared not.* She steadied herself. Bracing her feet, she lifted her chin, despite the flush that crept into her cheeks. God have mercy on her soul if she'd retained no more delicacy than that. 'Twas no defense at all that she'd lived most of her life without the presence of women, listening to men's banter, for she knew better, after all.

He took a breath, as though to harness his temper, and it was all she could do not to take a backward step in response. "Tell me what prompted you to come so long before the ceremony, Dominique," he demanded of her, his voice lowering with enmity, "when even the banns have yet to be cried."

Dominique's blush deepened, for 'twas the one question she'd asked of herself along the journey to Drakewich. The only explanation she could quite descry was that her brother wished not to allow Graeham the opportunity to change his mind and repudiate her before the ceremony. She knew how desperately he craved this union. "'Tis plain you cannot begin to comprehend," she told him fiercely, "but my brother is eager for peace!" She lifted her chin, gaining confidence with her conviction. "I fear not everyone relishes bloodshed as you seem to, my lord!"

"Nay?" Once again his devil brow arched, and then his face twisted and some sound escaped him, something akin to a snarl. Dominique shrank from him—so much for her show of mettle, she berated herself. Without another word, he spun about and stalked away, this time without prompting her to follow.

Dominique shrieked in indignation. "Nay!" She hastened after him. If he thought he could cast aspersions upon herself and her brother without hearing her speak her mind, he'd need think again. "With every dispute, Arndel loses men-at-arms we are ill equipped to," she yielded angrily. "The butchery must cease at last! Can you not see that?"

"Indeed?" he mocked her, halting once more and swerving abruptly to face her.

This time Dominique collided with him, so agitated was she with his treatment of her. With a startled gasp, she snatched herself away, as though scalded by the unexpected contact. She took a defensive step backward, straightening her gown with quaking hands. "H-Have you no courtesy a'tall?" she asked him shakily. Lord have mercy, her knees felt suddenly too weak to stand. Still, she refused to cower before him.

Ignoring her angry objection to the casual way in which he continued to dismiss her, he imparted, "As I see it, demoiselle, were Arndel in truth at such a loss, 'tis doubtful you'd reveal such to me. Nevertheless, you have the right of it, the butchery *must* cease, and to that end I am willing to accept you and your brother in faith."

He was willing to accept *them* in faith? God's truth, but he was imperious! Her eyes narrowed. "How obliging you are, my lord."

'Twas as though her choice of words had suddenly pushed him past his endurance, and only belatedly did she recall William's taunt. He took a wrathful step toward her, closing the distance between them in a single stride, and it was all Dominique could do not to shriek out in terror and flee. Bending till he near brushed her brow with his lips, he snarled, "Be that as it may, demoiselle, know this; I shall be watching the both of you—for my brother's sake."

A quiver sped down the length of her spine at his foreboding words.

"Are we understood?"

The look upon his face left no doubt as to his meaning. God's truth, but she sensed he would slay even her to protect his endeared brother. "Aye," she answered breathlessly, swallowing, trying to sound as fierce as she was able in the face of his charge, but failing miserably. "You shall find naught untoward with either of us, I-I assure you."

His green eyes bored into her own blue ones, again the impact so palpable, she was forced to take another step backward.

"We shall see," he apprised her. "Time *will* tell, will it not, demoiselle?"

Chapter 3

I ndeed!

Time *would* tell.

Pacing the confines of the chamber she was to call her own until the ceremony, Dominique found herself seething over the way he'd all but accused her. Nor could she so easily forget the manner in which he'd abandoned her within his bedchamber—aye, *his* bedchamber, curse him to damnation! However could she bear it, with all of his possessions amassed about her?

"*Pardon the inconvenience,*" he'd told her, "*but as you are already aware, we did not expect you so soon. There are no other arrangements available. Nonetheless, you must feel free to make my chamber your very own.*" His eyes had mocked her.

"*I shall need my coffers,*" she'd informed him at once.

"*I see,*" he'd said, sounding taxed. "*Perchance you've still another behest? Tell me, demoiselle, is there aught else I can do to assist in making my lady more comfortable?*"

She'd felt the condemned prisoner, given her last request in that moment. "*Nay,*" she'd answered petulantly. And then, *"Naught save to send me my maid."*

His fingers had tightened about the edge of the door, his knuckles whitening—evidence to his displeasure. She could tell it pained him to aid her in any fashion. *"Anything else?"*

"Nay!" she spat, though, in truth, she wished she could think of something just to vex him.

"Then you should have yourself a pleasant rest," he'd imparted coolly, and with that, withdrew, turning and virtually slamming the ash door in her face, the wrathful sound of it rattling her very bones.

Arrogant, misbegotten cur.

When she was mistress here, she would speak to Graeham; Mayhap Graeham would enfe off his brother and remove him far from her presence once and for all.

And mayhap not . . . they did seem rather bound to each other, she reflected, nibbling irately at her lower lip. The notion aggrieved her. Particularly so when she considered what little voice her mother had had in her own home. Truly she had hoped for something more. Looking about her wearily, she noted the simplicity of the chamber. Though 'twas large by most standards, all that occupied the room was a bed, a basin, and a brazier, along with a few coffers. Still, it was filled with him, all that he owned: his shield, his armor, his scent . . .

Ludicrous! she reproved herself, shuddering at the notion. How could she possibly know his scent? *Yet, somehow, she did.*

With another shudder, she sat upon *his* bed, testing it with a slight bounce, and trying des-

perately not to think of it as *his bed*. Instead, she
returned her thoughts to her mother. The truth
was that she scarcely recalled her mother—or
her father, for that matter—for her mother had
perished of fever when she'd been naught but a
child. Her father had died long before she'd come
of age—murdered by the lord of Drakewich in
a dispute over land in the eleventh year of
Stephen's reign. She shook her head at the
incongruity of it all—to be offered now in
wedlock to the very son of her father's foe—
her father's murderer, even!

Still, she could not quite summon the enmity
her brother bore the d'Lucys—at least not
towards Graeham. Her betrothed seemed amiable enough, and she'd been much too young to
feel, much less understand, her childhood loss.
Nay, she could feel no hatred toward him.

The Dragon was another tale entirely.

For him, though she knew him not at all,
Dominique felt little *but* enmity. Despite tales
to the contrary, she imagined he was just the
image of his despised father—if not in coloring,
then in temperament.

Be that as it may, she'd already determined
to do what was necessary for the sake of peace.
Too many at Arndel depended upon her for
her to fail them now. Moreover, she wanted
so desperately to have again the William who
had once been; the William who had shared his
confidences with her, the William who had loved
and laughed with her as a child, the William who
had lived . . . for something other than revenge.

The last thing she intended was to allow the

Dragon to muddle their plans. If *he* intended to look for cause to mistrust her brother and herself, then she vowed he'd not find it. She would make absolutely certain all appeared as it should. And henceforth, till he found indication enough to trust them, she would slay him with kindness. That would show him. She nodded determinedly. She only hoped he would feel reprehensible when the truth came known. At the notion, she struck the mattress with a clenched fist, thinking that the bastard Dragon probably knew naught of compunction at all, and she was likely wasting her time. With a heartfelt sigh, she fell back upon the massive bed to await Alyss and the arrival of her coffers.

"M'lady!" Alyss exclaimed in surprise, peeping in hours later to find Dominique lying in silence, staring at the ceiling. "Ye're awake?" She entered prudently, closing the door softly behind her as Dominique sat up. Alyss was young and pretty, with dark hair that fell braided to her waist and a face that stole men's attentions, but she was no lady's maid. In truth, till merely a week past, she'd been her brother's leman, and neither of them were as yet at ease with the new arrangement, for neither had Dominique ever had the luxury of someone to serve her in all her years.

"Aye," Dominique relented. "I could not sleep." Who could sleep surrounded by *his* effects? Still, she refrained from saying so, for she had yet to know Alyss well enough to feel so free to confide.

"Forgive me," Alyss entreated, her expression dejected. "They told me you were resting and that I should not disturb you."

Dominique sighed wearily. "I tried but could not," she repeated. And then, recalling the Dragon's parting promise, that he would send Alyss forthwith, she asked, "Did the *Dragon* not find and speak with you?"

Alyss's face seemed to suddenly animate at the mention of his name. Her shoulders rose and she hugged herself. "Oh, yea, m'lady! But William . . . er m'lord . . . as I said, he bade me not to disturb you." She came forward excitedly and seated herself upon the bed beside Dominique in a most familiar way. And though Dominique was slowly becoming used to the assuming way in which Alyss conducted herself, it took her aback. "Oh, m'lady," she exclaimed, "is he not magnificent?"

Dominique's brows knit and her face screwed with disbelief. "*The Dragon?*" Clearly they were *not* speaking of the same man.

"Aye!" Alyss declared. "That face!" She bit at her lower lip, and shivered. "He has the face of a man, m'lady. And those eyes . . ." She smiled at Dominique. "Lonely eyes, is what they are— but compassionate as well."

Dominique's brows rose. "*Compassionate?*" She shook her head incredulously. "Fie, Alyss! How can you say such a thing when you know him not at all? The man is a Philistine."

Alyss's brows collided. "A Philistine, m'lady?"

"Aye, a Philistine . . . a . . ." Alyss looked so

hopeful that Dominique shook her head in frustration, thinking it best not to enlighten her this once. She seemed too taken with the devil for Dominique to disappoint her. "Never mind," she relented. She was simply being contrary, she decided, and the last she wished was to spoil Alyss's good humor. If Alyss thought the man compassionate, then so be it. *She, herself, had thought him passionate.*

But passion was a far cry from compassion, she reminded herself.

Shrugging, Alyss whispered on a sigh, "Oh . . . to know a man so gentle." And her expression was wistful.

Dominique thought it a strange remark to make when Alyss and her brother had been lovers so long. She'd never known William to be *precisely* cruel, and in truth she would have thought him gentle with his lover, for he could be so generous when he wished to. Still, a prickle raced down her spine at the turn of her thoughts. She wanted to ask Alyss, but refrained, for she knew it an impertinent thing to do. 'Twas none of her concern, she told herself.

"Well, now," Alyss entreated, leaping up from the bed. "What shall we do now, m'lady? Do we plait your hair, or nay?"

It never ceased to amaze Dominique, the fervor with which Alyss served her. 'Twas as though this were a great adventure for her, though truth to tell, Dominique would have thought it a finer thing to serve the master of the domain, and an affront to be lowered to serving his sister. Still, Alyss never complained.

And neither could Dominique, for Alyss tried so hard, and treated her kindly—much more like the sister she never had.

"Mayhap I should change for the meal?" Dominique suggested. The fact that her gown had displeased him so greatly had absolutely naught to do with the reason she wished to change. *She simply wished to*; she told herself.

"Oh, yea, m'lady," Alyss exclaimed excitedly. "And we shall endeavor to make you absolutely irresistible for your betrothed. He's a handsome one, too, that one," she sighed. "And you, m'lady, are a very fortunate woman, indeed." And with that, she proceeded at once to explore the coffers.

Dominique was loath to disappoint, so she replied not at all, but the truth was that at the moment she felt anything *but* fortunate. She allowed Alyss to choose the gown, and then to dress her, and then when she could delay no longer, she made her way down to the great hall for the evening meal, her legs trembling disgracefully at the mere notion of facing *him* again.

Chapter 4

Damned *if the wench wasn't wearing a stolen gown.*

'Twas no small wonder she'd *glistened* wearing that pillaged fiery, gold-threaded cloth.

Sitting at table, listening to William Beauchamp and his brother exchange pleasantries—something he never could have envisaged—Blaec could scarcely credit the boldness of the wench—or that of her witless brother, for that matter, for 'twas William who inevitably was the thief.

Mayhap Beauchamp had thought the year long enough for Blaec to forget the cloth that had been plundered from his carts en route from London, but Blaec rarely forgot anything. Though even if he had, the crimson samite with its gold points was not so easily dismissed upon sight. He'd purchased the cloth from a London merchant simply because it had been so extraordinary, and he'd not seen the likes of it since. 'Twas unlikely William Beauchamp would have encountered the same merchant, nor did he feel William capable of procuring the funds for such indulgences, for he spent too much of his time and coin in mindless retribution against Drakewich— mindless because so much of it was unmethodical and ineffective. It was his experience that Beauchamp preferred inflicting his wrath upon the guiltless under cover of night like a coward whelp. *The same way in which he acquired his wares.*

He set down the goblet he held in his hand, shaking his head, his jaw taut, and his senses too on edge to allow him to relax. He hoped Graeham was able to see through the artifice, yet at the moment it certainly didn't seem as though he did. God's blood, but sometimes he wondered of his brother.

" . . . and should you care to consummate the union beforehand," he overheard William suggesting, "I would not at all be offended." He made a charitable gesture with his hand.

For the first time since their untimely arrival, Graeham seemed as revolted as Blaec, for that declaration managed to put an immediate lapse in the exchange between the two. His jaw going rigid, Graeham shook his head. "I . . ." He continued to shake his head, and then immediately choked upon his next words, coughing and stammering while William awaited his reply.

As far as Blaec was concerned, there was no charity in the offer at all. Fury charged through him, for he was certain that William was up to little good. Just what it was he was after, he could not quite perceive . . . as yet. He would before long.

Still Graeham choked.

"Are you so eager to be rid of her?" Blaec answered for his brother, his tone brimming with challenge. At once Graeham held a hand up to thwart him, but Blaec overlooked it, pressing for an answer. 'Twas his responsibility to discover William's purpose, whether Graeham willed it, or nay.

William straightened within his chair. "We are *eager* only for *peace*," he countered, sounding at once affronted. His eyes narrowed, and in that instant, Blaec was rewarded, for he saw in them the loathing he tried with such difficulty to conceal. *Without doubt, there had been no charity in his offer.*

"Of course," Graeham broke in immediately, having gained hold of himself at last. "As we all are. We are all eager for peace." He gave one more discreet cough. "Are we not, Blaec?"

William sounded so hopeful, Blaec nodded tersely, acknowledging the fact, but his gaze never left that of his foe. Aye, his foe—whether the fiend's lovely sister was bride to his brother, or nay. Glancing down briefly at his goblet of wine, he lifted it slowly, then proffered it, raising it betwixt them. Another challenge—may William's soul rot with the oath. "To peace, then," he said grimly. "May it come to—"

Like metal to a lodestone, his eyes were drawn to the entrance of the great hall. At the sight of her, 'twas all he could do to find his tongue, much less to complete his toast. No longer was she wearing the red samite, but a gown of emerald sendal that shimmered and glowed by the torchlight as she wafted through the room. Neither gold thread nor silver embroidery could have enhanced the cloth more than she, with her stately height and graceful, willowy form. Yet if she was lean, there was naught left wanting in the fullness of her breast, for as fine as the sendal was, it clung to her bosom like an envious lover. The thought aroused him even against his will.

Blaec covered his momentary loss by clearing his parched throat. "—pass," he concluded gruffly, clearing his throat once more. "May it come to pass." He brought the cup to his lips. Swallowing the spiced wine, he savored it with his tongue, observing her over the rim of his goblet.

Like a haughty queen, she caught his gaze, met it, lifted her chin, and gave him an icy glance before lifting her skirts and making her way towards the dais. Truth to tell, he thought her well able to give the Empress herself a fight for the crown in that moment. She took great care, he noted, not to meet his eyes again. Though it suited him well, didn't she realize, were she never to deign look his way again.

"Are you unwell, d'Lucy?" William asked with mock concern, interrupting his musings. "You seem so . . . tempered of a sudden?"

Blaec shot him a glare, but didn't bother replying. It was all he could do to keep from throttling the bastard as it was—or glancing up at his too beguiling sister as she drifted behind him. A quiver bolted through him as her gown whispered by, the sound of it as alluring as was the scent of her that lingered to taunt him when she passed. He alone gave her his back as Graeham stood along with William to greet her, yet he was unable to keep himself from lifting his face to seek again the sweet but delicate fragrance of her. She smelled of . . . *something too tempting to consider*.

He heard a kiss, and imagined William pecking her lightly upon her smooth, high cheek—his pulse quickened—and then another kiss, and he tensed at the reminder of whom she was to become. *His brother's bride*. Turning askance and closing his eyes briefly, he repeated the charge: *Thou wilt not covet thy brother's bride*.

"'Tis lovely you art, m'lady," he heard Graeham declare, in his usual diplomatic tone. "I should count myself a fortunate man, indeed." He drew her to where Blaec sat at his right, sharing his trencher with no one—as he preferred. "Alas, we were not certain you would join us this eve, you seemed so fatigued earlier," he said by way of apology. "Your brother and I have already endeavored to share our repast. Perchance it would please you to share this once with my brother, Blaec, instead?"

Stunned, Blaec turned in time to see her take a startled step backward.

Dominique had no notion how to respond. The last thing she wished was to share a trencher with the devil himself. She'd as lief curse him to Hades, but all eyes were upon them, so she took a step forward, however aversely. Though she could not quite bring herself to sit beside him.

"I assure you, demoiselle, I will not devour you," Blaec told her darkly, his voice low but resonant.

Graeham chuckled with good humor. "Of course he'll not," he reassured.

"Just as I do not spew flames," Blaec added, his voice even lower, deeper, grimmer, "nor do I dine on tender babes . . . or, for that matter . . . *sacrificial* virgins." His lips curved slightly, and his green eyes slivered, deep and dark as emeralds, telling her without words exactly to which *sacrificial virgin* he was referring.

Dominique gasped at his coarseness, but he didn't bother to make amends, nor did he arise from his seat. He merely glanced at his brother with something akin to disbelief—and disgust, if she read him aright. Well, she determined, casting him an affronted glance, it should occur to him that this would be no pleasure for her either! She thought to tell him just so, but then recalled her vow—that she would slay him with kindness, instead.

Collecting herself, Dominique smiled wanly at Graeham. "'Twill be my pleasure, my lord," she relented, but her heart tumbled violently as she seated herself at last at the Dragon's side.

"Will it really?" Blaec asked beside her, his tone bleeding with sarcasm.

Graeham elbowed him discreetly, yet not so discreetly that Dominique could overlook it, and then he smiled at her apologetically. The Dragon did not so much as stir, much less bother with an apology of his own, and to her dismay, Graeham stayed only an instant longer to see that she was comfortably seated before once again abandoning her to the mercy of his unpalatable brother.

For the longest moment she was aware only of the silence of the man beside her, for it seemed to

permeate the very width and length of the hall.
Sweet Mary, but whether they were, or nay, she
felt all eyes upon them.

A young page came forward, his light brown
hair neatly trimmed, and offered her water to
lave with. She promptly accepted, all the while
making certain to keep as distant as possible
from the man seated at her side. The mere
thought of touching him left her stomach in
twisted knots. As it was, she felt the heat of
his body much too acutely.

From the corner of her eye she watched his
great hands slice the trencher in half, giving her
an equal share, and she could not help but recall
the deftness of those fingers as he'd liberated
her gown earlier.

Only once he'd set the trencher before her did
she spare him a glance, but it was a mistake, she
realized immediately, for the look in his deep
green eyes left no doubt as to his thoughts; he
despised her as well as her brother, and would
no doubt take great pleasure in finding them
culpable. Of what, she knew not. Yet it seemed
he was searching for something.

Well, he'd not find it, she vowed.

The hall itself, so orderly and clean—like the
young page—was a far cry from that of Arndel.
Her brother had never been one for fastidious-
ness, yet she could tell that Graeham d'Lucy
was that and more, for the tables were set
in perfect arrangement. The rushes beneath
her feet were sweet with new herbs, and the
bright-colored tapestries hanging upon the walls
were immaculate. The Dragon, she knew, was

inordinately meticulous as well, for the state of his chamber told her as much; the room, as large as it was, was completely devoid of clutter. And tonight even the evening meal was a simple but painstaking fare: cheeses, breads. . .

"Mutton?" he asked beside her, startling her. The deep reverberation of his voice sent a quiver down her spine. God's love, but she'd not realized the carver stood behind her. Like a fresh-faced maid, she blushed at her own inattention. *Yet how could she concentrate with him sitting aside her?*

"Nay . . . thank you," she said with as much aplomb as she could summon, and her gaze was drawn momentarily toward the Dragon. She could not help herself—'twas impossible to sit next to the devil and not feel him so profoundly. Her heart raced as she took in his swarthy complexion. Truth to tell, he was so dark, he recalled her to the Saracen. And the scar high upon his cheek . . . She wondered how he'd received it, for she'd not noticed it afore now. It could very easily have been mistaken for a dimple were it not so high, for it seemed to appear only when he smiled. She stiffened, realizing that he *was* smiling now, however sardonically, and very likely at her expense.

"Lady Dominique?" she heard him whisper, saw his beautiful lips move, and her heart leapt into her throat. Those same lips again curved arrogantly. "If you are quite through gawking—" he gestured toward the carver "—the lad wishes to know if you'd care for aught else." He cocked a brow.

If Dominique thought she'd ever blushed ere now, she was sorely mistaken. Her cheeks heated till she feared she would swoon. Curse the arrogant cur! "Nay," she choked, and averted her gaze at once, thinking him the worst churl she'd ever known. Had she thought him the like of his father? Nay, the man was worse. *Infinitely worse.* One need only look at him, insultingly dressed for war at table, to know.

She'd do well to remember it.

She eyed him circumspectly. *'Twas rumored he was bastard born—conceived on the same day as his fair-haired brother, though sired by another man— yet that Gilbert d'Lucy accepted him despite the fact.* She wondered if it was truth. It seemed an incredible tale, yet 'twas argued that it *was* possible for two men to impregnate a single woman at the same time . . . thus siring twins that bore little resemblance to each other upon birth. She wondered of that, too, for no two brothers could ever have been so disparate as were these two, and then she recalled herself at once, her blush deepening at her unseemly deliberations.

She heard him chuckle beneath his breath— curse him again, a thousand times curse him!— the sound as reverberating to her ears as thunder. It shook her to her very soul. Truth to tell, if she didn't know better, she'd think he'd guessed at her very thoughts, even—yet 'twas ludicrous, was it not? *Still, the way he looked at her made her feel as though he knew her every contemplation.*

Well . . . if he did, she told herself, then it only served her right. What the devil ailed her that she should consider such inappropriate things? That she'd overheard her brother's men speaking of it gave her no leave to contemplate it herself. 'Twas unbefitting. Particularly so when the infuriating man was seated so prominently at her side.

She cared not a whit for him, she told herself. If he'd led a cursed life, 'twas no more her concern than . . . well, than whether he trusted her, or nay. Graeham seemed to, and that was all that mattered.

The meal proceeded in discomfiting silence. Trying in vain to listen to her brother's discourse and endeavoring to ignore the man at her side, Dominique stabbed at her trencher with her bone-handled poniard. Yet no matter how hard she tried, she could not quite remove him from her thoughts. Sweet Mary, but when he chewed, she could hear the faint yet deliberate sound of it—and could not keep from envisioning the strength in those very masculine jaws of his . . . the deceptive, soft-looking suppleness of his lips. The sound of his chewing only intensified with his brooding silence, until Dominique could little bear it. Her nerves were fraught. And so the meal persisted until abruptly she felt the heat of his breath upon her neck, and she froze.

"You might cease now," he informed her smartly. "*I do believe 'tis already deceased, demoiselle.*"

It took Dominique an instant to realize what he meant, and then at once she cast her poniard down upon the table, chagrined to have been caught mutilating her meal. And again she heard him chuckle low in his throat. It was the last gesture she needed to demolish her composure. 'Twas all she could do not to cry out as she rose from her seat. Never in her life had she been so affected.

Apologetically she glanced at William first, then at Graeham. "I—I—if you will forgive me, my lord . . . William . . . I-I find myself indeed much too weary to dine this eve, after all."

"Of course," Graeham allowed, his expression empathetic, though surprised. "Mayhap in the morn you shall feel more at ease?" he suggested with concern.

She nodded much too quickly. "Aye . . . perchance in the morn," she agreed.

Graeham nodded and made a motion with his hand, dismissing her. "Blaec, see m'lady to her chamber."

Blaec's gaze snapped about to meet that of his brother, his visage wrathful.

"Nay!" Dominique exclaimed at once. "Thank you, but I am perfectly able to find the way of my own." She didn't bother even to linger until Graeham and William spoke to give her leave— nor did she pause to retrieve her poniard, so much did she dread *his* company.

At table, they watched her impetuous departure with some bewilderment, and then when she was gone, William turned to demand of Blaec, "What have you said to her, d'Lucy?" He stood wrathfully, clapping his hand upon the table.

Still Blaec said naught, merely sat, staring contemplatively at his brother and then at William.

"Come now," Graeham appealed, standing as well, in an attempt to keep the peace. "I am certain my brother has done naught to offend the lady. Blaec, tell him so."

Blaec said naught, merely stared, his face an impervious mask. And then he was saved from responding at all, for in that instant a guard appeared, hastening to his side. With a sense of urgency, the guard bent to whisper into his ear, and as naught else had been able to, the whispered missive caused Blaec's face to pale.

He stood abruptly, gripping the table with fingers that whitened with the potency of his anger. "It seems there has been yet another raid," he informed Graeham, casting William a lethal glare. "You will pardon me . . ."

"Certainly, I understand you must go," William interjected at once, the anger leaving his eyes in the face of the unexpected crisis. "Mayhap you could use my—"

"Nay!" Blaec exploded, casting a swift glance at Graeham, who returned a cautioning glare. At Graeham's silent behest, it took him an instant to temper his fury, but he did so. "'Tis most obliging of you," he relented, casting back William's words with barely masked malevolence, "but you *are* weary, I am certain, and you *will* remain within the safety of Drakewich's walls."

He didn't bother to specify just whose safety it was he was concerned with, but by his expression, it was more than apparent that it was not William's—nor, for that matter, that of his precious sister.

William tensed visibly at what could be taken for nothing less than a command, and Blaec's eyes glittered determinedly. "As you have discovered yourself," he said in an effort to appease, for his brother's sake, "we have been troubled much with brigands of late . . . I would see our guests safe until we can hunt the bastards down. After all . . . *you* cannot know *our* lands as intimately as do we . . ."

William shook his head, his expression as fierce as that of Blaec; still he did not avert his gaze.

Neither did Blaec relent. "I'm pleased we understand each other," Blaec said with the slightest smile, and with that scarcely veiled accusation, he pivoted about and stalked away.

At once Graeham made his excuses to William, and hastened to catch Blaec's angry strides.

William, for his part, merely watched them go.

Chapter 5

Reaching nonchalantly to lift up his sister's abandoned poniard, William sat contemplating the two brothers as they walked side by side from the great hall. Scowling, he examined the blade, and then considered that mayhap Blaec d'Lucy was a greater threat than ever he had anticipated.

And then his lips turned awry as he scrutinized the polished blade of the small poniard, for the answer that came to him in that instant was inordinately pleasing . . . and simple. His beautiful little sister, without realizing it, seemed to have given him the edge. His smile deepened, for distracted as he was, Blaec d'Lucy would prove to be no match at all. Regardless that he thought himself so formidable—despite the fact that so many thought him invulnerable.

And ultimately if all went well . . . *Drakewich's Black Dragon would depart this life much sooner than he'd hoped.*

The notion pleased him so immensely that he was immediately ravenous. Peering about, and making certain no one was observing him, he stood, gathering his sister's portion of untouched food into his own trencher. And then he dared seize Graeham's, as well—and aye, the almighty Dragon's, too. Nay, he laughed to himself, nobody would stop him now. No one.

Not even the dreaded mighty Dragon himself.

"What, by God's great fists, are you trying to do?" Blaec exploded when they'd quit the hall.

"I've no idea what you're speaking of."

"Aye, you do," Blaec contended, but he said no more and they parted ways to armor themselves.

Blaec awaited Graeham within the solar, for he already wore hauberk and chausses, and he had no intention of subjecting himself to the wench's presence simply to retrieve his helm. When the alarm had been sounded to signal Beauchamp's arrival, he'd had no notion what to expect and so he'd armored himself then. Later, he'd simply not bothered to change, for he did not trust the bastard—with good cause, so it seemed.

His anger reached a thundering point by the time Graeham reappeared, fully armored, with his own helm cradled beneath his arm.

Seeing Blaec's lack of protection, Graeham glowered at him. "Next time you rage over my foolishness, I shall remind you of this," he warned, eyeing Blaec disapprovingly as he passed by.

Blaec was too enraged to acknowledge the concern in his brother's voice. Falling in step beside Graeham, he ignored the accusation and flung one of his own. "Damn you. Why must you persist in casting the wench at me like a bone to a mongrel dog? If you've no care to wed with the bitch, why then do you not send her—along with her jackal of a brother—back to their infernal Arndel?"

Together they descended the tower stairs and hurried across the hall, exiting the donjon. Through the cool night air, they made their way toward the stables: Graeham silent and troubled, and Blaec wrathful.

In the distance, though they had yet to leave the sanctuary of Drakewich's walls, the orange blaze of fire lit the velvet horizon like a foreshadowing of hell itself.

"Bastards!" Blaec exploded once more. "We've only just rebuilt the accursed huts after the last time. I should turn myself about and slit the jackal's throat whilst he sits gloating in our hall."

"Blaec," Graeham cautioned, "you cannot know for certain 'tis Beauchamp that is responsible this time."

Blaec turned a bitter glance in his brother's direction. "Who else would dare?" he asked, and Graeham had no response, for now, in the twentieth summer of Stephen's reign when Stephen had at last come to terms with the Empress, there was no one who would dare dispute their claim when both Stephen and the Empress supported them equally. Nor did any man relish the thought of tangling with the Black Dragon, Blaec was well aware, for they thought him possessed during battle—and likely 'twas so, for as determined as his brother was to die by the sword, Blaec was twice more determined to keep him from it.

Only Beauchamp in his blind vengeance would dare defy them.

Though, in fact, Beauchamp's sire had been one of Henry's *new men*—those raised from the dust and rewarded with the estates of the disinherited—Stephen had chosen not to confirm all of Beauchamp's lands and had restored those belonging to his own sire. Having known the d'Lucys to be well girded in Normandy, and the Beauchamps to be in surplus of English lands— lands that had once been rightfully the d'Lucys to begin with—Stephen had chosen to restore the d'Lucys as allies by attempting to appease them both.

Only now it seemed that the judgment of Solomon was not so wise a ruling, after all, for neither party had been truly appeased— Beauchamp because he'd been divested of lands he'd felt were his rightful earnings under Henry, and the d'Lucys because the Beauchamps were ever a thorn in the rear, ever challenging, yet never openly. Such a condition could have led to nothing less than hostility, a blood feud that Blaec was certain would never end in peace—not at any price—not when so many had already died for its cause . . . including William's sire at the hands of Blaec's own father.

"Guard yourself well, Graeham," he warned, "for I warrant he is not come because he is so eager for his sister to take our name."

"He claims—"

"I care not what the bastard claims!" Blaec interjected angrily as they entered the stables. "I trust him not."

Graeham's brows drew together in a gesture of defeat as he lifted and settled his helm over his coif. "Nor do I," he ceded at last. Both of their mounts were held in waiting, and Blaec wasted little time in gaining his saddle. Graeham, too, mounted swiftly, though he brooded still. "Christ and bedamned!" he exclaimed. "Have we no hope, then?" he asked with some desperation.

Blaec's features softened somewhat as he turned to look over his shoulder at his only remaining kin, yet he was never more determined. "Aye, Graeham," he yielded, whirling his destrier about wrathfully. Reaching backward, he jerked up the mail coif, settling it over his head, and then adjusted the ventail over his face—meager protection without the helm, yet better than naught. "*You* can hope," he said grimly. "For your sake, I cannot afford to. Look to your back," he commanded once more, and with that he spurred his destrier from the stables.

Graeham followed, his eyes affixed to his brother's mail-clad back, his expression grim. "What need," he muttered softly beneath his breath, "when I've you to see to it for me, my brother?"

Dominique had scarcely been abed when she heard the angry shouts below her window. At once she arose, instinct drawing her toward the immense painted shutters in the far wall. She knew only too well how deceiving the illusion of safety could be.

Skirting her scattered trunks in the darkness of the Dragon's chamber, she hurried toward the window. Unlatching the shutters hastily, she threw them wide and cringed as one clattered noisily against the stone. Peering down below, she spied the Dragon and his brother flying like hellhounds toward the stables, their enraged voices carrying even unto her ears upon the night air.

Despite the clatter she'd made opening the window, in their haste they seemed completely oblivious to her spying, and it didn't take long for her to discern why. In the distance the eerie orange glow of fire caught her eye, and it was only then that the distant shouts and frantic cries became discernible to her ears.

Far enough away that it appeared no more than a mute vision of hellfire, it was little enough threat to the donjon itself. Yet it nevertheless inspired fear, for Dominique knew full well the devastation such a blaze could bring upon simple waddle-and-daub huts and to the people who dwelt within them. Her ears could almost perceive the roar of the flames as they devoured all within their path; thatch roofs collapsing, incinerating, leaving little more than black ash and charred remains.

Who, by the love of Christ, could have done such a despicable thing?

In horror, she watched the brothers ride out from the gates until they appeared no more than a distant silhouette against the crimson inferno. Still . . . she knew which rider was the Dragon—the one in the lead—for his bearing in the saddle was unmistakable in its arrogance. A warm gust of wind swept in, swirling about her, lifting her unbraided hair and making her shiver.

Yet it wasn't cold that made her quiver, for the night air was sultry warm. It was the memory of the Dragon's piercing green eyes upon her . . . the way that he'd glared at her. The man was ruthless. Dangerous—everything bespoke it, from the scar high upon his cheek to the cynical curve of his too beautiful lips.

It astounded her that Graeham seemed so willing to cede command of his army to his brother, yet she'd witnessed enough to know that the claims were true; the way that he'd ordered the search for her brother's messenger without bothering to ask, or even heed, his brother's counsel was proof enough. The Dragon *was* in command of the garrison of Drakewich, and if the rumormongers had it aright, then the earl held his high seat only reluctantly. What then did that mean for her? Where did it leave her? Yet she had no choice but to do her duty. And it was too much to hope that she was mistaken, for as difficult as it was to credit, even her brother had instinctively acknowledged the Dragon as lord, for when he'd spoken to Graeham, it had simply been Graeham, while in speaking to the Dragon, he'd named him d'Lucy. She wondered if William realized what he'd done—wondered, too, if Graeham had noted the slight, for he'd not seemed to object in the least.

Such a strange pair, they were.

Dominique had no notion how long she stood,
watching the terrible blaze from the high window, but she was helpless to do anything more.
These were not her people as yet, nor did she
feel herself welcome to offer aid. Still her heart
wept for them, for this was precisely the horror
she had hoped to put an end to with her coming
marriage to the earl.

Thank the Almighty Christ that her brother
was not responsible for this! She knew he had
upon occasion executed just such a retaliation,
but not this time. Thank heaven above that he
was safe from suspicion here within the walls
of Drakewich, for she had little doubt that the
odious Dragon would have leapt at the first
opportunity to heap blame upon her brother's
shoulders. And then a sudden terrible thought
occurred to her . . .

What if William had left Drakewich? Surely
he would not have departed without a good-
bye, at least? Yet what if, by some twisted turn
of fate, he had? She knew how difficult it was
for him to share the same land, much less the
same roof and breath, as the d'Lucys. What if
he had borne his limit of them and had taken
his leave after the meal?

Panic welled within her as she turned and
rushed toward the door. The thought of being
left alone in the enemy's midst left her mouth
cottony with fear. Surely William would never
do such a thing? Yet what if they had argued?
What if, in his anger, he'd forgotten her? She well
knew his fits of rage, and knew him capable of

just such a craze. She needed to speak to him at once. She had no notion at all where he would sleep this night, she only knew she must find him. *She must.*

She had to set her mind at ease.

Alyss would help her, she knew.

Scarcely had she reached the massive wooden door when she heard the voices from the antechamber. At once she pressed her ear to the door and heard Alyss whisper, *"Aye, my lord, she has long been abed."*

"Good," she heard William's soft reply—yet it *was* William's voice, and she stifled a cry of relief. Backing away from the door, her heart skipping beats like lightning bolts through a summer storm, Dominique felt the bed materialize behind her knees and sat weakly upon it, holding her palm close against her breast.

"Thank God," she whispered, and her eyes stung with tears of relief. Truly they had come too far to lose it all now. There was much too much at risk. She lay back upon the bed and wept silent tears, thanking God that William's mere presence at Drakewich removed him from suspicion. For surely not even the Dragon would cast blame simply out of spite?

Chapter 6

Across the chamber, tallow candles burned, emitting ribbons of ash smoke that curled upward toward the shadowy ceiling. William smiled, thinking of the blaze that raged beyond the castle walls, and his nostrils flared as he sat upon the small cot. He drew Alyss nearer, despite that she resisted. It mattered not that she did, for he relished this the most.

"M'lord," she protested weakly. "I thought . . ."

"Shush, Alyss," he demanded, for he knew precisely what it was she thought, and it pleased him not at all. He'd be damned if he'd refrain from partaking of her fleshly pleasures simply because she was now his sister's lady's maid.

Of course, she was no substitute for Dominique—never had been—and he silently cursed her for that.

Too bad his lovely sister was worth so little without her virtue, for he'd long now coveted her within his own bed. Too bad, too, that the fool church took such offense with *incestus*, elsewise he would have taken her as his own bride. 'Twas how it should have been.

Nay, he felt no guilt for his private fancies—
if anything, 'twas resentment he felt, for his
little sister was much too lovely for the likes of
Graeham d'Lucy. The fool was likely too chaste
to understand what to do with a woman the likes
of Dominique. He wouldn't appreciate her.

Not like he would.

Well, that suited him well enough, for when
all was said and done, Dominique would be back
in his keeping, and the less she was befouled, the
better.

Aye, and then he would tell her. He knew
precisely what he would say . . .

Were it not that Dominique's beauty alone
had brought him so many marriage offers even
before her first blood, he would have long ago
proclaimed her a bastard and claimed her for
his own. Yet now she would bring him the ultimate bride-price, and he smiled inwardly at the
prospect. And in the end, she would be his
again . . . and he would be whole again. The
mere thought of it filled him with gratification.

Something in his expression must have eased
Alyss, for after a moment she relented and stood
before him, stilled at last. That's what he liked
most about her . . . that she learned quickly. Still,
she *had* resisted him, and he could not risk her
defiance just now. Not when so much depended
upon her complete obeisance to him.

Positioning the maid none too gently into the
space betwixt his legs, he then bent, reaching
into his boot to retrieve Dominique's poniard.
Alyss's eyes widened at the sight of the small
blade, but she dared say nothing, and he pro-

ceeded at once to slice the front of her gown, grinning with satisfaction at her expression of distress.

"M-M'lord," she stammered.

His skin prickled in anticipation. "Shush, Alyss," he whispered once more, but the command was no less menacing for its deceiving softness. Alyss complied at once and he peered up at her, his grin engaging in the shadows of the chamber. He drew her closer still, tossing the gleaming blade upon the bed. With satisfaction he watched as her eyes followed it, and then he commenced to parting her coarse gown, roughly, rending it until she was fully exposed to his eyes.

"Return the blade to my sister," he commanded her softly, and then as she watched, he placed his lips to her breast. He took great satisfaction in the gasp she emitted, and despite the gleam of fear in her eyes, her flesh flushed rosy by the light of the candle. Her head fell back helplessly, and he chuckled deep in the back of his throat at her anticipated reaction. Drawing the nipple firmly into his mouth, he rolled it between his teeth, and then bit down until she cried out. He felt himself harden at her cry of pain and smiled softly against the warm flesh of her breast as her head came up and her eyes filled anew with apprehension.

"William," she croaked, staring at him fearfully, yet she didn't move, for he held her nipple firmly between his teeth. She was an intelligent little thing, and he felt she understood him perfectly.

"You've the ampule?" he asked through his teeth. She nodded, and he could feel the beat of her heart rise against his lips. He relished it. "And you understand when it is I wish for you to use it?" She nodded once again, and he sent his tongue on a gentle little foray of her young flesh, a reward, of sorts, for her acquiescence. "Good," he whispered, releasing her. "Very good. As soon as they are wed, you should empty the vial into his wine," he suggested. "I shan't return until 'tis done."

"W-What of the Dragon?" Alyss asked timidly. "W-What if he should suspect?"

"I shall deal with the Dragon," he whispered with loathing, and felt her quiver against him. That, too, pleased him, for it assured him that she feared him still.

His plan was infallible. Already, tonight, with the fire, he'd cast suspicion elsewhere—and it didn't matter whether d'Lucy suspected him, or nay, only that later Stephen would be able to look back and see that there was another possible adversary. After all, what man would be witless enough to sabotage the d'Lucys and then sleep under their very roof? Certainly not he. He chuckled quietly at the notion.

Moreover, Stephen was unlikely to suspect William when there was already the promise of alliance betwixt him and d'Lucy. Nor did he believe Stephen ultimately cared, for 'twas common knowledge already that upon his death, England would be forfeit to the empress's heir. Why should Stephen concern himself now with petty wars?

And then . . . when Alyss poisoned Graeham so soon after the ceremony, once again he would be safe from suspicion at Stephen's court. Of course, he would play the wounded brother and claim that he'd not even been apprised of the ceremony. Mayhap he would suggest—with great regret, of course—that there may still have been some enmity on Graeham's behalf toward him. And then, of course, he would express his sorrow. Afterward, with Stephen's blessings he would go and reclaim his sister as his ward. And along with her, his rightful lands.

Just as simple as that.

Still, it seemed an eternity before it would all come to pass. And Alyss was still not Dominique. Be that as it may, it would be easy enough to pretend in the darkness of the chamber. Sighing against Alyss's plump, moist breast, he remembered a time when he and Dominique had been close. She'd been so young and tender then . . . the only one who had ever made him feel loved. All those times he'd trained during the sweltering summers—damn his father, for he'd not even had the regard to foster him— Dominique had wiped his brow with such sisterly affection.

His face heated even after all these years as he remembered that he'd walked about the first years of manhood plagued with guilt for the lust he bore his young sister. And then his father had mockingly confronted him—because he had been so obvious in his pining.

God's blood, but his father had leapt at the opportunity to tell him that he, too, sometimes fancied Dominique within his own bed. 'Twas then Henry Beauchamp had first expressed his doubt that he'd sired Dominique—mayhap to ease his own conscience, for 'twas too much to hope that it might be true. 'Twas evident to any who might spy them together that father and daughter had the same look about them. 'Twas that same look William and Dominique shared, as well.

Hearing his own contemptible desires upon his father's lips had disgusted William so that he'd heartily denounced his own dark yearnings. Enraged, he'd dared to strike his own sire in the belly for the quip. And then to prove him wrong, William had cast Dominique aside and out of his mind—as though she'd been no more significant to him than the mother he'd grown to despise.

With her infidelity, their damned mother had made his father bitter, and unpleaseable . . . yet 'twas her saving grace that she'd borne Dominique before her death . . . for the only one thing William loved with a greater passion than that of his hatred for the d'Lucys . . . was his lovely little sister.

No longer did he feel the guilt. On the contrary . . . he'd long ago accepted that he was his father's son. Aye, for if it meant having Dominique, he didn't care. The merest thought of either of the d'Lucys touching her burned at his gut, and the only one thing keeping him sane enough to follow through with this pretense was the thought that neither Graeham nor Blaec was long for this world. And by the eyes of Lucifer, the very thought of their deaths made up for so much.

It was nearly daybreak when the brothers returned. Graeham, weary as he was, made his way to the chapel. As far as Blaec was concerned, the one in need of prayer was not his brother, but William Beauchamp, for if he encountered the fiend just now, he thought he might send him straight to hell, where he belonged.

Fury alone gave him the strength to mount the steps to his bedchamber. Soiled and sweat-soaked from the night's ordeal, he cursed beneath his breath, for at the moment, he felt acutely the weight of his mail.

The fire had been contained, yet it had taken all of the night to put out the flames and to salvage what they could from the villeins' huts. While there had been few casualties, so many had been left without homes that he and Graeham had felt it their responsibility to remain with them throughout the night, offering what protection and aid they could while the folk rallied their kin as well as their belongings.

Yet their protection had been unnecessary, for the craven bastards who had set the fires had slipped away, into the night woods, without leaving so much as a clue to their identity. Nor had they returned. Yet Blaec had no need for evidence when his intuition told him exactly who it was who had sabotaged them. Beauchamp. The very name made the hairs at the back of his nape stand on end. *And all the while, the bastard slept peacefully within his own home.* If

Blaec could so much as prove his guilt . . . he would carve the heart from his body and feed it to the buzzards.

Blind with rage, he didn't bother to knock as he entered the antechamber, though once he set foot within, he wished he'd given warning. The maid, Alyss, though alone in her bed, lay replete and without blankets to conceal her. Her gown had been rent down the front, fully exposing her plentiful bosom, and from the looks of them, bruised and swollen, she'd been well used the night before. Likely by Beauchamp himself, for Blaec was certain none of his own men would dare leave her so damaged. Every one of them understood that the Beauchamps—useless as they were—were under his protection. And that included their servants. Damn Beauchamp, he thought sourly. The bastard seemed to be making himself at home, even while he wreaked havoc.

The maid didn't stir even as he closed the door, and he scowled, averting his eyes to give her what privacy he could. He didn't delay, but went straight through to his own chamber, once again opening the door to find a sleeping form. This time within his own bed.

He wasn't prepared for the sight of *her*, lying so serenely atop his tumbled sheets and blankets. It sent a charge through him the likes of which he'd never experienced in his life. He endeavored to ignore her, turning askance from the bed and going to the window. The shutters had been left wide open—no doubt so she could watch her brother's handiwork, he reminded himself

bitterly. He closed them, only to turn and find
her stretching like a cat in her sleep. Against his
will, he could feel the blood slithering into his
nether regions, hot and rousing.

She moaned softly, and he couldn't help but
consider the sounds she would make during
loving. Would she be seductively quiet but violent in her passion? Or would she be sensual
and vocal, telling him with her soft sounds and
provocative gestures precisely what it was she
wished of him?

The merest notion sent white-hot lust exploding through him, burning hotter than the tor-
rent he'd only just fought. Only this one was
far more dangerous, and he mentally thrust the
images from his mind.

Christ, but what ailed him? He had no right
to these thoughts—nor should he have come
here, he acknowledged. He should have sent a
servant for his garments, instead. Still, he was
here now and he couldn't help himself; he went
to the bed and stood staring down upon her.

Dressed in soft, white pleated cambric, she
looked every bit the virginal bride that her
brother claimed her to be. And her hair . . .
while it had burned copper beneath the late
day sun, it now appeared dark and rich in the
twilight and held a healthful gleam that was
evident even in her skin. Even her brows—dark
and perfectly arched—were a work of artistry
against her creamy flesh.

'Twas no wonder William had waited so long
to offer her in wedlock, for with her brand of
beauty, she was as great a prize as Jerusalem

itself. No doubt it behooved William to hold back for the best contract, for age, as with fine wine, could only make her more valuable a prize. She had that about her. And balls of the saints! Anticipation of the marriage bed alone could unman even the best of men.

Then again . . . he was not the best of men . . . and he wasn't foolish enough to pretend it. A muscle ticked at his jaw.

Unbinding the laces that secured the ventail, he let the partial mask slip from his face and then he shoved the mail coif back from his sweat-dampened hair.

According to his father, he was naught but a bastard. And if he'd thought himself free from envy and bitterness, he knew now 'twas otherwise, for as he stood staring down at the woman within his bed, the mere thought of his brother touching her, loving her, filled him with a greater wrath, even, then that he'd experienced at seeing the huts afire this eve.

Disgusted with himself, he turned from the bed and went to his coffers, opening the largest and removing from it a black tunic and breeches. God's truth, but he was in need of a bath to set him at rights—to cool his ardor. And that was precisely what he intended to do—the sooner he left this God-forsaken chamber, the better.

Chapter 7

Dominique wasn't certain what roused her from her sleep, but she sensed the presence within the room even before she opened her eyes. Her lashes flew wide, and she spied *him* at once—unmistakable with that black devil's mane of hair. He was stooping to probe one of the larger coffers in a corner of the room, and she sat with a cry, drawing the coverlets to her breast.

"What business have you here?" she demanded of him.

He turned—infuriating in his deliberate slowness—yet she wasn't prepared for the sight of him once he faced her at last. The malice in his eyes unnerved her—though no more than the sooty blackness of his flesh. Begrimed from the smoke, and his hair disheveled with sweat, he appeared before her eyes a demon from Satan's everlasting kingdom.

"Once again, demoiselle," he told her icily, "I could ask the same of you."

Her chin lifted. "'Twas you who brought me here," she reminded him pertly. "*I* would not have chosen this chamber. Alas, the least you might do is afford me the privacy I deserve."

"Nay, demoiselle. 'Twas greed that brought you here to Drakewich," he countered, "greed and naught more—if you think for one instant you are deceiving anyone, you art mistaken."

Dominique bristled. *How dare he begin this anew!* "We were not speaking of Drakewich, sir, but your chamber, and well you know it!"

His jaw tautened and his eyes fair gleamed. "You confess it?" he asked her, holding himself menacingly still as he awaited her reply—like a black beast, anticipating the pounce, she thought bitterly.

Dominique narrowed her eyes at him, rising to her knees and casting down the covers in her anger. "How dare you twist my words! I confess to absolutely nothing, my lord, and if you do not leave this chamber this very instant," she advised him, "I vow I shall scream!" Despite that she wanted nothing more than to hide beneath the covers rather than face him, she wasn't about to cower from him now. If he thought for one instant that she was going to quiver every time he thought to set upon her, 'twas he who was heartily mistaken.

His eyes flickered with amusement at her expense, and it chafed her all the more. So did the manner in which he appraised her, from her knees to the top of her head, as though she were no more than chattel to be inspected.

"Scream?" he scoffed, lifting a brow. "And precisely who do you think will come, demoiselle?"

Dominique lifted her chin, despite that his

question sent prickles of dread down her spine—despite that his look made her heart race so that she thought it would leap from her breast. "Graeham," she answered a little uncertainly, and then she averted her eyes, for she'd caught herself appraising him, as well— the breadth of his shoulders, the length of his body so thoroughly encased in mail. What was wrong with her that she would ogle him so? He was a despicable, vicious devil. *And the brother of her betrothed.*

He made some sound in the back of his throat, something akin to laughter, yet when Dominique dared look again, the amusement that had been there previously had vanished. He came forward, flinging his garments upon the bed, glaring at her. She flinched as they fluttered before her. "Graeham?" he scoffed. "Well, then, I should save us both the disgust of discovering elsewise," he told her, "and answer your earliest question, for you seem to have forgotten that you are occupying *my* chamber, demoiselle."

There was little need to remind her, for scarcely could she forget it. "Would that I were not," she answered flippantly, glaring back with equal measure. "Yet do I not have a choice, my lord, and the least you might do is offer me the respect I deserve as your brother's bride."

He answered her anger with calm assurance and a determined shake of his head. "Not as yet, you are not, demoiselle, and were the choice my own . . . you'd not wed with Graeham at all."

"Aye, well," Dominique returned saucily, "the choice is not your own—and thank God

Almighty, for elsewise the bloodshed would never cease! You cannot even strike a truce with me, and I have done you no harm. Forsooth, not even so much as for the sake of your own brother will you cry peace!" She had no notion her voice had risen so, until the door burst wide and Alyss stumbled into the room.

The maid glanced fearfully from Dominique to the Dragon, and then back, and only belatedly did Dominique realize that Alyss was holding her rent gown together timidly and was staring in terror at the Dragon.

"M-M'lady?" Alyss croaked. Her gaze reverted to Dominique, her eyes wide.

Alarm shot through Dominique at Alyss's ill-used appearance. She bolted from her knees to stand upright upon the bed, glaring down in anger at Blaec. "What in the name of God have you done to her?" she accused him.

Blaec didn't bother to look at the maid, for he'd seen the evidence already and it repulsed him. Nor did he reply, for he cared not a whit whether Dominique thought him responsible, or nay. He knew he was not.

"Oh, nay . . . nay, m'lady," the maid exclaimed. "Not he!"

He watched Dominique bolt from the bed, to the wench's side, taking no heed over her state of dress. He had to give her credit at least for her care of the maid, for she seemed genuinely distraught at the prospect of Alyss's having been harmed.

"Who, then?" she demanded, turning to eye him wrathfully.

Blaec cocked a brow at her silent accusation. God's truth, it was all he could do to keep himself from gaping stupidly at the sight she presented. Sheer as her gown was, it left little to the imagination. Long legs, slim and luscious, were revealed to him by outline, and above them a waist so narrow that he experienced an incredible yearning to measure it with his hands, to see that it was truly so small. And her bosom; for the sake of decency he tried not to note the way the dark nipples strained against the snowy fabric.

Never in his life had he coveted anything more. He felt his mouth go dry and he swallowed, wondering why it was that Graeham seemed so determined to avoid her. For himself, he could scarcely bear the thought of having to see her, yet he, at least, had a reason, for she was not his and he would not tempt himself.

God, she was not his.

What was he doing?

At once he averted his eyes.

He didn't think he could bear to remain with Graeham once they were wed. Yet for Graeham's sake, he could neither bear the thought of leaving. Without him, Graeham would not endure, he knew—though he'd be damned if he could understand why 'twas so, for Graeham was not an ungainly fellow. In fact, Blaec thought that were he merely to try, he would be at least Blaec's equal in skill, for Graeham certainly matched him in strength and in size.

In truth, he'd thought many a time that his

brother had some death wish... as though through his martyrdom he thought to atone for some great sin. He certainly spent time enough in penance, praying for long hours in the chapel as though he were some pious monk. And he might as well have been for Blaec could little recall the last time his brother had even looked with yearning at a woman.

He'd been surprised enough when Graeham had informed him of his decision to accept an alliance with Beauchamp. Yet he *had* accepted it, and mayhap, for everyone's sake, Blaec would finally welcome the fief Graeham had for so long tried to bestow upon him... a benefice so rich that it had seemed an injury to receive it, for the cloth goods produced therein lined the coffers of Drakewich so that they had little need of war as a means to replenish them.

Be that as it may... mayhap it was time, at last, for him to go...

" ... tell me who would do such a thing to you," Blaec heard Dominique demand of her maid.

Shaking her head and whispering her response, the wench held her ripped gown together determinedly, as though to hide the worst of the evidence from her mistress. Only now did Blaec note that her lips were swollen, besides. And, in addition, there was a blackening knot high upon her cheek, as though she'd been dealt a blow. Seeing the swelling, he fingered his own cheek, remembering, and his visage darkened. His lips curved grimly, for the evidence was much too overwhelming for him to simply walk away from now. If one of his own men had committed such a crime, Blaec intended to discover the name of the whoreson. He stepped toward them, reminding them of his presence.

The maid turned to face him with a cry of alarm, as though, somehow, she'd forgotten him, and now turned in fright.

His brows collided in displeasure at her reaction. "I, too, would have you relinquish the name," he bade her.

The wench shook her head more frantically still. "Oh, nay, m'lord! Please!"

Blaec's eyes slivered, though he retained his calm at her outright refusal. "You have no right to deny me dispensation of justice in my own home," he reminded her.

"Do you not mean your brother's home?" Dominique interjected at once, her tone biting, her eyes narrowing.

Blaec eyed her keenly, but disregarded the barb, knowing full well that she was baiting him. He refused to be manipulated. He turned to the maid, persisting, "I demand the name."

To his disgust, the young woman began to quiver before him. "Oh, m-m'lord . . . please . . ."

"God's teeth, woman, I cannot believe you would allow the fiend to go unpunished," he told her scathingly.

"'T-Twas no one, m'lord," the maid declared at once. She fingered her cheek anxiously, averting her gaze. "I-I swear it! I merely fell from my bed 'tis all."

"Fell from your bed, my arse!"

"How dare you speak to her so," Dominique interjected.

At her censure, Blaec eyed her once more, though with little compunction. He could scarcely credit that the wench was so unwilling to name the culprit. He knew full well that she'd not fallen from her bed, and was on the verge of telling her just so, for he'd witnessed the other bruises, as well, but then he looked at Dominique—truly looked at her—and found his tongue stilled. Only were the maid protecting her lord could she possibly lie so, and in protecting her lord, mayhap she protected her mistress as well. At the look in Dominique's eyes, he found inexplicably that he could not accuse William with her standing before him looking so distressed.

His lips curved contemptuously, though he was uncertain which disgusted him most: his sudden weakness toward Dominique, or the maid's blind devotion to her master. "And what of the gown?" he could not help but point out, turning to eye the maid sharply. "It rent itself on your descent to the floor, I presume?"

Alyss peered down at the gown in question, as though in a stupor, and then shook her head as she met his gaze once more. "I-I do not know," she persisted. Panicking at his doubtful expression, she said a little more hysterically, "I-I do not, m'lord!"

"Leave be, at last!" Dominique demanded, intervening between them suddenly, her expression fierce. Blaec watched with growing disgust as she enfolded the woman gently within her arms and patted her reassuringly. "Can you not see that you are distressing her?"

His brow lifted. "Unlike her mistress, it seems, the wench frightens much too easily, demoiselle, for I've not threatened her a'tall. I merely requested to know the name of the miscreant who abused her, so that I might deal with him justly."

Dominique's lashes fell momentarily, thick as smoke upon her creamy cheeks. "Aye, well . . . she says she does not know."

He could tell when her eyes met his once more that she'd drawn the same conclusion he had. Still, he found he could say nothing to accuse her brother, for in her beautiful blue eyes—those eyes that were so much like her despicable sibling's—he recognized both her acknowledgment and her denial.

She knew.

She had to know.

Yet she lifted her chin, denying, all the same, and dared to command him, "Let her be, at last, my lord."

When she'd thought him responsible, she'd been quick enough to speak, yet now he sensed fear that the possibility should be spoken at all. Which led him to wonder if she knew . . . or whether she merely suspected . . .

Could she possibly not know how detestable her brother was?

To his disgust, he had the overwhelming desire to go to her . . .

Her eyes were wide and liquid suddenly.

Mesmerizing. God, but he could lose himself in those brilliant blue pools.

"If you've something to say, my lord, say it and be done," she told him breathlessly, her chest heaving softly.

With fear? grief? anger?

She looked as though she would burst into tears, yet she did not, and he found that suddenly it did not matter. If she would protect her brother, then so be it. He shook his head, unwilling to press the matter further.

Even so, he could not quite shed the urge to enfold her into his own arms . . . just as she'd done with the maid . . . fool that he was, for she was not his to comfort.

Neither did she need him to comfort her, he reminded himself. 'Twas naught but his fancy that she seemed suddenly wounded, for she was likely as contemptible as was her brother—with a heart as black.

That likelihood hardened his own.

"Very well, demoiselle," he relented. "I *shall* speak plainly." He gestured toward the maid. "The men of my garrison do not commit such dishonorable acts, for they know well the consequences."

The blood seemed to drain from her face even as he watched, yet she surprised him by standing her ground. Her shoulders straightening, she asked him, "Precisely what are you trying to say, my lord?"

Despite the mettle with which she asked, Blaec spied in her eyes the sudden regret over having asked the question, and so he merely shook his head, telling her simply, "The answer is plain, demoiselle. Merely open your eyes and you shall spy it." He turned to the maid. "And you . . . should you find your memory returns, feel free to seek me," he told her. And then he turned a nod toward Dominique. "Good day, demoiselle."

Dominique gave him no reply, and he didn't wait to see that she did. Without another word, he took his leave, retrieving the tunic and breeches from the bed, and slamming the heavy ash door behind him—before he could be tempted to tell the impudent wench *precisely* what he'd meant by the remark; that her brother was an ignoble bastard who not only had the vileness to burn serfs' huts while they slumbered, but the depravity to beat his own sister's maid, besides.

Blaec wanted nothing more than to throttle Beauchamp with his bare hands.

He made a fist at his side, for more than that, even, and more than before, he was determined to see this farce ended, once and for all. Graeham would *not* wed Dominique Beauchamp—not, even, if Blaec should die trying to prevent it. He refused to consider that his own motives might be somewhat less pure.

He only knew that, at all costs, he was determined to keep Beauchamp's sister from his brother's bed.

At all costs.

Chapter 8

Graeham just wasn't certain how he was going to do it—not when her own brother all but forced her upon him. *Yet, by all that was holy, he intended to keep Dominique Beauchamp from his bed.*

He'd spent the better part of the morning in prayer, and now as he made his way up to his chamber, his heart was heavy with uncertainty. Truly, he'd thought he'd effected the right decision. His people could scarcely endure more of such treachery. He'd thought his alliance with Beauchamp would put an end to the attacks, yet now it seemed he was mistaken. Blaec seemed certain that Beauchamp was responsible, and he could but agree.

Damnation, but it weighed heavily upon him, for other than Beauchamp, he could not imagine who else would lead the raids against his villages. Beauchamp would seem to have little motive, when, through his sister, his blood would once again hold these lands. Graeham simply could not conceive that William would risk it, for it made little sense to toss away the gold in one's hand merely to snatch at the possibility of more. Yet there didn't seem to be anyone else . . .

The one thing that was clear to him now was that he found he could not bear to break a sacred vow, not when it seemed no good would come of it. In spite of his adolescent vow of celibacy, he'd agreed to the alliance with Beauchamp because he'd considered the greater good; an end to their private war. It was the poor man's thatch that went up in flames with each retaliation, and so if it had meant spending all eternity in hell for the sake of his people, then he would have done so joyfully.

Yet he'd be damned if he'd do so for naught.

His chest aching from both the remnants of smoke in his lungs and the anguish of his incertitude, he shoved open the door to his chamber and found his brother waist-deep in the carved wooden tub that had once belonged to their father, and to his father before him. Their noble grandsire had ridden beside the Conqueror himself, and 'twas he who had first called this English land his own. And then the Conqueror had died, and under his youngest son the land had been bathed in the blood of treachery—a treachery even Graeham felt tainted with, despite that the betrayal was not his own but his father's.

Enough that he lived the lie.

Seeing Blaec now, bathing in a borrowed chamber, and with no maid to lave him as was his due, Graeham felt his gut twist, but he put on a brighter face, masking his guilt from his brother's fatigued, shadow-rimmed eyes. Again, last night, Blaec had guarded his back with the same determination and ferocity as a wild boar facing the hunter.

"I'm pleased to see you took my advice," Graeham remarked lightly.

Blaec wearily cast a glance over his shoulder and smiled grimly. "As you pointed out . . . we wouldn't wish to offend our guests, now would we? For your sake, my brother, a bath was the least I could do."

Graeham chuckled as he tossed his helm upon the massive bed. "You do too much," he remarked, removing his gauntlets and snapping them against his leg. He cast them alongside his helm. "At any rate . . . since when do you listen to me?"

Blaec ceded a chuckle. He ran a hand through his black mane, sighing wearily, and then laid his head back against the rim of the tub to stare up at the ceiling.

Graeham sat upon the bed. It shrank beneath his weight with an ominous creak. "We still cannot know for certain 'twas Beauchamp," he said after a moment.

Blaec continued to stare at the ceiling. "Nay," he agreed. "Not as yet . . . though I intend to find out for certain this day."

Graeham's eyes narrowed with interest. "Truly?" he asked. "How?"

"One of the villagers claims to have wounded one of the bastards during their escape."

At last Blaec turned to face him, resting his scarred cheek upon the wide rim of the tub. The memory of the blow that had marred his brother's face was yet another constant source of guilt for Graeham. Their father had taken great pleasure in stepping in and offering Blaec the *colee*, the traditional first blow given a knight, striking him unmercifully hard with the hilt of the very sword he'd later presented to Graeham. The gash had been deep, and though the blood had run thickly down his cheek, Blaec had knelt proudly, his back straight, and had received it without so much as a word. Yet Graeham had seen the gut-wrenching sorrow in his eyes. And behind those eyes . . . he'd spied the little boy who had so long craved his father's embrace.

It had never been forthcoming. To his lament, Graeham had always been his father's son, Blaec little more than an inconvenience. And no matter that Graeham would have changed it were he able, it was as it was. His hand went to his sword hilt, and he lifted the old relic from his scabbard, tracing his bare thumb over the inscription along the blade. INNOMINEDOMINI: *In the name of God*. How discrepant.

"To whom do we owe such a debt of gratitude?" Graeham asked, clearing his throat. He could not begin to fathom how it was that Blaec could even look at him with affection, much less such devotion as he gave. He didn't deserve it.

Blaec's answering grin was wily. "The carpenter's wife," he said with obvious relish.

"Sweet Maude?" Graeham's tone was incredulous.

Blaec chuckled. "One and the very same. It seems they caught her husband with his breeches down."

Graeham's brows knit. "Surely you jest?"

Again Blaec chuckled, only this time with considerably more humor. "Nay, and to hear Adam tell it, she climbed down from atop him like a madwoman, shoved down her skirts, and ran to the window with a wood axe, flinging it out at the nearest rider." His grin widened. "Apparently it left imbedded within the rider's face."

"Ye God!" Graeham shuddered at the vision that came to mind.

"My sentiments precisely."

"I believe I shall tease the wench ne'er more," Graeham vowed, shuddering again. "In fact, mayhap we should recruit her, instead."

Blaec smiled morosely. "Certainly she's fared better against the fiends than any of us have managed thus far."

Graeham sighed. "A rather sad fact, though true," he said.

"At any rate," Blaec continued, "last night it was much too dark to search the adjoining woods, though I thought mayhap today . . . we would invite our guests on a . . . *hunt*, shall we call it?"

Graeham's brows lifted. He nodded. "I should very much like to spy Beauchamp's face do we happen upon the body," he agreed soberly.

"'Tis settled then."

"Aye," Graeham agreed. Lifting himself from the bed, he made his way to the door, resheathing his sword. "I'll go now and extend the invitation to our guest," he proposed. *And pray he's found blameless,* he cursed silently. God's blood, but not even Graeham could stop Blaec from reacting in his anger. Nor did Graeham care to continue this vicious private war. For everyone's sake he hoped Beauchamp was not responsible.

"Be certain not to forget to invite your *bride*," Blaec called after him, his tone sardonic. He grunted as he lifted himself into a more comfortable position within the tub.

Graeham stopped and turned, nodding. "Of course," he conceded, but his brows knit.

Something about the way Blaec had called her his *bride* had caught his regard, and he stood there considering his brother a long moment. Considering the way the two of them dealt together. He'd been watching them, though even a blind man could have detected the undercurrents betwixt them. And suddenly he grinned, for he knew precisely how to remove himself from his entanglement. Inadvertently he'd already stumbled upon the answer, for Blaec had been right, though Graeham would never admit it was so. Out of guilt, *he had been casting the two of them together.*

Even if William *was* guilty, he reasoned, in all likelihood his sister was not, for she didn't strike him as so. Loyal to her brother, she might be, but her outburst yestereve when they'd considered the fate of William's messenger had told him much.

Aye . . . what better way to shed himself of the burden?

Indeed, and it was only the beginning, for if all settled itself correctly, then it would go considerably easier when he spoke to Stephen later. He'd long vowed to do so, but now he resolved he would, at last. It was long past time, and as he shut the door behind him, and Blaec settled back into the massive tub, Graeham felt remarkably lighter in spirit.

Lighter than he had in ages.

Dominique managed to wait until both she and Alyss were respectfully dressed, but no longer could she keep herself from uncovering the truth. When Alyss lifted up a comb from Dominique's possessions in order to dress her hair, Dominique removed it from her hands, returning it to the table.

"Alyss," she began, her tone grave, "you must tell me who did this to you." Gently, wincing at the sight of the bruise, she reached to touch Alyss's cheek. "I'm so sorry," she whispered.

Alyss fidgeted uncomfortably. "Nay, m'lady . . . there is nothing for you to be sorry for," she insisted. Gently she removed Dominique's hand from her face, as though heartily uncomfortable with the ministrations. "I thank you, but 'tis just as I said . . . I fell from my bed in my sleep."

Dropping her hand at her side, Dominique averted her face, turning from Alyss toward the shuttered window. "Dear God, Alyss . . . how can you expect me to accept such a tale? Much as it pains me to agree with one word Blaec d'Lucy might utter, I cannot believe that tale any more than he did."

"'Twas kind of him to consider me," Alyss interjected at once.

Dominique's brows collided as she whirled to face her maid. "*Kind*, Alyss? I can think of much to call the man, but kind is not one of those things!"

Alyss nodded impassionedly. "Oh, aye, m'lady! In truth, he would not have been so angry were he not concerned. Only think of it . . . Would he have spent long hours without sleep, battling fires, when he could have sent his men out, instead, and then gone to bed without a backward thought? Could he not as easily have dealt with it this morn? Aye," she affirmed, seeing that Dominique considered her words, "and were he not concerned for his people, he'd have done just so!" She seemed wistful a moment, wringing her hands, and then she shrugged, shaking her head. "'Tis fortunate, you are, indeed, for Graeham is not only kind and handsome, but he is gentle as well. Only would that I . . . " She halted on a sob, her gaze skiding toward Dominique.

Dominique hesitated, her eyes misting, but only an instant, for no matter that she dreaded the question, she had to ask, "Was it my brother, Alyss? Was it William?" Her hand clenched at her breast. "Did he do this to you?"

Alyss's eyes widened at the accusation. "Oh, nay, m'lady!" She gave a little cry of alarm and shook her head adamantly. "Nay!" At once she made the sign of the cross. "God preserve us both—nay, m'lady—how could you even think so?"

Relief washed over Dominique. Still, she had to ask, had to know for certain, "Art certain you tell me true, Alyss?" God's truth, she'd wondered once too oft to leave off so easily. Verily, too many times Alyss had turned up bruised— yet never so conspicuously as this time.

Alyss opened her mouth to speak and then closed it, lowering her face as though taking offense with the question. An instant later, she lifted her chin, and said with certitude, her eyes devoid of emotion, "'Twas not your lord brother, m'lady."

"Who then?"

Alyss shook her head determinedly. "You must forgive me, this I cannot tell."

Just then, a knock sounded at the door. Dominique and Alyss both turned just as the door creaked opened—something these two brothers seemed to share in common, Dominique thought crossly as Graeham's face appeared in the doorway. Neither seemed to care one whit for even the smallest of courtesies. God's love, but she was beginning to truly regret this unholy alliance.

Dominique gave her maid a furtive glance. "You understand I had to know?" she asked softly, fully intending to address the matter with Graeham. Not even the infernal Dragon would stop her from discovering the name of the miscreant responsible for this offense against Alyss.

She fully intended to pursue it, though later. Because this was, indeed, the first time her betrothed had troubled himself to seek her out, she forced a smile, not wanting to barrage him with complaints all at once. "My lord," she said sweetly in greeting. Lifting her gown, she made her way at once toward him. "I did so hope I could speak with you today."

He smiled down at her, and Dominique found that some of her anger dissipated with the warmth of it. In truth, he was a comely man, and Alyss was right; she was quite fortunate in that, at least. "Here I am in the flesh," he told her jovially. "I trust you are feeling better this morn?" Reaching out, he sought her hand and, taking it, gently pressed his lips to the back of it.

Unaccustomed to such gracious handling, Dominique observed the gesture skeptically. "Aye, my lord," she relented, and despite her discomfiture, she felt at once a little foolish and guilty for the things she'd only just thought of him. Certainly he was nothing like his brother, she assured herself. Nay, for 'twas more than apparent that the man standing before her was of noble breeding—she cast an irritable glance at the door—at least, in most respects. His brother, on the other hand, was naught but an uncivilized brute.

"Splendid," Graeham declared. The dimple in one cheek deepened with his smile, and she found herself wondering whether he and Blaec shared that peculiar feature in common. Though even as she thought it, she was horrified. Why, by God's love, should she care one whit over such a ludicrous thing? *She need only concern herself with Graeham.* Retrieving her hand, she lowered her lashes guiltily.

"I'm pleased to hear 'tis so," he told her. "You see, I hoped to persuade you this morn to join me in today's hunt." His eyes were sparkling when she met his gaze again. "If you shall consider it, at least," he continued, "I shall count myself quite a fortunate man indeed."

With every word he uttered, Dominique felt more ill at ease. Never had she known such courtesy, or, for that matter, such honeyed words from a man. She gave him a tentative smile. "No need to consider at all, my lord," she replied reticently, lifting her chin slightly out of necessity. Yet another way in which these two brothers were alike—their uncommon height. "Truly, I should be delighted to ride at your side," she told him . . . and could not help but wonder if the Dragon would bother to grace them with his presence . . .

At the merest possibility, her stomach tumbled. She told herself it had absolutely nothing to do with the prospect of seeing Blaec d'Lucy again. Indeed, she hoped the demon Dragon didn't bother to join them at all.

Nay, she fervently prayed he would not.

Her brows knit, and she bit into her lower lip.

Not that it would matter, of course. Neither his presence nor his absence concerned her at all.

Sweet Mary, but what ailed her? She didn't seem to be able to put two thoughts together this morn without thinking of the beast. Assuring herself 'twas merely because he'd managed to distress her so this morn, she forced her thoughts to graver matters. "My lord," she began hesitantly, "there is something I wouldst speak to you of . . ." She glanced over her shoulder at her maid, and then back. "Alyss, you see . . ."

"Oh, nay, m'lady!" Alyss broke in.

Startled by the protest, Dominique turned to question her silently, and saw that she'd taken an urgent step forward. Truth to tell, she appeared very much as though she would swoon, and the expression on her face was nothing short of fearful, growing more so by the instant.

"I beg you . . . please . . ."

Dominique thought that she might be somewhat disconcerted at the notion of broaching such a tender subject before Graeham, and she relented with a nod, resolving to ask Graeham later, when Alyss was not present. Mayhap they would even have a moment aside during the hunt when she could speak to him privately.

Graeham's brows lifted. "If there is aught I can help you with, demoiselle, you need only ask," he assured her.

Demoiselle. The sound of it upon Graeham's lips was strangely unappealing after hearing it

from his brother's—though how absurd when
Blaec d'Lucy had used the word only in anger
and never in affection. Somehow the realization
filled her with a sudden hollow deep within.

What could she have possibly done for him
to treat her so? Nothing, she acknowledged.
Absolutely nothing. For a flustered instant she
could not find her voice to speak. Recalling the
way he'd looked at her, with such potent, silent
fury, she shook her head, clearing her throat,
wondering again what ailed her that she should
care whether *he* despised her unjustly, or nay.

This man standing before her would be her
husband. This was the man she should concern
herself with, and no other.

This man, and not his brother.

"Very well, then," Graeham relented. He was
watching her with the most peculiar expression upon his face. "If there is nothing . . ." He
waited for her to speak out, and when she did
not, he said, "Well, then . . . there *is* something
I wouldst have you do for me . . ."

Guilt pricked at her, unreasonable though it
might be. She wanted to please him. Nay, 'twas
her duty to please him, and she would do aught
she could to realize her place in his home. She
tilted her face to his and prayed he could not
spy the confusion that filled her soul. "Anything, my lord. You need only ask," she told
him, and meant it.

His smile was amiable, and she thought in
that instant that Graeham d'Lucy was the most
gentle man she'd ever known. God's truth, not

even her own flesh and blood had been so tender with her—not ever. She must remember to count her blessings.

"My brother," he said softly.

Dominique's heart lurched at his mention. She lowered her lashes at once.

"He is bathing in my chamber," Graeham pointed out, lifting her chin with a finger so that she was sure to see his eyes as he commanded her, "As my bride to be . . . *I wouldst have you go there now and accord him the honor of bathing him.*"

"Nay!" The word exploded from her lips, startling even Dominique, for she'd never dared deny a behest before. Still, having done so, she could not seem to find in herself an apology for her outburst. He frowned at her. Brushing his hand away from her face, she took a panicked step backward. "My lord! you cannot mean for me to—"

"Ah, but I do," he broke in, his expression hardening at her refusal. "He is my brother, Lady Dominique. And as my brother, none other in this house holds higher regard, save me. Not even you," he pointed out callously. "So you see . . . you *shall* go and you *shall* bathe him, for I'll not have myself a disobedient wife."

Dominique swallowed the bitter retort that came at once to her lips.

"Do we understand each other, Lady Dominique?"

Her heart sank. Why had she hoped it would be otherwise? Had she truly dared think she could ever be more than a political hostage in this contemptible barter? Had she dared think Graeham would be different from his brother only because his smile had been so angelic? God's mercy, but she didn't know who was worse: Blaec, who openly loathed her, or Graeham, who allowed her to hope and then would so easily grind her beneath his heel.

"Aye, my lord," she yielded, trying as best she could to keep the ire from her tone. "We understand each other very well indeed." God's truth, she thought in that instant that she didn't know which of the two she despised most. And then she frowned, for as violently as her heart was pummeling her ribs, she knew the answer was still Blaec.

Chapter 9

In truth, it might have been a perfectly reasonable request did she not so loathe the thought of being in *his* presence. Nor had Dominique e'er bathed a man before, because her brother had never allowed it. He'd warned her vehemently against their lechery, pointing out that their own mother had fallen prey to just such carnality while bestowing the honor herself. And it was true, for while Dominique recalled little of her mother, she remembered vividly her father's rages and accusations.

It wasn't difficult to ferret out the lord's chamber. It lay beyond the women's solar—or at least what should have been the women's solar. Here, as in her brother's household, there were no women save for those who served. With the realization, sadness bled into her anger, for she had envisioned herself partaking in a woman's pastimes, sharing secrets with the wives and daughters of her husband's garrison—not slaving over two ruthless, ill-tempered brothers. Mayhap Graeham was not quite the demon his brother was, but he'd made it perfectly clear what place she was to hold in his home. *None.*

In the solar, she made her way past the specters of her dreams, trying to will away the visions that came to her of women bantering at their sewing, children laughing at their feet, chasing naughty kittens with mouths full of stolen yarn. She lifted her head, refusing to give in to the sorrow. Always she had done what was necessary, and this moment was no different from any other. If she must bathe the beast, then so be it. *She would bathe the beast*.

Still, at the door she paused, her palm on the soft wood, looking over her shoulder at the empty solar. Someday, she vowed, it would be filled with laughter—by God, she would make it so! And bolstering her courage, she knocked upon the door.

Cramped within the confines of the bath, Blaec thrust a leg over the rim just as the knock sounded. His brows knit, for plainly 'twas not Graeham. While his brother seemed so determined to accord him undue honors, Blaec was certain he'd never be so absurd as to knock upon his own chamber door. Nor would anyone aware of his presence here willingly come to this chamber—certainly not without express invitation.

"*Entrez*," he commanded, fully expecting a winsome maidservant to appear, courtesy of Graeham. He didn't bother to conceal himself. Damn his brother, for if he spent half as much time seeing to himself, rather than trying to make up for something that had long been out of both of their hands, Blaec might then be able to go on with his own life, as well. Always

he would serve his brother in some capacity—
had ever sworn to—but God's teeth! Drakewich
seemed to be getting smaller by the instant. In
no small measure due to the arrival of the ill-
tempered little vixen.

Christ and bedamned! As the door opened,
he straightened within the tub at once, jerking
his leg within furiously and sloshing water
over the sides onto the floor. He'd not been
prepared for this visitor. *Not this one.* His eyes
narrowed. Most certainly not wearing *that* dress.
He gripped the tub wrathfully, prepared to leap
from the water—modesty bedamned—and bellow for his brother until the rafters shook.

"What the bloody hell are you doing here?"
he asked her incredulously.

As he watched, her cheeks brightened with
chagrin or indignation—or mayhap both, he
decided, for she gave him a fierce glare before
averting her gaze.

"Prithee, what think you I am doing here?"
she returned tartly.

His teeth clenched. "Won't you enlighten me,
demoiselle."

Her blush deepened and she seemed to take
great interest in the ceiling suddenly. With her
neck arched and bared to him so, revealing a
strong pulse at her throat, his own heartbeat
quickened. He tried to ignore the temptation,
but despite his anger, it was all he could do
not to rise from the tub and go to her, shake
her until her good sense returned, and then
satisfy his hunger for the scent and the taste
of her flesh.

Willing himself to remain seated within the bath, he allowed himself to imagine what it would be like to feel the heated pulse at her throat against his tongue. His nostrils flared. *By the love of Christ, his brother was demented to send her here.*

"I am come to bathe you, of course," she disclosed sourly.

His lips curved. "Really?"

"Not of my own accord, I assure you, my lord." She cast him a swift glare, leaving him with an impression of clear blue, fiery eyes. Christ, he could burn in those eyes. *Willingly.* He could scarcely help himself, for he burned even now. Images and sounds of bodies entwined, tangled limbs and exotic moans, accosted him . . . sweat . . . heat . . .

At the peril of his own soul, he tried to place his brother in the embrace with her, but could not; the lips he saw suckling at her breast were his own.

Damn Graeham to hell and back.

Cursing softly, Blaec shifted uncomfortably within the tub, lifting his knee as a barrier between those extraordinary blue eyes and the evidence of his arousal. Could his brother truly have no notion what he was doing sending the wench when he was unarmored and weak as Adam? By the eyes of Christ, he might be faithful to Graeham, but unlike his brother, he was far from a saint.

Aye, and in truth, he'd never come close.

And this moment he was quickly losing what will remained.

The best thing he could possibly do just now was to command her out of the chamber.

He shut his eyes, clenched his jaw, and heard himself say, *"Come hither, Dominique."*

Dominique quivered at the sound of his voice. Raw and primal, it sent fear pummeling through her. And sweet Mary, it seemed the steamy air somehow sucked the breath from her lungs, for she suddenly found she could breathe not at all. "I . . . I think not," she sputtered.

"I see." When he reopened them, his eyes were vivid green, feverish almost. Arrogantly they traveled the length of her, once again appraising her *and* her gown.

Well, good! She was glad her dress displeased him. The last thing she wished to do was to please the cur.

"And you think to bathe me from whence you stand?" he taunted softly. "Or did you plan instead to simply watch, demoiselle?"

"Of course not!" *The very notion.* Even realizing she'd been goaded into it, Dominique took a reluctant step forward, and then stopped where she stood, unable to close the distance between them, after all. Coward, she called herself.

To her dismay, he lifted a sopping rag from the water and held it out to her, his eyes boldly issuing challenge. Her body trembled at the merest possibility of touching it—that cloth that had shared the same water as he—taking it so intimately from his hands. *Touching him.*

Sweet Mary, but she could scarcely believe this was happening. And she could not think clearly with him holding the rag out so determinedly.

Was this the way her mother had felt? Was this how her betrayal had begun?

She moved forward tentatively, reaching out for the rag warily, for she imagined him closing his hand about her wrist lest she escape him. And what would she do then? Scream? Turn and flee? Somehow she didn't think she'd be able to, so much did the sight of him mesmerize her. The notion unnerved her so that she snatched the rag from his grasp, determined not to find out, only to watch him reach down into the nebulous water once again and retrieve the soap. This, too, he handed to her. Another challenge.

A gauntlet tossed at her feet.

Nevertheless, at the sight of it, Dominique found she could not move, even to save her pride. *Watch him, indeed.*

He cocked a brow. "As I've assured you once already, Lady Dominique . . . I'll not devour you."

Dominique shuddered, for she wasn't so certain. The unmistakable predatorial gleam in his eyes led her to wonder if he did not make his meal of tender babes and sacrificial virgins, after all. "Aye, well . . ."

"Unless you fear me, there is no cause to remain at arm's length . . ."

"I—do—not—fear—you," Dominique bit out as fiercely as she was able, lifting her chin. *Arrogant swine.* She eyed his outstretched hand as warily as though it were a treacherous dagger

he were offering. Swallowing hard against the
lump that suddenly appeared in her throat, she
reached for the soap, only to find that she was
so nervous, and the soap so slick and wet, she
could not seem to grip it well enough to remove
it from his hand.

Whatever clever words she'd thought to utter
fled from her mind entirely as she struggled to
gain hold of it. Coming to her aid, his hand
curled around the soap, holding it secure for
her to take, though in lifting his powerful fingers about the small piece, he *touched* her. His
fingers, hot as tiny flames, sent jolts through
her, leaving her dazed. God preserve her, but
she could only look down upon him blankly as
her heart thumped wildly against her breast.
Her fingers curled at last about the soap. How
was it this man affected her so, when his brother did not? Something must be wrong with her,
surely. Graeham was a beautiful man.

His answering smile was cold, chilling, for
'twas as though he'd glimpsed into her eyes
and there had spied her shameless weakness
to him. And like his namesake, in that instant
Dominique could well imagine that he would,
indeed, take great pleasure in feasting upon her
body and soul. The thought made her quiver with . . . surely not anticipation? Her brow
furrowed.

Fear, she told herself. 'Twas fear and naught
else.

He seemed to read her thoughts, for he asked
her, "Certainly you aren't afeared of me, Lady
Dominique?"

"What a ludicrous notion," she exclaimed, but her quiver made an immediate lie of her denial. "Whyever should I be afeared of you, my lord?"

Only belatedly did she realize she'd not removed her hand from his grasp. With his palm, he pressed the small sliver of soap into her own as his fingers mercilessly closed about her hand, clasping it cruelly. Dominique cried out, but couldn't think in that moment. Couldn't think at all. Blinking, she stared down at their joined hands, her heart tumbling violently within her breast. His gaze speared her. The curve of his lips seemed to mock her. There was something she should do, she knew, but could not conceive what it could be.

Between them, the bar of soap slithered like warm, wet velvet betwixt their palms as he twisted his hand, threading his fingers through her own, tugging firmly, and drawing her nearer. Dominique could merely go, her will having fled entirely, all thought escaping her.

Blaec told himself that his intent was to frighten her, so that she would flee the chamber and leave him in peace, once and for all, but even as he drew her nearer, and forced her hand upon his chest, he knew that he had no will left at all. Like a madness, his only thought was that he would die did he not feel her small, delicate fingers dancing upon his flesh, laving him. They burned where they touched him so tentatively, and he shook with the fierce desire that overtook him suddenly, filling his loins with heat.

Her intake of breath was audible. "My lord!"

She tried to draw away at the contact, but he found he could not release her.

"Lave me, then, Dominique," he dared her. "If you are not afraid . . ."

She stiffened, but did not immediately remove her hand, and he counted it a victory . . . a failure. God, he was weak. His brother deserved better than to be cuckolded by his own blood kin, yet he could not help himself. He felt himself a man possessed. *Obsessed*. She was in his blood just as surely as that gown of hers belonged to him. To him. *Even if she did not*. In his anger, he wanted to rend it piece by piece from her body . . . and then bury himself within her like the blade of his sword; swiftly and with sweet vengeance.

"*Lave me*," he whispered fiercely, his eyes glittering.

Still she did not move, and their gazes met, locked, held. "I am not afeared of you," she told him. Her breast heaved, drawing his gaze to the pebbled peaks that strained so deliciously against her bliaut. "I am not afeared of you," she repeated, as though it were a litany. Her eyes were wide, her pupils dilated, emphasizing the incredible blue.

"Nay?"

"Nay," she exclaimed breathlessly, and lapped at her lips with her pink little tongue.

He wanted to feel that breath upon his skin, suckle that tongue with his own, wanted to lure her into the tub atop him and crush her over his painful arousal, relieve himself of the pressure that was fast becoming insurmountable.

"Dominique," he croaked. God save him, he had no will left. No will left at all. He was weak. Despicable. And worse, without honor—his father had been right all those years past. Every muscle in his body was tightly coiled, taut to the point of snapping. He meant to command her to go, but all at once her hands began to move upon his chest and he was as lost as the angel Lucifer himself.

"*Dominique.*" The single word was a plea that she see the beast within him, that she recognize it and flee in terror, for he could do nothing but sit in the steamy water and relish the feel of her hand upon him, stroking his chest, brushing at his nipples with the soap.

"*Christ.*" Another plea. She affected him too deeply for rational thought. She should go, he knew, but he closed his eyes and laid his head back against the rim of the tub, releasing her hand at last.

Like a beardless youth, he groaned, and shuddered in raw, naked pleasure when she continued.

Chapter 10

*S*he was her mother's daughter.

God have mercy upon her soul!

The truth horrified Dominique, for even though she despised this man, she secretly thrilled to the feel of his body beneath her trembling fingers, his reaction to her touch. She had never truly understood how her mother could risk so much for the attentions of a stranger . . . until now. *And now she understood everything*. Yet her mother had been driven into the arms of another man, and Dominique had not even that to sustain her, for she'd only been here at Drakewich a single day, and had certainly not endured the suffering her mother had.

This was worse than her mother had done. Far worse.

He lay back within the tub, his brawny chest revealed to her fully, magnificently sculptured from years of battle training. And the way that his muscles quivered at her merest touch . . . it gave her a heady sense of power, even as it dismayed her, for how could Graeham test her so? She didn't understand.

Was it his intent to share her with his brother? Were they so depraved?

Something fluttered deep in the pit of her belly at the question, and she shook her head, for 'twas she who was depraved—*she*, when the merest thought of this man excited her, even despite that he infuriated her like no other. Even despite that he was not her betrothed, but his brother. Graeham, after all, had but sent her to honor his brother.

And Blaec was merely enjoying his bath.

And she?

His eyes, glittering with jewel-hard brilliance, pierced her composure.

Did he suspect her thoughts?

Her heart pummeled wildly against her ribs as she dared to explore his shoulders, mindful not to glimpse down into the murky depths of the water. She dared not, for she didn't wish to know that he shared her depravity. Jesu, what would she do then?

Lie with her enemy?

She was not so ignorant that she didn't comprehend what her body was feeling; awakened, titillated . . . tempted . . . She closed her eyes, warding away the images that rose up like Eve's serpent to seduce her.

But nay, he was not her enemy, but her betrothed. Oh, God, but not so either . . . *his brother*. Merciful Christ, but she was so confused. And she was trembling. She must gather herself at once. Cease thinking such thoughts.

She must not fail as her mother had.

Aye, she must simply do her duty and be done.

More than anything, Dominique wanted to leap to her feet and bolt for the door, but she settled fully upon her knees instead, her hands shaking like leaves before a storm. She cried out as she dropped the soap into the water and squeezed her eyes shut, thrusting her hand down at once to retrieve it, groping frantically.

Like a bolt of lightning from the darkness, his hand snaked out to seize her by the wrist, halting her search. Dominique cried out at the painful grip upon her wrist. Her eyes flew open to meet his; green and sapphire clashing. For an instant neither spoke, so charged was the air between them.

When finally he did speak, his voice was both strained and full of malevolence. "Search no more," he cautioned her, his eyes blazing, "or I warrant you'll not relish what you discover."

Dominique felt as though the breath had been whisked from her lungs, with such impact did his meaning jolt her. Her heart tumbled violently. She shook her head, averting her eyes. "S-Surely, my lord . . . I've no notion of what you speak . . ."

She felt his eyes upon her still, skewering her. So desperate was she to flee him that had she a blade, she would have gladly sacrificed her arm.

"My lord!"

He said nothing, but continued to grip her wrist as though he would snap it in twain did she so much as dare to move.

"I-I was merely looking for the soap," she explained a little hysterically.

"Were you?"

At his doubtful tone, her gaze flew to his.

His eyes glittered coldly, mocking her. "Truly?"

For an instant, Dominique had no notion how to respond. His gaze so accused her. She swallowed convulsively. *He had guessed at her thoughts!* The fury in his eyes made her feel as though he had. She began to pant softly, mentally grasping, her head pounding. *What had she done?* Merely search for the soap—naught else. She shook her head. Even if her thoughts had been wayward, *she* had done nothing untoward. Of that, she was certain.

And he was hurting her.

"Unhand me," she demanded suddenly, her eyes burning with unshed tears. He did not, and Dominique struggled to free herself, stopping only when it proved futile. She glared at him with unrepressed malice, her chest heaving with the exertion. "How dare you accuse me!" she cried out. "How dare you, when 'tis *you* that has taken so much joy in this bathing! You," she shouted, "and not I!"

His jaw twitched so imperceptibly that if Dominique had not been watching his granite-like features so intently, she would have missed it wholly.

Unknowingly, she'd struck him with the truth. *He had enjoyed it far too much.*

Furious with himself, Blaec released her. She drew away at once and made to rise. He allowed her to, saying nothing, thinking morosely how close he'd come to dishonoring both himself and his brother. So badly had he wanted to take that fine little fist of hers and wrap its velvety softness around himself. Even now, the mere thought came near to unmanning him where he sat, and he wasn't certain whose was the greater sin: Graeham's for sending the wench to begin with, hers for tempting him so sorely, or his own for succumbing so easily.

He didn't have to think on it long; 'twas his.

Because even now, he wanted her.

Even now.

It twisted his gut, revolted him.

"Wash yourself and bedamned!" she charged him, hurling the rag at him furiously and whirling to flee.

It smacked him full in the face and he reacted instinctively, surging from the water in a black rage and catching her at once, jerking her back wrathfully.

Against his better judgment, he held her too close.

The scent of her tormented him.

The feel of her burned him.

His body reacted violently. Gritting his teeth, he warned her, "'Tis said, *demoiselle*, that if one plays with fire . . . one gets burned. You are dangerously close to the flame."

She lifted her chin defiantly. "You do not frighten me," she returned fiercely, struggling once more to free herself.

"Nay?"

"Nay. I know you are beholden to your brother. You would do naught to harm his bride. Now, unhand me," she demanded. "You are wet—and you are wetting me!"

He lifted a brow. "You think I would not behave with dishonor, demoiselle?"

"I know you would no—"

He thrust her violently away. She stumbled backward, tripping upon the bed. "Then you know nothing," he snarled, following her and leaping upon her, pinning her to the bed before she could rise.

"You are sodden," she protested, panting, gasping for breath. "Get off!"

Water dripped from him, soaking her bliaut. Against his will, his eyes took in the damp fabric at her breast, the way her nipples strained against it, uplifted, heaving, tempting him, teasing. "I would venture, demoiselle—" His gaze returned to her face "—a soaking is the least of your concerns just now," he admitted, meeting her sapphire gaze with abject honesty.

"Let me be!"

Let her be? The bloody seductress. She squirmed and bucked against him as though she meant to entice him. And she succeeded, for a madness claimed him in that instant. A madness like never before, too aware was he of the soft body twisting beneath him. Seizing a handful of her curls, he thrust her head backward into the bed, forcing her still, and then, unable to help himself, he covered her mouth with his own, pressing his lips full against hers, his mouth closed, his lips trembling, some part of him still painfully aware that he could not give in to his desire.

For the love of Christ, she was his brother's bride.

He muttered a curse through clenched teeth, but the word was barely recognizable, more a savage snarl. Quaking, his mouth covering hers still, pressing until his teeth cut against the inside of his own lips, he saw his brother's image rear up before him, and he dared not part his traitorous lips, dared not kiss her intimately. He lay there atop her, instead. His eyes closing, he shuddered with an impossible determination to restrain himself. Shuddered with need.

His sex was full between them, evidence neither of them could deny.

He didn't bother trying. She whimpered, and he murmured feverishly against her lips, "Claim to me now that you are unafraid, demoiselle." How could she not be, when he was suddenly terrified of himself? His eyes speared her. "Claim to me, too, that you are unaffected," he heard himself demand, his voice strange to his ears.

She said nothing, merely stared, wide-eyed. *But she didn't deny him.* God . . .

He prayed she would.

Damn him, but he could not help himself. *She didn't deny him.* His desire too great to withstand, he thrust his tongue into the depths of her mouth, reveling in the sweet, heady taste of her, if only for the merest instant . . . the briefest . . . most extraordinary instant. *He was lost.*

It would be so easy to give in to the madness, to lift up her skirts and bury himself there. It would be so easy. God help him, he could almost imagine the way it would feel. She tilted her pelvis, and he groaned with the exquisite pain, following her, too aware of his own nakedness.

Too aware that beneath her dress, there would be no barriers between them aside from her maidenhood.

And *it* belonged to his brother.

At the feel of him, Dominique could do nothing but cry out.

Even had she not been pinned so ruthlessly to the bed, she could not have done more, for the rigidness of him against her was too shocking. Too real. She closed her eyes, helpless to the feel of his heart pounding against her ribs, tripping her own, his mouth upon hers. Closing her eyes, she felt every heated, powerful inch of him. Never before had she experienced such a terrifying, exhilarating instant of longing.

"In truth," he rasped, jerking away and turning his face, as though to gain hold of himself, "though naught has happened here betwixt us . . . neither of us can deny what *has* transpired." Beads of perspiration flecked his upper lip. She knew it was the sweat of his body, because she could taste it still upon her own lips. His eyes, when he faced her once more, were swirling with torment. She lapped her lips nervously, swallowing as he stared down at her. "Nor what might have transpired . . . can we, demoiselle?"

Dominique could not find her voice to deny him, for he spoke the truth. She was the last to understand what there was between them, but there *was* something . . . something impossible to deny. Something she *must* deny.

"Nay," he continued scornfully, his body shaking, his face gone bloodless. "But neither shall we speak of it again," he told her, "for you are correct in one thing, Lady Dominique. I will *not* dishonor my brother. This shall not pass again. Stay the hell away from me, for I am only a man—and you . . . you are a bloody temptress!" With that he shoved away from her.

Straightening to his full height, he towered above her, gloriously naked, the sight of him near as shocking as the feel of him had been.

She had not tempted him, but neither could she speak to deny it. Nor did she dare move. She could do naught but stare, wide-eyed, as he proceeded to dress himself, despite that his eyes condemned her. When she did not look away, he jerked his gaze away suddenly, as though the sight of her disgusted him, yet she was too aware that his body declared otherwise.

He was no more immune to her than she was to him.

Bewildered, she touched her fingers to her lips. Already they had begun to swell and were tender to the touch.

When he was fully dressed, he turned to address her once more, his eyes glittering dangerously. "Another thing, demoiselle . . . If you ever don that gown again, I swear to you that I shall rend it strip by strip from your body—regardless of where we are. *Regardless that you are my brother's bride.* Understood?"

Still dazed by what had transpired between them, Dominique said, her voice trembling, "Why? Why does my gown offend you so? Why should you care what I wear?"

"Because 'twas stolen from me!"

He turned to go, and she found she could move again at last. "You lie!" she accused him. "'Twas a gift from my brother!" Quaking, her limbs feeling as though they had less substance than water, she started to rise from the bed, only to find herself arrested when he turned to face her yet again. For an instant he merely glared at her, and then he turned and stalked toward her.

"I never lie, demoiselle, and I never threaten without intention!"

Dominique didn't wait to discover his *intent*. She turned and fled, scrambling over the bed, but he was much too quick. She gave a hapless shriek as he caught her about the waist and suddenly lifted her up, into his arms.

"Release me at once, you! You! *Ayeeahh*—" Her protest ended abruptly as she was dumped unceremoniously into the bath. Water cascaded up each side of her, enveloping her, sucking her down into the depths of the tub, soaking her thoroughly. She glared up at him wrathfully. "Beast! How dare you!"

His mouth curved with the first traces of genuine humor she'd ever glimpsed upon his lips. Nevertheless, Dominique was far from amused. She wanted to curse him to damnation, if only she could, for he'd all but ruined her gown—the beautiful cloth her brother had brought back for her from London, the only gift he'd ever given her. She felt like raking the demon's eyes out as he hovered above her so smugly.

"A small guarantee," he said glibly, his ensuing smile deepening the scar high upon his cheek and revealing the single dimple upon the other. *They did share the distinguishing trait*, she thought irrationally.

Without further ado, or explanation, he turned and left her, chuckling richly at her expense.

"Blackguard!" she railed at him, even as she slipped farther into the tub with the effort. Reaching beneath her, she jerked the odious lump of soap out from under her, glaring at it wrathfully, and then she hurled it at the door as it closed, taking great satisfaction in imagining the *Dragon's* head as her target instead.

Chapter 11

Clenching his fists at the sight of his brother sparring with Nial, his cocky young squire, Blaec made his way toward the scrimmaging pair, barely cognizant of the crowd of onlookers who parted before his wrathful glare. His emotions warred, for while he was pleased to see Graeham training rather than on his knees at chapel, he also had the overwhelming desire to strike a fist to his brother's face. *Her* doing, for not since their nose-wiping days had he experienced such a senseless urge.

Nial was the first to spy him. The youth's smile vanished and he lowered his sword—a testament to the fierceness of Blaec's expression, for the lad of usual, with his indomitable spirit, was intimidated by little. Proof was in the way he'd bantered so carelessly with his lord only seconds before. Not so now. He looked much as though he would soil his braies.

Graeham, spying Nial's unsettled countenance, turned to face Blaec, but unlike the youth's, his expression twisted with unconcealed amusement. "Ye God!" he exclaimed, chuckling as he took in Blaec's dripping wet head and tunic. "What in creation has happened to you?"

With some effort, Blaec unclenched the fist at his side. "Why is it you think something has happened?" he asked with deceptive calm.

"Oh . . . well . . ." Graeham shrugged, and seemed to be battling the urge to laugh.

Blaec wasn't in the mood. He cursed silently.

"Mayhap 'tis that you appear as though you've been champed and spat out," Graeham offered, and let loose a hearty chuckle.

Renewed fury surged through Blaec. "I was restless," he said tersely. Only the muscle ticking at his jaw betrayed him as he eyed the sword his brother held. "In fact, I came down to spar with you." He cocked a brow in challenge, a self-mocking smile curving his lips as he disclosed, "You might say I *couldn't resist.*" And he wondered wryly if Graeham understood the double meaning he intended.

For an instant Graeham's expression was bewildered. "Aye, well . . . that explains it," he announced with considerable humor. "You were so eager to join us that you took not even the time to dry yourself?"

Nial barked with laughter, a startled sound that quickly dwindled to a nervous groan when Blaec spared him a glance. Not trusting himself to speak, he smiled grimly at the youth and raked his fingers through dripping locks, lifting them up and out of his face. He turned to Graeham. "Seems so," he yielded softly.

A grin spread across Graeham's features. He turned to Nial. "Well, then, stand aside, lad.

Time to watch and learn," he declared with a chuckle. In a whispered aside, he added, "He wants to whip my arse, I think."

Quiet male laughter echoed about them. Nial nodded jerkily, immediately doing as he was bid, his expression clearly disbelieving that anyone should jest over such a likely prospect—brothers or nay. But Graeham's eyes twinkled as he turned again to face Blaec, undaunted. And then suddenly his expression was sober. He tipped his head, the faintest glimmer still evident in his deep brown eyes. "First," he said, "you should understand that no harm was done . . ."

For the first time in their lives, silence was a barrier between them.

"You are my brother."

Blaec stood unmoving, fully conscious of the fact that there were too many witnesses present for him to betray the truth. Guilt plagued him. Harm *was* done. It was an assertion only the two could comprehend. An acquittal. Yet it served only to infuriate Blaec all the more. Harm *was* done. He swallowed, the knob in his throat bobbing as he faced his brother . . . his friend. God save him, he'd sampled betrayal, and the taste of it was bitter, indeed. Though Graeham didn't realize, he had every right to cleave him in two. And if he didn't wish to try, then Blaec damned well did.

"I understand perfectly," Blaec said in a clipped tone, forcing a lighthearted smile. "You're much too fainthearted to lift that weapon against me . . ."

Graeham chuckled, and shook his head. "Lacking, mayhap . . . but fainthearted, never." He lifted his sword as evidence. "You might regret this," he added.

"Really?"

"Really. I've been practicing, you see." He laughed when Blaec still made no move to unsheathe his sword. "I see the very notion has you quaking in your boots."

Blaec chuckled despite himself. "Give it your best," he charged him, and with misleading calm, unsheathed his own sword, wielding it.

To any man's eyes, this would be a simple contest of skills, naught more, one of many betwixt them, but Blaec felt an underlying violence at the notion that his brother had purposely thrust him so near the edge. And guilt. He could never discount the guilt. Preparing himself, he shook his head, sending spatters of his bathwater flying into Graeham's face.

"God's teeth, Blaec, but dry yourself next time!" Graeham swiped at his cheek.

Blaec's expression turned sober. "Graeham," he said, "what if I were to tell you 'twas otherwise? What if I said harm *was* done?"

Testing its weight, Graeham swung his sword, and then shrugged. "I suppose, then, I would inquire as to whether you enjoyed it," he said flippantly, and let another chuckle at Blaec's answering expression, changing the subject. "Fainthearted, am I?" He laughed richly. "What, then, do you think of this?" Grinning, he struck the first deft blow.

With practiced ease, Blaec deflected it, returning a ruthless one of his own. God's truth, but Graeham's lightheartedness evaded him. The last thing he needed was Graeham's unwavering trust, or his sanction—and his fury, while tempered, was far from dissolved. More swiftly than he could have anticipated, Graeham shunted it, his expression turning serious with the force of the impact.

As though he'd read Blaec's thoughts, Graeham said between breaths, "*I trust you, Blaec.*"

Blaec cracked another grim smile. Pride and pleasure bled into his anger at seeing his brother's rarely exhibited mastery. It doused his fury momentarily. . . . until he recalled the feel of his brother's bride beneath him, and guilt and rage filled him anew. With a savage outcry, he whirled, striking another blow, less controlled this time, though still with confidence that Graeham could manage it. He smiled when Graeham parried so deftly. "You *have* been practicing, I see."

"I'm pleased you noticed," Graeham rejoined, his smile engaging.

"How could I not when you made it a point to say?"

"God's bones," Graeham lamented. "And I thought 'twas my skill that alerted you to the fact."

Blaec laughed, low. "Pity you thought so," he returned, unable to resist the sportive quip. Too many years of raillery lay betwixt them.

Once again metal screeched as blades clashed, tangled, sparked. They struck and parried, the contest continuing until both were winded. Blaec, emotionally torn, lacked his typical finesse. He knew too well that to allow one's emotions to rule obscured one's judgment and could prove a lethal mistake were one's opponent not one's brother. Still, he could scarcely help himself when the feel of *her* lips crushed beneath his own taunted him, made a mockery even now of his self-control. *By God, he had none!*

Not now. Not then.

And God damn him to hell for it!

Again he struck, wildly this time, blinded by self-contempt. Another. And another.

Graeham parried each, and with a hoarse cry, spun and caught Blaec's blade, striking hard, and knocking the sword from Blaec's grasp more easily than he should have been able to. It flew, striking the ground with a thud, its silver blade reflecting the sun with painful brilliance.

Stunned murmurs filled the air.

For an instant their gazes linked, held, and then Blaec turned away, uncertain as to why he'd released the hilt so easily. Mayhap he'd hoped Graeham would finish him once and for all. And mayhap he'd known his emotions were getting out of hand.

"*I trust you,*" Graeham reiterated, heaving in a weary breath and tossing their father's sword down between them.

Blaec stared at it, his fingers going unconsciously to his cheek as he doubled over. Bracing his hands upon his thighs, he gulped in air, muttering a curse as he swiped the sweat from his face with his sleeve, averting his face. He was fully aware that everyone stared. *He was mad.* There could be no other explanation for this. He was tired, aye, but so was Graeham. Damn the both of them. The night had been too long . . . and he was still too angry with Beauchamp's treachery.

Not to mention his own.

Christ . . . if he could but prove Beauchamp's guilt . . .

"Lauds!" came an unwelcome cheer. "Lauds to the both of you!"

Blaec had no need to turn to know the bearer of the voice. The hairs upon the back of his nape prickled and stood on end.

William chortled at his back. "Especially to you, Graeham." He laughed outright.

Graeham straightened.

So, too, did Blaec, meeting Graeham's gaze briefly, acknowledging the cautioning glance his brother flashed him, before turning to face the man he was beginning to loathe more, even, than he did himself at the moment.

What he didn't expect was to find *her* so soon in accompaniment, and he started, tensing visibly at the sight of her.

Her hair was damp still, but plaited now to keep the wavy locks from her face. Coiled about her head, it appeared darker, though the drier strands stood out like rich copper veins. A few escaped confinement and fell in damp ringlets about her face. Her cheeks were rosy, and growing more so by the instant—a testament of her guilt, he thought. Of his own. Their gazes met, and hers darted quickly away.

He didn't give her the luxury of turning away. Satisfaction filled him at seeing that she'd changed her dress. Yet he could only be so pleased with the victory, for her new gown left little to the imagination. The fine gold sendal was so gossamer from years of use that it clung to her like dew upon the grass blades—the effect no less mystical, and every morsel as enticing. Like minuscule, glistening beads to the eyes of a thirsting man. And the girdle she wore only served to emphasize her narrow waistline. The cords, with their silky ends, hung to her hem, tangling with her limbs as she walked, accentuating the long length of her legs and even delineating them.

The sight of her made him shudder in remembrance.

Graeham must have noted his reaction, and hers, for within the instant, he was at Blaec's back, murmuring, "You cannot usurp that which is freely yielded."

Blaec turned to regard his brother and found Graeham pensive. His brows knit. Surely he could not have meant . . .

"Let him not provoke you, Blaec. The man's an officious boor."

Blaec nodded, stunned at what he thought he'd heard, and watched as, with his politic smile in place, Graeham edged his way past him to greet their disdained guests.

"Beauchamp," Graeham bellowed in greeting. But his gaze was upon his bride, Blaec noted with some discomfort. He shifted, crossing his arms when his brother lifted Dominique's hand

and pecked it respectfully. She didn't look up at Graeham at first, and when she did, nervously, her gaze skittered toward Blaec once more.

Blaec clenched his jaw, but didn't look away. He could not, for she bewitched him even now, though he knew the dangers. She did look away, though he continued to stare, unable to help himself. In the bright light of the midmorn sun, she was no less lovely—despite that hers was not the celebrated beauty. Nor was she dark like the Eastern women. Hers was an undefinable beauty . . . a kind of radiance that invited more than a glance. Something about her mesmerized, though no one feature stood out. Even knowing her brother observed them, he could not tear his gaze away. Like some beast of prey, he could feel William's razor-sharp gaze riveted upon him, watching shrewdly.

"I do declare . . ."

Blaec lifted his head, meeting the ice-blue gaze directly, eyes that were far too familiar now in their likeness to his sister's.

William smiled, a cold smile despite its brilliance. "I thought I would never witness the mighty Dragon trounced so soundly," he commented dryly, his lips twisting with his mirth. "If the troubadours could but spy you now, d'Lucy."

Blaec said nothing. Unlike Graeham, he had no use for diplomacy. Nor did he have the patience for it. Nor did he give a damn what the bloody lyrics had to say of him. In truth, no one could deny that his brother was better suited as earl—not in this—for like their father, Graeham had been born to politics. Still he refrained from responding, though William seemed to be waiting.

"Now that we are all present . . ." Graeham broke in, in an attempt to change the subject. He turned to regard Blaec, his brows flickering in question. Blaec instinctively understood what he asked. Too much alike did they think. He nodded almost imperceptibly, and Graeham's smile returned as he again faced their guests. "Well, then," he announced, "on we go to the hunt!"

Chapter 12

Dominique only wished she knew what it was they were hunting.

The look in Blaec's eyes had been thoroughly chilling. Even now it caused her to shudder. And her brother—she eyed his brightly clad back skeptically—had insisted she carry an accursed crossbow when she had not the slightest notion how to even use one. Why, she could not fathom, for even were her very life in danger, she could not use it to save herself. She held it awkwardly now, trying not to lose it as she guided her mount and tried with all her might not to fall out of the saddle with her burden.

Forsooth, but she was beginning to wonder that this alliance was not an alliance at all, but a treacherous game they played, instead. *In truth, it felt like war*. The tension amid the small hunting party was palpable, increasing by the instant, and Dominique could little bear it.

Time and again, her gaze was drawn to Blaec. He rode ahead of her, ignoring her, though she knew full well that he was aware of all she did.

He didn't trust her, she knew. That he loathed her was evident in the way he treated her . . . in the way he could not seem to bear even to look at her. He obviously felt it his duty to keep her within sight, yet he could not abide even to glance her way. Not once had he done so. Though still she could feel his regard acutely. Strange that . . . 'Twas as though he watched her through eyes in the back of his head.

The very notion made gooseflesh arise upon her arms, limbs . . . breasts. 'Twas disconcerting, for even as much as she loathed him, the very thought of him caused her body to react peculiarly.

She tried not to think of him. Determinedly she turned her attention, instead, to the beauty of the parklands stretching before her. It was a lush land of woods and fields so abundant in its greenery that it seemed surreal. For at least a furlong beyond the castle walls, encompassing it fully, there was only grassland, a grass so verdant that it stunned the senses. Beyond the burned village, a backdrop of deeper green marked the beginning of the woodlands. Deep, dark, and misty, it took them near an hour's ride to pass through them entirely.

And now, once again stretching before them, the land rolled gently, blue in its richness and sprinkled with wild lilies in stark yellows and whites. Splashes of violet marked the distant horizon, though she could not make out the source of the color—heather, mayhap. It was mesmerizing. So much so that for an instant Dominique managed to forget her impending marriage, as well as the odious brother, forget that she carried in her hands a loathsome weapon she had no intention of using, and was simply bewitched by it all. It filled her with a sense of beauty and homage so deep that it was nearly a tangible weight within her breast.

God's truth, but seeing it now, she could well imagine that any man would covet it, fight for it, even . . . simply for the chance to breathe of its air. Closing her eyes in pure pleasure, she filled her lungs with the scent of the land, the sweetest air she'd ever breathed.

So captivated was she by the sight before her that she'd not even realized she'd reined in her mount in order to admire it more fully.

It fair stole the breath from her.

It struck her then that two tracts of the same land could be so disparate. With a touch of bitterness she could but compare it to Arndel, an unripe expanse of earth that had helped to turn her father as bitter as the soil he would come to be buried within.

'Twas no wonder her brother coveted this demesne so fiercely, while their father before him had treasured it, and the earl had fought so desperately to reclaim it. The very sight of it moved her to tears, for now . . . now, at last, 'twas conceivable that peace would come to it.

For her children.

And for their children after.

Suddenly, desperately, this alliance made sense. If it did not for these men of war surrounding her—her brother included—then it certainly did to her.

She eyed the Dragon sullenly. Somehow 'twas easy to see him as the root of all evil. Nor could she look at him now without remembering the things he'd made her feel. Even now, she could recall the imprint of his lips upon her own—her imagination mayhap, but shamefully real even so.

She feared that never again would she be able to forget.

Aye, in truth, she felt branded.

And strangely warm—a warmth that had little to do with the heat of the sun, for it seemed to radiate from somewhere deep within. 'Twas a warmth that heightened with the merest thought of him—her fingers went to her lips—of his kiss, his trembling lips and obvious restraint, the fury and passion that had swept through her as she lay beneath him, the feel of his maleness erect against her thigh . . . the heat of him. Her heart leapt at the memory. Aye, she was branded.

God's love, but so much as she loathed him—and she did, she surely did—she craved his lips again. What sort of woman did that make her, for the love of Christ, that she would lust for the brother of her betrothed? That kiss was Lucifer's own temptation, her damning bite of the serpent's fruit. And she was surely as weak as Eve . . . as weak as her mother had been.

Was she fated as they were?

Her mother had made a mistake; she'd given in to these dark yearnings, but she'd not deserved the life she'd endured afterward. Her father had all but tortured her, and she had died a harrowed, broken woman.

Nay *she'd* not given in to them, per se, but she *felt* as though she had, because she *had* in her heart and in her thoughts.

The worst thing about it all was that she doubted this could ever be forgotten. If he stayed . . . if he did not . . . she thought she would remember it always. She would crave it always. In truth, she was thankful he seemed so disinclined to look at her, for she doubted she could ever face him again without blushing fiercely. And it didn't matter that she would never break her vows once they were made—in her heart she had already betrayed Graeham, for she could not imagine lying with him now without wondering of Blaec.

God's truth, but she was no innocent to the pleasures shared betwixt men and women. She'd heard too much ribaldry in her brother's home not to understand. Aye, and she'd spied too many lovers in carnal embraces to call herself ignorant. Even now, her heart raced at the image of Blaec, towering above her, unashamedly naked . . . She couldn't help but wonder what it would feel like to be possessed by him. *Wholly*.

She shook the image away, and pressed her thighs together, willing away the heated sensations that threatened to spread through her nether regions. She was wanton and faithless. And she didn't even like the man she yearned to lie with—God have mercy on her soul.

Her eyes flew to his back. As though he felt her regard, he suddenly turned to peer over his shoulder for the first time this day and her heart somersaulted violently. No one else seemed to have noted that she lagged behind. The rest rode on, conversing lightly. He did not. He halted, letting the rest of the party pass him by, and then he turned to meet her gaze fully over the distance, his own impugning. In that instant it was as though only the two of them existed.

Dominique stifled a gasp at the intense, burning look in his eyes—a boundless knowing look that made her heart vault into her throat. Like some macabre rider, he whirled his destrier about and trotted toward her, his shoulders straight and stiff, despite the weight of his mail.

Once again he'd worn the accursed armor—a slap in the face, for by it he rudely proclaimed that he cared not a whit whether he offended them, or nay. The only thing he lacked by way of armor was his helm and shield, for he wore both chausses and hauberk with the coif back as though 'twere everyday raiment.

Dominique's first inclination was to turn her mount about and flee. But 'twas ludicrous. There was no reason to flee him. She'd done naught wrong. Again her heart leapt. At least nothing he could know of . . . *could he?*

She gave a little cry of distress as he reined in before her.

His eyes were hard, assessing. "Are you finding the hunt less than enjoyable, Lady Dominique?"

For an instant Dominique could not find her voice to speak. A breeze filtered between them, sweeping in the sweet scent of honeysuckle . . . and another more elusive scent. The scent of male sweat. Beads of perspiration dotted his upper lip, and another trickled down his temple, and she lapped at her lips, tasting his kiss even still.

God's love, but it served him right to be uncomfortable, she thought with a measure of satisfaction. After all, it had been his choice to dress so oppressively. Yet he seemed not to note it, and that fact managed to dim her pleasure somewhat. With a touch of bitterness, she thought the accursed man made of stone for all that he seemed to feel.

The same as his heart. Cold, hard stone.

The same as his body, she could not help but recall.

Her face heated. Still, she was piqued enough by his false concern that she arched a brow. "I didn't realize you cared overmuch for my pleasure, or lack thereof," she snapped, and regretted her remark at once, fearing that he might misconstrue it. *Of a certain she was not referring to this morning's ordeal.*

He smiled coldly. "And what makes you think I ask because I care, demoiselle?" His destrier pranced impatiently beneath him. "I merely find myself wondering if you've some reason to be anxious over this hunt . . . You appear so . . . distraught."

Dominique found herself staring at his lips, unable to keep herself from it; full lips, slightly down-turned, as though in an eternal scowl, and pale against his swarthy complexion—a complexion made all the darker by the shadow of his beard. And his black hair was as feral-looking as the man himself. Yet though too long, the shiny locks fared better than hers, for her own had long since begun to escape confinement, and now fell into her face in shameless abandon.

Like her thoughts.

If she thought her face warm before, 'twas nothing as it felt now. Her cheeks burned as though with fever. She averted her gaze, unable to vocalize the true source of her misery.

He was the cause of her discontent.

He was the bane of her existence.

She shook her head, her heart tripping painfully.

"'Tis a guilty flush you bear," he said, his tone bleeding with sarcasm.

Her gaze flew to his. "And you are an uncouth, heartless fiend—how dare you accuse me once again!"

His eyes narrowed, condemning her. "The innocent have naught to fear of mere questions," he countered.

Dominique straightened her back. God's truth, but she felt like hurling the crossbow at him. *If only she could lift it.* Her fingers were growing numb from gripping it so long. "I *am* innocent," she maintained, her tone wrathful. "God's truth, I have done naught wrong."

"*Are* you truly innocent, demoiselle?"

Dominique bristled, her chin lifting of its own accord. "For truth, I know not even what you accuse me of, but it seems to me that from the moment you laid eyes upon me, you were inclined to believe the worst. Tell me, my lord, what is it about me you despise so?" Even as she told herself she didn't care, Dominique held her breath, waiting for his response.

His face tightened as though she'd struck him with an unexpected physical blow. His lips thinned. "Less than I should, demoiselle—more than you know," he said hatefully.

"I have done nothing to deserve this treatment from you," she persisted, and it was all she could do to keep her eyes from misting. Sweet Mary, but what had she gotten herself into? How could she possibly bring about the peace she craved? *It wasn't going to work.*

"Mayhap as yet you have not," he relented, his face an impervious mask. "Ride faster," he apprised her, wheeling his mount about, "lest you find yourself lost. 'Tis a vast, treacherous land," he called out as he rode off, rudely giving her his back. *"We wouldn't wish to have you perish as did your messenger."*

As though he cared. Clenching her teeth, Dominique watched him canter away without giving her so much as a backward glance, a grim specter of silver, an abomination against the perfect, peaceful landscape. Yet there was a macabre beauty about him as well, with the sun glinting off his armor like diamond jewels.

She watched until he'd reached the half distance between herself and the rest of the party, all the while cursing silently at his back—

words she had no right to know, though she was pleased at the moment she did. And then stifling them, once and for all, she spurred her mount after him.

Chapter 13

⁓∾◦◦∾⁓

They'd ridden most of the afternoon, and as yet had discovered nothing—no sign of the attackers, nor of the rider Maude had wounded.

Blaec had been watching their *guests'* faces closely while they *hunted*. Either Beauchamp was truly innocent . . . or he was the most arrogant bastard he had ever encountered. More than likely 'twas the latter, for the Lady Dominique seemed as anxious as the buteo Nial held perched upon his arm, twitching in its anticipation of a feast on carrion . . . and to his way of thought, her distress gave them away.

He didn't bother to glance back at her. He knew she was there, her face pinched and white with stress. Nor had it escaped him that her brother had insisted she carry a crossbow. He wondered what they schemed. Whatever it was, he vowed they'd not succeed.

Still, the constant vigilance was beginning to wear at him.

Nor could he so easily put aside the morn's incident—guilt would be his bedfellow for many a night to come, he suspected.

To make matters worse, the buzzard's shrill, keening cries were beginning to escalate, despite that its hood was still in place. The sound, like the cries of the wounded after battle, grated upon his nerves. God's teeth, but 'twas no wonder only beginning falconers employed the ill-tempered beast, for neither was it a choice hunter. Oft was it lazy, opting to feast upon carrion, rather than finding itself fresh kill of its own—precisely the reason Blaec had brought it along today.

He was counting upon it, in truth.

He smiled grimly, imagining Beauchamp's reaction when he saw the bird unveiled at last. Truth to tell, there was a certain satisfaction to be had in this subtle baiting—even if 'twas not quite the same pleasure as he would attain in strangling the bastard outright. Yet however much he relished the thought of harrowing Beauchamp, as of yet he'd been reluctant to unhood the bird. He'd hoped not to utilize such an obvious manner of search, for he'd hoped to discover the evidence of his own. *Accidentally.*

Now, however, it was past time, for he grew weary of the game . . . as did Graeham. His gaze was drawn once again toward his brother. He could tell by the way Graeham slouched in the saddle that he was played out . . . though incredibly he continued to make idle talk with William . . . laughing when 'twas appropriate . . . nodding when he thought it prudent.

God's truth, but his brother must own an infinite amount of patience.

Blaec, however, was lacking in that virtue, and so he tuned the conversation out, dropping back from the lead to ride beside Nial, knowing it would take very little to provoke him in his present state.

"I believe we've wasted quite enough time," he remarked quietly to Nial, his tone charged with annoyance.

"My lord . . ."

Retrieving the protective glove from whence he'd placed it before him upon the saddle, Blaec thrust his hand within it, jerking it up the length of his forearm and twisting his fingers into place. He made certain the double leather padding was in proper position about the thumb and first two fingers, and then tugged on the reins, halting. Nial at once did the same, reining in beside him. Blaec stretched out his arm. "Hand me the bird," he said.

Nial's mount seemed to sense the tension, for it pranced fretfully beneath him. "My lord . . ."

Blaec eyed the youth sharply.

"Art certain?"

"At this hour, Nial, I give not a damn whether he takes insult, or nay. Hand me the God-accursed bird, lad, and do not question me again."

Nial's fair face flushed with mottled color. "Aye, my lord." Swiftly, though with care, he guided his skittish mount closer, and transferred the bird of prey to Blaec's arm, making certain the leash was well secured within Blaec's hand before releasing it fully into his care. The buteo screeched restlessly, jingling its bells in a fit of agitation—a state Blaec wholly shared in at the moment.

Hearing the bird's shrill cries, William turned to peer over his shoulder, as did Graeham. Both, at once, whirled their mounts about to watch the launch, as did the few retainers they'd brought along.

"Well, well! 'Tis about time," William called out, his spirits seeming to lift as he cantered forward, leaving Graeham at his back. "Forsooth, I thought we'd never get about to the real sport," he remarked blithely, laughing hoarsely.

Blaec gave him a cursory glance, and then simply ignored him. Nor did he bother to acknowledge the lady Dominique as she approached them at last, reining in her mount at a prudent distance . . . *but he knew she was there.* Like a blind man drawn to the heat of a fire, he sensed her brilliant sapphire gaze upon him.

If he met them . . . would they be full of loathing? Or would they be charged with the same confused desire he'd spied in them this morn? Nay, he'd not mistaken the look in her eyes . . . the passionate flush of her skin.

A vision of her lips, swollen and pink from the savageness of his kiss, emerged within his mind. God's blood, but he was like a drunkard seeking wine, drawn into the madness against his will. He shook it away, clenching his jaw. Saying nothing, he proceeded to remove the bird's hood—ignoring, too, the tightening of his loins, as his Judas body reacted to her mere presence. He had no right to it, though God save him, he burned for her despite that it was so.

The tension mounted, if only within himself.

Yet if there had been some easing of the tensions amid the hunting party itself, it vanished once the buteo was fully revealed. He heard *her* immediate intake of breath, and peered up to find her soft lips parted in shock.

Dominique could scarcely believe her eyes.

Until now, she'd paid the bird little mind, though she'd known it was there by its shrill cries. Yet there was no mistaking it now. 'Twas a revolting buzzard, and her shock was palpable.

"Something wrong, Lady Dominique?"

She was dumbstruck, though she met his gaze, more than aware that her own eyes betrayed her revulsion and startle.

"God's teeth!" William exclaimed, and his expression mirrored Dominique's feelings precisely. "What vulgarity do you plan to serve us this eve, d'Lucy?" He spurred his mount forward, invading the space between them. His mount protested, rearing slightly, and pranced away, turning as though in response to some silent warning. Restraining it, William turned to face Blaec, his face mottled with anger. "What insult is this?" he demanded.

Blaec offered no explanation, though by his expression, Dominique suspected that he enjoyed this immensely. His eyes gleamed and his lips curved ever so slightly. He opened his mouth to speak, but before he chanced to do so, Graeham rode forward, interceding.

"No insult intended, I assure you, Beauchamp. The peregrines are still molting, as yet. Only one is finished, though she is yet too fat to fly. The buteo was all that was available to us."

Still Dominique could not find her voice to speak. She might know little enough about hunting with crossbows, but she *did* know about falconry. As a child, she'd been fascinated with the mews. Graeham's explanation was likely true, for in order to molt the birds quickly, they were engorged with food to promote the growth of plumage, a process that took months in itself, and once finished, the bird was oft, indeed, too stout to fly, *and* in need of training besides.

'Twas a time-consuming task, to be sure, the keeping of birds. Nevertheless, the buteo was less than worthless in the hunt, for it did not take birds on the wing. Like the vultures, it hunted by hovering and swooping, taking small prey, such as insects and rodents, for it had not the strength or wit for bigger game—*nor was it indisposed to taking carrion*. The thought of either pickings set before her upon her trencher repulsed her wholly, and she shuddered at the very notion.

William was clearly suspicious, and his expression revealed it, yet he said nothing more, simply watched, stone-faced, as Blaec launched the buteo. With a horrendous shriek, it cast off his glove, soaring high over the trees, its guide bells tinkling eerily on the gentle breeze.

As Dominique watched, riveted by its morbidly graceful flight, cold fingers pricked at her flesh. A sense of foreboding swept over her, intensifying as the bird began to hover above

head, a black silhouette against the clear blue
sky . . . a silent harbinger of death.

Like the vulture.

Or the *Black Dragon* . . . as the tales went.

Her gaze was drawn to his silver-clad figure. His profile as he peered up at the buteo
was hard, but striking—yet so was the gleaming blade of a sword, she reminded herself, and
like it, he was just as treacherous. It behooved
her to remember it so.

'Twas said, even, that he became possessed
during battle, that he fought with the fury and
strength of three men, that he relished the scent
of blood, and woe betide to any man who came
too near to his brother. In truth 'twas rumored
that Graeham ruled more by grace of his brother's battle prowess than he did by his estimable
holdings in Normandy, and that when the Dragon faced an enemy during battle, some had
been known to clutch their hearts and die of
fright.

Dominique had always considered it naught
more than babble, but knowing what she knew
of him now . . . she could well believe it all . . .
which brought her to wonder once again how
he'd received the scar upon his cheek. Alyss
had been told that 'twas acquired during a
bloody battle on the day that he was knighted—
though any more than that was a mystery. For
truth, all that was known for certain was that
he'd received both his spurs and the scar that
fated day.

As though he'd sensed her deliberations, he
glanced her way suddenly, his lips curving

softly, arrogantly, and Dominique averted her eyes, her face flaming with mortification. Sweet Mary, but why did it seem as though he knew what she was thinking? And worse yet, *when* she was thinking about him? Before him, she felt so blessed transparent. As though there were nothing about her he could not discern, or divine.

Dominique made it a point not to look at him again and to keep her thoughts clear of him, as well.

They followed the buteo's flight about a furlong, and then it circled one last time before swooping somewhere beyond the tree line. Watching its purposeful descent, Dominique felt her stomach twist into knots. She glanced at her brother, and found him glowering as they reentered the misty woods in search of the bird and its kill. Whatever it was, Dominique vowed to have no part of it—let them all sup on field mice if they would! She would rather starve.

As the leaf-strewn path narrowed to the width of a single mount, William fell behind her so that she was directly behind Blaec. Single file they rode through the shadowy woods. In grim silence. A silence as grim as their murky surroundings.

Even as much as she despised the man before her, she dared look at nothing but his mail-clad back while they remained within the forest. Somehow, she acknowledged ruefully, his presence fortified her, for she'd heard far too many tales of woodland ambushes to feel at ease. Nor could she look into the shadows and mist without seeing all manner of intrigues. For truth, having the notorious *Dragon* in their presence settled her twofold, for while he was celebrated, he was also notorious, and it seemed ridiculous to be afeared when he was a capable and feared warrior.

Nor was it aught but foolish to fear the unknown when her greatest menace rode directly before her.

And it galled her that Graeham had yet to offer her a moment's interest. Forsooth, she'd ridden the majority of the morning in silence, with not even her brother to speak to, and though it had not bothered her in the least to begin with, it now grated upon her nerves. *It seemed to Dominique that her betrothed was bound and determined to ignore her.* What then was she to be? Naught more than a bauble to show when he found the inclination? The arrogance of men! It seemed incredible that the only one person to show her any heed at all was the very man she despised—the very man who despised her, in turn.

Her emotions were in turmoil. How was she supposed to feel, to think, when one moment there seemed to be great hope for the future . . . and the next there seemed to be no hope at all? Nor had she been given the slightest occasion to discuss Alyss's ordeal with Graeham, despite that she'd been watchful for the opportunity to speak with him privately. It seemed now that she'd watched for naught. But it didn't matter; somehow she would find a way. If not now, then later—or she would try Alyss again, for the mere thought that Alyss's abuser was free to harm another choked her with impotent fury. The more she thought about this morn's encounter, the less she could turn her attention from the odious brother, and the angrier she got.

At him.

At herself.

What was wrong with her? Why could she not cease thinking of him?

Because she was faithless and wanton.

And because no man had ever kissed her before . . .

Dominique closed her eyes, once again blocking out the burning memory of his lips trembling upon her own.

God's truth, but why could she not fantasize about Graeham instead?

Why must she crave the forbidden?

Her eyes closed tightly, and she arched her face skyward, breathless with desperation, feeling nothing but the coolness of shadow beneath the canopy of trees. Still, she burned from within, a heat that made her heart quicken and trip. Her hand fluttered to her throat as she willed away the treacherous thoughts. She had to fight the urge to make the sign of the cross. *Holy Mary, mother of God,* she intoned silently, *pray for us sinners—*

"Something ail you, Lady Dominique?"

Dominique's eyes flew wide to find Blaec peering back at her over his shoulder. Her heart turned violently. "I . . ." She shook her head, flustered. "Nay," she croaked, fanning herself with a hand. "'Tis but that . . . I . . . I am hot . . ." Her face flushed. Anxiously she lowered her hand to the crossbow she held in her lap.

His eyes flickered with amusement. "Here in the shade of the forest?" he asked her.

Her heart continued to hammer. "I-I mislike the woodland," she countered quickly, gripping the crossbow too tightly now.

Still his gaze was unwavering. "Do you tell me that you are afeared, Lady Dominique?"

He taunted her now, she knew. Dominique clenched her teeth together, refusing to be baited.

His lips curved arrogantly. "Tell me what it is you fear, Lady Dominique?"

She could not bear it. "Certainly not you!"

His smile deepened. "Truly?"

"Aye."

"Ah . . . but you would if you were wise, demoiselle."

Blackhearted, misbegotten swine! Cur! As much as she wished to rail at him out loud, Dominique held her tongue, gritting her teeth as she forced a smile. "Are you trying to tell me something, my lord?" she asked as sweetly as she was able.

"My, but you *are* wise," he remarked softly, mockingly, though he said nothing more, merely turned his back on her once more, chuckling low. Dominique bristled. More than anything, she wanted to fly at his back and claw him to death like his odious buteo would do to its prey. Never in her life had anyone infuriated her so. Never had one single person elicited from her so many emotions. God have mercy, she would grow mad did she have to suffer his presence eternally!

In her anger, she was vaguely aware that he dispatched two men to ride ahead—the squire, Nial, accompanied by another. Her sense of unease intensified as she watched them ride into the obscurity of the forest.

They didn't return, a fact that Dominique cared not to contemplate.

It seemed for an eternity thereafter that they rode in disquieting silence . . . until ahead of them a nimbus of sunlight pierced the shadowy realm. A mere instant later, Nial's shout reached them, and though Dominique could not make out the words, she felt instant trepidation.

At once Blaec spurred his mount, edging past his brother and breaking into a full canter as he passed into the nimbus, bursting from the misty forest and into the bright sunlight.

Chapter 14

❧

Though Dominique could no longer spy him, she could hear the voices clearly: Blaec's cursing, and Nial's rapid speech. Turning instinctively to seek out her brother, she found William brooding.

An instant later, shielding her eyes with a hand, Dominique followed Graeham into the piercing sunlight, and William after her. Like some gruesome song, she heard the frenzied tinkling of the buteo's bells long before she spied it. As her vision cleared, she found them gathered, muttering to themselves, staring down as the buteo gorged itself upon its kill.

It took an instant longer for Dominique to grasp the full atrocity of the scene unfolding before her. As Nial slipped from the saddle with the lure in hand to retrieve the buteo, she was afforded a clear view, and it was all she could do to keep from swooning where she sat upon her palfrey. She cried out, horrified, and at once averted her gaze, feeling the bile rise in her throat.

Dear God! If she was not seeing things—if her eyes were not playing tricks upon her—

'twas a man they'd found! *A man and not an animal.* Swallowing convulsively, she whirled her mare about and urged her away from the bloody scene, scarcely able to bear the thought of being in such close proximity.

William, she noted, made no move to join the others, and for the longest instant, Dominique was too paralyzed to even consider why he seemed so withdrawn. She sat there, clutching the crossbow in hand, her heart hammering and her stomach churning as she fought an incredible surge of nausea.

A man, dear God . . . a man . . . The enormity of that fact overwhelmed her now.

William roused himself at last, casting her a glance as he passed her by and moved toward the gruesome scene. And still Dominique could not stir herself. She wanted, more than anything, to flee. She wanted to spur her mount and fly back to the castle, but she remained aloof, her body trembling, chilled despite the heat of the sun.

"Aye. 'Tis my messenger," she heard William say low, evidently recognizing the dead man. Shock pummeled through her. "God's blood, but they butchered him, did they not?"

Silence; it was deafening.

"Art certain?" she heard Graeham ask, breaching it finally. "Hardly is he recognizable with that wound upon his face."

Dominique tried not to imagine what sort of wound he might bear.

"Aye," William ceded grimly. "'Tis my livery he wears."

"Good God, man, how can you tell?" She shuddered at hearing Blaec's deep, resonant voice. "It looks as though he fell from his mount and was dragged the distance. Little enough remains of his garments to wipe my arse with." There was an edge of barely suppressed violence to his tone, but Dominique attributed it to the situation at hand. It wasn't likely any man—even the hardest of men—could remain unaffected by the gruesome sight, regardless of whose ally it was who lay sprawled before them.

"'Tis he," William persisted.

"My lord," Nial ventured. "Look there . . . you can still spy the marks where he was dragged. Do you see them? Strange that they come from the direction of the village," he remarked.

By chance, Dominique glanced down, spying the marks that led directly beneath her horse, marks that scattered leaves and underbrush aside, leaving an unbroken trail of disrupted earth . . . and . . . *and blood*. As she followed it with her eyes, toward the burned village in the distant horizon, another rush of nausea threatened, and she had to steady herself lest she fall.

"Strange, indeed," William agreed.

"Indeed," Blaec echoed, his tone clipped. "Mayhap you have an explanation for it, Beauchamp?"

"Perchance, do you?" William countered icily, and Dominique had no need to spy their faces to understand the silent battle that waged betwixt them—both so ready to cast blame. It made her ill.

Too stunned to remove herself farther from the newly detected evidence, she sat numbly. Behind her she heard the approach of hooves, and in the next instant Blaec passed her by, searching the ground intently, lifting his gaze only briefly to cast her a hate-filled glance—as though somehow this were all her own fault. The audacity of the man!

'Twas her brother's loss and not his. If aught, 'twas William who should be casting blame. It seemed Blaec d'Lucy was determined to mistrust them. Still, she held her tongue, saying nothing, for 'twas her brother's place to speak and not hers. Nor did she feel William would welcome her meddling. The look he'd given her yestermorn when she'd speculated aloud about the messenger's fate was enough to keep her tongue stilled even now. *And she had been wrong. William had been right.*

Had it only been yestermorn since their arrival? It seemed an eternity ago, for within that time so much had transpired.

One by one, the rest of the party passed her by, following Blaec as he searched the ground for some telltale evidence of the man's identity. Only her brother remained beside the body, staring down at the gruesome sight in contemplative silence, his face clouded with rage.

Dominique guided her mount backward, off the trail, and out of their midst that they might search unencumbered. Her position between them offered a clear view of both her brother and the rest of the party—though still she could not bear to look fully upon her brother and the ghastly body.

For truth, it seemed she sat her mount an eternity, every sound magnified . . . every moment of tension stretched until she could feel them acutely.

Her heart hammered mercilessly, the beat of it a cacophony within her head. And suddenly the sounds imploded within her mind, for in her peripheral vision she spied her brother lifting up his crossbow . . .

Sweet Mary! She knew he was furious, but clearly he was not thinking. Clearly he reacted in anger.

Before she could even look his way to plead with him . . . to stop him . . . an arrow flew. Terror filled her heart with the sound of its release. It whizzed by her head, the sound of it a merciless roar in her ears. Dominique didn't stop to think what it was she was doing. She knew only that William could not be caught in the midst of these men who did not trust him—*who would relish any opportunity to skewer him through.*

He could not be the sender of the arrow. Nay, it had to be her.

It happened so quickly, she had not the time to think. At once, she lifted up the heavy bow, her hands quaking violently, and was relieved to see that her brother lowered his own. In the next instant the arrow struck, embedding itself into the bark of an oak, barely missing Blaec's head in its deadly flight. The sound of its impact was like to the first cracking of thunder in a violent storm.

Blaec's head snapped about, his gaze going instinctively to her brother, and then to her. His eyes narrowed as he spied the crossbow in her hands, and he wheeled his mount about, advancing upon her, his destrier rearing slightly in his furious handling of the animal.

Dominique had no notion what to say when faced with his fury. Nor, in her shock, did she move to lower the bow. Still, she could not regret her decision, for William was likely too emotional to have considered his actions. She was certain that he'd not meant to challenge.

She prayed he'd not meant to challenge.

From the corner of her eye, she saw that he seemed to be watching. He made no move to load another arrow.

And still Blaec said nothing, merely stared, first at the extended crossbow and then at her face, his gaze unwavering, his green eyes slivering in his fury. Dominique swallowed convulsively, wishing he'd speak, that he would say something—anything.

"I-It was an accident," she ventured, her voice faltering. She prayed her brother would not discount her.

"An accident, demoiselle?" Blaec's tone accused her. He peered down at the crossbow, and then back.

Dominique nodded jerkily, praying he'd believe her—trying not to imagine what he would do to them if he did not. She dared not glance at her brother even to bolster her courage—dared not give him away.

Blaec seemed to sense her thoughts, for he

looked directly at William and said softly, menacingly, "Like Rufus in the New Forest?" He asked her pointedly, "That manner of accident, Lady Dominique?"

For an instant Dominique did not grasp his meaning, and then recalling the rumors of William Rufus's death, that he was murdered by his brother during a hunting accident, an accident that had occurred too many years before her birth for her to speculate, she shook her head frantically. "Nay, my lord! Nay! I was simply afeared, is all. I—I thought the attackers might still be lurking and reacted without thinking."

When his eyes met hers again, they were brilliant in their fury. Truth to tell, Dominique thought she might not live to see another instant, for she could well imagine him striking her dead where she sat—woman, or nay!

"My lord," she said contritely, "I . . . I am sorry . . ."

"Are you truly?" he asked her, once again peering down at the crossbow, his green eyes canny. He cast another glance at William before returning his gaze to her. "And did you truly think to protect yourself with that bow, demoiselle?"

Dominique's eyes narrowed: She knew instinctively that to cower now was folly. "Do you not think me capable, my lord?" she asked him indignantly.

His lips curved, and his eyes were hard as glittering jewels. He nodded curtly. "Something did give me just such a notion," he mocked her.

"Really, my lord! Because I am a woman?" she asked him, becoming incensed now. The truth was that Dominique didn't know how to use an accursed crossbow, didn't even know how to load one, but that he would simply assume 'twas so infuriated her beyond reason.

"Nay, demoiselle," he bit out, advancing upon her once again, until his destrier was at her side and he faced her squarely, leaning forward, his lips so close to her own as he spoke that Dominique could feel the heat of his breath. "'Tis because you are holding the bloody device upside down," he informed her arrogantly. "God preserve mankind from ignorant females!" he said, snatching the unloaded crossbow furiously from her hands.

Chapter 15

Hours later Dominique's cheeks still grew warm with the memory. God's truth, but she'd never been more humiliated in all her life. Her only comfort lay in the fact that Blaec d'Lucy had believed her tale—had accepted her lie as truth.

Meager comfort that, when he likely thought her an imbecile, as well.

Nor had she as yet discerned *why* William had discharged the arrow, though she thought it very likely that he'd done so in anger. Seeing the body of his own man, lying there . . . Dominique shook her head, unable to bring it to mind, so horrid was the sight. And if she could not even think of it . . . how much worse had it been for her brother to see it?

Aye, she could well understand his fury. And knowing William, that he'd sucessfully tempered his anger enough not to challenge Graeham was remarkable, and she could not regret having taken the blame for him. She could never have borne the sight of her brother dying before her, and he would never have prevailed, outnumbered as they'd been.

Nor had it truly been Graeham's fault—not when he'd not even been aware of their imminent arrival. How could he have known to send guards when the messenger had never arrived to request it? With that thought, she sent a silent prayer skyward and crossed herself, thanking God for their safe passage. How easily such a fate could have been theirs. She shuddered at the thought.

If only now she could speak with William . . . if she could but see his face . . .

They'd returned to the castle in grim spirits, all of them, no one breaching the taut silence— not even Graeham, who was of usual so diplomatic. And then her brother together with Graeham and Blaec d'Lucy had closeted themselves at once, speaking in low tones behind closed doors. For her part, Dominique had made great haste in seeking the sanctuary of her bedchamber—she closed her eyes— Blaec's chamber, she corrected herself. Not hers.

She sat now, her stomach roiling as she imagined the discourse taking place belowstairs. By the look in Blaec d'Lucy's eyes, she thought mayhap both she and William were in mortal danger. Nay, he'd not held her accountable there in the woods, but she sensed it would come to that, and soon.

Scarcely could she bear the wait.

It seemed hours that she sat upon the bed, wringing her hands, staring at the door. 'Twas with great relief that she greeted William as he entered the chamber, at last. Though his expression was grave, Dominique could only be reassured that he stood before her unharmed.

"William!" she exclaimed, springing from the bed. She ran to embrace him—something she'd not done since they'd been children together. Yet she was so glad to see him that she could scarcely contain a sob of relief. "Oh, William," she cried, embracing him tightly. "I worried so."

Her gesture seemed to startle him, for he returned the embrace awkwardly at first, and then with restraint, looking down upon her with the queerest expression upon his handsome face. "What is it?" she asked him. "Tell me!"

He cleared his throat, and then embraced her more fully, laying his cheek down upon the pate of her head. "I . . . I think it best I should go, Dominique."

Dominique gave a small gasp of surprise at his disclosure, and tried to withdraw, but he held her firmly against him with a hand splayed at her back, as though he could not bear for them to part as yet. Hearing the powerful hammering of his heart only managed to heighten her fears. God preserve them both, for little, if anything, ever concerned her stalwart brother. To Dominique's way of thought, their situation must be dire for him to be so troubled now. At her back, his palms were sweaty. She could feel the dampness even through her gown, and a frisson rushed through her, prickling her spine.

"God . . . Dominique . . ." His voice was hoarse.

Dominique peered up at him. "Dear God, William, tell me!" She clutched at his tunic. "Do not keep me unknowing . . . please . . ."

He cleared his throat once more.

She could little bear the wait. "Did they bid you leave?"

"Nay, Dominique, they did not." He cupped her chin, lifting her face with a tenderness the likes of which he'd never shown her before—the likes of which she'd never known. Ever. The gesture overwhelmed her. "You were very brave today," he told her gently. "I was fiercely proud of you." His expression, for the first time in so long, was tender, caring, as though he bore her some measure of love. How long had it been since he'd looked at her so? Her heart leapt, and like a child long starved for affection, tears swam in her eyes. What mockery of life this was, that they should find each other now when he was to leave her.

"I could not bear for them to harm you," she told him truthfully.

"Aye, well, 'tis precisely why *I* think it best I go," he told her. "Today you were able to salvage the day, Dominique. Tomorrow, mayhap not."

"Nay, William . . . please . . ." How long had she yearned for a true family? God's love, how long had she craved her father's, mother's, brother's arms? Any one of them, to no avail. How long? Nay, she could not lose him now. Not now. "I cannot bear the thought of remaining here alone," she told him, her eyes pleading with him. "Not without you. Do not leave me."

"Dominique . . . *my love* . . . my little sister . . ." His voice trailed suddenly. And then he frowned, seeming to regain hold of himself. "My presence here does naught but undo the good we've worked so hard to achieve," he said with resolve. "Can you not see that? The truth is that while I crave this alliance above life itself, I cannot trust myself to remain under the same roof with Blaec d'Lucy. You witnessed the truth of that today—nor do I trust the bastard any more than I trust myself in his presence. I cannot abide the man. 'Tis best that I go. There is too much to be lost elsewise. And you shall see . . . all will be right in the end," he assured her, releasing her chin abruptly and thrusting her face away, as though it disturbed him suddenly.

"You must trust me," he told her sternly. And then he grasped her arms suddenly, startling her. "Do you trust me, Dominique?" He shook her gently when she did not at once respond. "Do you?"

Dominique nodded, and allowed him to draw her once more into his embrace, although he held her a little too tightly this time, a little too intensely. God's truth, but she thought he would squeeze the breath from her lungs! Gasping for air, she felt the sudden inexplicable need to pull away, distance herself, but she did not. She held him back, though somewhat rigidly, telling herself it was merely that she was unaccustomed to such affections betwixt them. She frowned at herself . . . *This was good . . . this was what she wanted . . . wasn't it?*

"Good," he said, and sighed heavily, releasing her.

Relieved, Dominique at once withdrew from his embrace, stepping back out of his reach, drawing in a shaky breath.

He frowned at her reaction, but overlooked it and said, "Listen to me closely, Dominique . . . You must find a way to hasten the ceremony. You must lead Graeham to the altar as soon as 'tis possible. It simply cannot wait, for I fear Blaec d'Lucy would thwart us if he could. Do you understand me?"

Dominique nodded dejectedly. "He does not trust us," she agreed, and then averted her eyes as her heart twisted painfully. Her brows knit. "I believe he does despise me, in truth." She dared not glance up at William in that instant, dared not . . . for fear that he would see how very much the notion pained her.

Not when she could not comprehend it herself. Sweet Mary, but why should she care what Blaec d'Lucy felt for her? Yet somehow . . . somehow . . . she did.

"I understand," she said softly, gazing up at him suddenly as tears once again welled in her eyes. God's love, but she was so confused. "I swear I'll not disappoint you, William." She shook her head. "I swear, I will not."

He studied her a moment, and Dominique fidgeted under his intense scrutiny. "Nay," he agreed, his expression hardening abruptly, "you'll not, Dominique." His eyes pierced her as he cautioned, *"See that you do not."*

Try as she might, long after William had departed Drakewich, Dominique still could not abolish from her thoughts the warning in his glare. Something about the way he'd looked at her as he'd ridden from the gates filled her with dismay, for it left her with a sense of impending doom.

Following their discourse, William had not even remained long enough to take the evening meal with her: rather he and his retainers returned to Arndel, hoping to utilize the remaining daylight for their ease of travel. At table, Dominique was especially quiet, reticent even, listening to the bantering of the men, and trying not to feel a hostage in the enemy's court. For truth, that was what she felt like, even despite that Graeham d'Lucy seemed intent on smoothing the way before them. He entertained her with stories of his and his brother's youth, while Dominique tried not to wonder what his devil brother was up to, conspicuously absent as he was.

Scarcely able to bear the tension of awaiting his inevitable arrival and the burden of smiling when she did not feel like it, Dominique was unable to muster the slightest appetite. She excused herself early and escaped to the solitude of her chamber.

With Alyss's help, she prepared herself for bed and crawled beneath the covers, fatigued by the ordeal of the day. Though still, even into the blackness of night, sleep eluded her.

Forsaken and afeared as she felt, the overwhelming sense of doom intensified. *Something was not right, she knew.*

She could feel it just as surely as she breathed.

Or mayhap 'twas simply guilt . . . guilt because along with her brother's face, another swam before her eyes, as well.

Not Graeham d'Lucy's.

This face was swarthy . . . scarred . . . the eyes too knowing, scathing . . . and still—God have mercy upon her wicked, unrepenting soul—she craved those beautiful, demanding lips upon her own . . .

The very memory stirred to life within her the most disturbing heat. She tossed and writhed upon the bed, breathless and perspiring, betrayed by her traitorous body, unable to find respite. Nor could she bring into focus the man Alyss spoke of and the one whom she knew. Kind? Compassionate? She could not conceive it, yet Alyss's words held truth, as well. It seemed 'twas only she who inspired such viciousness in him, for he *had* been concerned for Alyss. She was confused.

And God help her, when at last she succumbed, 'twas of *him* she dreamed.

Chapter 16

The almoner had collected and distributed much of the previous night's offerings, but Dominique felt it her duty to see that the villagers received more. After all, these would soon be her people—regardless of what she felt for their lord—and somehow she felt responsible after seeing their homes ablaze in the night. Many still worked diligently to repair their incinerated huts, while others searched for strays from their flocks, gathering them together.

Early this morn, Dominique had requested permission from Graeham to dispense items of need: blankets, clothing, and some food. Closeted with his odious brother, he'd refused to see her, but had granted his express permission for her to take whatever she would to them. In *that*, he'd been generous, as somehow she'd known he would be, but the fact that he avoided her still made her feel less than welcome in his home. Dominique could not help but worry, bitterly, that if he could find her so repulsive, he would risk the alliance. How could she inspire in one man such hatred, and the other such indifference?

God's truth, but she was becoming so very confused.

Free to come and go as she chose, she conveyed what she could to the village and was surprised that they received her offerings with such mistrust. Truth to tell, they eyed her as though they expected her to hand them poison instead of the comforts she bore. Dominique didn't care. Let them mistrust her if they would. For now. Soon enough they would see that she meant to be mistress here in every way—and that meant caring for them in the manner she'd never been able to for the villein at Arndel. 'Twas something she aspired to, and she would prove herself to them all.

Without being asked to, she began a stew of leeks and cabbage for one of the larger families, showing the woman, Maude, how to employ the most common spices to flavor the broth. While Dominique was no master of the simples, she certainly knew enough to enlighten them. Alyss, on the other hand, was quite skilled, and Dominique vowed to bring the maid along on her next visit. There would be much Alyss could teach them, Dominique was certain—including how to grow some of the more useful herbs themselves. Maude, for her part, stood guard over her shoulder, as though she expected Dominique to add a pinch of mandrake instead. No matter that she told herself she was not insulted, she *was*. She could not help but be.

Later, wearied of trying to prove herself to the parents, she played hide-and-seek with the children, keeping them occupied while their mothers and fathers labored to set things aright. And from the children, she received a more ardent welcome. In their innocence, they held no prejudice against her, and she found herself, for the first time in days, able to forget that she was an unwelcome stranger in their midst.

Still, their honesty was staggering, bewildering.

"My da says your devil brother burned our homes," one older boy told her.

The laughter died in Dominique's throat. Caught in the middle of tying the scarf about the boy's eyes, she unraveled the knot and whirled the lad about to face her. "Nay! 'Tis not so," she told him fiercely, seizing him by the shoulders, trying to make him see. "Your da is not right! My brother was with me during the fire—within the castle! Do you understand? He most certainly did not burn your homes!"

She released him when he nodded mutely, but her own expression remained stricken, for the damage was done. She could play no longer with her heart so heavy. God's truth, but it seemed that when her brother was innocent, he was guilty still. 'Twas unfair!

She offered the day's farewells with a smile, though it never reached her heart. Even with hugs from the children and a penitent glance from the boy, she could not regain her former resolve and lightheartedness. Nor could she so soon return to the castle. Instead, she mounted her palfrey and sought sanctuary in the distant meadow. There she dismounted and sat wearily upon the plush grass, and before she could thwart them, tears sprang to her eyes.

It seemed hopeless. Could these people ever forget the bitter battles fought by their fathers before them and accept her as she was? She had been willing to lay her grudges to rest. 'Twas her own father, after all, who had perished at the hands of Gilbert d'Lucy! If she could forget these things for the sake of peace . . . could not these people even try?

Dominique knew 'twas pointless to feel sorry for herself. She knew 'twould solve naught, yet she could scarcely keep the sadness and sense of loss—a loss she'd not even experienced at the death of her own father, at least not so acutely—from enveloping her. And then there was the loneliness. With William gone from Drakewich, she truly had no one.

No one at all.

Nor, she realized, could William care for her overmuch when he'd left her here alone to endure as best she could in his enemy's home. Aye, his *enemy*, for he'd gone so far as to call Graeham so—even despite that they'd forged this alliance. Nay, he could not care for her. Nor had he said he would return for her nuptials. On the contrary, he'd admitted that he could not stomach the sight of her with Graeham d'Lucy. The look upon his face, in truth, had been as though she were being exiled. So, then, he would sacrifice her and then abandon her? Would he never then be able to bear the sight of her again? What sort of an alliance was that to be?

'Twas no alliance but war, a little voice answered.

And she was its casualty.

Plucking a new blade of grass from its pale green sheath, she studied it, turning it between her fingers. Then, suddenly, she tossed the blade into the breeze and watched as it was carried away. Lifting her gaze toward Drakewich, she thought that, like the solitary blade, she was lost, caught in the wind betwixt heaven and earth . . . or rather, hell.

As the blade fell to the ground in the distance, she knew that selfsame fate would be her own.

'Twas hell that awaited her.

A soft sob escaped her and was muffled at once, for as she glanced behind her to be certain she was alone, she caught sight of a figure on horseback, watching her silently from the shadows of the woods.

Gasping in startle, she scrambled to her feet, her heart racing as she turned to face the rider.

She thought . . . God's love . . . she could not be certain, but it looked to be William! She would recognize his odd helm from any distance, uncommon as it was. Made of a darker metal, with rivets and bands and a nose guard that fell well below his chin, dividing his face full in half, 'twas a sight that would have frightened her silly were it not so familiar. Yet it was, and the possibility that it might be William lifted her spirits at once.

Might he have changed his mind? Might he have returned?

Waving, Dominique hailed the rider, but the figure did not so much as stir. Yet she knew it was him—she knew it! Why he did not make himself known, she had no inkling, but 'twas him, she knew. Tossing caution to the wind, she lifted her skirts and began to race toward him.

It had to be William.

Even as she closed the distance, the figure retreated into the trees. Dominique called out his name, and ran faster, though her sides ached with the exertion.

"William! Wait! William!" She shouted to no avail, stopping and gulping in a breath as the rider disappeared completely from view, engulfed by the trees. Still, she was too close to simply stop where she stood. 'Twas him. She knew it. It had to be. Once again she lifted her skirts and ran, stopping to catch her breath only when she entered the threshold of the woods. Unable to go farther, she leaned against a tree rather than collapse to her knees, resting as she took in her surroundings, seeking some sign of the rider.

There was none.

Her side ached, and she clutched it, winded and disheartened. Still the area was undisturbed, as though the horseman had been naught but an apparition. But it could not be . . . The hairs at the back of her nape prickled, rising. She could not have imagined him.

She *had* seen a rider.

Shaking her head, she covered her face with her hands and gave way to a rare burst of hysterics. Had she wished so much for her brother's return that she would envisage him here? God's truth, but she thought she would go mad in this place alone!

"Perchance you are looking for someone, demoiselle?"

Startled by the unanticipated voice, Dominique straightened at once, pushing herself from the tree to face Blaec d'Lucy. She frowned. *Her tormenter.* For an instant there was only silence between them. "You!" she exclaimed suddenly.

Like some doomster, he sat his mount, looking down upon her, saying nothing, though his brows lifted, mocking her once again.

Her hackles rose, and her hands went to her hips in outrage. "'Twas you!" she accused him. "You all along! What right have you to stalk me so?"

He cocked one brow higher. "Is that what I am doing?"

His tone sounded bored, as though he could not care a whit that she'd *caught* him at his spying. Dominique's blush heightened with her anger. "You know very well that it is, my lord," she said through clenched teeth. "Tell me . . . what is it you hoped to discover following me— spying!" she accused him outright. Let him be offended, if he would, for she had no desire to mince words.

"What is it you hoped to hide?" he countered, dismounting, and tossing the destrier's reins over its withers.

Dominique eyed him warily as he approached. And then it struck her that, for the first time, he'd not donned his raiments of war. Nor had he worn the ominous black. Instead, he'd worn a shorter, light gray tunic with simple blue embroidery, and dark blue hose. Nothing remarkable. But the breeches, unlike the ones he'd worn the day before, were shorter, and all but indiscernible beneath the tunic, *leaving his hose completely exposed to her view*. Dominique had seen the fashion worn on occasion, though never quite so indecently. Having never been to court to witness the changing fashions, she was rarely subjected to such revealing sights. And her brother's men—her brother, included—had not the coin to follow the newest trends. Praise God for that, for the sight of his near bare legs left her dumbfounded.

Standing before him now, faced with his state of dress, she forgot everything, forgot his scarcely veiled accusation, forgot her wariness, forgot her anger, forgot even her breeding. Her gaze rose the length of his well-muscled calves to his perfectly delineated thighs, and she was struck speechless. "I . . ." She swallowed convulsively, her gaze returning to his face briefly and then back to his disclosed limbs.

A shudder coursed through Blaec at the look she gave him. "You what, demoiselle?" His voice sounded strange to his own ears. God curse him, she didn't know what trouble she was courting with that look. Were he any other man . . . and she any other woman . . . Christ . . . were she not to wed his brother . . .

It didn't matter what *she* wore, or for that matter, that she was dirty after serving in the village and rollicking with the children, she was beautiful—too beautiful for his own good. He'd watched her from the castle walls, for it had struck him as odd that she'd wish to aid the villagers when 'twas her own brother who had caused so much destruction . . . or mayhap 'twas why she wished to help. Guilt was an effective motivator. Or at least, he'd begun to believe 'twas so until he'd spied her here, waiting— he'd not missed the rider on horseback, watching from the distance. Dominique must have known him, expected him, for she'd waved. But the rider had disappeared upon seeing Blaec's approach. That she'd not realized he rode toward them told Blaec only that she'd lost all thought at the sight of her . . . lover, was he? The mere possibility sat like acid within his belly.

"You seem to be struck dumb of a sudden, Lady Dominique."

"I . . ."

His jaw tightened with displeasure. "Perchance it was something I said?"

Her gaze remained fixed upon his limbs. "Something you said," she repeated dumbly. Her brows knit, and her tongue darted out to lap at her lush, full lips.

Heat surged through his veins. "Lady Dominique . . ." He shut his eyes, willing his own body to restraint. When he reopened them again, it was to find her staring still, and he shuddered, undone by the desire so evident in her brilliant blue eyes. Eyes that were too knowing by far. 'Twas a gaze that enticed and teased, for she knew very well he would not have her.

Could not.

Did she tease him apurpose? He wondered.

It led him to wonder, too, though he had no right to, how oft she'd issued such blatant invitation before. Led him to wonder how oft such temptation was met. Once again, it led him to anger.

And then he reminded himself that he had every right to consider his brother's interest. The last he intended was to allow her to foist some bastard's by-blow upon Graeham. Graeham was too accepting by far. His anger rose, and with it his determination to discover the truth about the little vixen standing so defiantly before him.

Whom had she intended to meet . . . Was it her lover, by God, or her brother's spy? Either possibility burned his gut raw.

She was no innocent, he vowed. Nothing about her bespoke it—not her too ripe bosom, nor her long, lean legs, made to wrap a man's waist in bawdy pleasure.

Again he shuddered, more affected by the sight of her than he cared to acknowledge.

Was that, then, why William wished to hurry the ceremony? Was she no innocent? Unpure? Was that why they'd come to Drakewich unannounced? Had they hoped to secure the alliance before her belly swelled with child? God damn the both of them!

He'd not realized he advanced upon her until he saw her retreat a step, back into the tree, and thwack the back of her head in her haste to evade him. She cried out, and tried to scurry away, but before she could flee, he lunged forward, pinning her between his arms against the oak tree. "I've warned you already, demoiselle . . . when you stir the fire, you risk being scalded by its flames."

Though Dominique winced as he pressed her against the rough bark, something fluttered deep within her at the intimate feel of his stone-hard body against her own. Every nerve within her came alive at his words of warning. His touch.

"That gaze of yours is a dangerous thing," he continued coldly, softly.

Dominique's heart vaulted against her ribs. "I . . . I've no idea what you are speaking of," she denied at once. "If I've looked at you any way at all, my lord, 'twas with disdain, and naught else!"

"Truly?"

His husky whisper sent a shiver of alarm down her spine. Dominique felt her voice leaving her even as her lips parted to speak. "Aye," she croaked. "'T-Tis the t-truth . . ."

He lowered his face till his lips hovered just above her own. Dominique felt herself grow cross-eyed as she stared at them in dread, remembering. *Dear God, did he plan to kiss her now?* Her heart tumbled with the thought.

Surely she did not *want* him to?

"Did you not intend to provoke me with that look?" he asked her softly, his eyes darkening to smoke green. "Do you think me so dull-witted that I would believe you, demoiselle?" He pressed her more firmly against the tree, his lips brushing against hers as he spoke.

Dominique cried out at the brief touch of their lips, and averted her face, though something in the depths of her leapt to life in that instant. Liquid heat spread through her limbs like wildfire, burning . . . just as he'd warned it would. "I . . . I . . . did not," she denied, but closed her eyes in dismay, for, in truth, she could not refute that she'd stared at him so openly. Brazenly. Nay—and God's mercy, she could not be feeling this . . . this feeling! Should not : . . could not . . . She shook her head in bewilderment, for she did. She wanted him to kiss her, God rot her own soul. She was faithless . . . wanton . . .

"Who were you planning to meet here today?" he asked her, changing the subject abruptly. Dominique could scarcely part her lips—much less answer.

"Lady Dominique!" he snapped. "Who did you plan to meet?"

The meaning of his words penetrated the haze of her mind at last. Once again he mistrusted her, when she'd given him no reason to do so. *How dare he!* Dominique turned her head sharply to face him.

"I planned to meet with no one!" she exclaimed vehemently. "No one, do you hear me? Why do you accuse me yet again? It seems to me you are bound to believe the worst of me, my lord. What mischief is it you think I scheme?"

"Any number of things," he murmured hatefully, his gaze unblinking, unrepentant. The cur! He cared not a whit that his words wounded her.

Dominique narrowed her eyes and glared at him. God's truth, but she wanted so desperately to lash out at him. And she would have, too, if his thighs against her own had not trapped her legs so mercilessly. She twisted furiously, trying to free herself, to no avail.

"God curse you, Blaec d'Lucy," she railed. "God curse and rot you!"

He made some clucking sound with his tongue, admonishing her as though she were naught more than a naughty child. "Such language from the lady," he said, his eyes piercing her. "Did I not know better, demoiselle, I would think you less than your breeding."

"Oh!" Dominique twisted again, managing only to set him more fully against her, for he was as unmovable as solid stone. "You—are—truly—*all* that they say you are!" she spat at him. "You are despicable! Get off me, you arrogant beast!" She shoved at his chest, but he would not budge.

"I think not," he said, hovering closer yet. His very nearness sent her pulses skittering wildly. "Not till I know for certain you come to my brother pure and untouched."

Dominique screeched indignantly. Her brows collided. "Pure? Untouched! You blackhearted swine! Let me go! Get off—"

His lips covered hers with a swift brutality that sent lightning bolts racing through her entire body, ending her protests once and for all, and curling her toes within her soft pointed shoes. Dominique meant to shove him away, she truly did, but her hands came about and clung to him instead. To her dismay, she could do nothing more, for her traitorous knees buckled beneath her as he claimed her mouth with a fierceness for which she was unprepared.

She could only whimper as his tongue traced the outline of her lips, demanding entrance.

Blaec was determined. It was a madness within him now. No more could he stop himself, despite that he knew this was not his right. The sight of her, the feel of her against him, aroused him beyond rational thought. When she wrapped her arms about his neck and her fingers curled at his nape, he could only recall the lust, the white-hot need that surged through him like an explosion of fire.

God . . . when she parted her lips . . . he experienced triumph like a burst of lightning throughout his veins. His tongue thrust within her mouth, tasting, plundering—not a gentle invasion but a punishing one. The taste of her was sweet, much too sweet. Pressing more fully against her, he allowed her to feel his arousal, hoping to God she would thrust him away, because he feared he would not stop. God save them both, because now that he was touching her . . . kissing her . . . at last . . . he didn't know if he could ever stop.

Ever.

She felt too good, too right in his arms.

God's truth, he could not even remember the reason he'd begun this, nor what he'd hoped to prove. And she didn't resist. He groaned in torment . . . in pleasure. His hand slid down to cup her bottom, lifting her against him more fully.

Dominique moaned low, scarcely aware that his hand crept lower still, down the length of her leg, lifting her skirt clear to her thigh. How could she be so recklessly drawn to this man?

How could she ever go back? Never could she forget this. She was branded just as surely as she was lost. Branded by the flames of the Dragon's breath . . . her soul, heart, body . . .

Nay . . . nay . . . but nay . . . how could this be? How could she yearn for a man she'd known so little time and mostly despised? How was it possible? Nay, she told herself.

" 'Tis not," she murmured, but her body called her a liar even as she said it, for it arched against him in shameless abandon, aching for his touch. Tears pricked at her eyes, burning, slipping silently from her closed lids. She was wicked, like her mother, and worse, for she did not even love this man. She could not. How could she crave the touch of the infamous, heartless *Black Dragon*? The man who had done naught but taunt and mistrust her at every turn?

The brother of her betrothed.

"Blaec . . . no . . . please . . ."

Like some distant call to arms, some part of Blaec heard the voice that summoned him back to reason. Her voice. Still he could not quite rationally find his way through the black lust that clawed at his body, drove him to insanity.

And then suddenly the blackness cleared and he thrust her away, panting heavily. Backing away from her as though she were sin incarnate, he wiped his mouth with the back of his hand, tasting her still. Like some intoxicating poison, the taste of her lingered to torment him. And like some seductive enchantress, the sight of her beckoned to him still. Weak-kneed and glassy-eyed, she leaned against the oak for support, her breast heaving beneath her blue bliaut, and her lips rosy from his kiss, swelling, even as he watched. Evidence of how close he'd come . . .

Christ, what had he done?

Too much, and not enough.

He shook his head, resisting, for even now, even knowing he must walk away, he wanted nothing more than to take her into his arms again and lie with her here under God's sight.

God help him . . . even now . . . and if he touched her again . . . he knew he would . . . even now.

Their gazes held, locked, revealing too much. Far too much.

Dominique's heart leapt at what she saw there, and suddenly . . . she understood everything. Every moment that had transpired between them. Every word. Every look.

Everything.

With that first fated glance they'd shared in the bailey, he'd felt it, too. And he'd resisted, as well. To no avail.

Her legs almost failed her. So jolted was she by the knowledge that scarcely could she catch her next breath.

His face flushed with angry color. "Damn you to hell," he hissed, tearing his gaze away. "Damn me, as well!" He spun toward his mount, closing the distance in a few angry strides, retrieving the reins and remounting hastily. Giving her one last baleful glance, he whirled his mount about, spurring it with a vengeance toward Drakewich.

He rode as though wolves snarled at his heels.

Away from her.

Swallowing the knot that rose in her throat to strangle her, her eyes glazing with tears, Dominique watched him go . . . knowing in her heart that ever after . . . she was changed. Branded. There could be no denying it now . . . she loathed him—a low keening sound escaped her constricted throat as she acknowledged that she wanted him, as well. Sweet Jesu, but she did! She slid down the tree, uncaring that the bark might ruin her gown, wondering to God how such a thing could have happened.

Never could she have foreseen it—never!

Nor could she ever, *ever* have him.

Benumbed with shock, and trembling, she slid to the ground, her breasts heaving with sobs she would not free.

With nary more than a simple kiss . . . their fates had been sealed.

And God have mercy upon their souls.

Chapter 17

Desperate for solitude—if for no other reason than to give her mouth time to heal from his ruthless kiss—Dominique sought out the mews instead of her chamber, thinking it the one place she could escape prying eyes—Alyss's in particular. Nor did she care to find herself face-to-face with Graeham as yet.

Like the keep itself, the facility was impeccable, housing a number of precious birds: a few goshawks, a pair of peregrines, a merlin. But a single white gyrfalcon was the biggest surprise of all, for it was a rare and costly bird. In truth, Dominique had only seen one once before, so rare was the beast. As had been claimed, all were molting—a fact that seemed to ease her somewhat, though she knew not why. Mayhap later she would lend her own expertise to their keeping, for there was a way of exercising them that minimized their idle time. At the moment, however, she felt only like brooding.

She stood staring at the gyrfalcon, lost in her musings, until the sound of *his* voice intruded once more, startling her. Had he lain in wait for her, then? Either that, or his men rushed to apprise him of her every movement, she thought bitterly.

"I believe I asked what you were doing here, demoiselle."

Dominique refused to face him, hoping against hope that he would simply leave. Still she could not keep herself from baiting him. "Stealing your falcons, of course, my lord."

Silence. More than his anger, even, it unsettled her. Unable to think clearly, she reached toward the gyrfalcon, needing something to occupy her trembling hands, but she ventured too close. The bird screeched, snapping at her, barely catching her finger. Dominique squealed in surpirse, jerking her hand away, though more alarmed than hurt. To her dismay, *he* was at her side within the instant, lifting up her hand for closer scrutiny.

"'Tis naught!" she proclaimed at once, and tried to draw away, but he would not release her. A trickle of blood pooled at the tip of her finger, and she stared at it resentfully, unable to look into his eyes—she couldn't bear it, couldn't bear to recall what had only just passed between them within the forest. Nor could she endure the warmth of his fingers upon her flesh once more. *Why was he here?* It was all she could do not to jerk her hand free and bolt past him. Sweet Jesu, but she could not suffer another confrontation with him so soon—not when she was still reeling from the last.

"You seem to have an affection for danger," he pointed out, his voice treacherously soft, sending a quiver of alarm down her spine—

for aye, he was danger incarnate, and *she was drawn to him*, God save her!

"Do I?" Dominique answered softly, swallowing. She lifted her face at last, meeting his uncanny green gaze, wholly conscious that he held her hand still. "Tell me, my lord," she asked him evenly, "will you follow me at every turn?"

His eyes narrowed, and his lips curved sensuously—those lips that had already tasted of her own. Heat crept into her cheeks. "If that is what it takes to uncover your intrigue," he replied huskily.

Dominique's trembling fingers went to her mouth, wiping her lips in remembrance, concealing them, as well, for heat suffused her at the merest recollection. "Th-There is no intrigue," she swore vehemently.

"So you say."

In truth, Blaec had come to beg pardon for his actions in the forest, but facing her now, he could not bring himself to speak the words, for once again she tempted him . . .

"You're bleeding," he pointed out, and couldn't help himself; he reached out with his free hand, brushing her hair from her face. God, she was too beautiful for his peace of mind. A few strands fell back, covering her mouth.

She gasped, flinching at his touch, and tried to remove her fingers from his grip, the look in her eyes both wild and confused; the same ungovernable emotions that raged within himself. Yet he found he could not release her.

"My lord!"

He lowered his head, bringing his lips to the small cut upon her finger, aware that he would be damned with the taste of her flesh upon his lips, yet unable to keep himself from it. He kissed her, lapping up the trickle of blood, shuddering with a primeval pleasure. His heart hammering, he drew her finger into his mouth, suckling it gently, intimately, willing it to heal with his kiss.

For an instant she let him, too stunned to protest, and then seeming to regain her reason, she cried out, "My lord! *What are you doing?*"

If only he knew himself. "No less than a bitch would do for her brood," he told her bluntly, still suckling her finger, knowing full well that *his* was a far more dangerous instinct—he wanted to protect her, aye, yet that was not all he craved. *Not even a faint degree of what he craved.*

"Aye, well, you are not my mother—nor are we beasts!" she informed him haughtily, jerking her finger from his mouth, though not before he noted the shiver that coursed through her at the withdrawal.

"Ah," he countered, his tone filled with self-reproach, "but there you are wrong, demoiselle. Strip away reason—" *as she had somehow done to him* "—and we are, indeed, beasts," he assured her. "Little more." He was silent a moment, letting her digest his warning, and then said, *"Believe it."* Reaching out once more, he brushed the strand of hair from her lips, wanting to assess the damage he'd inflicted in full. As he'd feared, her lips were swollen and pink from the lustiness of his kiss, and guilt clawed at him, even as the sight aroused him. He swallowed, restraining himself. "You should go," he said ruefully. His fingers lingered at her cheek, caressing her. *Either she would, or he must, for they could not continue in this vein. He was powerless to resist her.*

"A-Aye," she croaked, jerking away from his touch, averting her gaze, and shuddering. "I-I should, indeed, go!" And with that she lifted her skirts, bolting past him—like a frightened hare on the run, he thought. He didn't turn to watch her go, but stood, instead, staring down into the eyes of the gyrfalcon, fighting every instinct within him to turn and swoop down upon her as would the bird of prey before him.

It was his duty to let her go, he told himself.

His duty to go.

Unable to bear even the notion of facing *him* again the next morning, Dominique took the coward's way. She feigned illness, staying abed with the shutters closed against the day, darkening her chamber. Not since her childhood when her father had gone into his rages had she been so weakhearted, but it could not be helped. She did not dare chance seeing *him* below. If the shutters were ajar, she reasoned, then she would inevitably be drawn to the window, and if she were drawn to the window, then he *would* be there below. 'Twas her ill fortune. And God's truth, she never wished to see his face again—though just how she would manage such a feat, she had no notion.

Nevertheless, she intended to try.

Even now she could not banish the feel of his mouth upon her own—the memory of him suckling her finger, tending her as would a mother beast with her young. Yet the look in his eyes had been anything but benevolent. He had looked at her in warning, though his actions were so at odds with his words. He acted as though he despised her, yet he rushed to her aid when he thought her harmed.

Never in her life had she been so confused.

Both fortuitously, and to her despair, Graeham came to inquire only once while she lay abed, speaking to Alyss from the antechamber. She heard him ask of her well-being, heard Alyss reply that 'twas merely her monthly flux that kept her abed, and then he left and did not return.

She loathed that Alyss had been forced to lie for her, but it garnered her much-needed time. To think. And 'twas with great relief that she received news of Blaec's departure two days after. Only then did she dare leave her chamber.

She learned at once that he'd gone to fortify his brother's borders, for it seemed there was cause to believe the village's attackers had remained in the province. The very possibility made Dominique shudder when she considered that she'd left the sanctuary of Drakewich's walls while those barbarians might still be at large—and evidently unsated by the damage they'd so brutally inflicted.

Graeham, for his part, continued to shun her, even once she'd been up and about a few days, but Dominique vowed to speak with him as soon as the opportunity presented itself. God's truth, but her betrothed was more a stranger to her now than he'd been when first she'd met him, for at least then she'd seen him in a flattering light. Now she could scarcely gain a picture in her mind of the man he might be, for while he treated her kindly and with all due respect, he'd also revealed a side of himself that was less than amiable, particularly where his brother was concerned.

If only the same could be said of his brother.

Even once he'd been gone a full sennight, the image of his smoldering green eyes as he'd gazed upon her there in the shadows of the forest haunted her still.

And still she tried to forget.

The following morning, after searching most of the premise, Dominique found Graeham, at last, in the chapel, on his knees at prayer. To her wonder, he never acknowledged her presence, nor did he so much as turn to discover who it was that had invaded his sanctuary, though the echo of her footfalls reverberated throughout the shrine. The sound was a blasphemy within the quiet stillness of the hallowed chamber. Still, she could not turn and leave, not without speaking to him at last.

Then, too, she was loath to intrude, and so she sat, watching, waiting. To her disbelief, he knelt as though made of solid stone, unmoving, his head bent over in prayer. Did she not know better—know that he was flesh and blood—she

would have thought him some beautiful creation, the effigy of an angel, for with his gold-
en hair and flawless profile, he seemed un-
real.

And then mayhap he was, for though Dominique sat near an hour's time, he still did not
turn to recognize her. She chafed, for if 'twas
his intent to wound her with his indifference,
then he full well succeeded. 'Twas as though
he sensed it was her, and refused to acknowledge her. Or mayhap he truly was oblivious to
her presence, so deep was he in his meditation.
Either way, it boded her no good.

Tears sprang to her eyes, as she began to feel
with an undeniable certainty that this alliance
was little more than a farce. Though not in the
same way that his brother did, Graeham roused
her distemper. Like a madwoman, she wanted
to fly at him and pummel him with her fist,
wanted to command him to give her answers.
Was she destined to go from her brother, who
treated her with little more affection, to this?
Was she never to be valued? How could she
have hoped?

Swallowing the lump that rose in her throat,
choking her, she rose and fled the chapel before
she could disgrace herself.

"I've no idea what else to do, Alyss. He is
like a statue, unfeeling! He will not see me
elsewise."

"Forgive me, m'lady," Alyss suggested, "but
mayhap you should try harder when you are
with him, rather than lie in wait like this? If

he is unprepared to see you, mayhap he will be unkind?"

Dominique turned from the solar window to face her maid, her cheeks suffused with angry color. "Nay, Alyss, but he is too politic to be unkind! He wounds with his actions, instead." Her shoulders slumped dejectedly.

"M'lady, forgive me, but I think you mistake him." Dominique's brows lifted, though she said nothing, and Alyss continued, undaunted. "You see . . . I have watched him," she said somewhat wistfully. "He is kind and gentle to those who serve him. Aye, he is," she persisted, when Dominique looked disbelieving still. "'Tis my feeling he does not seek to cause you woe. There is something between these two brothers, though I cannot place it as yet . . . something . . . and it seems to me you are merely the straw that bent the camel's back."

"I know not how you can claim such things."

"As I said, m'lady . . . I've been watching him," she confessed guiltily, her face staining crimson. "'Tis fortunate you are to have him," she added quickly, lowering her head, sampling the mead she stirred within the small pitcher she held over the candle flame. "Ack!" she exclaimed, making a sour face. "But 'tis the most horrid concoction I have ever troubled myself to warm! We must have something to mask the taste."

Dominique found it difficult to care overmuch at the moment what, if anything at all, was used to spice Drakewich's beverages.

"Mayhap 'tis flavored to a man's taste," she said with some resentment, and refrained from adding that she cared not a whit of improve it. If 'twas bitter, then it would match their lord's temperament—regardless of what Alyss claimed.

"Nay, m'lady," Alyss countered, "for your own brother preferred it sweet. For truth, I used to warm it for him with pearmain and honey." She stopped stirring and sighed, seeming suddenly forlorn, and then as swiftly as the look appeared, it fled, and she began again to stir, her expression shuttered.

Dominique wondered what she might be thinking, but refrained from asking. The maid, she knew, had borne a grievous life as well, for her father had awarded her even before her thirteenth summer to William, in exchange for what, Dominique knew not. But to go from lord's daughter, to leman, to lady's maid, could not have been an easy burden to bear. Particularly so when she should have married and been mistress of her own domain.

Dominique sighed. She'd heard, though not through William, that her brother had taken a fancy to Alyss during a visit he'd once paid to her father at Kester. Alyss had come to Arndel the following summer after her first blood, and though she and Alyss had never spoken overmuch, Dominique knew that William had not always been gentle with her. Which led her to wonder . . .

"At any rate," Alyss continued, breaking into her thoughts. The maid glanced up from her task, smiling. "I should share with you something a very wise woman once said to me."

Dominique could not help but return the maid's smile, though it failed to reach her heart. "What wise woman is that?" she asked somberly.

Alyss's smile deepened, reaching clear into her gentle brown eyes. "My mother," she replied softly, and with reverence. And once again her expression was dreamy. "She wouldst say to me ... 'Alyss, dearling ... sometimes a woman must take matters into her own hands. She must do what she must.'" Her eyes glazing slightly, she nodded, meeting Dominique's gaze. "'Tis what she said to me, all right, though I didn't understand it then."

Dominique felt a momentary pang of loss; both for Alyss and for herself. Her own mother had never lived long enough to dispense such advice. And Alyss ... Dominique didn't know which was worse, to have it, and then lose it, or to never have known it at all. "And do you now? Understand, that is."

Alyss's eyes shadowed as she returned her attention to warming the mead. "At times I do," she said without glancing up again, her voice without inflection.

"Alyss ..." Dominique's heart lurched at the question she felt obliged to ask. If her brother had been the one to harm Alyss ... she just didn't think she could bear it. "I was wondering ..." Her gaze averted to the window, and then came back to scrutinize Alyss. "The bruises," she prompted. "How—"

Alyss's head snapped up, and her eyes were once more like those of a caged beast. She shook her head. "Do not ask me, m'lady, for I will not speak of—"

"Ladies?"

Startled by the unexpected male voice, both Alyss and Dominique glanced up to spy Graeham standing there, his own expression one of surprise. Dominique's heart tumbled a little. She'd known he would have to pass this way in order to find his chamber, and she'd hoped to speak with him at long last. But he didn't appear overly pleased with their presence in his solar. Nevertheless, she bolstered herself, knowing they could scarcely go on much longer as they had.

"My lord," she began, "I . . . I had hoped . . ." Her gaze skittered toward Alyss. With her eyes, Alyss beckoned her on, urged her to continue. "Aye, well . . ." Her gaze returned to Graeham. "You see, we . . . we . . ."

"We were warming the mead for you, m'lord," Alyss interjected softly, without glancing up from her task.

"Aye!" Dominique exclaimed at once. "Please, please, my lord, do come in and sit awhile." She rushed forward when he removed his mantle, and offered to take it from him. He hesitated, holding it back from her. Dominique peered up at him, refusing to shed a single tear did he refuse her, but her hand clutched the rich woolen cloth with a desperation that shamed her. To her relief, he released it into her keeping, saying nothing, nodding. She hurried with it into his chamber, beyond the screen, and placed it upon his bed, returning within the instant.

Hope sprang within her as she stood there staring at the man promised to become her husband. Mayhap they could make it work, after all? Perchance all was not lost. "We were . . . wondering, my lord . . . i-if you had spices . . . for the wine?"

His chest heaved, as though with a weary sigh. "In the pantry," he relented. And then he turned and made his way to, and seated himself within, the nearest chair, facing them.

Giddy with excitement, Dominique fair raced to the pantry, giving it a cursory search and removing from it honey and nutmeg and, a little reluctantly, a small container of *vin aigre* in the absence of pearmains, or bitter fruit. Racing back, she brought them to Alyss, but Alyss, to her surprise, refused them. Instead, the maid rose, requesting her leave, complaining of a sour stomach and mumbling something of women doing what they must. And then, with nary another word, she departed the chamber. Dominique smiled as she watched Alyss go, head bowed and clutching her belly, thinking her a crafty soul indeed.

"Well . . ." Dominique's gaze reverted to Graeham. She smiled shyly. "My lord . . . I pray *you've* a hearty stomach," she said with an awkward attempt at humor. "I'm sorry to say I've not Alyss's talents."

Graeham smiled haggardly. "We shall manage," he answered with a terse nod. He sat, watching her, as though it pained him to remain in the same room alone with her.

It didn't matter. Dominique refused to be thwarted. If it pained him, so be it. He would bear it—as she had borne his lack of attention these weeks past. "Aye, well . . . 'twill be done in no time at all," she promised, and smiled brightly. At once she took over where Alyss had left off, lifting up the pitcher by the wooden handle and setting it carefully over the flame. While Graeham sat, watching, she stirred in the nutmeg, and then the honey, tasting it at intervals.

To her dismay, the silence between them lengthened, and became an awkward thing, but Dominique was determined to find a bridge betwixt them this day.

"I am sorry, Lady Dominique, if this has been difficult for you," Graeham said suddenly, discomposing her.

Setting down the pitcher with trembling hands, Dominique left off her task to face him, uncertain of what to say. His eyes seemed as tormented as her own. God's truth, but he was a handsome man, even more so when he smiled at her. Why couldn't she make him smile the way he had that first time?

"My lord . . . I just don't understand," she said.

His sigh was weary, rueful. "I know."

"Have I—"

"'Tis naught you've done," he broke in. "In truth, I wish I could explain—" he shook his head "—but I can't."

"I see," Dominique said, though she didn't at all. She lowered her head, lifting up the pitcher of mead, tasting from it. "'Tis too sweet," she said softly, trying to remain composed.

Silence.

Dominique swallowed her pride. "My lord . . . I wish to be a good wife to you," she said, her voice wavering.

He was silent a moment longer, and then said with quiet certainty, "You *shall* be a good wife, Lady Dominique. I never doubted it."

Heartened by his remark, Dominique faced him once more, and his eyes were warm, regretful even.

"All will turn out as it should," he promised, nodding softly, his eyes filling with some unnamed emotion. "I never meant to hurt you, Lady Dominique," he told her. "Please remember that."

Dominique's spirits fell. *Why did she feel 'twas an apology for something yet to come?* Nodding, afeared to hear any more, she lifted up, though reluctantly, the pitcher of *vin aigre*. Her hands quivering, she poured a meager amount within . . . and then . . . God help her, she heard *his* voice below, and his ensuing footfalls as he climbed the stairs.

Her heart leapt into her throat.

A myriad of emotions swept through Dominique as she awaited his appearance in the doorway: disappointment, terror at seeing him again, and aye . . . whether she wished to deny it, or nay . . . anticipation. Her belly fluttered nervously.

Graeham rose at once to greet him, embracing him in the doorway and clapping him enthusiastically on the back. Blaec responded in kind . . . until he chanced to spy Dominique over Graeham's shoulder . . . and his hand stilled in midair.

Their gazes met, locked.

That same look passed between them: dread, turmoil, denial . . . guilt . . . too many emotions to name.

He turned abruptly away, patting his brother, embracing him more fully.

"'Tis an alluring scene I've discovered here," he said lightly, casting Dominique a suddenly dispassionate glance. She swallowed convulsively, for with little more effort than it had taken him to blink, he'd cast all emotion from his dark visage—at least where it concerned her. His eyes, while they were upon his brother, were full of affection.

With all her heart, she wished she could do the same. What a fool she was to attach herself to this man! She averted her gaze at once, though her heart continued to thump traitorously.

"God's blood," Blaec complained, "but with no remorse at all, you send me to sleep on leaves and stones whilst you carry on in comfort with your bride." In her peripheral vision, she saw that he cuffed Graeham's arm lightly with a fist. "Well done," he said. "'Tis about time."

"Ah, but *I am* guilty," Graeham countered. "I confess it."

"You confess far too much," Blaec remarked softly.

Watching them, Dominique had the distinct impression that their banter was less than mirthful. Yet there was genuine affection between them; that much was evident in their manner and in their gazes. These two brothers—these twins from birth, who appeared nothing alike—shared much more than conception in a single womb. It seemed to her they shared, if not love, then a mutual admiration for each other. And both seemed equally protective of one another.

Graeham chuckled richly. "Aye, well, mayhap, but did I not . . . who then would pray for your soul, my dear brother? You are lost without me," he declared glibly.

Blaec's lips curved slightly. He ceded a chuckle. "That I would be," he admitted without vacillation. "That I would."

"There you have it, then," Graeham exclaimed with good humor, and then he pivoted toward Dominique. "Lady Dominique! Bring forth a cupful of that warm, spiced mead for my weary brother. God's truth, but I vow he shall perish without it!"

It took Dominique an instant to realize that she was staring. God curse him, but he only seemed to grow more handsome every time she saw him. Even unshaven as he was, he was breathtaking. Nay, 'twas not the angelic beauty his brother possessed, but Alyss was right . . . he looked unmistakably a man. No boy was he. In truth, looking at him now, it was difficult to believe he'd ever been one, for his eyes were those of a man who'd witnessed far too much. They were the eyes of a man who'd lived a lifetime already, and were in deep contrast with his youthful features.

She wondered how old he was, for he seemed in ways as ancient as sin. And in other ways . . . there was something nestled deep in his expression that made her yearn to reach out to him . . . comfort him. She shook her head. Too dangerous were these thoughts. *Dangerous and reckless.*

Nor did he need comforting, she was certain.

" . . . not a damned thing," she heard Blaec say crossly. "There was no sign of them."

Once and for all, Dominique shook herself free of her thoughts, and glanced down into the pitcher of simmering mead. And then she peered at the empty container of *vin aigre* still in her hand. A strangled sound escaped her. Sweet Christ, in her alarm, she'd emptied the *vin aigre* in its entirety into the pitcher!

"Lady Dominique?"

Merciful God—all of it. Wide eyed with the discovery, Dominique faced Graeham's inquiring gaze, her heart racing, her stomach knotting. "M-My lord!" she exclaimed.

"The mead," Graeham demanded, his pale brows drawing together in disapproval. "Bring it."

"But . . . but, my lord!" Her mind raced for an excuse. "'Tis not yet done," she exclaimed at once.

"Ludicrous!" he said. "I've watched you give it exceptional care these past twenty minutes.

God's truth, but if it warms any longer, there'll be naught left of it to drink. Bring it now."

Dominique gritted her teeth. She had to fight the urge to narrow her eyes at him as well, telling herself that it would serve him right did his brother die poisoned before him. If he wanted her to feed his brother rancid mead, then so be it! "Very well, my lord," she answered dutifully, straightening her spine. The truth was that she thought she might take great pleasure in such a scene. By the saints! They deserved one another, these two! She set down the container, and using both hands, poured from the pitcher, filling the cup she'd left to one side full to the brim.

Pasting on her sweetest smile, she rose and conveyed the cup to Blaec, offering it to him. For an instant he simply stood gazing at her, and Dominique's temper flared. So, too, did her heart trip, but she refused to be cowed by him, not this time.

Her chin rose a notch. "My lord . . . mayhap you wouldst like me to spoon it to you, as well," she suggested impertinently, blinking prettily. *In truth, she'd like to pour it down his blessed throat!* She found herself wishing fervently that Graeham d'Lucy had no brother at all. More than that even, she wished she'd never set eyes upon this accursed place!

He received it from her at last, and Dominique immediately excused herself. She was no fool, and she had absolutely no intention of remaining here to see whether he collapsed to the floor, clutching at his throat in agony. Graeham relented with a nod, and Dominique hurried toward the door.

"Aarrgghhh!"

Hearing the strangled sound, Dominique froze. Though she willed her feet to run, flee, she could not move them from the place she stood to save her soul. She whirled to face him and found him gagging, spewing mead and swiping at his mouth.

"God's bloody teeth!" he exclaimed. "'Tis poison!"

"I can explain," she offered at once.

He spun to face her, his visage wrathful. "Please do *try*, demoiselle!" He hurled the contents of the cup down upon the wooden floor at her feet.

Dominique took a step backward at the menacing look in his eyes. Her expression screwed. "I . . . I . . . It was an accident," she swore, her voice faltering.

"Another bloody accident, demoiselle? *How damned convenient!*"

"I swear 'tis the truth, my lord. It *was* an accident," she insisted. "I was warming the mead when . . ." Sweet Mary, how could she explain? *She was warming the mead when she heard his voice and started. The thought of seeing him again was so distressing that she'd spilled the entire contents of the* vin aigre *bottle without even realizing. She'd rather swallow boiling pitch.* "Fine!" she snapped. "I tried to poison you, then, my lord! Believe it, if you will! I only wish I'd succeeded," she spat venomously. And then without another word, she lifted her skirts and raced from the solar.

* * *

In her chamber, Dominique paced until the pads of her feet ached her. Trying to kill him, was she? Fie! At the moment, she'd dearly love to do more than try. "I cannot believe he would accuse me of such a thing, Alyss!"

"I'm certain he cannot believe it, m'lady," Alyss said reasonably.

"Nay?" Dominique faced her maid, her cheeks suffused with impotent rage. "You did not see his face. The man is bent upon finding me guilty of something—anything. I has hoped that once William left, he would cease his accusations once and for all—but nay!" There has to be a way to end this farce. Mayhap once she and Graeham were wed, all would resolve itself. Dominique didn't see any way out of the betrothal. Not when her brother was so determined to see it through, and Graeham had agreed. She just could not comprehend why Graeham seemed so guarded against her.

Mayhap 'twas simply that he was uneasy with women? He'd never been unkind to her, not really. Mayhap he simply had no notion how to speak with her? Mayhap he was too abashed in her presence?

Suddenly she knew what she must do. The instant the inspiration came to her, she knew it was the *only* solution. If Graeham was too timid to come to her . . . then she would go to him.

Tonight.

And if he truly did not want her . . .

Well, then, she would discover that as well.

Chapter 18

Dominique waited until she was certain the household was aslumber, and then, following the trail of torches, she made her way to the lord's chamber. Wearing naught but her linen chainse, she padded barefoot down the tower steps.

No one stopped her.

No one was left awake to do so.

Making her way quickly through the solar, she pushed open the massive door and slid quickly within. From a single unshuttered window along the far wall, moonlight spilled into the chamber, lighting it with a ghostly glow. Like a blade of silver, it fell across the bed, illuminating the figure entangled within its sheets much too clearly. The sight of Graeham lying there so intimately gave her pause, though she refused to allow her feet to hesitate. Bolstering her courage, she hurried across the room, only to lose her nerve as she stared down at the bed that held the sleeping form of her betrothed.

Sweet Jesu, but he was a beautiful man.

His yellow hair was even more pale by the light of the moon, and his features flawless in slumber. Angelic, she thought, not for the first time. Even so, the very thought of crawling—willingly—into his bed was disconcerting at best. Still Dominique knew it was something she *must* do.

She *must* not leave herself open again for temptation.

She *must* do this. She had no choice.

And she *must* succeed.

Drawing in a shaky breath, she carefully lifted up the coverlet and slipped beneath it beside Graeham, her heart pounding so wildly that she thought it would burst from her chest. Sweet Christ, how could he sleep with it beating so loudly? Trying to soothe herself, she lay as close to the edge of the bed as possible, taking care not to touch him—or any part of him, for that matter.

Not yet, she told herself.

In a moment, she would.

A moment passed, and then minutes went by, and with every second that elapsed, the beating of Dominique's heart became more painful to bear.

For the love of Christ, she thought hysterically, how was she going to seduce a man she could not even bear to touch?

Move closer, she willed herself. She shook her head at once, freezing at the slight movement she created, her breath arresting. Had she moved the bed? Had he sensed her presence?

Oh, God! What if he awoke? What would she say to him? How would she explain her bold behavior? *What would he say?*

Truly she was mad! And thank God, for elsewise she would never be able to carry out such an insane plan.

But she could not carry it out, she realized suddenly. No matter that she told herself she *must* seduce the man lying at her side, she could not move even to save her soul. The inches between them lay as wide as a chasm, and the reality of being within his bed was more distressing than ever she could have imagined.

Closing her eyes, Dominique willed her hands to move, to touch him, but they remained, to her dismay, steadfastly clamped at her breast—like a woman dead! she thought frantically.

Move! she commanded herself.

Her breathing quickened so, till she felt as though she'd raced up a thousand flights of steps—and down again! Squeezing her eyes shut, she moved her small finger, and found that the pounding of her heart increased with the puny effort.

Dear God, she would die here in his bed! God's truth, her heart felt near to bursting even now!

What a fool she was!

Whatever could she have been thinking?

A panic unlike any she'd ever experienced in her life came over her, paralyzing her wholly. Suddenly even the thought of rising from the bed seemed an impossible task, for what if she should wake him?

She *must* get up! Oh, what a coward she was!

A foolish little coward!

A feeble, foolish coward at that!

And she'd never felt more like weeping.

To her dismay, hysterical laughter bubbled up from the depths of her, exploding from her lips against her will, shocking her—startling Graeham.

At the shrieking sound, he shot from the bed, and ran like a child from a nightmare. "Who's there?" he demanded at once.

Try as she might, Dominique could not cease with her laughter, not even to catch a single breath. She clutched at her belly, paralyzed with giggles that were anything but mirthful.

Graeham hurried to light a taper, and then held it over her, staring down as though he thought her demented.

And she *must* be, for she could not stop even when he scowled down upon her.

"Lady Dominique?" His expression was stunned, and a little dismayed.

Dominique could not have responded to save her life.

"By God's holy light!" he exclaimed. "What are you doing in my bed?"

His startled face, lit only on one side by the light of the taper, appeared wholly sinister suddenly, twisting with the flickering candle flame, and it was more than Dominique could bear. Her emotions swung like a pendulum. Gasping in fright, she bolted from the bed, only to find herself tangled in the bedsheets.

With a strangled yelp, she fell to the floor. And God was merciful, for in her mind the lights flickered and died.

Scarcely able to believe his eyes as she fell, Graeham hurried to the other side of the bed, hoping to catch her in time. But he wasn't quick enough. He reached her as she emitted a final shuddering gasp and succumbed.

Hurriedly discarding the taper at his side, he placed the back of his hand against her nostrils, testing her breath. Finding it strong, he breathed a sigh of relief. He hardly cared to add to the hostilities betwixt her brother and himself.

She was limp as wet cloth as he lifted her into his arms and placed her upon his bed. He went back for the candle at once, and with it, lit the torch within the brace alongside his bed.

What in God's name had she been doing?

As he gazed down at her, there was a pallor to her face that sickened him, twisted his gut. He slapped her cheek softly. Again. "Lady Dominique!" She didn't respond. God's truth, but he thought her beautiful in that instant.

Quite beautiful, though she failed to stir him.

He'd thought he'd be able to do this. He'd truly hoped to put an end to the feud betwixt their houses with their union. He knew now that it was not possible. The truth had become apparent to him in the last days. And he'd prayed to no avail. It seemed God would not hear him.

When first he'd spied her . . . he *had* thought it possible, then. He'd thought, for truth, that if any maid could stir him to life, 'twas she. But she had not, and he began to wonder now that any woman could.

Once he'd been a man whole . . . until a peasant maid for whom he and Blaec had shared a lust had come into his life. Once Blaec had become aware of the fact that Graeham had coveted her, he had never so much as looked at her again. And Graeham might have had her then . . . he might have had he willed it so . . . but since that day, he'd understood that he was ever destined to take what his brother desired. Blaec had always dutifully stepped aside, gladly even, and that was the crux of the problem. Some part of Graeham would not have what was stolen. Mayhap Blaec did not care that Drakewich was rightfully his by birth, but Graeham did. Though even had his body not rebelled against him so long ago . . . even were he able to take a woman . . . there would still be his vow of celibacy.

He'd long ago determined it just penance.

It might have been different had he *not* known the truth, but he *did* know.

On his mother's deathbed, she'd confessed it all to him, bidding him always keep his brother near. She'd told him everything he'd always suspected: Their father had been so certain Blaec had not been his, for with his dark coloring, he'd looked nothing at all like their fair father, nor their mother, and Gilbert d'Lucy had determined soon after his birth that he'd been ill conceived. And though he'd loved their mother too much to cast her aside, Blaec had paid the price of Gilbert's suspicions—no matter that their mother had denied it to the end of her days.

So as not to shame her before the eyes of men, he had given Blaec his name. Behind their backs, Blaec, eldest son to Gilbert d'Lucy, had been a bastard, and no more. Unloved. Unwanted. Repudiated. A travesty, for Graeham knew the truth. Not only did they share the same womb, but they had shared the same father.

Like some unseen blade, the truth pierced Graeham's gut, and time would not heal the wound, though the wound was not his own. While Blaec did not realize . . . the wound was his. And Graeham could not live with the blood and guilt upon his own hands any longer.

He'd taken too much undeservedly.

He shook her softly. "Dominique."

Her eyes flew wide, and she gasped in a breath at the sight of him hovering above her.

He shook his head, trying to understand. "What were you doing in my bed?" he demanded of her, though not unkindly.

She said nothing, though her lips began to quiver. A single tear slipped from her lashes, and rolled down her ashen cheek. Still she lay staring at him, wide-eyed, and he asked her once more, his tone gentle, lest he frighten her further, "Lady Dominique . . . *what were you doing in my bed?*"

She shook her head, averting her face, and began to weep softly. "I-I do not know," she cried miserably. She rolled to one side, away from him, covering her face with her hands. "I am so ashamed!"

"Tell me why," he demanded softly.

He placed a hand upon her shoulder, and she rolled to face him, her eyes glazed with tears.

"Because I was seducing you, my lord!" she confessed.

Graeham's brows lifted in stupefaction. There must have been something he'd missed. "I assure you, Lady Dominique," he said, shaking his head. "Whatever it was you were doing . . . you most certainly were *not* doing *that*."

At that, she began to cry all the more earnestly, and Graeham peered nervously over his shoulder at the door, praying no one would overhear. That was all he needed now—for everyone to know she'd been within his bed. There would be no dealing himself out of the betrothal then.

"But I was!" she insisted, sitting to face him. He tried not to note the dark shadows of her nipples behind the fine pleated linen. "And I'm so ashamed!" she wailed.

Graeham averted his eyes, wincing, glancing up at the ceiling. Hoping to stop her tears, as well as to remove her from his line of vision, he reached out and urged her into his arms. "There, now," he said awkwardly. "All is well, Lady Dominique . . . No harm was done."

She shook her head frantically. "I was not trying to poison you," she swore vehemently.

"I know," Graeham relented, stroking her back. "Shhh . . ." If he'd wondered of her innocence ere now, he did no longer. Somehow he knew that the woman in his arms was guiltless, no more than a pawn in her brother's politics. Her sobs were too sincere to doubt. The simple fact that she'd been so honest about trying to seduce him, and that she'd gone about it so ludicrously, only served to prove that she was a desperate bride, ignored and confused.

He wished he could follow through with his promise to her brother—that he could wed her and all would be well. But he could not. Holding her within his arms was the final proof. God, he'd avoided her for naught, telling himself that he did not wish to tempt himself, but there was nothing there . . . no feeling at all. Though he could smell the sweetness of her hair, feel the warmth of her female flesh . . . he was not stirred.

There was only one resolution now.

And by damn, he would do what was right.

He drew her away from him suddenly, wiped her tears, and rose from the bed, going to the door.

Chapter 19

S he hadn't known he was there.
In the shadows.

Watching as she stole by him on her way to his brother's chamber. Her fine pleated gown had billowed about her with the night draft, her shape gracefully limned beneath. She was lithe and beautiful, her bosom ripe ... high ... round. Her waist small ...

A strangled sound caught at the back of Blaec's throat at the excruciating thought of his brother's hands upon her. God ... why? Never in his life had he begrudged his brother aught.

Why her?

Why now?

He didn't think he could bear it.

For certain, he would have to go.

He lifted the flagon he clutched within his hand to his parched lips, and then drew it away irritably, shaking it. Discovering it empty, he tossed it aside.

Though deep in his cups, he still could not sleep, imagining her within there ... in his brother's arms ...

Blocking the vision from his mind, he stretched out upon the pallet within the solar, staring at the ceiling, his body taut. With a low moan, he closed his eyes, raking his fingers across his scalp. Already his head hurt, but he didn't know whether it was the drink or the tension. Mayhap 'twas both.

Just as he wondered, again, what they might be doing, the door to Graeham's chamber burst open, and someone bellowed his name. Graeham, he thought. His eyes attempted to focus upon the figure standing silhouetted in the doorway. Graeham. Surging to his feet, Blaec swayed slightly, half expecting to find a blade protruding from his brother's chest.

"Get her the hell out of my chamber!" Graeham charged him.

Blaec shook his head, unable to comprehend, for Graeham stood there unharmed.

Angry, but unharmed.

"By God! I don't care if you have to sleep atop her," Graeham bellowed, "get her out of here, and keep her out!"

Dominique could scarcely believe her ears. Her face flamed with mortification.

For an instant she thought he might be speaking to a guard, despite that she'd not spied one on her way into his chamber—certainly not there in the solar. She would have noticed . . .

Her heart lurched when Blaec d'Lucy appeared in the doorway, leaning idly upon the doorframe as he peered within. Yet though his appearance was calm, the look in his eyes was anything but.

They accused her once more, though he said nothing.

He wore only his loose breeches, no tunic, and his hair was disheveled as though from sleep. In the dim light of the room, his flesh was even swarthier, glistening with a light sheen of sweat, for the night was warm.

Had he been there in the solar all along?

How had she missed him?

Had he heard?

It didn't matter, she wasn't going anywhere with him. He stood there, as though waiting— well, he could stand an eternity. She wasn't going. He moved suddenly, as though to come for her. "Nay!" she shrieked hysterically. "I can find my own way!" She bounded from the bed at once, and giving Graeham a wounded glance, hurried to the door, hesitating there, for she was forced to go between them. Her heart began again to pound as she glanced from one brother to the other, gathering her courage. She bolted past them all at once.

"I've no need of escort!" she informed them both haughtily, and prayed *he* would not follow.

To her dismay, she didn't get far.

Blaec, the cur, was behind her within the instant—curse him!—lifting her up and heaving her over his shoulder. In the space of seconds, Dominique found herself dangling like a sack of meal down his bare back. Shrieking indignantly, she pummeled his back with her fists, trying not to note the heat of his bare flesh.

"I despise you!" she hissed at him. "Release me at once, you loathsome cur!" Feeling dizzy, and a little as though she would swoon again, she braced her palms against his back and felt his muscles flinch at her touch.

Adding to the insult, he said not a word as he hauled her up the tower steps to his chamber. No apology—naught! And Dominique found herself seething by the time they reached the antechamber. To her way of thought, he enjoyed this far too much—the arrogant brute! Well, he wasn't simply going to walk away this time, because she wasn't going to let him! Not without gouging his eyes out!

Kicking open the antechamber door, and then the door to the chamber, he carried her within and tossed her down upon his bed, again as though she were no more than baggage. But Dominique vowed it wasn't going to be so easy as that. She locked her arms about his neck, refusing to let go, fully intending to scratch his eyes out when she got them within reach.

Screaming, she pulled him down with her.

With a grunt of surprise, he toppled upon her.

Dominique lost her grip—as well as her breath—with the impact. But that didn't stop her. She groped wildly for a lock of his hair, grasping it as though her soul depended upon it—God curse his own rotten soul! 'Twould serve him right did she yank every hair out of his head!

At once his hand shot up, seizing her wrist, gripping it tightly. "Let go," he snarled.

"Never!" she replied vehemently. "Arrogant bastard! I'd as lief pluck every strand from your churlish head. How dare you treat me so!"

His thumb pressed harder against the tender spot in her wrist, until Dominique cried out in pain. Still she refused to ease her hold.

He sounded as though he could not catch his breath, but Dominique could not tell, for the chamber, despite that the shutters were open wide to the night, was pitch-dark. He emitted some sound, something akin to a snarl.

"What the hell were you doing in my brother's chamber?" he demanded suddenly, arrogantly.

"As though 'twere any of your bloody concern!" she hissed at him. "Overbearing bastard!"

He clucked his tongue at her in the darkness. "Such language . . . Did you speak this way with Graeham, too?" he asked her. "Is that why he tossed you out of his bed?"

"I most certainly did not! And he did not—"

"He did," Blaec countered with deceptive calm. The seductively gentle tone of his voice sent a quiver of alarm down Dominique's spine, for the hold he retained upon her wrist was anything but tender. "You forget I was there, demoiselle," he taunted her. "Mayhap your brother failed to inform you, Lady Dominique . . . but my brother likes his women purer than that."

"Why, you!" Catching the gleam in his eyes, Dominique made to strike him, but he held her wrists too firmly.

She twisted and bucked beneath him, and he grunted, as though in pain. "I would not move quite so, were I you," he warned her softly, and then rocked his pelvis suggestively against her, letting her feel him. "I myself take my pleasures where they are offered."

Dominique gasped in shock and in outrage.

Though she could not see him in the blackness of the chamber, she could feel his eyes upon her, burning into her very soul . . . feel his panting breath, warm and sweet with wine . . . feel his manhood nestled scandalously against her thigh.

Sweet Jesu, she felt *that* even through her chainse and the cloth of his breeches. It could not be missed!

She swallowed convulsively, stilling her movements at once.

For the longest instant, neither moved.

He laughed softly, the sound mirthless, mocking. He bent to whisper against her ear. "I see that I have your attention at last," he said.

Dominique's grip tightened upon his hair. God's truth, mayhap she could not move the rest of her body, but she could make him regret every blessed word he spoke to her!

Pain shot across Blaec's scalp, but he welcomed it, for it kept him from forgetting himself entirely. The feel of her beneath him was too potent a distraction by far. Like some lost soul, he prayed she would not move, and prayed, at the same time, that she would—prayed that she would release him, and was heartily relieved when she did not.

Unable to help himself, he moved against her, and felt himself pulsate. Christ . . . he thought he would lose control . . . "Dominique," he rasped, pleading, and then it was too late. He couldn't have stopped himself had he tried. Far too long had he lain upon his pallet . . . wanting this . . .

And now she was beneath him . . . and it was no dream . . .

Last night in his tent, he'd awakened, moving against his pallet, thinking 'twas her . . . needing it to be so.

And now it was, and he was undone.

One arm slid beneath her back and he lowered his mouth, unerringly, to her lips.

Startled by the unexpected warmth of his mouth, Dominique gasped in surprise, opening to him. At once he thrust his tongue within. With a soft cry, she released his hair, dropping her arms to his neck, and the helpless gesture sent a new burst of heat singing through his veins, filled him with a triumph that was not his right to feel.

From the first instant, Dominique was lost.

She could not think, only feel . . . and the feeling was too exquisite for mere words. 'Twas as though she had lived an eternity for only this moment. All thought of denial fled from her head and from her heart . . . and from her lips . . .

All she could think of was the warmth of his tongue, the sweetness of his breath . . . and the softness of his lips as he lapped and tasted of her mouth.

Seduced her.

He tasted of sweet wine, she thought vaguely. *Delicious*. Of their own will, her hands wound themselves within the length of his hair . . . only this time, her fingers reveled in the softness.

That feeling . . . that same incredible feeling that had sparked to life before—that same feeling that made her yearn so desperately to close her thighs against him, around him—began to unfurl once more . . . simmer . . . burn . . .

Moaning softly, Dominique writhed mindlessly beneath him . . . needing more. He responded with a low, husky moan, and slid down the length of her body. For an instant, Dominique thought he meant to leave her. And to her shock and dismay, she felt only relief when he remained, nibbling and kissing at the heated flesh of her neck. She arched to give him better access, mindless with the pleasure he gave her, sobbing softly at her own wantonness.

But she didn't care . . . she'd not let herself care.

She was her mother's daughter.

"Forgive me," he whispered.

Dominique wondered distractedly, if he asked it of her . . . or whether they were her own words . . . and then she wondered no more, for the hand beneath her back lifted her up, and he moved downward yet again. With a low groan, his lips found and closed about the peak of one breast, toying with it, lapping it, tugging it softly, suckling like a babe.

Dominique cried out, tensing, though only for an instant, for the shock of his intimacy faded at once with the incredible sensations that burst through her, aroused by his suckling. Whimpering softly, she arched beneath him, writhing, weeping with the inconceivable emotions that swept over her.

Oh, God, but she was wicked ... wicked ... wicked ...

And she loved him.

Her hands locked about his head, holding him fast to suckle at her breast, while beneath him, her body began to undulate of its own accord. He moved down slowly, alternately nipping at and kissing her breasts.

In all her life, she'd never felt more confused ... more certain of anything ...

She loved him.

Blaec groaned with pleasure when she accepted him so fully, raising her breast for his will. He suckled her, moving against her in euphoria, knowing he should stop, but unable to force himself to do so.

'Twas as though his body were not his own.

He reveled in the taste of her flesh—pleasing even through the fine linen cloth of her chainse— the warmth of her body, the long length of her legs against his own.

Too much for him to bear.

His hands, flexing, slid down along her delectable curves, slowly, savoring every inch of her, committing her to memory ... for somewhere in his half-consciousness, he understood ... this could not happen again.

But this once . . .

He could not stop it.

He could not have torn himself away from her even had someone stood above him with sword in hand, ready to plunge it between his shoulder blades.

Gladly he would die for this moment.

God strike him down, but he could not stop.

Dominique was only vaguely aware that he lifted her chainse, but she welcomed it . . . wanted to feel his mouth on her bare flesh . . . his hands . . . though with a desperation that dismayed her, she fought the separation of their bodies, clinging to him as though she would die with their parting.

And God's truth . . . she thought she might.

Unable to remove her gown with her mindless struggles, Blaec gripped the neckline instead, rending it savagely, jerking it from between them once and for all.

The shock of bodily contact was physical.

He groaned in torment at the feel of her bare breasts arching against him, her pebbled nipples rising to brush against his chest . . . her warmth, her softness.

Like a man possessed, he rocked against her, losing himself a little more with every mindless undulation. He could not see her, but he could feel her, and she felt exquisite.

"Beautiful," he whispered. *The feel of her was ecstasy.* "My God, you are beautiful." And if he didn't bare himself at once, he thought he would go mad. He fumbled between them for the ties that bound his breeches, and shrugged out of them, gasping aloud as he freed himself, at last. Reaching down, he hooked his arms beneath her knees, raising her legs.

She was a vixen . . . her brother's whore . . . and she incited him to madness—best the truth be discovered sooner, he told himself. *For his brother's sake.* The woman beneath him could not possibly be pure. The fire within her burned too hotly for him to believe it had never been kindled before.

In all likelihood his brother had already discovered that fact, and that was why he'd ordered her out of his chamber.

With that last piercing thought, he positioned himself against her, holding her legs up for his pleasure. He didn't care. He wanted her to take him deeply, sheathe him wholly. She moaned beneath him in wanton abandon, writhing in expectation of his entrance into her body.

Well, she need wait no longer, he thought viciously.

Nor could he.

Damn the whore!

He slid the tip of his shaft easily within her, and then surged down against her, groaning with the exquisite tightness of her body ensheathing him.

Dominique cried out with the pain of his intrusion, going still beneath him. Her body began a cold sweat, but she clenched her teeth and bore it, knowing the pleasure would come again. Alyss had told her so.

She knew it instinctively as well.

Above her, Blaec, too, went wholly still.

"Damn you," he muttered. At once he began to withdraw, but the pain had faded, and Dominique could not bear for him to leave her now.

Now they were just beginning . . .

Now she was just beginning . . .

She wrapped her legs about his waist, holding him in that ageless lover's embrace.

"*Damn me,*" he whispered. "*Damn me . . . damn me . . . God forgive me, I cannot stop.*" He lowered himself against her once more, rocking her gently, letting her adjust to his size, his arms trembling with restraint.

Dominique's fingers skimmed the taut muscles of his arms. Instinctively she wrapped her arms around his shoulders, feeling him, stroking his back, reveling in the width of his muscled shoulders, the heat of his body. Without thinking, she drew his head down to hers, craving his kisses fiercely.

He responded at once, as though he understood what she needed. His tongue flicked out, brushing her lips, and Dominique opened to him wholly. When he teased her mouth, she suckled his tongue, tentatively offering her own in return. His response was a low, guttural moan.

With that small victory, she whimpered softly, wanting him to move against her again . . . as he had before. Mindlessly she rocked against him.

He reached down at once, stilling the movement of her hips with his hands. "Do not," he rasped, and made once more to withdraw.

Dominique followed him with her hips, forcing him within her. Crying out when he withdrew again, farther this time, she grasped the sheets, and followed him stubbornly.

"Dominique," he cautioned, withdrawing once more, so that the tip of his shaft was all that remained. "You cannot know . . ."

"I do," she murmured breathlessly. "I do . . ." Feeling never more brazen, for this could not be real, she locked her legs about his waist and surged upward, crying out as he filled her at last. "I do," she whispered euphorically.

Tendrils of heat slithered through her forbidden regions, making her cry out in triumph.

Never had she imagined such sensations possible.

Never had she dreamed.

"I cannot stop," he warned her now. "I can—not!" With a harsh cry of his own, he withdrew and surged forward again.

Dominique screamed. "Nay!" she cried. She did not want him to leave her. She never wanted him to.

She wanted this never to end.

She wanted him to fill her this way always.

Just now, there was no world, only the two of them.

There was no betrothal, no brother, no daylight.

Only the two of them. And the darkness.

Tomorrow was soon enough to consider those things.

Tonight she could only think of this. This incredible sensation that tore through her, pulling her into a whirlwind of unconscious feeling. Clutching the bedsheets desperately as he moved against her, rocked her, Dominique sobbed softly, welcoming him.

Christ . . . *he was mad* . . . she was his brother's bride.

He could not spill himself within her. *He could not*, he commanded himself. 'Twould be the final betrayal—though God curse him, or save him, he could not stop!

She moved against him with complete abandon, and he could not stop.

He could not.

Once more he tried in vain to withdraw, and was undone by the silky softness of her. He lost all control then, thrusting savagely, filling her, and withdrawing. When her body tightened and convulsed about him, he arched his head backward, crying out, a guttural, tormented sound. Beneath him, Dominique sobbed with her own release, her body convulsing, coaxing his seed from him, demanding his surrender.

With a last powerful thrust, Blaec spilled himself deep within her.

And still 'twas not enough.

He clutched her buttocks, pressing her tightly against himself, undulating once more, and once more, and once more, driving his seed into the very depths of her body.

And even then he could not stop.

Tonight, against all morality, he'd made her his own . . . and he could not blame the wine.

He was weak and without honor.

And the fault was wholly his own.

Tomorrow the price of his sin would be weighed in the full light of day.

But tonight, for the first time since his youth, his eyes glazed with tears. With a low, harsh cry, he collapsed atop her, holding her tightly . . . burying himself within the silence and the darkness.

God help him, his father had been right.

Chapter 20

Morning rays streamed in through the open shutters, spilling golden light into Dominique's face. Yet the light was not what first awoke her. From the bailey came the shouts and sounds of men and horses, the chinking and clanging of armor, the neighing of restless mounts.

The next thing she became aware of was the hand cradling her bare breast . . . the soreness between her legs. Her heart lurched as sultry images from the night came back to plague her. She winced, biting into her lower lip, and shielding her eyes with a hand, stole a glance at the other occupant of the bed. Seeing him lying there beside her, she knew it had not been a dream, and she was at once filled with conflicting emotions—too many to recount.

His eyes were as yet closed, and he lay upon his belly with one arm thrown over her chest, pinning her to the bed. The palm of his hand cupped one breast. Sweet Jesu, even now, without so much as trying, his touch stirred her body to life. She tried not to note the contrasts of their skin, his dark hand against her pale flesh, tried not to focus upon the feel of his battle-hardened fingers upon her smooth body.

She looked, instead, at his face. In sleep, his expression lost much of its harshness. Even the scar upon his cheek was less visible somehow. Wondering again how he'd received it, she stifled the urge to reach out and touch it.

Afeared that the moment would come to an end.

Would he awake despising her once more? Or would his eyes gaze at her tenderly? She was afeared to discover the truth. Afeared because she knew that no matter how he felt about her now—even did he loathe her—she could no longer deny her own heart. She'd given herself freely to him last night, and the worst part of it was that now, in the morning light, she could not even find proper regret.

She was no different from her mother, loving a man she could not have.

Yet at least now she understood.

With a sleepy groan, he flexed his hand suddenly, squeezing her breast, a lazy though reverent gesture. Dominique bit down into her lip, suppressing the telltale moan his touch aroused.

And then his eyes flew wide as he heard the heavy, grating sound of the portcullis as it rose. Within the space of seconds, he bounded from the bed to the window. Try as she might, Dominique could not avert her eyes from his nude form as he stood looking through the open shutters. He was a stunning masculine specimen, his buttocks and legs as well muscled as his chest—more so.

"Damn me to hell!" he muttered furiously.

He spun to face her, completely uninhibited in his naked state, his green eyes impaling her. By his expression, Dominique knew it was grave.

She sat at once, searching for her gown. Finding it in shreds, she flushed, and lifted the linen sheet to her bosom instead. "What is it?" she asked fearfully. He didn't respond, save to come to the bed. He snapped the sheet about, jerking it from her in his fury as he searched for his clothing.

Dominique could feel the blood drain from her face. "What?" she persisted, scrambling to cover herself once more. "You must tell me! What is it? My brother? Has he returned?"

Finding what he searched for—his breeches— he jerked them up from the bed and tugged them on, glaring down at her as he laced his ties. His green eyes smoldered with contempt— for her? himself? Either way, it pained her to spy it, for she knew at once that he regretted what had passed between them last night.

Still, she could not.

Her cheeks grew warmer, for she watched him shamelessly despite that he glowered down at her. Despite that her brother might very well be riding through those gates, and might soon discover her perfidy.

His eyes narrowed with displeasure. "They are leaving," he apprised her.

For an instant Dominique could not think clearly. "Who?" She shook her head, uncomprehending. "Who is leaving?"

"Graeham," he snapped. With his laces bound, at last, he turned to go. *"Your betrothed, lest you forget,"* he reminded her cruelly. Dominique's heart twisted with the unfair accusation. God's truth, but she'd not participated alone! She wanted to shout at him, rail at him, but was too stunned even to speak. He didn't bother to glance back at her, and slammed the door as he left the chamber.

Choking back a sob, Dominique found her regret at once. Springing from the bed, she flew at the door, striking it once with her fist, and crying out in anger. Yet her rage was directed more at herself than at Blaec, for sweet merciful Christ, *how could she have been so witless last night?*

Turning her back to the door, she leaned against it, her limbs quavering. Never had she despised herself more than she did in that instant—never had she felt more the fool.

She loved a man who could not love her back . . . and in loving him, had betrayed the man she was to wed—not to mention her brother, who would surely be enraged.

Aye, she was a fool.

How, in God's name, had she embroiled herself so? Had Graeham come upon them this morn? Dominique could not help but wonder. And fret. If he had spied them in just such an intimate lover's embrace as she'd awakened in this morn, she could not blame him for despising her. Aye, and she could well understand why he would go.

Sweet Jesu, what would William say? Mayhap that was where Graeham had gone—to William. That possibility both dismayed her and filled her with hope. For even still she prayed the alliance could be salvaged. It had to be salvaged, for elsewise . . . well, she could not bear to think of elsewise.

Blaec took great pains to avoid her the rest of the day, for Dominique knew very well that he'd not accompanied Graeham to London. She discovered that he'd been commanded to remain at Drakewich—an edict that had enraged him beyond reason, she knew, because his angry bellows had reached her all the way into her chamber.

Returning the courtesy, she evaded him—Alyss, too, for she was in no mood for companionship—busying herself with any diversion she could find. If ever she became lady of Drakewich, she would assume the duties of chatelaine. Until then, she had no right to the keys—nor was Drakewich in dire need of her direction. It seemed the seneschal performed his duties all too well. *She was not needed here, nor was she wanted, it seemed.*

With little better to do, she went to the mews to gain another glimpse of the birds Graeham kept, and was astounded once again at the wealth hoarded therein. But standing there, staring at the gyrfalcon, she was accosted anew with every memory and emotion she was trying so hard to forget.

After the mews, she visited her palfrey within the stables, making certain the animal was getting its proper care, and then, with nothing more to explore, she closeted herself within her chamber—waiting, though she knew not for what.

Mayhap she hoped he would come to her—and perchance she simply feared to garner his wrath did she meet with him unexpectedly. As of yet, she wasn't certain what to say to him when she next saw him.

Surely he could not blame her for what had happened between them last eve? Certainly she blamed herself, but *he* had no right to place the blame solely at her feet—nor would she receive it wholly.

With every hour she spent alone, Dominique's fury grew. So, too, did her anguish and her confusion. She missed the evening meal apurpose . . . yet she wanted nothing more than to see him. She tried to sleep, but could scarcely close her eyes. Whenever she did, the previous night's memories came back to torment her.

At last she could bear it no longer, and she arose from the bed, tossing off the coverlet, fully intending to seek him out once and for all. She found and lit a taper against the vacuous darkness of the tower chamber. As she lifted it up, she startled suddenly, nearly dropping the taper when she heard the antechamber door open, and then close.

For an instant Dominique froze, uncertain what to do. Holding the candlestick before her with trembling hands, she turned to face the door, her heart racing.

*   *   *

It had proven impossible for him to keep his distance.

Even knowing it was wrong.

Even knowing the price they would pay—might have already paid—for he was certain that Graeham had spied them together.

Like a drunkard after taking his first swill, he was forced to seek another, and another . . . and another.

Blaec had fully intended to spend the night within Graeham's chamber, as far as he could from her—but his feet had continued up the tower steps, defying him even as he commanded himself to go back.

God damn him to hell, but he could not.

And tonight he had not even the wine to use as an excuse.

He went with a clear mind, and free will, and a leaden feeling in the pit of his stomach that was the essence of his betrayal.

Upon opening the door to his chamber, he found her standing barefoot before him, dressed only in her chainse. Her auburn locks were loose, her curls wildly disheveled as though from slumber. He tried to speak, but the sight of her staggered him, rendered him speechless. He'd expected to find her abed—had hoped to, or so he'd told himself—so that he could see her, satisfy his curiosity, and then turn and go.

But she was not abed.

And he knew damned well he would not have left her, even had she been deep in slumber.

She said nothing, though her lips parted to speak.

If she asked him to leave, he wasn't certain he could comply.

The light of the candle illuminated her beautiful face . . . her brilliant sapphire eyes, and her bosom, clad in the most diaphanous white cloth he had ever beheld. Fine from use, and unpleated, it fell short of her ankles, telling him that the garment was far from new.

It occurred to him suddenly that, while she had fine, new gowns—one less after he'd all but destroyed the one fashioned of his own stolen cloth—the majority of her garments were thread-worn and long outmoded. It led him to wonder that her brother did not value her overmuch. The fact that he'd simply left her, without remaining to witness a ceremony, had seemed strange at the time . . . yet now it began to make sense. William *could not* value her, or he *would* have remained—regardless of the hostilities that lay between them.

If *she* had been his own blood, he would have remained by her side until the last instant, guarding her honor.

He found himself regretting that he'd destroyed the crimson gown. 'Twas no wonder she'd worn it so oft—and no wonder she'd taken such pride in the accursed thing. It was likely the only thing her brother had gifted her with in years. His gaze was drawn to her coffers—merely two, confirming his suspicions. That she should have so little baggage for all her worldly possessions was inconceivable. His gut twisted with the realization, and he found himself wishing he could bestow other gowns upon her. Found himself wishing that it were his right to do so.

He found himself wishing she were to become his bride . . . that he might shower her with all that her heart desired.

His gaze returned to her. She stood proudly, though her eyes were fraught with apprehension, and he could not help but recall the way she'd protected her brother, defended him, even when the bastard did not deserve it—he'd not missed William's bow being lowered in the forest. Yet he'd not been wholly certain, and so he'd let it pass. Still, while he could bring himself to believe that it had been an accident— and it may well have been, though he sorely doubted it—he knew as he gazed at the woman standing before him that *she* was innocent of her brother's treachery.

A vision of her hastening after him in the bailey when first she'd arrived at Drakewich, defending her brother's honor against his insinuations and outright accusations, came back to him.

Why was it the unloved fought so hard to gain what could not be held?

The question tormented him, for he could have been speaking of himself. He cleared his throat, glancing out the window. From this side of the keep, the moon was rarely visible. Once more, the night was black, the stars too far and too few to lend their meager light. He was glad she held a taper.

Tonight he wanted to see her.

She stood unmoving, her exquisite sapphire eyes fixed upon him . . . as though she feared what he would do next . . . what he would say. Her breasts rose and fell softly. Recalling the way he'd awakened this morn, cradling her soft flesh beneath his palm, he was undone.

"Where were you going, Dominique?" he asked her hoarsely. "At this late hour." His heart hammered against his ribs.

Her brows drew together and she shuddered, though the chamber was not cold. "I . . ." She glanced away, closing her eyes, swallowing.

And he knew.

Yet how could he blame her for something he could not even control in himself? He thought to put her at ease, to tell her so. "Last night happened by no fault of your own," he told her honestly. "The fault was mine."

She peered up at him, shaking her head, her eyes welling with tears. "Nay . . ." She averted her gaze to the bed. "If . . . if only 'twere so," she replied miserably.

"Last night was inevitable, Dominique." *As tonight would be.* He swallowed thickly, for betrayal was no easier the second time around. But he could not help himself. "I . . ." He, too, glanced away, his heart hammering. "I could not stay away," he said with no small amount of self-contempt.

For an instant the silence engulfed them, surrounded them, a silence in which the beating of their hearts ticked the seconds by, drew them out to agonizing lengths.

Her features screwed with anguish as she faced him again, her eyes gleaming with unshed tears. "I—I did not want you to stay away," she confessed softly, with trembling lips.

Blaec needed to hear no more.

Dominique cried out softly at the intensity in his eyes. He moved toward her with purpose, and God's truth, she thought she would swoon. Without a word, he removed the candlestick from her hands, placing it down upon the coffer beside them. Its light shone up between them, casting their distorted images upon the white-washed ceiling.

She gasped in surprise as he knelt at her feet, touching her hem. He glanced up at her as he lifted up her chainse, silently pleading for her consent. She gave him a jerky nod, and her heart pummeled against her ribs as he bent and touched his lips to the bare skin of her calf. Gooseflesh arose and spread, like wildfire, to her arms, her breasts, which ached for his touch.

With a soft cry, her head lolled backward as his lips began a slow ascent upon her legs, first one and then the other. Above her, the orange light of the taper played their every motion against the ceiling. *Erotic.* Every muscle in her body tautened as he moved up the length of her body, inch by inch, lifting the chainse mere fractions each time.

Merciful heaven, she thought she would die with the exquisite pleasure!

His tongue and his lips, they worshiped her, lapping and kissing, nipping at the sensitive flesh of her inner thighs until Dominique swore she could bear it no longer. Yet she could not speak to stop him when he lifted the chainse yet higher, to the apex above her thighs. Her legs trembled traitorously. Clutching the cloth of her gown within his fist, he held it at her belly as his mouth rose, finding and exploring her most secret parts. She swallowed convulsively.

And all the while she watched the ceiling, seeing their shadows in motion, her heart tripping wildly.

Dominique felt her legs buckle beneath her, but he was there to catch her. Crying out, she fell to her knees, facing him.

His arms entwined about her, crushing her. "Shall I continue?" he asked her, his whisper harsh and rasping.

Dominique could not speak. Though she was not certain she could bear it, she nodded, and he proceeded to lift her chainse up and over her head, discarding it.

"I want to see you," he whispered. "All of you . . . here by the candlelight."

Dominique could not have spoken to refuse him, even if she'd wished to. But she didn't. Once she was bared to his eyes, he merely stared, without touching her, his hands at his sides. And then he lifted one hand to her breast, touching it, cradling it reverently. And then the other. Dominique swallowed, moaning, unable to speak, unable to think when he touched her so tenderly. Her breathing quickened.

One hand left her breast, traveling down her side, her waist, her hip, as though measuring her, and then he retraced his path upwards, exploring her sensuously, and in that moment Dominique wanted to see him as well, give back to him what he gave to her.

Her heart pounding, she reached out to touch the hem of his tunic as he'd done with her chainse. Their eyes met, and he nodded, giving her leave. Her heart tumbled at her brazenness, but she would not stop. Following his lead, she lifted his tunic, up and over his head, letting it fall from her hands to the floor to lie with her own discarded gown.

Before she could think to stop herself, before she could lose her nerve, she leaned over and touched her lips to his smooth chest. He groaned, his hands going to her waist to hold her, telling her without words that he approved. As never before in her life, Dominique was filled with euphoria.

She wanted to please him. Wanted to love him. Wanted him to love her. She wanted to give him anything he desired, everything she owned . . . her mind, her body, her heart.

Remembering all that he'd done to her the night before, she sought and found his nipples, lapping them, kissing him, each in turn. Her teeth closed about one peak, and his head fell back, the cords in his neck revealing the tautness of his body. Once again, Dominique felt triumph, even as his response to her touch brought her own body pleasure. Somewhere deep within her, she reveled in the feel of his body, and it roused her as she'd never thought possible.

Eagerly she explored his chest with her hands and her mouth, rejoicing in the way that his muscles leapt at her every touch.

"Dominique," he rasped. "I cannot bear it." He reached out, seizing her hand, taking her fingers where he willed them most—the ties of his breeches.

Her heart leaping with the silent request, Dominique obeyed, unlacing them at once. They fell discarded to his knees, revealing him to her eager eyes. Again her heart tumbled, but for the longest time, she could only stare. He was magnificent.

Once again, he reached out, taking one of her hands from her side. Bringing it between them, his eyes never leaving hers, he unfolded her fingers, one by one, until she was left with an open fist. Bringing her fingers to his lips, he kissed them one by one, suckling them, wetting them, and then without a word, he lowered her hand to his shaft, guiding her fingers to close about it. She inhaled sharply, the beat of her heart quickening, but she did not resist. She held him, her own body convulsing privately with the feel of him against her palm.

Nor was he unaffected, for he closed his eyes, and his body jerked slightly, his hand falling away.

"I've yearned for this—" he swallowed visibly "—since the day you bathed me," he told her honestly, and then he gazed at her once more, his eyes glittering as though with fever.

Dominique could not find her voice to speak. Nor could she move. She continued to kneel before him, without the first clue as to what he wished of her, her breast heaving. He seemed to understand her dilemma, for he chuckled softly, richly, and the sound was as arousing to her as the feel of his body within her hand.

Smiling, the first true smile she'd ever spied upon his beautiful lips, he moved within her fist, once, twice, and then again, and Dominique was undone. Her body suffused with heat. "Please," she cried out, panting softly.

He withdrew, and reached out, sweeping her up into his arms. He lifted her, carrying her swiftly to the bed. Though unlike the night before, he laid her down gently, and then stood, staring down at her, saying nothing. And then he lay down upon her, slowly, fitting his body against her own. Dominique welcomed his weight, gripping the bedsheets, lifting her knees instinctively. Again he chuckled, and the sound was ambrosia to her senses. He found her, impaled her slowly, embedding himself, and then he stilled.

"Show me what you want," he commanded her softly, lifting himself and bracing his weight upon his arms to give her room.

At first Dominique could not quite comprehend what he asked of her, and then she did. She began to move beneath him, moaning with the extraordinary sensations that burst through her.

She wanted this to last an eternity, wanted it to never end . . .

At first the pace was slow, and then, though she tried to restrain herself, she quickened it, gasping aloud when he joined her movements. Instinctively Dominique wrapped her legs about his thighs, bringing him closer against her, wanting him deeper still.

She surged upward, impaling herself further, and then the pace was lost to them both as their bodies took over the mating ritual.

"I cannot bear it," Blaec growled, and then he drew back and began to thrust and withdraw without restraint.

Crying out, whimpering, Dominique met his every thrust, drawing him deeper each time. Until it seemed he touched her very core. In that instant her body shattered into a thousand brilliant pieces.

And still he did not stop. He pumped fiercely, seeking his own release, and Dominique's heart leapt higher and higher with each stroke. Until she thought she would die. He brought her to yet another release, and then with a last rousing thrust, he cast his head backward, crying out savagely.

He collapsed atop her burying his face against her neck, and Dominique held him, stroking his back, running her fingers through the length of his hair.

With all her might, she fought the yearning to tell him that she loved him.

Chapter 21

Waiting for his summons, Graeham paced the hall outside of King Stephen's apartments. Though he'd arrived in London early yestermorn, he'd waited until today to seek counsel with the king. Though he was certain Stephen would never have denied him, he'd waited out of respect, not wanting to appear before his sovereign begrimed from the journey. Well rested now, and tidied, he was prepared to make his request, unconventional as it might be.

Well aware that Stephen would think him mad, he was nevertheless determined. Too long he'd contemplated this—since the day of his mother's death, in truth. Had she lived, he knew she would have approved.

The door opened at last, and he was beckoned within. Sucking in a fortifying breath, he followed the king's chamberlain to the hall where the king waited. In a chamber full with the bounty of his twenty-year reign, Stephen stood in plain dress at the window with his back to Graeham, gazing out, his pale hair revealing little of his gray.

"Sire," the chamberlain said.

Stephen peered back over his shoulder, and remarked, "D'Lucy . . . I am surprised to see you. In truth, I would have thought you pre-occupied with your new bride." He nodded to his chamberlain. "You might leave us now," he said softly, and then waited patiently for the chamberlain to comply.

Graeham straightened his shoulders, re-solved. "Aye, well, that is precisely the matter I wished to discuss with you, my lord . . . my, er, *bride*." He shifted uneasily under the king's watchful stare.

"Really?" Stephen inquired, lifting his chin. He turned now to face Graeham, adding off-handedly, "Are you aware, Graeham, that William Beauchamp is here at court, as well?"

Graeham was unable to suppress his surprise. His brows lifted. "Nay, I certainly was not, my lord."

"Aye, well, that he is. He awaits an audience with me, though as yet I've not had the stomach to grant it. Imagine my surprise to find you here, as well," he said as he came to stand before him.

In deference, Graeham knelt before his sov-ereign, but Stephen waved him up. "We are alone," he said. "No need for such formal-ities. Tell me what brings you to London, Graeham."

Graeham swallowed, and faced Stephen squarely. Once reputed to be the most come-ly man in England, at fifty-seven Stephen still wore his looks well. Yet his lackluster eyes bore a sorrow that Graeham knew came from the loss of his queen two years past. She had been his ally through the worst of his trials, and he would never truly overcome her passing. That, and the simple fact that he had no issue to whom he'd pass the crown, had led to his truce with Matilda, Graeham believed.

"I've a queer request," Graeham yielded, "though one of which I feel strongly." When Stephen nodded, he continued. "I wouldst have you confirm my father's lands, all of which I now hold, to my brother."

Stephen was taken aback, and his expression clearly revealed it. He made some staggered sound, and agreed, "'Tis indeed a most irregular request. God's truth, I have *never* come across such a petition in all my days." He shook his head incredulously. "Though I would welcome Blaec as lord of Drakewich, I must wonder, Graeham, why you would seek such a thing. 'Tis mad."

"Sire . . . I realize how this must sound, but 'tis simple. Blaec is both my brother *and* the rightful heir to my father's demesne. He is firstborn, and as such, deserves to hold what is his due. I'd not hold it any longer, for I feel I am not suited to lead my men—not as he is."

Stephen's expression turned grave. For the longest instant there was only silence between them. "I knew your mother, Graeham," he said. "I knew her well indeed, and I am well aware of that unfortunate truth. Yet . . . I wouldst remind you that your father assigned *you* as his heir, not Blaec. That he is firstborn does not give him absolute right to succession. I fail to understand why you should *wish* that altered. I would loathe to think 'twas so, but you are not being coerced in this are you?"

"Nay, m'lord. I am not. 'Tis simply that I am not the warrior my brother is," Graeham said, standing firm. "In truth, as you know me well enough to know I am not a coward in battle, I must admit to you that I've neither the stomach nor the heart to lead any longer."

Stephen's brows rose at his forthright answer. "I see. Yet I must admit that I find it difficult to credit Blaec would agree to such an ill-advised proposition." He cocked his head questioningly.

Graeham's face colored fiercely. "Aye, well," he said, hedging, "the truth is that Blaec does not know as yet."

Stephen blinked incredulously. "He does not know?" He shook his head. "Allow me to repeat this lest I've misunderstood . . . You wish to bestow your lands upon your brother, and he is unaware of the fact?"

Graeham gave him a sheepish glance. "I believe that is the pith of it, sire."

"God's teeth, son! Why, by the birth of Christ, wouldst you wish to do such a thing? Did I not know you better, I wouldst think you unsound of mind! I feel certain in saying that did your brother know of this, Graeham, he wouldst not only refuse it but think you as mad as I do."

"Mayhap," Graeham replied softly, resolutely, his expression sober, "yet I must insist that you consider my wishes."

Stephen emitted a sound something like choked laughter. "Brotherly devotion is a virtue indeed, d'Lucy, but the two of you take it too far, I fear." He sighed wearily, heaving in a breath. "Ah, well, I cannot say as I understand this, but if 'tis your wish, then so be it," he relented. "It will be done."

Graeham knelt at once, seizing his sovereign's hand, kissing it fervently. "Thank you, sire! Thank you!"

Stephen nodded, retrieving his hand and drawing it over his chin in bewilderment. "One thing, Graeham. Say to me one thing to make me comprehend this. Is your bride so hideous that you wouldst give up so much not to wed with her?"

Graeham's face reddened. "Nay, my lord. She is fair enough."

"What, then, prithee?"

Graeham shrugged, searching for a plausible reason, one not quite so complicated, or embarrassing, as the truth. He shook his head. "I've a calling for the church," he said rather unassertively, his expression screwing.

"Good God, man! You must have one better than that!"

Graeham shook his head. "I fear not, sire. 'Tis as good as any."

Stephen sighed and shook his head. "Very well, then, d'Lucy. Have it as you will—though I wish you success in convincing your brother, for I doubt he will be as accepting as I."

Graeham smiled. "I'm certain I shall manage, sire."

Stephen chortled. "Aye—smooth-tongued bastard that you are," he quipped. Once again, he waved Graeham up from his knees, and then placed an arm about Graeham's shoulders, leading him toward the door. "Tell me, then . . . does this mean I will have yet another God-spouting prelate fighting to save my soul?"

Graeham laughed, and cocked his head. "Mayhap so, sire, though I vow to give you no more grief than the Empress's minions have."

Stephen laughed outright and whacked him upon the back. "Ye God! I wouldst have you quartered," he swore emphatically. "I would indeed!"

His mood was black—blacker yet for the news he'd just received . . . from the king, no less! Though he tried to keep his calm, he stormed from the king's apartments, bursting out into the sunlight, his face a mask of stone, lest anyone's eyes were upon him.

That whoreson d'Lucy! What possible reason could the fool have for giving up his lands to his infernal brother? If he had dared so much as touch Dominique wrongly . . . he would strangle the imbecile with his bare hands. If he thought for one instant that he, having given up his holdings, was going to wed with Dominique still, then he was mad!

He was a fool! As was Stephen for granting the petition, for Blaec d'Lucy's loyalties lay with no other save his brother. His interests were purely his own. And his power, while it had been harnessed beneath his brother's thumb, was incontestable. There would be no bounds to his greed now that his business was his own.

And Blaec! God damn the man to hell! William would as lief strangle Dominique himself, rather than allow the bastard to touch her. The very last thing he intended was to allow Blaec d'Lucy to usurp what was his. Graeham, he could have borne—Blaec was another matter entirely, for he could well recall the way Blaec had gazed at Dominique. No duty there. Nay, for he recognized lust when he saw it.

Damn d'Lucy!

It had been all William could do to mask his anger when speaking to the king—king, bah! the man had no wisdom at all for the dispensation of justice. Nor had he the stomach to rule as he might. Had not England suffered enough these nineteen winters? Stephen was a spineless fool, wanting to please everyone, and pleasing no one at all. At least Henry had known to choose allies. Stephen was little more than an idiot.

Well, by damn, if Stephen could not execute justice, then William was perfectly capable—and more than ready, as well.

Mayhap as yet all was not lost . . . Aye, perchance all that was needed now was a reverse in plans. *Mayhap Dominique might still become lady of Drakewich. His lady of Drakewich.*

Aye, mayhap.

But then . . . if it proved to be so, and Blaec d'Lucy had bedded her . . . if he had so much as touched her . . . mere poison alone would not be a fitting enough death. By the eyes of Christ, he would personally rip out Blaec d'Lucy's entrails and feed them to his accursed buteo!

Chapter 22

All she need do was walk into a room to command attention—even dressed as she was in her threadbare blue bliaut, all eyes followed her. Her curls, rich and full, cascaded behind her as she lifted her skirts and raced across the hall, oblivious to his and the steward's presence. She didn't see him even as she rushed past them toward the stairwell, and Blaec was hard-pressed to listen to the steward's report as he watched her—as was the steward struggling to keep his train of thought, he couldn't help but note. Yet his mood was too good to fault the fellow for what he himself could not help.

Excusing himself once she disappeared from view, he followed her, racing up the tower steps after her, his pace swift but silent, for he intended to surprise her.

He quickly overcame her stride, hooking his arm about her waist, lifting her, and hauling her up the stairs along with him. She gave a small shriek of surprise. "You are being made off with," he told her, chuckling. He carried her into the nearest doorway.

Dominique shrieked indignantly. "Not here!" she exclaimed.

He set her upon her feet, grinning. "Ah, now, where better a place for solitude?" he countered.

"Aye, but 'tis the garderobe!" Dominique returned incredulously.

He lifted his chin, gazing with a look of surprise about the small chamber. "Is it?" he asked flippantly, sniffing. "I didn't notice."

"You!" Dominique laughed and shoved him away, trying to evade him. "God's truth, but I think you are mad!" she informed him with certainty.

He caught her, backing her once more against the wall. His lips curved roguishly. "Mad for you," he agreed readily. He arched a brow.

Dominique laughed softly. "You are a wicked, wicked man," she said, berating him.

"Well, there you have it," he said without remorse, brushing her hair from her shoulder. He bent, pecking her neck with his lips. "And since we are here . . ."

Dominique gasped. "I think not!" she said. "I do not think I could bear the odor, my lord!"

Lest she escape him, he pinned her to the wall, bracing his arms on either side of her. "I smell only the fragrance of your body," he murmured silkily, leaning into her, nuzzling her hair. One knee went betwixt her legs, lifting up against her.

Dominique inhaled sharply at the gesture. "I cannot be certain, my lord," she said on a sigh, her head lolling to one side, "but I believe you have only just insulted me . . ." He placed a hand upon her breast, and she murmured softly.

The door made to open suddenly, and she stifled a cry of surprise, her head jerking up. Blaec's arm thrust out before it could open to reveal them, ramming it shut once more. " 'Tis occupied," he called out.

For an instant, there was only silence from the other side of the door. "Sorry, my lord," answered a male voice.

"Good God, can a man not relieve himself in peace?" Blaec added for good measure.

Dominique stifled a gasp, her eyes widening at his crudeness.

"Aye, my lord," came the chagrined reply from beyond the door, and then the sound of retreating footsteps.

She lifted a hand to cover his mouth, lest he speak again.

Blaec shook away from her, remonstrating, "Ah, but I *am* relieving myself, my love."

"Shhh! My God, he will hear you!" Dominique hissed at him. "You are truly mad!"

"He is gone," Blaec murmured softly, reaching down and lifting up her hem with purpose. "And aye . . . I am mad . . . mad with need," he told her huskily. "Let me love you, Dominique . . ."

He didn't wait for her to reply, but bent and kissed her lips. She melted against his knee, and her soft crooning was answer enough.

They were being pursued, Graeham was certain.

For the last few hours since departing London,

they had borne a shadow. And now, at intervals, the foreboding glint of metal flickered ahead of them, making him wonder that they were being led into an ambush.

His brows drew together as he considered who it might be, and then he frowned outright, for the truth was that he could not fathom. These were lawless times at best.

Everyone was suspect.

Instinct told him that their pursuers had been with them from the first, yet anyone leaving London would have heard the rumors, and would know . . . there was no longer anything to be gained by challenging him. He held his father's lands no more. Nay, there was naught to be gained . . . unless they wished demand a ransom . . . *or to settle a debt*.

He glanced at Nial, riding proudly at his side. Nial held his banner high, unmistakable with its glittering gold-threaded field, and its black, fire-breathing dragon—a device more suited to his brother, for Blaec was the true dragon of Drakewich. For truth, Blaec held the title already, even without the lands.

Strange that . . . that people could sense a leader even when the leader swore to follow.

Graeham had never had reason to doubt Blaec. His brother had always given him fealty without regret. The bloody truth was that Blaec would likely hang him by his testicles when he discovered what he'd gone and done. Nevertheless it *was* done, and there was naught that could be said to change Graeham's mind and will. God's truth, he'd done what was best for all, and for the first time in his five and twenty years of life, he felt like his own man—not his father's puppet.

Once again the metallic flicker appeared in the distance, nearer this time. Nial spied it as well, Graeham noted, and he nodded at the faithful squire. "Go and warn the men," he commanded him.

Nial immediately fell back. "Aye, my lord."

"Discreetly," Graeham charged him, studying the surrounding land with keen eyes, "lest we force their hand."

To the right, no more than a furlong's distance, lay thick woodlands, ideal for hiding an army were there need, yet instinct told him it was not there that the danger lay, for their pursuers had not bothered to make use of it. Rather they had lain behind at an indistinguishable distance— mayhap farther now, for he'd not caught a glimpse of them in the last twenty minutes.

In the immediate stretch before them, the land sloped upward, concealing what lay beyond. And to the left of them, the terrain was the same. The road on which they traveled lay at an angle to the two hills, cutting betwixt them at the point at which they met, along a lower, narrow passage. It was there he focused his attention.

There, and the small pockets of woodland they had yet to pass. He skirted them, all but the last, and was forced to make a decision, for the last thicket posed a quandary. Did they go around it, they would be forced to pass to the right, dangerously close to the even thicker forest-land to their right. Yet it would also give them a clearer view of the dale as they entered. Did they pass through the thicket itself, it would place them in danger of an ambush within, and then they would emerge blindly into the dale. If they forced a pass to the left, then they would need ride up the hill, placing themselves also in danger of an attack upon the hillside, and then again as they entered even more vulnerably into the valley.

Damn, damn, damn . . . 'twas always when Blaec was not there that he needed him most. Yet 'twas his own fault, Graeham acknowledged irritably, that his brother was not there, for 'twas he who had commanded him to remain behind. Clenching his jaw, Graeham reined in, his skin prickling, for he knew instinctively that it was at this point in which their greatest danger lay.

And the decision was solely his own.

Though he retained his calm, the palms of his hands began to sweat profusely. At this moment his attraction to the church had never waxed deeper. This was not his strength, by God. It was Blaec's. He laughed derisively. What absurdity . . . Driven by guilt for what his father had done to his brother, for his own part in the injustice, he had placed his life in danger so many accursed times . . . and now did he die . . . he would bequeath his brother with a legacy of the selfsame burden. Scarcely could he bear the thought.

It seemed his men understood his dilemma, for one knight came forward at once, offering to scout the hill. He ordered another to the right of the thicket. And another to explore within. Though uneasily, all three obeyed at once, cantering away, while Graeham watched them, sweating like a hog neath the sweltering August sun. Yet though his face was soaked with perspiration, he resisted the urge to remove his helm, knowing without looking that his men watched him.

No sooner had the three ridden away, less than twenty yards distance, when the ruse was revealed. The knight riding for the thicket scarcely had time to turn about, so fast was he descended upon. He was cut down as the attackers stampeded past him. His scream of pain rent the air.

"To me!" Graeham thundered. "To me!" Wily bastards! From the thicket, they might have fallen upon them had they passed from either side. Were it the last bloody thing he did, he planned to skewer their ignoble leader through. It'd be the finest thing his father's sword had ever done.

With the clashing of metal, the battle was joined, and Graeham found himself, sooner than expected, face-to-face with the iron-helmed leader.

Masked with ventail and a helm, the nose-guard of which distorted his face, cutting it visually in half, the fiend left only his eyes exposed to reveal his identity. Graeham instantly knew the eyes: brilliant sapphire blue.

"Bastard!" he called out to him as his mount reared beneath him. Vicious laughter rang in his ears, even as did the metallic peal of their first clashing blows.

Chapter 23

They were alone upon the tower roof.

Another moment of solitude, *stolen.*

As she gazed out over the wall, Dominique felt as though she were suspended somewhere betwixt heaven and earth. From this great height, the land stretched far below them, revealing the horizon as never she had beheld it before.

Breathtaking.

Nor had she ever been so deliriously happy.

Like a whisper from God, telling her all would be well, a gentle breeze whipped at her face, her hair, her dress, lifting her spirits as though on angel's wings. She was bewitched. So much so that she did not hear Blaec as he came up behind her once more, embracing her, the heat of his body warming her from her nape to the curve of her hips. She gasped as his big hands slid about her waist, and she reveled in the way that he held her . . . as though he cherished her.

He squeezed her gently, and she smiled, turning her head, her eyes radiating the pleasure that flooded her at his touch. "'Tis beautiful, is it not?" he murmured. Her gaze returned to the landscape, and his arms tightened about her waist. "You are beautiful," he whispered fiercely.

Smiling, Dominique laid her head back against his chest, gazing up at the pale blue sky, her heart swelling with joy. A dove winged its way past them, landing gracefully at a higher place upon the tower wall, and she gazed up at Blaec to see if he was watching. He was, indeed. In profile, his face was harsh in the most beautiful sort of way, striking, though her eyes fell once again upon the scar that marred his cheek.

This time she could not have held herself back had she tried. She reached up, stroking the pale outline of it with the tips of her fingers, her eyes dulling at the smooth feel of it. It ached her to know that he had suffered pain at all, and it brought to mind the reality of what he was.

He was a knight. A warrior, loyal to his brother and his king. Even were they to resolve the insurmountable obstacles that lay between them, there would always be the possibility that he would be taken from her in war. She shivered, scarcely able to bear the thought. With the reckless desperation of one who had been too long without air, she wanted to breathe him within her so that they might never part.

"How did you receive it?" she asked him suddenly, candidly.

He smiled, the corners of his eyes crinkling as he gazed down upon her. "What?"

She frowned at him, removing her hand from his face, and placing both of hers upon his own at her waist. "You know very well what I wish to know," she accused him petulantly.

His green eyes twinkled as one hand slid up to squeeze her breast. "What is *that?*" he returned playfully, changing the subject effortlessly.

Dominique shrieked with surprise, and laughing, tried to disengage herself from his embrace. But he held her firmly within his arms, unwilling to release her.

"Nay, you do not," he said. "I'll not let you go."

"Then tell me," she demanded of him.

His eyes sobered slightly. "Very well, if you must know . . . I was sliced with a shaving knife by a careless barber."

"Nay!" Dominique was incredulous. "Say it cannot be so!"

He hugged her, nuzzling her neck playfully. "Ah, but 'tis true," he swore, his breath warm against her neck.

"*That* is *not* what I have been told, my lord." She sagged against him, feeling the answer of her body in the tautening of her breasts as he nibbled her neck, nipping her lightly.

"Truly?" His tone was unconcerned. "Tell me what it is that you heard, demoiselle." He lifted a hand to cup her breast, while the other explored the flat contours of her belly, and his lips explored her neck.

Dominique's breath quickened. "I heard . . ." And then she laughed. "If you will not stop, I cannot speak," she berated him, but her head lolled to one side, giving him better access. "I heard, my lord, that you received the scar during battle," she relented, "during some great feat of valor."

"Babble," he muttered, dismissing it. He gave her a gentle squeeze, holding her. "Yet though I like that tale better, my lady, I can assure you . . ." He was silent a moment. And then he sighed, relenting, "'Twas nothing so noble as that."

Dominique sighed, as well. "Tongues do wag," she agreed feebly, undone by his gentle attentions.

"Mmmmm . . . like this?" He tickled her neck with the tip of his tongue, and Dominique laughed softly.

It amazed her the difference that had come over him in the last days. He was almost like a mischievous boy, she thought. "You, my lord," she said dreamily, "are a very . . . very wicked man."

"Hmmmmm . . ." He nodded, nuzzling her lazily. "So I've been told, demoiselle. Yet do you sound disappointed . . . Wouldst you rather I admitted the scar was suffered during battle?" he asked her blithely.

"Nay," she told him, clutching his arms about her tightly. "You mistake me, my lord." And then she blurted with a wistful sigh, "Would that this moment might never end." He said nothing in response, and Dominique closed her eyes, leaning against him, wanting so desperately to ask him of their future.

Did they even have one together?

Did they have anything at all?

For the last days they had somehow, without speaking it, agreed not to think of this as the betrayal it was—nor of Graeham, or that it should end. Nay, for it had been easier to pretend . . .

In the distance, a lone tree swayed with the breeze, its feathered limbs arching this way and that, like some graceful dancer beneath God's watchful eyes. The silence betwixt them in that instant was so keen that Dominique could almost hear the rush of the breeze stirring through its brilliant green leaves.

"What will Graeham say when he returns, do you think?" she dared to ask him. She nibbled at her lower lip as she awaited his reply.

It was not forthcoming. He laid his chin atop the pate of her head, as though reflecting upon her question. She could feel his jaw working, tautening.

"Think you he knows?" she persisted. "About us?"

"My brother is no fool," he told her with quiet certainty. "He knew before he left."

He turned her about suddenly, his expression sober now, his eyes searching. Dominique willed him to see what was in her heart. *Sweet Mary, but she loved him!* As he gazed at her, his eyes both turbulent and tender at once, his hands went to her shoulders.

Slowly, his eyes closing, he bent to kiss her mouth, his lips quivering, his fingers biting into her shoulders. The look she had seen upon his face made her heart fly into her throat, made her want to cry out in sheer pleasure, for it seemed as though he relished the very thought of kissing her, hungered for it, even. As did she.

His tongue slid seductively along the curve of her lips, his breath trembling as he lapped her, embraced her. Feeling the pounding of his heart against her breast, she opened to him readily, sighing with the joy it brought her. Dear God, she loved this man. She wanted to tell him so. She truly did, but she wasn't certain how he would respond. She knew he wanted her, aye . . . but did he love her?

It seemed as though he did . . . At least she dared to hope. And yet . . . his brother's shadow fell over them both, haunting them even at this moment.

Any day Dominique expected Graeham's return . . . any day . . . and then what would come of her? Of them?

She squeezed her eyes shut desperately, for she didn't wish to think of that now, she wished only to think of the feel of his smooth lips moving like warm silk upon her own.

She clung to him fiercely, wanting him to take of her whatever he would.

Anything.

Everything.

If he wanted to make love to her, even here, she would let him gladly. Aye . . . and she would love him back . . . with every fragment of her body and heart. If he wanted only to kiss her, then she wanted that, as well. And if he wanted merely to hold her . . . then she would hold him back as though her life would end without him.

And God's truth, she thought that it might . . .

Through the haze of pleasure, Dominique heard, vaguely, the sound of a horn being blasted.

Blaec tore himself away at once, peering over her shoulder, out over the tower wall, toward the gatehouse. It took Dominique an instant longer to gain hold of her wits, though by his expression, she wasn't certain she wished to.

His face had gone taut, his eyes narrowed.

Dominique whirled about to spy the approaching cavalcade. From this height and distance, little more was distinguishable aside from the glittering golden field of his banner. When she saw it, her heart lurched viciously.

Graeham.

"Something is wrong," Blaec told her, his voice taut, his hands squeezing her shoulder. He released her suddenly. Pivoting about, he raced down the tower stairs.

For an instant, her heart thundering painfully, paralyzing her, Dominique merely stood there. And then, taking in a fortifying breath, she hurried after him, telling herself all would be well.

It simply had to be, because she could not bear the thought of living without him.

The portcullis was already being raised when Blaec reached the bailey. His heart thundering like an armorer's hammer, he raced toward the gatehouse.

"Get that damned door open!" he shouted. "Faster!"

When at last the portcullis was lifted, he went himself to unlock the gates. Unlatching them, he drove them forward with a strength that came from fear. With the aid of his men, the massive door began to creak on its immense hinges. The abrasive sound, compounded by the silence from the other side of the ironbound oaken door, made the hair of his nape stand on end.

As the gates burst open, revealing his brother, and merely half the contingent of men with whom he had departed Drakewich, Blaec's gut wrenched violently. He felt a roar rise up within him at the sight of them, for he understood by the blood-smeared appearance of them that they had battled. And God . . . the first thought that struck him was that he'd not been there to defend his brother. Guilt pummeled him, gutting him from within, tearing him to shreds.

Whilst Graeham had fought for his life, he'd likely been abed with his bride.

God . . . this had been his greatest fear. That Graeham would fight without him at his side. That his brother would die and that he would not be there to save him.

He felt numb as he watched his brother ride within the bailey, his mount enervated and frothing at the mouth, his back so stiff in the saddle that it appeared he'd been propped with a lance up his arse . . . and yet his head lolled to one side with a sickening lameness.

The blood drained from Blaec's face as he watched Graeham ride toward him, and he shook his head denying the sight, even as his eyes held witness to it. Hastening to Graeham's side, he was relieved to find that Graeham's eyes were open and aware, though scarcely. Seeing him, Graeham stiffened. His eyes brightened, and he attempted to lift his head, as though to reassure Blaec, and for an instant their gazes met, held. His cracked lips parted to speak.

One word. *"Beauchamp."* And then his eyes suddenly rolled backward into his head and he collapsed where he sat, sliding off his blood-encrusted mount and into Blaec's arms.

Seeing his brother's leaden face, Blaec could scarcely speak. His throat constricted.

"Graeham," he rasped. He heard himself give a low, keening cry, and then he clenched his jaw, and closed his throat, knowing he could not reveal his emotions.

With a savage cry, he lifted up his brother's limp body into his arms, his eyes glazing, and started toward the keep, meeting brilliant sapphire-blue eyes as he turned.

His rage spiraled to new heights, for he saw only her brother's face.

He was vaguely aware that someone tried to aid him in carrying Graeham's body, but he turned on the man, snarling, "Touch him and I'll skewer you through." Though Graeham slipped from his grasp, he wanted no other hands upon him. He wanted to carry the burden alone. *He needed to carry the burden alone.* Would that he could exchange places with him—gladly, he would do so if he could.

Nial backed away, his arms falling to his sides. "We were ambushed," he revealed, crestfallen. His boyish face was dirty and streaked with sweat and blood, but his eyes were somber like those of a man who'd witnessed too much death. Blaec knew only too well what the boy was experiencing, for he, too, recalled his first battle. Only too well. And if he ever dared to forget, he need only see his reflection to recall.

"They attacked not long after we left London," Nial continued.

Carrying his brother's deadweight, Blaec made his way toward the donjon, his expression unyielding as stone. "Beauchamp?" he asked with barely suppressed fury. "He did this?" He wanted to be certain—needed to be certain, because he intended to rip the bastard's throat apart.

Nial nodded, averting his face and casting Dominique a withering glance.

Trying desperately to keep pace, Dominique stumbled along beside them, her face stricken.

For her brother? Blaec wondered bitterly. God damn her to hell! Certainly not for Graeham.

"Nay!" she exclaimed, her breasts heaving, her face crumpling with the news. "It cannot be so! You lie! My brother wouldst never do such a thing!" she swore vehemently.

Blaec gave her a piercing glance for her indefatigable defense of the bastard. Lest he spit in her face, he ignored her, unable to deal with her at the moment—and less with their treachery against the man who lay so helpless within his arms.

His brother.

Christ . . . his brother . . .

What kind of a man was he, that he would allow his brother, his kin, his liege, to fight and die on the battlefield whilst he was here . . . cuckolding him with his new bride, the sister of his nemesis?

He glanced down at his brother's face and thought his chest would cleave in two. "My God . . . did you not seek a physic?" he asked Nial. "He appears as though he's bled for days."

"My lord," Nial defended, his young face collapsing with his guilt, "he would let no one rest till we arrived here. We tried—we did . . . we tried to reason with him, but he feared Beauchamp would come here next, and he would not be eased until you were warned."

Blaec cursed roundly. "How many fell upon you?"

"Too many to count," Nial answered quickly.

"And how many perished?"

"We lost nine," the youth revealed. "But we returned the number of dead," he said with some dignity, "and I . . . I killed a man," he yielded, without emotion.

Blaec listened to the youth prattle on, scarcely aware of those who followed as he carried Graeham into the keep, up the stairs, beyond the solar and into the lord's chamber.

Benumbed with grief and regret, and beleaguered with unanswered questions, he placed his brother's limp form upon their father's bed, and then, raking a hand across his shadowed jaw, snapped out at Nial, "Go . . ." His voice failed him. He swallowed. "Go, lad, and seek the priest . . ." he commanded him.

Chapter 24

⟨✦⟩

Dominique stepped forward, desperate to aid them if she could. She wrung her hands, feeling dizzy with the thoughts that whirled through her mind. William could *not* have done this thing . . . he could not have. She refused to believe that he would . . . There had to be some mistake.

"You . . . you must allow Alyss to tend him," she entreated. "Leave the priest for those dead." Though she was aware that all eyes fell upon her suddenly, she felt only his.

Only his condemning glare tore at her heart.

"Alyss wouldst know what is best for him," she reasoned, her eyes stinging with hot tears.

"Why should I trust your brother's whore?" Blaec barked at her, his green eyes glittering coldly.

Dominique gulped in a breath, taken aback by his anger. She tried to catch her next breath and found a sob caught in her throat. "She is . . ." She blinked back tears, unable to find a response for the truth. "She is skilled in the simples," she finished feebly, averting her gaze, fighting back bitter tears. "I swear to you, my lord . . ." Her voice faltered and her lips trembled. She shook her head miserably, covering her mouth as she met his gaze once more, her eyes pleading with him. "God's truth . . . Alyss would no more harm him than she would . . . than she would me. Let her tend him . . . please . . ."

For a moment he said nothing, though his eyes impaled her, and then he said evenly, "It seems there is little choice but to trust her, demoiselle, for Drakewich has not a physic in residence. Fetch her, then, and quickly," he snapped.

Dominique nodded and turned to go at once, relieved to leave his presence, for her heart was breaking and she wanted no eyes to witness her pain.

He blamed her, she knew.

She could spy it in his eyes.

"Tell her this for me, Lady Dominique," he called after her, stopping her cold with the scarcely veiled malevolence in his tone. "Should he die by her hands . . . I will lay her head upon a pike beside that of your brother. Tell her that for me, if you would . . . and then, while you are at it, demoiselle, pray to God for your brother's black soul, because 'tis his blood I will seek come tomorrow's first light."

Dominique's limbs threatened to fail her, but she nodded jerkily, choking back a sob at his hateful words. To think that only moments before, they had laughed together . . . hoped together. In anguish, she covered her mouth with her hand as she fled the chamber.

Sweet Jesu, but she could not bear it. This could not be happening. Her brother had not done this to Graeham! He could not have!

Because he would have known that he would place her at risk with his actions. And he would not do so.

Would he?

Nay, but there had to be some other explanation.

With that self-assurance, she swiped the tears from her face, and vowed that as soon as she found and apprised Alyss of her duties, she would set out to discover the truth.

Even if it meant going to William.

There was no way she could stand idly by and allow Blaec to simply kill her brother for some imagined wrong. She had to warn him.

More than that, even, *she* had to know.

"He but sleeps, m'lord," Alyss told him, coming to stand timidly before him, "The wound at his breast is deep, yet he is strong and I've faith he shall live," she said, encouragingly.

Relief sucked the breath from Blaec, choking off whatever words he might have spoken. Though he tried, he could not find his voice. He nodded.

Hanging her head, taking in a visibly shaky breath, the maid reached into her apron, hesitating, and then produced a vial for him. "I . . ." She took another shuddering breath and then handed him the ampule for his inspection. "You must give this to him . . . a few drops when he awakens," she instructed him, swallowing, meeting his gaze with some difficulty. "But no more than a few . . ."

Blaec examined the small liquid-filled vial, and then returned his gaze to hers, narrowing his eyes warily. "What is it?" he asked.

She held his gaze, he noted, even as he saw her flinch at his question. "T-Tincture of hemlock, m-m'lord."

Blaec arched a brow at her, his lips thinning at her disclosure. "You carry hemlock about with you oft?" he inquired of her suspiciously. "Why?"

Her face reddened at the question, and she averted her gaze, shrugging nervously, and then shaking her head. And then again she met his gaze, lifting her chin, her eyes revealing that same cornered stare he'd spied in them once before . . . the night he'd questioned her about her bruises. "'Twas g-given to me," she answered softly, guiltily.

"*Given to you?*"

She closed her eyes, and shivered, nodding jerkily. "Aye, m'lord. *Given to me.*"

God help him, he understood, and once again rage barreled through him.

"Damn the bastard!"

He'd intended all along to murder Graeham. His thoughts fled back to the forest . . . and then to the mead Dominique had been brewing . . . and he was afeared to hear any more lest he learn what he did not wish to know.

Still . . . he had to discern the extent of their treachery—had to be certain. "William gave it to you, Alyss?"

She would not look at him now. "Aye, m'lord."

Blaec braced himself, and then demanded, "Does your mistress know this?" Though he told himself his heart was hardened against her, he held his breath for her answer.

She shook her head, meeting his gaze, and said with quiet certainty, "Nay, m'lord, she does not."

He felt the breath leave his lungs—he wanted to believe her. Too much. For Graeham's sake, he could not allow himself to be led blindly. Not when Graeham's life depended upon his prudence. "And why do you tell me this now?" he asked her skeptically, unable as of yet to perceive her motives.

"Because, m'lord . . ." She glanced at Graeham's body, lying so still upon his bed, and then back into his eyes. "Because I cannot do it. And . . . and he shall need the tincture when he wakens, m'lord," she concluded. "Hemlock is good for pain, as well, though in small doses. Yet . . ."

"Speak," he commanded her impatiently. "Now is not the time to hold your tongue, woman."

"Aye . . . well . . . you see . . . too little will not serve him at all . . . though too much might leave him lame—or even kill him, as you well know," she replied truthfully. "And this recipe . . . 'tis particularly dangerous, for I-I prepared it strong . . . and . . . and I did not wish to risk it . . . not if . . ."

He cocked a brow. "Not if I meant to place

your head on a pike?" he finished for her. "I see." With some reservation, he handed the vial back to her, his face as rigid as stone. He went to his brother's side, lifting the coverlet up, as though to shelter him from the draft.

His fingers lingered upon his brother's hand, the hand he had once sworn fealty to.

She hadn't had to tell him anything at all, he acknowledged. She might have simply used the tincture while his back was turned ... or once he was healed, even ... once she no longer thought herself at risk. "Do you love the bastard?" he asked her suddenly, his tone calm despite his raging fury.

For an instant, she didn't respond. And then she replied emphatically, "Oh, nay, m'lord. He ... he did beat me oft."

He sensed the truth in the embittered way she said the last, but he demanded ruthlessly, "Was it he, Alyss, who gave you those bruises I witnessed?"

He could tell it was a difficult question for her to reply to, for she hesitated, but she did so at last, swallowing before she spoke. "Aye, m'lord. 'Twas he, though I beg you not to tell m'lady so. She does not know. She believes him nobler than he is, and I would spare her the truth. Forsooth, he is all she has—all she has ever known."

"I see," he said. And then, "Do you wish my protection, Alyss?" He met her gaze at last. Her eyes were glassy, and her youthful features seemed to have aged since the last time he glanced at her.

He saw the hope kindle in her eyes. "You wouldst do so, m'lord? You would do this . . . for me?" She bit her lip, until he thought it would bleed.

For a moment there was silence between them, and then he told her, swallowing hard, "Aye . . . only, do what you must." He glanced down at his brother, his eyes glazed and wounded. He met her eyes once more. "I place my trust in you, Alyss," he told her soberly, shaking his head, his eyes narrowing. "Do not fail me, and does he live, I will grant you leave to remain at Drakewich."

Her expression twisted with emotion. "Thank you, m'lord! Thank you! I swear I will not fail you, m'lord," she said fervently.

"Though if he dies," Blaec continued, meaning every word he was about to say, despite the mildness of his tone, "I will indeed place your head on that pike—better yet, I will return you to that bloody bastard and tell him you have betrayed his confidence."

She swallowed visibly. "Aye, m'lord . . . I'll not fail you," she vowed. "I swear it."

"See that you do not," he warned her, and then he stepped back to allow her to attend to her ministrations. Yet he fully intended to watch over her every moment.

She came forward at once, eagerly almost, clutching the ampule within her fist, and Blaec silently prayed.

Chapter 25

Long after the maid, Alyss, had fallen asleep, her head pillowed within her dainty arms, Blaec sat, sleepless, in their father's chair, watchful of Graeham's slumber.

Bitterness crept into his bones like a cold mist into his very frame as he marked the rise and fall of each labored breath his brother took. If either of them should be lying there, suffering, it deserved to be he, not Graeham.

He could only be grateful to the hollow-eyed wench who now sat dozing at his brother's bedside, for she'd given faithfully of herself in her duties. He'd watched her keenly, though it had not been necessary, for not even now, when she was so weary that she could scarcely keep her pretty little head raised, did she abandon Graeham's side.

Likely she was afeared that he would keep his promise to her—that he would place her head upon that pike. Or mayhap she was simply so eager to be free of her devil lord that she was resolved to see Graeham healed. Either way, her determination served him well, for

Blaec did not care what her reasons were, only that she succeeded in her endeavor.

If Graeham did not live . . . God help him, some part of him would die inside, as well.

Late into the night, the bedside torch began to flicker, and then guttered, pitching the chamber into blackness. And still he sat, unmoving, listening to the sounds of the night.

Moonlight trickled in to lend its light, streaming like molten silver across the sleeping forms of his brother and Dominique's weary little maid. As he listened to the whisper of Graeham's breathing, taking comfort in each successive draw of breath, he could not help but wonder of the woman who had tended him all eve.

She spoke eloquently, if diffidently, and Blaec would wager she was no baseborn wench. Everything, from the delicateness of her limbs to the fairness of her skin and the gentility of her manners, proclaimed her gentle-born. He found himself wondering how she had ended in William's clutches—found himself wondering, too, how the bloody hell Dominique could be so blind to her brother's treachery.

Still, he was certain Dominique was innocent of it all. He could see it in her expression when she had begged him to accept her maid's service. Christ and bedamned—he shuddered to think of what might have happened had he, in his desperation, allowed Alyss's ministrations—which he had—and she had not chosen to come forth with the ampule, and with it, the truth.

What if she had used it as William bade her?

The probable end result twisted his gut. And

Christ . . . she might have done so . . . and he might have never known. He would have simply attributed Graeham's death to his injuries.

Yet Alyss *had* come forth, and for that he was indebted to her. Whether William lived, or nay—lame or not—he knew he would give the girl leave to remain at Drakewich under his protection. He owed her that much.

Still he could not credit the depths of Beauchamp's treachery.

Though he could not begin to consider what was the best course concerning Dominique, he was glad, at least, that she was not beneath her brother's roof this night.

He tried not to think of her—he clenched his jaw with the force of his determination—tried not to think of her lying abovestairs within his bed. But even now, like the faithless bastard his father had claimed him to be, he was torn betwixt wanting to remain by Graeham's side, needing to remain by his side . . . and wanting to go to her.

Even now that his brother was again under the same roof, he wanted her. And aye, he loathed himself for it, even as he *craved* to spend himself, his pain, his fury, his seed, into Dominique's lithe, sweet body. Like some drogue, she was in his blood.

Guilt kept him from rising.

Guilt, weariness, and the sight of the brother he valued so dearly, lying so near to death before him.

God's teeth, what a fine brother to Graeham he was—aye, and what a treacherous way he had of showing his affection. His lip curled with self-contempt, for he had dared to reason, dared to hope, that Graeham had willed him to it.

Like a fool, he had convinced himself that his brother had driven him into Dominique's bed . . . into her body.

What a fool he was . . . a faithless, presumptuous fool.

He should have gone after Graeham.

His self-derisive thoughts persisted, besieging him, until at last fatigue began to claim him, and he slouched within the massive chair. Permitting his head to slump to his shoulder, he closed his eyes . . . only for a moment . . . and dozed.

Dominique lay awake most of the night hoping that Blaec would come to her, pondering her decision to go, and wondering of Graeham's condition. But she waited in vain, for he didn't appear, and just now, her heart felt as though it would rend itself in two. Yet the fact that he'd not bothered to come reinforced her decision to leave, even as she was crushed.

She'd managed to convince herself last eve that she'd wanted him to come to her one last time because she'd needed the memories to embrace until they chanced to meet again. She knew now that once she departed Drakewich, she never would return, and the mere thought that she might never see him again made her eyes sting with tears.

Still, she knew . . . even were Blaec to accept her again within Drakewich's walls—which she was not at all certain he would, for she'd not missed the expression upon his face when the boy had claimed her brother responsible—he blamed her, and judging by his look of contempt, she thought he might never forgive her.

But even if he did forgive her . . . once her brother knew of this—once he understood that the d'Lucys had accused him, once more, without affording him even the opportunity of a defense—he would never allow her to return here.

Aside from that, the betrothal was well and duly broken, for never could she agree to wed with Graeham d'Lucy after having loved Blaec.

How could she bear it were she forced to?

Nor did she believe that Blaec would allow the marriage to be consummated. Not now— not when his brother's honor was involved. If she'd wondered at all of his devotion to his brother—and she'd not—the look upon his face today as he'd carried Graeham's wounded body within the donjon was proof enough.

It was over.

With all her heart Dominique prayed that Graeham would live, prayed that Blaec would forgive her did he not, but she wasn't going to remain to see that it was so. Nay, and she could not afford even to tell Alyss of her plans, for as of yet Alyss had not once emerged from the lord's chamber—the very last thing Dominique needed was to face Blaec this morning. Nay, she could not go in there.

If she did, then she would never have the strength to leave him, to do what she must.

And she had to discover the truth.

She had been faithful each morning in taking the almoner's offerings to the village in hopes that the villeins would, in time, come to accept her as their lady—and she felt that she'd nearly succeeded, for if they did not trust her wholly, then they had, at least, come to receive her warmly. She was glad now that she had thought to carry out the task, for more reasons than that, for at least now she had a reason for leaving the castle walls this morning. With luck, no one would think to question her—not when she had carried out the very same routine each sunrise before now. With a sack from the kitchens she would be able to carry along with her a few of her own belongings, as well as some foodstuffs for the journey home.

Home. Sweet Mary, whither was that? she wondered bitterly.

Pain tore into her heart, numbing her with the impact of the question. Never had she truly known one—never would she ever, by the looks of it.

She was doomed ever to live in Limbo.

Trying her best not to weep, she dressed herself quickly in her blue bliaut, and then hurried down to the kitchens, grateful that no one seemed to remark her presence there. Unlike the previous mornings, however, she didn't bother to inquire of the rations, leaving them, instead, for the almoner. Were she to take them with her now, she would simply have to leave them within her bedchamber, which would serve nothing, save to give her away.

Nor would it reach those who needed it most. Nay, she would leave them.

She found the sacks easily enough, seized one, along with a few pickings from the food being prepared for the breaking of the night's fast, and left at once, hurrying back to her chamber. Once there, she began to choose what she would carry along with her—only the most valuable of her belongings. The rest, she would leave behind. She was forced to, for there was no way she could take them without drawing attention to herself.

When she was prepared at last, she hurried down the tower stairs, her heart hammering, praying she would not meet with Blaec.

She breathed a sigh of relief once she'd made it through the hall, and then out to the stables. As luck would have it, her palfrey had already been tended this morn—she could tell because the animal was still feeding when she arrived.

Once again, no one remarked upon her presence, for she'd come every morn in just this same manner—only this sunrise, she had no intention of riding into the village . . . nor any intention of returning. She found her saddle and trappings, prepared the animal, and smiling nervously at the stablehand who passed by, drew her mare out of its stall. She crooned softly to the animal as she placed the meal sack over its haunches and secured it, trying to appear casual as she hurried. That done, she led the animal out of the stables, into the dawn light, and mounted.

By now the sky had lightened considerably, sending tendrils of pink and violet into the distant horizon.

Her palms sweating, her limbs shaking, and her heart pounding madly within her breast, she took in a fortifying breath and rode toward the gatehouse, telling herself that this morning would appear no different to the gatekeeper from any other. But the insistent pounding in her head gave lie to her self-assurances.

This morning *was* different.

How could it not be when only yesterday the lord's body had been carried within, wounded—mayhap fatally? She could not forget that Graeham d'Lucy lay within the keep, fighting for his life. Nor could she forget that 'twas her brother who stood accused.

Nor could she forget the look Blaec had given her.

Would the guard allow her to pass?

The pit of her stomach plummeted and then surged again as she neared the gatehouse. Scarcely able to breathe as she faced the sober-faced gatekeeper, she said nothing, merely smiled and patted the sack she had secured to her mount. He waved back and proceeded to direct the opening of the portcullis and gates. Dominique was grateful she was mounted, for she thought that had she been upon her feet in that instant, her legs might have given way beneath her, so relieved was she.

While she waited, listening to the clamor of the portcullis lifting, she prayed no one would rush from the keep and prevent the opening of the gates themselves—prayed that she would have the stoutheartedness to go forth once the moment arrived.

The longer she sat, the more her fear over-whelmed her, paralyzed her. She tried not to appear guilty, but she felt the guilt all the way to her core.

At last the portcullis was elevated, silenced, the drawbars released, and then at last the gates were opened. With far more fear than cour-age, Dominique spurred her mount forth, into the barbican, not daring to glance backward. She could not, for in her mind she saw Blaec storming from the keep, racing toward her, a lethal vengeance in his eyes.

She sighed in relief when she exited the barbi-can and the gates closed behind her. The sound of the drawbars being replaced was like both a harmony from heaven above, and a death knell as well, for if she never saw Blaec again, she was certain some part of her would cease to live.

Sweet Jesu, scarcely was she free of the gates and some part of her was dying already.

In order to dispel suspicion, Dominique rode toward the village at first, her heart pounding like a battering ram. Once she was far enough away from the castle walls that she felt it safe enough, she veered toward the fog-enshrouded trees and didn't slow until she was safely with-in them.

And even then, she did not rest. Anticipating the shouts of pursuit to reach her at any moment, she made her way through the misty woods, tears streaming silently down her cheeks.

No sounds came to her other than the crunching of leaves beneath her mount's hooves and the noises of the forest surrounding her. Those, and the sound of her heart rending.

Not even when she exited the forest and dared to make use of the old road did she hear their pursuit, and Dominique didn't know whether to be relieved or aggrieved.

Though she told herself it was the former, her heart felt only the latter.

Chapter 26

"**M**' lord!"

Blaec straightened abruptly within the chair, gripping its carved wooden arms. He'd been dreaming, and the frantic female voice had intruded, waking him, befogging him.

"Awake, m'lord!" the maid exclaimed.

Seeing her blurry face waver before him, he blinked, clearing his mind of its webs. It was morning, as best he could determine, for the shutters were open wide to the daylight and the torches as yet unlit. He'd slept.

"He called for you, m'lord!" Her face was animated, elated, her dark eyes sparkling. "He called your name!" she told him excitedly, smiling.

Scarcely able to believe his ears—afeared that he was dreaming still—he blinked again, and his voice was gruff with sleep when he asked, "He called for me?" He cleared his throat, tilting his head in question. "Graeham?"

She nodded enthusiastically, and then leapt away as he bolted suddenly from the chair, practically overturning it in his haste to leave it. His heart hammering, Blaec knelt at his brother's bedside only to find that Graeham's eyes were still closed. "Art certain?" he asked her, disappointment quickly filtering through him.

"Aye, m'lord," she replied, peering over his shoulder. Her voice seemed undaunted at the sight of Graeham's pallid face. Not so, Blaec. It terrified him, for Graeham was too still by far. "Not once, but twice did he call for you," she assured him.

Blaec touched Graeham's arm warily, squeezing gently, feeling its warmth. And still he was afeared to hope. "Graeham?" he called softly, and held his breath.

At first there was no response, and then as he started to call Graeham's name once more, Graeham opened his eyes suddenly. Seeing Blaec, he smiled wanly, and Blaec exhaled in relief.

"God's teeth," Graeham said weakly, swallowing with difficulty. "Can a man not rest in peace?" he grumbled. His eyes sparkled dimly.

Blaec's features softened at his brother's quip, at the familiar bedeviling look in his eyes. "You whoreson," he replied, smiling back. "What makes you think you can lie about all day sleeping your fool head off?"

Graeham chuckled, though with some difficulty, grimacing in pain over the effort.

Blaec's smile faded somewhat. "You went and did it this time, didn't you, Graeham?" Both of them well understood his charge, he knew. "It seems to me that you are determined to see yourself consigned to the grave," he remarked, when Graeham did not respond.

Graeham's expression sobered as he made an effort to peer down at his bandaged wounds. As he met Blaec's gaze once more, he shook his head. "'Tis not what you think, Blaec." The expression in his eyes was regretful. "I tried. I truly did. Had I not . . . well, then . . . we would not be speaking just now," he pointed out. "Would we?"

Blaec nodded, and sighed. "I suppose not," he relented. And then admitted, "I feared to have lost you, my brother."

Their gazes held.

Graeham blinked, his eyes glazing slightly. "Well, you did not," he answered, "for here I am in flesh and blood."

Blaec's lips curved. "Mostly blood."

Graeham took a deep breath, and then grunted in pain. "That bloody whoreson," he hissed.

Blaec gritted his teeth. "Beauchamp?" He sensed Alyss's withdrawal in that instant. He heard her footsteps as she moved across the room to afford them some measure of privacy, and was grateful, though he was too angry to acknowledge the gesture at the moment.

Graeham sighed, his eyes following her. "Aye, Beauchamp—the bastard—though I know not why he wouldst do so." A muscle ticked at his jaw.

"And you are certain 'twas he?"

"Never could I mistake those eyes," Graeham asserted. "'Twas he—the bastard! I swear that if I ever get my hands around his traitorous neck—" He clutched his hands together and then shuddered. He nodded in Alyss's direction. "Did she do this?" He indicated the bandages.

Blaec nodded. "She was quite eager to, in fact." His lips curved slightly. He peered back over his shoulder at the woman in question and then his gaze returned to Graeham. "Mayhap she feared to lose the opportunity to ride her new lord?" he said in low tones, lest he offend her.

Graeham chuckled, closing his eyes, as though to consider the remark . . . but then did not reopen them . . . nor did it seem as though he breathed.

Blaec's heartbeat quickened. "Graeham?" His face paled.

Graeham's eyes popped open and he sought out the maid once more. "I was wondering if she wouldst mind riding the lord's brother, is all," he said blithely, with the slightest smile.

Blaec averted his eyes to the window momentarily, hating himself never more than he did in that moment. "The lord's brother needs no consideration," he said guiltily, bitterly. "The lord's brother has already taken his fill." *Of that which he had no right to.* It was all he could do to return his gaze to Graeham.

"Bastard," Graeham said without heat, without meaning, laughing low. "Speak for your own self. If I say the lord's brother is in need of attention, he is in need." The sparkle in his eyes returned and intensified. "At long last," he added softly, almost inaudibly.

Confused by the remark, Blaec frowned down at his younger twin brother. "You must be addlepated," he said. "You haven't made this little sense . . ." He shook his head. "Not since . . ."

"I am not the lord of Drakewich," Graeham interjected, his expression sober, though his eyes were brilliant still, as though with fever.

Blaec's brows collided. "God's blood!" he exclaimed. "Beauchamp *has* rattled your brain! What the hell are you speaking of, Graeham?"

Graeham's face set sternly. "I said . . . I am no longer lord of our father's demesne," he repeated, his eyes sober. "I believe I spoke plainly enough. If not, I'll say it no plainer than this . . . Drakewich is no longer my own. 'Tis yours," he revealed without regret.

Blaec surged to his feet, glowering down at Graeham. "By whose edict?" he demanded to know.

"King Stephen's," Graeham replied easily, though he grimaced in pain.

"I'll not bloody accept it!" Blaec bellowed. "Who the devil does he think he is to strip you of your birthright?"

"Nay. 'Tis your birthright, not mine," Graeham countered softly, his chin lifting. "'Tis yours and we both know it well enough."

Blaec's jaw tightened. His teeth clenched.

"'Tis long past time to accept the truth," Graeham continued, undaunted.

Blaec shook his head furiously. "By the rood of Christ, Graeham!" He knelt again by the bedside, trying to make Graeham comprehend, trying to comprehend himself. "Can you not see that I've never cared who inherited this land? Do you not know that I've never begrudged you aught—" His voice broke, and his eyes closed. "Save one thing," he amended truthfully, meeting Graeham's eyes once more, no matter how painful. "We both know what that *one thing* is . . ."

Graeham nodded slowly. "Along with Drakewich . . . she, too, is yours," he yielded with moist eyes.

Blaec's expression grew incredulous. His eyes narrowed, glittering. "Is *that* what this is all about?" he asked. "Is it, Graeham? Because if it is—"

"Nay," Graeham countered, his tone firmer now. "This is not about Dominique. *This* is about which of us is rightful heir." He grimaced, clutching at his bandaged chest. "*This* is about which of us has the strength to protect this land. *This* is about—"

Blaec shook his head, his own eyes glazing. "I swore my fealty to you, Graeham." His tone was rife with emotion. "Did you not believe me when I pledged you my life?"

"Aye!" Graeham exploded, losing his voice with the outburst of emotion. He swallowed. "God damn you to hell, Blaec!" His nostrils flared. "I believed you, you bastard." He clenched his jaw, and his expression twisted with grief. "Can you not understand that this is not only about you? This is about me, too! I do not want this—" He squeezed his eyes shut, as though with pain, groaning.

Blaec reached out to place a hand upon his chest, to settle him, his own jaw clenching so tightly with emotion that he thought it would snap in twain. He shook his head. "God . . . I never wanted this," he said hoarsely, closing his eyes, trying to make Graeham understand.

Graeham seized him by the arm, squeezing furiously. "I *need* you to want it," he said, shaking his arm. "I *need* you to take it! Can you not see?"

Blaec opened his eyes. "And if I cannot?" he asked softly.

Graeham lifted his chin, his eyes glistening. "Then I shall walk away, Blaec—I swear it! I shall walk away and then we shall both be left with naught," he said stubbornly. "See if I do not," he challenged.

Blaec's eyes narrowed. "And what shall you have, do I accept this act of folly?" he asked him grimly. "How can I take what is yours, Graeham, when I've sworn to defend it for you instead?"

"I shall have my pride," Graeham replied earnestly, as though it were all he craved. "As for taking what is mine . . . what was mine was ever yours," he pointed out reasonably. "And what is yours . . . I know you will freely share."

Blaec said nothing, merely stared, stone-faced, unconvinced.

"In return I will swear to you my fealty."

For the longest instant there was only silence between them. A weighty, unbreachable silence, for they were at an impasse, neither willing, or able, to yield.

"You cannot know what you are asking of me," Blaec said at last, a muscle ticking at his jaw. "You are asking me to go against my oath of fealty to you. An oath I swore with my soul," he pointed out irately.

Again there was silence, stubborn and pressing.

"*With my life.*"

"'Tis done," Graeham said tonelessly, averting his gaze. "It cannot be undone."

"The bloody hell it cannot!"

Graeham's gaze returned to the maid who stood in the corner of the chamber, watching them with wide, incredulous eyes. He nodded at her. "Bring me my sword," he charged her.

"Y-Yes, m-m'lord!" she said at once, but she hesitated, glancing nervously at Blaec. When Blaec said nothing, she brought Graeham the scabbard that held his blood-smeared sword, still stained from battle. Graeham withdrew their father's sword from the scabbard and held it out to Blaec. "Then use it now," he hissed. "Use it!" he charged him.

Blaec refused, not moving to take it, merely glaring down at Graeham, thinking him mad.

"I cannot live with this guilt on my conscience any longer," Graeham told him impassionedly. "Let me live at last!" he demanded.

"This is madness," Blaec yielded, shaking his head. "'Tis not your guilt to bear, Graeham. Can you not see that?"

Graeham thrust the sword at him, his face turning bright red in his fury. "Let me live, Blaec," he insisted. "Or let me die!"

"God! Is there naught I can say to make you see reason?" Blaec asked. "Is there naught I can do?" He shook his head.

Graeham, too, shook his head. "Not a thing," he asserted. "Nothing at all. You cannot understand, Blaec, because you do not live in this body of mine." He narrowed his eyes and lifted himself from the bed, forgetting his injuries in his fury. "You cannot know what our father's retribution against you and our mother has cost me. Do not take this away from me now."

"Do not take this away from you?" Blaec repeated incredulously. "But God's teeth, you are asking that I take everything!" he pointed out.

"Aye, and yet you give me my freedom in return," Graeham countered. Trembling, he fell back upon the bed, his face perspiring from the effort and the pain this new battle had cost him.

"You are weak and wounded and not thinking straight," Blaec told him. "Think on—"

"Nay! There is no need to think on it. My decision was made long before I even left Drakewich. Why is it do you think that I did not tell you whither I was going, Blaec? Why is it do you think that I did not let you come? And aye, why is it do you think that I urged you together at every turn? Aye," he affirmed, nodding when Blaec's eyes snapped back to question him. "You were right."

"This is madness!" Blaec exclaimed once more, seeing Graeham's bloodless expression.

"Mayhap so . . . but I wouldst that you took what I offered even so. I swear to you that I will walk away."

"Where?" Blaec challenged. "Whither wouldst you go, Graeham?"

Graeham shrugged. "The church," he said

without fervor, and then squeezed his eyes shut, grimacing.

"Damn you!" Blaec raked a hand across his whiskers, afeared that Graeham had exhausted himself. "Complete and utter madness!" He nodded at last. "But aye, if it please you, I shall take it," he relented, "though on one condition . . . that you will accept it back from me if you find the will again to rule it."

Graeham's jaw set stubbornly. He opened his shadowing eyes, meeting Blaec's gaze. "I have never had the will to rule," he said with his innate honesty. "*You* have ever been leader here—even when you did not hold the title. Drakewich is rightfully yours, my brother—has ever been. Yours, whether you like it or nay— never mine. That is both my own will, and that of our king. As God is my witness, never shall I take it back."

Blaec didn't know what to say. Rendered speechless by Graeham's impassioned words, he sat, his jaw working as he weighed the most difficult decision of his life. Some part of him acknowledged the truth of Graeham's claims. Another part of him wanted to refuse for honor's sake.

But whose honor was of greater consequence here?

Graeham's, as far as Blaec was concerned. If he needed to do this so urgently—and it seemed that he did—then so be it. He could not stand in Graeham's way. He nodded in agreement, though with no small measure of reservation. "Very well, Graeham," he relented with a weary sigh, "as you wish it . . ."

"I do wish it thus," Graeham assured him at once. "Now, at last, all will be as it should have be—"

A knock sounded at the door, interrupting him.

"I shall get it, m'lord," Alyss declared at once. Intending to tell her not to bother herself, that she had done enough already, and that he would get it himself, Blaec turned to see that she was already hurrying toward the door. He didn't have the heart to stop her now. She opened it, revealing behind it a sober-faced Edmund, one of the older knights in his garrison.

"What is it, Edmund?" Edmund's face flushed, and he seemed hesitant to speak. Blaec stood to face him, the hairs at the back of his neck rising instinctively. "Edmund?"

The older man's face screwed. "My lord," he began. His brow furrowed. "I've no idea whether 'tis important, or nay, but I thought I should tell you just the same . . ."

Blaec tensed. "Tell me what?"

"Well, my lord . . . 'tis the lady Dominique . . ."

His feeling of unease intensified. "Speak up, man!" he commanded at once. "*What* of Lady Dominique?"

"Well, you see, my lord . . . it may be nothing at all . . . 'tis only that . . . well, when she appeared at the gate early this morn, I did not think much of it then . . . Only later . . . when the almoner came and bid me let him pass, did I think to wonder . . ."

Blaec frowned. "I do not understand."

Edmund straightened. "Well, my lord . . .
'tis like this . . . You are aware that the lady
Dominique has taken the almoner's offerings
into the village each morn?"

Blaec nodded, following thus far. "I am."

"Well, this morn she came to me no different-
ly than any other . . . and I thought . . . well, my
lord . . . I did not think at all," Edmund admitted, red-faced. "And later the almoner came
himself, and I had to wonder whether the lady
Dominique had not taken the morning's offerings, after all—though she left with a sack," he
explained. "I waited, thinking that she wouldst
return at any moment . . . but she did not, and
I thought I should come and tell you."

Blaec's gut twisted. He turned to look at
Graeham, and then the maid—she fidgeted
under his scrutiny—and then again at Edmund.
"How long ago did she leave?" he snapped.

"Hours ago, my lord."

"Hours? And just now you come to me?"

Edmund hung his head a little. "The almoner came just a short time ago," he explained,
"and then I thought . . ." He looked past Blaec,
toward Graeham. "Well, I hesitated to intrude,"
he said. And then to Graeham, "'Tis good to
see you breathing, my lord." He nodded. "Very
good indeed."

"Thank you, Edmund," Graeham replied.
"'Tis good to breathe again," he confessed.

"Aye, well . . ." Edmund's gaze returned to
Blaec. "'Tis all, my lord. Is there aught you
wouldst have me do?" he asked.

"Go after her, Blaec," Graeham urged him.

Blaec stood a moment, shaking his head, torn. He could not leave, and yet he could not let her go. The barest thought of her again in her brother's hands chilled him. *He had to go.* He turned to Alyss. "Can I count upon you, Alyss . . . to remain at my brother's side?"

"Aye, m'lord," Alyss answered at once, stepping forward eagerly. "I will tend him faithfully," she swore.

Blaec nodded and turned to Edmund. "Aye, then, Edmund, there is something I wouldst have you do. Have my mount prepared, and gather five men to ride with me. Send another here to watch over Graeham." He turned to Alyss. "I make no apologies, lass," he told her. "I can take no chances where my brother is concerned."

She nodded, seemingly stung by the dictum. But she lowered her head, and said only, "Aye, m'lord. I understand. I wouldst do the same."

He nodded appreciatively, and turned to Edmund. "Go," he directed. "Go quickly, and have the gates opened, and tell the five I will join them within the bailey anon."

Edmund pivoted at once, and hurried to do his lord's bidding.

Blaec turned to look at his brother. He stood only a moment, their gazes holding fast. So many emotions swept through him in that instant, too many to address just now, too many to acknowledge. He was grateful that he lived, grateful for his affection, grateful for their blood ties. "Do me a favor," he asked of Graeham.

Graeham's brow lifted. "Yet another?"

Blaec chuckled despite himself, but his eyes were turbulent with emotion. He shook his head. "Try not to die while I am gone," he remarked.

"I would not dream of it," Graeham said with meaning. And then added, "Find her, Blaec . . . Do not allow her to return into that devil's hands."

Blaec nodded, and said, his voice gruff with emotion, "I intend to, Graeham." And then he, too, turned to go.

Chapter 27

⟨ ∽◯◯∽ ⟩

Dominique had been traveling now for several hours beneath the heat of the sun. Glancing up, she determined by its position in the sky that it must be near to nones. Yet she could not be certain at all of the time when each minute seemed to crawl into the next.

By now, her dress was sodden with her body's sweat, and consequently, it stuck to her skin like wet, clinging rags. And her hair, like her gown, clung to her face in damp, unruly ringlets— aggravating her to God's end.

Still, she felt grateful that she'd not been followed thus far—at least she didn't think she'd been followed. Every so oft, her ears played tricks upon her, though as of yet, her fears had proven unfounded. The sounds were no more than those of the woodlands: a hare scampering before her mount's hooves, a rodent scurrying beneath the underbrush before her, the birds flitting in the trees. Every sound seemed to conspire against her nerves.

No one was there, she told herself . . . no one was following . . . though some little part of her dared to hope, even as she prayed 'twas not him.

More than that, though, Dominique prayed that Graeham had lived. She had to convince herself 'twas so, for if he did not, she didn't think she could bear it.

Sweet Jesu, what if it was, in fact, William's doing?

What would she do were she to discover it to be true? That William had heartlessly ambushed Graeham and had left him for dead? She shuddered at the thought.

Certainly there was much about her brother she did not know. After an age, he'd all but shut himself away from her. Still, she could not imagine him capable of such vile treachery. No matter that she tried, Dominique could think of naught to be gained by the violence, for it made no sense at all. After all, William's entire reason for negotiating the union with Graeham d'Lucy was so that Dominique's children—William's blood—would eventually again rule these lands in England's name. Were William to kill Graeham, how could that possibly serve him?

Unless . . . he had planned to kill Graeham *after* he and Dominique were duly wed . . .

Dominique shook her head, refusing to believe that he would plan such an atrocity. Her brother was no simpleton. Surely he would have considered that had Graeham died without issue . . . his claim to Drakewich would have been feeble at best—not when Graeham had an older twin brother to contest it. And Dominique was certain Blaec would have contested it.

Nor would William have overlooked the obvious. There was certainly nothing to be gained in attacking Graeham *before* the ceremony. And she and Graeham were not as yet wed. Even were he to have planned something so nefarious, he would have waited until after—until he acquired word of their nuptials—something he could not possibly have received, for it had never come to pass.

The more she deliberated . . . the less sense she could make of it all. And it all came to one thing . . . William had little, or naught, to gain from such an endeavor. Her brother would not have ambushed Graeham.

She simply refused to believe it.

With every minute that passed, with every rationale she employed, she knew she was doing the right thing warning William of the suspicions against him. Though she loved Blaec fiercely, William was her blood, and she could not disregard that. She could not allow her brother to suffer unjustly.

She simply had to tell him what they had accused him of—and aye, she had to hear for certain the denial from his lips.

Dominique rode on, ignoring her hunger pangs and her exhaustion as best she could. When she reached a rivulet, she thought she would pounce from her mount into the small stream, so unbearably hot was she. She dismounted at once and led her horse to the water. Letting the animal fend for itself, she then dropped to her knees and eagerly splashed her face and her neck. Closing her eyes, she savored the relief its coolness brought her.

She then proceeded to lie upon her belly, and cupping her hands, reached down to bring the water to her lips, drinking deeply and desperately. When that failed to satisfy her, she brought another handful to her lips, and another, until she was quenched at last.

And then, like a child lying in the dewy grass, she was too replete to move. She rolled to her side beside the stream and peered up at the changing sky, judging the time and the distance.

God's truth, but it seemed that it had taken far less time when they had journeyed *to* Drakewich. Surely she was close now to Arndel . . . She had to be.

Yet nothing was familiar as yet.

And then again, how oft had she left Arndel's walls? Her father, and then her brother after him, had never allowed her to venture beyond them. She had spied the surrounding land only from her tower window. The only thing she knew for certain was that Arndel's land was less verdant than that of Drakewich.

She lifted her head, peering over the landscape. There was far less greenery now, she noted. Even the woodlands she had only just left were sparser in trees. And up ahead, there was yet another patch; it, too, was less dense.

And sweet Mary, but she was hungry.

And she had to do the necessary, besides.

Frowning, she lifted her weary self up from the ground, dusted off her dress, and patted her horse, before searching through the bag she had secured to its back. With a little foraging, she found both the bread and the cheese she had stuffed within, and with no one about to observe her manners, she cared not a whit how she ate. Like a dirty, hungry peasant girl, she stuffed the stale morsels within her mouth, more than grateful that she had thought to bring them. She didn't care that they were stale, didn't care that she appeared a madwoman consuming them.

When she was done, she wiped the crumbs from her face with her sleeve, bent for another drink from the stream, and then rose, patting her hands, and brushing her dress off once and for all. That done, she took her mare's reins and started for the thicket ahead, fully intending to relieve herself there. While 'twas doubtful she would be spied should she do so here, there was no assurance someone might not come upon her in the midst of it, and she could never bear it. Though the trees behind her were nearer, she had no wish to go backward even a few feet. God's truth, but she wanted only to go forward, for she didn't know how much longer she could bear this.

Never in her life had she been in such a desperate state.

Yet it would all be worth it when she faced William at last, and he assured her once and for all that he was innocent.

The tracks were becoming fresher and fresher.

Blaec surmised that Dominique must have passed this way no more than thirty minutes before them. Yet though far from being pleased with the progress they were making, he was beginning to grow more ill at ease with each passing instant.

With every mile they covered, they were riding nearer and nearer to Arndel.

Had she reached it by now? he wondered. The possibility sat like acid in his gut. He clenched his teeth as he rode out from the forest and then immediately reined in his mount, urging his men to do so at once, for there in the distance he spied her, and his heart began to hammer like that of a beardless youth.

The knot in his stomach eased with the knowledge that she'd not reached her brother—not as yet.

Though she *was* near enough to her destination to make him uneasy still. The last thing he wished to do was panic her just now. If she spied them and seized the opportunity to remount and to ride only a few miles south, they would be within visible distance of Arndel's tower walls, and *that* was the last thing he needed just now— to be spied by her brother's men—not when he was ill prepared to face them.

For an instant he sat and watched as, oblivious to their presence, she staggered into a thicket of trees ahead of them. Blaec waited only a moment longer, and then, urging his men to remain behind, he alone followed her. He dismounted, leaving his destrier outside the thicket, and then entered as stealthily as he was able.

It took him only a glance or two to locate her, for he spied the top of her head at once, barely visible above a bush where she squatted, not twenty feet from whence he stood. Pissing, he thought, and singing softly besides, and his face screwed at the ill fortune of his timing.

He had to strangle the impulse to turn around and afford her the privacy she had sought, for he was unwilling to lose sight of her again. God's teeth, but he was glad he'd not brought his men, he decided, as he crouched and stole toward her.

Well, if he had hoped to catch her unawares and unprepared to flee him . . . there was no better moment than this.

The very last thing Dominique was in the mood for just now was singing, but she did so because it helped to dispel her melancholy. She sang a verse of a song she vaguely recalled her mother singing, and then promptly forgot the words as she was halfway through it. Trying not to think of her discomfort, or her weariness—or, for that matter, the humiliating fact that she was relieving her bladder in God's plain sight—she sighed in disgust, and tried once more:

"My husband is exceedingly jealous, arrogant, ruth-less, and harsh . . .
    but he will soon be a cuckold if I can meet my sweet lover,
    a man of refinement and charm.
    You see, I do not care one bit for husbands . . .
    because they dislike anything worthwhile.
    I am telling you: We should scorn the boor who is full of harm!"

She nodded, quite pleased that she'd remembered this time, and continued:

"Not for all the riches of Citeaux
*   should a lively heart and lovely lady*
*   take a husband, says Etienne de Meaux;*
*   she should take a lover instead . . .*
*   and I shall believe him and take a lover!*
*   Oh . . . I am telling you: We should scorn the*
boor who is—"

"Full of harm . . ."

Starting at the unexpected accompaniment, Dominique shrieked and vaulted to her feet, her face screwing in alarm as she thrust down her skirts.

Blaec cleared his throat, pursing his lips as he suppressed his laughter. Standing before him, she appeared more a waif than a lady in her threadbare blue bliaut, with her dust-smeared face—but ah, what a beautiful waif she was.

Her damp gown clung to her, revealing every delectabe curve. And Christ . . . he remembered those curves only too well. His mouth went dry with hunger. God's truth, but he was glad his men had remained behind, for if he found even a one of them staring just now, he thought he might run him through with his blade.

She was stunned speechless, he could tell, and he lifted a brow, feeling frivolous in his relief to have found her at last. "Really, demoiselle . . ."

"You!" Dominique exclaimed, finding her voice at last. And then more angrily, "You!" She flew at him then, like a woman mad, pummeling his chest furiously with her clenched fists. Laughing, though he tried to stop himself, he seized her wrists. Between his relief, and her comically enraged expression, he thought he would split his side with his hilarity.

"Dominique!" he bellowed. "Stop, lass."

"Never!" she swore. "I swear to you I will murder you here where you stand!"

"Really?" he asked her, and then burst into another peal of laughter as he attempted in vain to avoid her legs while she kicked at him. "Only, before you do, tell me," he said, when he could get a breath, "where did you learn such a bawdy song as that?"

"My mother!" she told him viciously, struggling to free herself from his ruthless grip. "You mannerless boor!"

"A boor?" he said, bursting once more into laughter. "Like the one in your song?"

"How long were you listening?" she demanded, kicking his shin.

"Ouch! Watch those legs, demoiselle. They are more dangerous a weapon than my sword itself."

"How long?" she demanded, her cheeks bursting with rosy color.

"God's teeth, if I'd've foreseen this, I would have worn my chausses, woman! Merely a verse or two," he relented, answering honestly, trying to preserve his legs from further damage.

She stilled at that, glaring at him, her blue eyes brilliant in her fury. "Oh! How vile you are!" she told him.

He cocked a brow, grinning. "Truly?"

"Truly!"

He gave her an injured glance. "You wound me, demoiselle."

"God's truth, I should dearly love to wound you!" she told him fiercely. "I cannot believe you wouldst spy upon me here! How dare you!" she cried.

His lips curved. "The truth is, demoiselle, that there is not a single part of that delicious body of yours that I do not know intimately."

He could see in her eyes that his words affected her as much as the truth of them affected him. Even now he was aroused. Painfully. Despite the fact that he knew there was no possibility of being relieved this moment. Not here. Not now. Though if she kicked him once more, just a little higher this time, he would be cured for all eternity, he thought wryly.

"In fact, Dominique," he continued, his tone low and husky, "the images are burned indelibly in my mind."

Her face flushed with color—angry color, he thought, for her luminous sapphire eyes narrowed. "You've not seen this!" she denied vehemently. She shook her head in discomfiture.

"What?" he asked, unable to keep himself from goading her. "What is it that I've not seen?" His grin widened, despite that he tried to arrest it.

Her blush deepened till he thought she would scream. "You know very well," she accused him, declining to speak the forbidden word.

"Oh," he said, his grin widening. He nodded, his brows rising. "I see . . ." He held her wrists tighter, lest she use them to pummel him again.

He cast a meaningful glance at the ground where she'd been squatting. "You mean your pissing?"

She shrieked indignantly and struggled all the more fiercely to free herself. "You swine! Cur! Oaf! I cannot believe you wouldst say such a thing to me!"

He clucked his tongue at her, resisting another burst of laughter. He had to fight the urge to draw her against himself and hold her, touch her, caress her, kiss her senseless. God, he wanted to. He wanted to make love to her right here and now, wanted to brand her, making her his own for all eternity. He wanted to tell her there was nothing standing in their way now, for they had Graeham's blessing. He wanted to say so much. As God was his witness, he didn't know what he would do without her.

"What language," he admonished her softly, his eyes caressing her, while his hands could not. "It seems I shall have to cure you of that, once and for all, demoiselle," he told her, sobering. "After all, we cannot have the lady of Drakewich speaking such obscenities."

Her blue eyes shadowed. "We both know that I am not the lady of Drakewich—that I never will be," she returned, glaring at him hurtfully. "And you are cruel to taunt me so! Release me, at last! Let me go . . ." She tilted her head, pleading with him.

"Never!" he swore, though he released her wrists finally. "Why did you leave, Dominique?" he demanded of her.

Dominique simply stared at him, the expression in her eyes seemingly as tormented as the emotions he felt within. "You should not have followed me," she told him at last. "You should have let me return to Arndel. 'Tis best for all."

"Christ, Dominique . . ." His face twisted. "Best for whom? You cannot truly expect that I should simply let you go just like that?" he asked her incredulously, and meant for her to see the truth in his eyes, that he could not live without her. He wanted to speak the words, as well, but found his tongue tied. She seemed not to read him at all.

Lifting her chin, she asked, "Why?" He recognized the instant she withdrew from him completely, hardening her heart against him. "Tell me, my lord . . . are you afeared I will tell my brother what you plan? Are you afeared I might spoil your turn at vengeance? Is that it?"

His own face hardened at her accusation, for it forced him to consider the possibility as truth. Mayhap that *was* her intent today—to betray him as he had first suspected she meant to do.

"Come to think of it," he remarked, blinking, his jaw clenching.

"Well, you can just take yourself back to Drakewich," Dominique told him fiercely, "for I'll not be returning with you, after all." She turned and stormed away, toward the palfrey she had tethered to the bushes only a few feet away.

Did she truly think it would end thus?

Did she think him mad? Stupid? That he would give up so easily?

He'd be damned if he'd come this far, only to have her ride away.

He didn't believe that she didn't want him. No woman who made love as she did held herself dispassionate. Nor did he think she meant to betray him—though if she did, he'd be damned if he'd let her go now. "Aye?" he challenged her. "Well, we shall see about that," he said, and moved toward her with purpose.

Dominique sensed his advance, and bolted into a run. But she wasn't quick enough. She shrieked indignantly as he lifted her up and hoisted her over his shoulder.

"I cannot believe you wouldst resort to this once more! You oaf! Have you no courtesy? Can you not see that I wish to go home? Let me go!" she demanded furiously.

"You *shall*, indeed, go *home*, demoiselle."

She mistook him. "I wish to go home *now*! Now! Do you hear me? Let me go!"

He slapped her fanny, hard, and she squealed irately. "That one's for calling me an oaf!" he told her without heat.

"Oh! You! Release me at once, you overbearing boor! Let me go," she entreated, squirming wildly. "Blaec!" she screamed. "As God is my witness, I shall make you regret this! Set me down!"

"I think not," he said, lugging her out of the thicket and toward his mount.

Chapter 28

He came to a halt as he stepped into the bright light of the sun, and Dominique sensed the sudden tension in the muscles of his arms, and the rigidity of his back. She knew at once that something was amiss and tried to turn, to see what had caught his regard, but she could not quite twist herself about in order to see. He wasn't making it any easier on her, either, with the way he held her restrained.

"I would suggest you do as the lady Dominique bids you," a familiar male voice apprised him.

Once again, Dominique attempted to turn, and was impeded by the wrathful shake Blaec gave her. She stifled the urge to strike at him with her closed fist. God's truth, but at the moment she wanted naught more than to get her hands about his neck and strangle him.

"Set—me—down!" she demanded through clenched teeth.

"Do as she requests, d'Lucy."

Though laggardly, he did so at last, setting her slowly upon her feet, and Dominique turned to discover the bearer of the voice—Rufford, her brother's captain.

And he was not alone.

Seven more of her brother's armed men surrounded them on horseback. Six surrounded Blaec's contingent of five, and one joined Rufford, standing opposite Blaec. What was more, the last man aimed a crossbow directly at Blaec's chest.

Her heart began to hammer, not in fear for herself, but in fear for Blaec, for the looks upon their faces told her all she needed to know. They would just as soon kill him. She cringed at the thought, and moved away from Blaec at once, closer to her brother's men lest he be tempted to contest them. By the look upon Blaec's face, she knew full well that he was considering it, and she wanted to make it clear what she wished.

His eyes as they met hers were icy, and it was clear he thought her gesture a betrayal. But it couldn't be helped, she told herself. She much preferred that he thought himself betrayed than to have him resist and find himself dead.

"You do not have to go," he murmured low, a muscle ticking at his jaw. "Only say the word, Dominique, and I will not let them take you . . ."

He waited for her reply, and Dominique could scarcely speak for the emotion that caught within her throat. She shook her head, and again moved closer to her brother's men. "I . . . I *must* go," she told him. "Can you not see that? I must discover the truth. I must, Blaec."

His eyes gleamed with wintry brilliance. "Only ask them," he urged her, indicating her brother's men. "*Ask them, Dominique!*"

"Nay!" she refused, turning and hastening toward her brother's waiting men. She lifted her skirts and ran, afeared that if she didn't go now, she would change her mind and stay, for the look upon his face rent her heart to shreds.

"Dominique!" he called after her.

Her brother's captain lifted her upon his mount, and through it all Blaec merely glared at them, unblinking, his gaze damning her as it never had before.

She couldn't allow herself the luxury of regret. She lifted her chin, though she felt more like crumpling into a miserable heap upon the ground. "I owe it to William to ask him to his very face," she told him, pleading with him in her heart to understand. "Can you not see that 'tis the right thing to do?"

He said nothing, merely stared at her, his face expressionless.

"Wouldst you not do the same?" she reasoned with him.

Still he said nothing, and when Rufford turned, motioning for the other seven to follow, she saw that Blaec held out his hand for his own men to remain where they sat, his face an impervious mask of stone. Even so, she breathed in a sigh of relief, even as she choked on her sorrow.

"Forgive me," she beseeched him, mouthing the words, for she could scarcely find her voice now to speak. And then, lest he spy the tears that followed, she turned from him, clutching Rufford as he spurred his mount away from the glade. Only when they'd started away did she recall her mare, but even then she could not speak, so choked was she. She embraced Rufford as though her life would end did she release him.

And still she could feel Blaec's eyes burning into her. She dared not turn, could not face him again. As it was, she feared she'd never forget the wounded, scornful look upon his face as he'd stood there, asking her to stay. *No matter that she'd wanted to so desperately, she had to go.* And knowing 'twas the last time she would ever see him, she could not bear to remember him thus.

Her heart twisting with grief, she sobbed against Rufford's chest, not caring that he might hear her—nor that his mail sherte cut against her cheek. The pain seemed trifling compared to that which tore through her heart.

Still, she knew . . . this *was* the right thing to do. *He would have done the same for his own brother.*

William was seated upon the dais when Dominique entered the hall, his chair drawn back from the lord's table, one booted foot propped negligently upon it. When he saw her, his expression lightened and he set his foot down at once, rising, looking first pleased and then suddenly discomposed by the sight of her.

Tears streaming down her cheeks, Dominique ran to embrace him, needing, in her grief, to feel her brother's comforting arms about her. She took solace in his reception, and wept, embracing him more desperately than she had Rufford.

"We found her in the glade, my lord," Rufford reported to William at once. "She was fleeing d'Lucy—the bastard! He had her heaved up over his shoulder like some worthless sack of meal, he did."

"Have they gone?" William asked, his tone angry though calm. He caressed her back with a sympathetic palm.

"Aye, my lord. They took their leave, but she has wept thus since we rescued her from d'Lucy, I fear."

William stiffened. His hand stilled at her back. "You may go," he charged Rufford. And then he waited, making certain that he went. "Dominique?" he prompted after a moment's time.

Dominique peered up at him, her face stained with tears, her eyes swollen.

His own eyes were gleaming with jewel-like brilliance, taking her aback slightly with the intensity she saw there. "Did he harm you?" he asked softly, his jaw taut.

Dominique averted her eyes, unable to face him just yet with the shameful truth—that she'd fallen in love with the wrong d'Lucy. "Nay," she said brokenly, choking back her salty tears. "He did not."

His body went stiller yet. "Why, then, do you cry?" he asked her, his voice toneless now.

Dominique shook her head, unable to speak the words, sensing his disapproval, though she could not discern over what. *What had she done?* She thought that mayhap he was angry because she had fled Drakewich. Yet if he only knew . . . if he knew how they had accused him . . .

She shook her head miserably, knowing 'twas her duty to tell him. "Oh, William," she sobbed. "They blame *you* for the treachery against Graeham—yet I told them it could not be. He was att—"

"He lives, then?"

Dominique shook her head. "I . . . I do not know," she replied honestly, swiping at her cheeks in dismay. Only now did it occur to her that she'd not even asked Blaec of his brother's well-being—in her fury, she'd not even bothered to consider it, and now the question plagued her. "I-I left as soon as I was able," she told him, her brow furrowing, "and . . . and I did not think to ask . . ."

Another thought occurred to her suddenly and she swallowed convulsively. William had asked whether he lived . . . without surprise, and without anger that they would accuse him of such a wrong. "Blaec was not angry," she reasoned, "so I must believe Graeham lives. William," she began warily, "you are not responsible . . ." She lifted her chin when he did not respond, bracing herself. "Tell me nay."

His face remained an unreadable mask, expressionless, though his blue eyes continued to glitter coldly.

"William, nay!" Dominique drew away from him at once, stung, horrified by the import of his silence. "Nay! Nay! Oh, God—nay! Tell me you are not!"

His face twisted suddenly, transforming before her eyes. "Tell me, Dominique, why do you care?" He reached out, clasped her arm tightly and jerked her toward him, his face florid in his fury. "What is he to you, little sister—did you lift up your skirt for him? Did you?" he demanded cruelly.

Dominique wrenched herself free, and backed away in growing horror, not wanting to hear any more. She blocked her ears with her hands, shaking her head as he followed.

Her heart lurched as he backed her against a wall, jerking her arms away from her face and pinning them to the stone at her back. He crushed her hands ruthlessly beneath his palms.

"Did you?" he demanded of her. He shoved his knee, hard, between her legs. Dominique cried out in pain and in fear. "Did you let him betwixt your legs, Dominique?"

She shook her head frantically, unable to respond.

"Answer me! Speak! God damn you, you filthy little whore!" He began to tremble fiercely as he pressed her mercilessly against the wall—as though he would shove her within its very core were he able.

Like a little boy, his eyes closed suddenly as though he would weep—and still he trembled, and then suddenly he did cry out, and Dominique was torn betwixt her fear of him and her desire to soothe him, for whatever else he was, he was still her brother. She gazed at him, unblinking, not understanding what was happening, though trying desperately to comprehend. He opened his eyes, and stared at her, the lack of recognition in his gaze terrifying.

"William?"

Without warning, he lowered his mouth to her lips. Dominique screamed and tried to avert her face, unable to believe this was happening to her. She spat, twisting wildly to free herself, even as he crushed his teeth against her mouth. He seized her by the hair, slamming her head into the wall without warning, dazing her with the force of the blow.

"You filthy whore!" he accused her, covering her mouth once more.

Dominique was too dazed to fight the nauseating invasion of her mouth. He thrust his tongue within, his lips quivering as he kissed her. Dominique fought to catch her breath, to shove him away, but he was immovable.

"God damn you," he cried, his voice breaking like that of an injured child, before he ravaged her mouth once more.

Regaining her wits, Dominique found his lip betwixt her teeth, and clamped her jaw down upon it until she tasted his blood. He bellowed in pain, and jerked away, though not before leaving the imprint of his hand upon her face.

Glaring at her, he drew his fingers across his lips, finding his own blood, and then he slapped her once more. "You are just the same as your mother!" he told her viciously, as though they did not share the same blood. "A lying filthy little whore!" he told her, backing away, as though the sight of her disgusted him. "I could have loved you, Dominique," he told her sullenly. "I would have loved you with my *body* and my *heart*."

Dominique gazed at him in revulsion of his meaning. She shook her head, swallowing, tasting the bile that rose like acid in her throat. "Wh-What are you saying, William?" She choked on a sob.

"I would have cherished you," he continued, his eyes shimmering.

She held her palm against her face, easing the sting of the blow—yet there was nothing that could ease the sting within her heart. God . . . Blaec had been right. Graeham had been right. William *was* a fiend. How could she have been so blind? How could she not have seen the truth? He'd held her so dispassionately all these years . . . Sweet Christ . . . she had thought him oblivious to her. She shook her head, swallowing, her eyes accusing him, glazing with new tears. Yet she made no sound, for inside she was numb.

Just then, he shouted for Rufford, startling her with the ferociousness of his bellow. Mere moments later, Rufford came loping into the hall to do his bidding.

William eyed her coldly, and said, "Take her to her chamber, Rufford, lock her within . . . and then I want you to send a messenger to d'Lucy."

"Aye, m'lord."

"Tell him he may come for Dominique if he dares. Though if he does . . . I intend to kill

him with my bare hands for his treachery—you
might tell him that as well. And if he does not
come for her . . . ah, well, then . . . I shall simply
kill her . . . and then I shall serve him her pretty
little head upon a goose platter."

Dominique thought she would faint at his
declaration. "William," she croaked, disbelieving her ears. Her knees buckled beneath her.

"My lord?" Rufford said in obvious shock.

"How can you despise me so?" Dominique
asked him brokenly. "How can you do this?
William . . ."

William shook his head in disavowal of her
words, looking even staggered by her remark.
He said, almost tenderly, "Nay, Dominique . . .
you mistake me . . . *I love you.*"

Dominique gave a hoarse cry, her hand flying
to her mouth, stifling her sob, lest she burst into
hysterics.

"My lord?" Rufford asked again in bewilderment.

"What the hell are you looking at?" William
roared at the top of his lungs, spinning about.
He started after Rufford as though he would
strike him down where he stood, his hand gripping his sword. And then he stopped suddenly, his jaw working furiously, his eyes a violent, swirling blue. "Get the bloody hell out of
here, Rufford," he said, gaining hold of himself. "Take her—and get the bloody hell out.
Go tell d'Lucy what I bade you, lest you end
with your arse in the moat along with the rest
of the offal."

"Aye, my lord."

William closed his eyes, and bellowed, "Go, now!"

Even before she could gasp in horror, Rufford was coming toward her. Dominique could see in his eyes that he would do whatever William bade him, no matter how long he had known her, no matter that he regretted it. Her knees buckled with the knowledge, and she fainted even before he reached her.

"I lost her."

"What do you mean you lost her?" Graeham asked him, sitting up within the bed, his expression bewildered. "You found her, then?"

"Aye, damn it all, I found her—and then lost her again."

Blaec came into the chamber, slamming the door behind him, spearing Alyss with a shriveling glance. Though it wasn't intended for her, he could scarcely help himself—the image of Dominique clinging to her brother's underling tormented him still. Like the picture of her standing before him, limned by the candlelight, in all her naked glory, this new image, too, now was ingrained vividly upon his mind. He shuddered with the potency of his anger, cursing roundly.

"Shall I go?" Alyss asked timorously, her face ashen as she stood to do his bidding.

"Nay," Graeham declared at once, meeting her gaze and holding it fast. "Stay," he bade her.

Blaec witnessed the exchange betwixt them, though he refrained from remarking upon it. His mood as black as the maid's anxious eyes, he sat himself upon their father's chair, slumping down into it like a man whose spine had been broken in twain—and it had been, he brooded.

It might as well have been.

She had refused him.

Though he had asked her not to go, she had done so anyway.

Part of him was stricken ill at the very notion that she was again at her brother's mercy. And though he told himself that William would not harm her, he thought the bastard's soul black enough to use even his own flesh and blood if it suited him.

Had he not heedlessly placed her in danger by abandoning her here at Drakewich? The whoreson had not even cared enough to see that his sister and Graeham were properly wed. He had left her at the mercy of Blaec's suspicions—not to mention his lust.

Nay, such a man could not care for her, he decided.

Another part of him . . . the part that she had rejected by refusing to return with him, felt well and duly betrayed. He tried to tell himself that he would have done the same . . . that with her innate loyalty she could have done nothing more than return to her brother. He *would* have done the same. But still he could not be eased.

She had refused him.

"Damn!" Without explanation, he arose from the chair, gave his brother an apologetic nod, and quit the chamber, unable to speak of

his conflicting emotions even with Graeham
just now . . . for despite that his brother had
handed him everything . . . *everything* . . . he *felt*
as though this day he had lost it *all*.

Chapter 29

Graeham sighed, frowning at the door as it closed. "I wish there were aught I could do to ease him."

"If you will pardon my candor, m'lord . . . it seems to me that you have done so much already . . ."

Graeham said nothing for an instant, and then stated flatly, "You do not understand."

"Again, m'lord . . . if you will but forgive my boldness . . . I believe I understand more than you think. You value your brother highly, it seems."

Graeham heaved another sigh, nodding. "I do."

"'Tis plain, m'lord. And I believe he knows. It seems to me he values you, as well. Pardon my saying so, m'lord, but lest you wish to give him your guilt, along with everything else you've bequeathed him . . . you must let it pass, at last . . . let him live as he must, and do for himself. He will discover the way. God has a way of providing."

His brows drew together. "You see all that?" he asked her.

She nodded, and Graeham considered her an instant. Alyss had been at his side from the first moment he'd opened his eyes, tending to his every need. She'd been the first thing he had seen upon waking, and the last before closing his eyes. Truth to tell, he liked having her thus, and thought that mayhap he wasn't in such a hurry to heal.

"You're a wise little bit of baggage," he said at last.

She smiled with her eyes, and Graeham found himself once again entranced by the incredible depth of them, the way they sparkled so intelligently. "Aye, m'lord," she said soberly. "Would you have me continue now?"

"If you like." His voice sounded strange to his ears.

She smiled shyly, blushing as she approached the bed once more. "Then you must give me your back," she charged him.

Graeham did so, and she sat again upon the bed beside him. He liked the way her dainty weight shifted the mattress, filled the space beside him. "By chance, where did you learn to do such things with your hands?" he asked her casually, lifting his nostrils and breathing deeply of her presence, of the oil she had heated and placed within a basin upon the floor by the bedside.

"My mother," she told him, returning eagerly to her task. "She taught me much about pleasing a man," she told him directly.

He listened to the sounds of her dousing her hands with the oil; it sounded much the way sendal cloth did when rubbed together. Anticipating the first touch of her fingers upon his flesh, he lay there, still as a stone.

"Really?" he said with a sigh of pleasure. He twisted, turning to meet her doelike gaze. "Your mother taught you?"

"Aye, m'lord. My mother."

"And what of your father?" he asked.

She was silent a moment. "My father was lord of Kester, vassal to William Beauchamp, and vassal, before him, to his father." Her eyes, deep, dark, and rich, were as inviting as a shadowy glade. She'd removed his bandages earlier in order to bathe him, and now she was pleasuring him in ways he'd never conceived possible . . . in ways he'd never allowed himself to consider.

"She taught you well," he said huskily.

Alyss's soft laughter filled the chamber. With lithe, delicate fingers, she began again to massage the warmed oil into the taut muscles of his back. "Thank you, m'lord," she murmured.

"There," she said. "Now, turn again upon your back, m'lord."

Graeham's heart staggered to a halt. "You're not through as yet?" he asked her, disheartened by the prospect. He turned as she bade him, and for an instant, as he lay upon the bed under her scrutiny . . . he felt himself stir once more and rejoiced in the sensation. It had been so long . . .

For an instant their gazes held, and she must have spied the disappointment in his face, for she asked, sounding as breathless as he felt, "Wouldst you desire me to continue, m'lord?"

Graeham's voice became husky, his breath short, his mouth too parched for words. "I would like that very much," he said hoarsely. "Please . . ." He swallowed convulsively.

She nodded, her smile like that of a feline, and began again to stroke his chest, avoiding his injury, even as she dared to hold his gaze.

Graeham felt himself harden fully. "Should you . . ." He swallowed. "Should you bandage me, once more?" he asked her, shifting upon the bed, unable to remain still with the blood simmering through him. She knew what she was doing, teasing him, and that knowledge, too, aroused him.

"Nay, m'lord," she answered huskily. "The wound is sewn and there is no infection . . . It needs only the air now to heal." Her eyes were still upon his, and Graeham felt himself as breathless and weak as a babe under her scrutiny.

He raised himself, wanting to be nearer to her, wanting to smell her, to touch her, and then he grimaced, lying back again upon the bed, frustrated, unable to do any of those things.

"You've lost much blood," she told him, seeming to read his thoughts. "'Tis why you feel yourself so weak," she explained. Her eyes slitted as she began again to work her lithe fingers down his chest . . . to his belly . . . and then lower . . .

Graeham flinched slightly, his hand going to hers, covering it with his own.

Her voice was throaty when she spoke again, and more than a little breathless, her cheeks flushed. "Shall I continue, m'lord?" she asked silkily.

For an instant Graeham could not respond, and then he nodded, his jaw clenching. He closed his eyes, feeling as though he would burst with the sensations that surged through him in that instant of surrender, filling his groin with a heat he'd not known in far too many years. His head fell back as she lowered the sheets from his naked body, revealing him fully to her eyes.

He heard her soft intake of breath and opened his eyes to spy the look of appreciation in her gaze. It filled him with exhilaration. She lifted her chin, and her features softened, and he thought her in that instant the most beautiful woman he had ever beheld in his life. She was an angel from God—his angel from God. His salvation. His own face went rigid with tension, and his jaw worked with emotion. "Alyss . . ." He shook his head. "You've no idea . . . Ah, God," he said when her fingers found him and closed about him suddenly. Feeling utterly helpless, he fell back once more upon the bed.

"Shall I continue, my lord?" she murmured.

Graeham scarcely trusted himself to speak. He nodded, casting his head back against the pillows as she stroked his burning flesh. His heart hammered against his ribs. He reached out suddenly, stilling her hand, stopping her, not wanting to spill himself for the first time like the virgin he was.

He wanted it to last. Aye, and he wanted to pleasure her, too.

"Did I hurt you?" she asked him with concern. "M'lord?"

"Nay," he told her with certainty, his voice hoarse as he met her gaze. "Not at all, Alyss. Come hither," he commanded her. *"Stand beside me."* She did, and he reached out to take her hand, drawing her closer still. "I wish to see you," he said eagerly.

She nodded, smiling elfishly as she reached down to lift up her hem, and Graeham feared he would unman himself, after all. He could scarcely bear it. When she was naked at last before him, he drew her toward him once more, and touched her hip lightly, urging her gently to seat herself atop him.

She seemed to comprehend everything he wanted without him ever having to say a word, and he lay back in supreme pleasure as she straddled him, lifting her hips above his pelvis, where he rose to meet her. With a gasp, he guided her down over his shaft, bucking with the almost painful pleasure it brought him.

Like some pagan creature, she began to move atop him, undulate, and Graeham felt himself in Heaven at long last. He heaved a sigh, laying his head back, allowing himself for the first time in his life to savor the pleasures of the flesh without a trace of guilt.

"Alyss," he groaned. "Ah, God . . . sweet Alyss . . ." And then he could speak coherently no more, and the sounds that escaped the both of their lips were like an erotic melody to his ears, drawing him to the edge, spurring him on.

Feeling a new burst of energy, he rolled atop her, urging her beneath him, refusing to lie at her mercy any longer. He wanted to love her like a man should love a woman. He wanted to pleasure her, as well.

But he was lost with the first thrust, lost in fleshly pleasure. He lay down atop her, fusing their bodies together in a slow and erotic mating ritual. Their bodies, slick with the oil that coated his flesh, twisted obliviously upon the bed, pumping slowly, and then faster, rolling, undulating, until, with a hoarse shout of triumph, Graeham fulfilled himself at last.

Bedamned if he cared that he raised the rooftops; he shouted for all of creation to hear him.

With a savage outcry, Alyss joined him, holding him fast against her lush breasts, crooning love words into his ear.

Graeham rolled again, taking her with him, mindful of his wound—though even were he to die this very night, he told himself, they would find him smiling in the morning light.

Christ, he thought deliriously . . . had he truly thought to commit himself to the church? Stephen, he feared, would simply have to pray after his own soul, for it seemed it was God's design that he make up for lost time.

Beginning now . . .

Blaec lay within his bed, one arm thrown over his face, listening to the carnal sounds that came from below, and for an instant the noises startled him. Uncovering his face, he stared into the darkness, contemplating them, for while they were seductively familiar, they were foreign to his ears. No man sleeping within his hall would make such a clamor out of respect for him and Graeham. Those sounds could come from no other than Graeham—and God's teeth, while he'd never believed his brother completely celibate, he'd never heard such a ruckus in all his days.

Could it be? Could Graeham have remained abstinent all these years?

Nay . . . His brow furrowed. 'Twas inconceivable. Nor could he fathom *why* he should wish to do so. While Blaec did not believe in licentiousness, neither did he believe in self-torture. Abstinence all these five and twenty years would have been more than any one man could bear. He shuddered at the notion.

Still . . . in all this time he recalled not once that he had witnessed his brother in the act— nor did he recall a time when Graeham had spoken of it. Yet his ears did not deceive him now; those sounds were not spectral. They were real, and they were Graeham's, and God's truth, he'd never heard them before now.

He was pleased for his brother—stunned, but pleased.

And God's blood, mayhap it had taken Graeham twenty-five years to lose his virginity, but he was doing it with relish and abandon. He gave a silent nod of appreciation, and then with a tortured groan, turned upon his belly, painfully aroused, and thought of Dominique.

He needed her—God, did he need her.

Chapter 30

William was inebriated.

Dominique could tell by the way that he slurred his words. He spoke to her through the door, and she sat atop her bed, hugging her knees to her breast, and trembling with fright. If he wished to, there would be naught she could do to prevent him from coming within her bedchamber. Nothing. No mere latch would hold him without. Aye, and he was lord here, and her wishes, which had never accounted for aught before, certainly wouldn't be considered now.

"I am sorry, Dominique . . . I did not mean to hurt you," he swore, slamming a fist against the door. His voice sounded tortured, and she wanted to comfort him, yet all she need do to remember herself was to touch her swollen face, her split lip.

"Forgive me," he pleaded.

Dominique dared not speak out, not even to deny him. She stared out from the window of her bedchamber, feigning sleep with her silence. If he entered . . . and found her here within the bed . . .

She choked back a sob, praying he could not

hear her above his own keening cries. She didn't know any longer what he would do . . . perhaps had never known what he was capable of.

"*Dominique,*" he croaked. "*I swear I did not mean to . . .*"

Dominique shuddered, persevering with her silence. And then the door latch moved and her heart lurched painfully. Panicked by the possibility of him finding her within her bed, she stood and, moving as silently and quickly as she was able, scurried from the bed to the floor. Watching the door keenly, she crouched in the darkest corner of the chamber. There she sat, staring at the closed door, praying it would not open—praying he would go away. God help her . . . the recollection of his tongue within her mouth, and his beard . . . scratching her face, plagued her, disgusted her, shamed her . . .

It made her feel violated.

He had said that he would kill her.

Could he possibly do such a thing?

Her own brother? How could he want her in that way?

The return of his attentions after all these years had been a blasphemous thing, after all— a thing of darkness. God have mercy upon her soul, for she despised him—her own blood— even as she pitied him . . . even as she sorrowed for herself.

To her relief, the door did not open. Instead, it seemed he removed his hand from the latch.

"*Dominique,*" he pleaded one last time, and when again she did not reply, he moved away from the door at last. She heard his footsteps as they receded from the antechamber, yet still she could not find the strength or the will to move from whence she sat.

Even when the silence reached her, enveloped her like a safe cocoon, she sat arrested in the corner of the room, her face twisting with grief.

God's truth, but she didn't think it possible to be more brokenhearted than she was in that moment. In the space of a day, she had lost so much . . . *everything*.

Weeping silent tears, she laid her head back upon the wall and thought of Blaec . . . What was he doing? Was he thinking of her?

Closing her eyes, she willed him to know what was in her heart—that she loved him, would always love him. If only she might have the opportunity to tell him so . . .

Would he come?

God give her strength to endure . . . she prayed fervently that he would not.

She could not bear it if William harmed him for her sake.

Yet neither could she bear it if he chose not to come for her, for that would mean that she had meant nothing to him—less than nothing.

Yet he *had* come after her once . . .

Aye, a little voice taunted, *only because he'd thought to prevent her from warning William.*

Nay, for she could not forget the way he had looked at her within the glade—betrayed.

"I love you," she whispered, and meant it with every fiber of her being. She prayed that, somehow, God would carry her message into his heart. For, aye, she loved him . . . more even than she did life itself. If she would die here to save him from harm, then she had lived for something, at least. "God grant me the strength," she prayed softly, "to do what I must. Let him not come . . . please . . . *please* . . . let him not come . . ."

The bearer arrived before noontide the following day. Blaec received the missive with barely restrained rage, eyeing the messenger with open malice. It was all he could do not to rip the youth's heart from his breast where he stood.

Beauchamp, wise bastard that he was, had sent a child with his threats—wise, because had the messenger been a man full-grown, Blaec wouldn't have allowed the fool to depart Drakewich with his life. As it was, the boy spoke with trembling lips and facial ticks that trumpeted his fear.

As Blaec rose abruptly from his seat at the lord's table upon the dais, the youth stumbled backward, nearly tripping over his own feet in his haste to gain distance between them. He said not a word to the boy, merely nodded at Nial, commanding him tacitly to throw the poor bastard out, and then he sought Graeham's counsel at once, closeting himself within the lord's chamber.

He sat restively upon the edge of his father's chair, facing the bed, raking a tense hand across his jaw, waiting for Graeham to comment upon the news he'd only just imparted.

"It could be a ruse," Graeham pointed out.

"I am aware of that," Blaec said, "but I cannot bring myself to gamble with her life."

Graeham sat up within the bed, his expression sober. "I do not trust him, Blaec, nor do I truly believe he would harm his only sister—less kill her. Only think on it, if you would . . ."

Blaec shook his head, unable to think at all. He clenched his jaw, for of usual, he was the judicious one here, yet in this he knew he was not capable of cold reason. 'Twas why he'd sought his brother's counsel. In his fury, he would have been halfway to Arndel just now, without the least thought for stratagem, or even the welfare of his men.

He forced himself to consider the possibility of a ruse on Beauchamp's part but could still not bear the thought of risking Dominique. He wanted her back . . . under his roof . . . in his arms. His chest ached with the thought—with the merest prospect of her being harmed.

"If he touches so much as one . . ." He shook his head, unable to speak it, rage consuming him.

"He wishes you to believe he will. Think back, Blaec . . . to the one meal we shared together . . . Do you not recall how angry he became when he thought you'd merely insulted his sister?"

Blaec closed his eyes . . . but saw only Dominique in his mind's eye . . . the way she'd stared at him at table . . . studying his face . . . the distress registered upon her own whilst she'd scrutinized his scar. He'd been torn between wanting to conceal it from her curious eyes and wanting to assure her that it no longer pained him—at least no longer the flesh.

The heart was another matter entirely, and Dominique had somehow, against his will, come into it and filled it, until even that pain was endurable. Though he could not forget . . . it no longer seemed to hurt him so much that he'd fought so hard to win his father's affections . . . and had failed. Somehow that part of him that had searched for acceptance . . . searched no longer.

Yet she was gone now, and he could scarcely bear the thought of being without her.

"You love her?"

Blaec was taken aback by the question. *"Love?"* He shook his head. "She's an impudent wench . . ."

"I didn't ask what you *thought* of her, Blaec. I asked what you *felt* for her."

"I'm not certain what I feel, Graeham," Blaec answered truthfully. "I only know that I cannot allow her to remain with Beauchamp. The very thought that she is with him now burns me alive."

Graeham nodded. "I thought so from the first," he said.

Once again Blaec swallowed his guilt, a knot that threatened to asphyxiate him with its magnitude. "I tried not to," he swore.

"I know," Graeham yielded. "I know. If 'twill ease you to know . . . I, in truth, never coveted her as my bride—not even from the first."

Blaec's brows drew together. "I did wonder—God's teeth, but you enraged me. I was wholly prepared to honor her as your own, Graeham, but you cast her at me again and again and again."

Graeham sighed. "Aye, well ... though I thought her lovely enough, she failed to stir me as a husband should be stirred by his wife. I was uncertain how to go about freeing myself from the noose I had placed about my throat, and you were the most obvious solution. 'Twas evident from the first glance that you coveted her. I thought my only dilemma was in convincing Beauchamp to agree to it ... convincing you ... and then once I resolved to return to you Drakewich—as I'd long ago contemplated—it was no longer a dilemma at all."

"Aye, well ..." Blaec eyed him sternly, lifting a brow. "As to that matter ... I wish you would reconsider."

Graeham shook his head. "Nay. I never wanted it."

Blaec laughed, the sound without mirth. "Strange that both of us should value this demesne so ... yet that neither of us should desire it exceptionally."

"Not so strange," Graeham debated. "Not when you consider the price to be paid ... and at whose expense. You," he said, "I value more dearly than I do my own life. Drakewich is yours."

Raw emotion caught within Blaec's throat, clouding his eyes. Though he could scarcely speak, he held Graeham's gaze. "As do I, you," he professed, his eyes sparkling. "As do I, you. As for Drakewich . . . as long as I've breath, what is mine is yours," he swore, letting his hands dangle betwixt his legs. His head followed, dropping wearily forward.

"Beauchamp is lying," Graeham swore. "I cannot fathom that the same man who seemed prepared to strangle you with his bare hands for your meager offense to his sister would turn about and harm her himself."

"Aye . . . well . . . as to that . . . yet do I also recall that he abandoned her here, in our custody—and all the while he planned treachery against you. He must have known, Graeham, that she would suffer were his perfidy to be discovered."

"True. But you forget that he never intended to be discovered. He wore the strangest helm, Blaec . . . one in which the noseguard covered much of the face. In truth, I would never have recognized him at all, but for the eyes." Graeham inhaled suddenly, wincing, and clutching at his chest. "That, and his laughter," he relented, grimacing. "The bastard is evil—and I swear I shall never heal."

Blaec smiled, though the smile did not reach his eyes with his heart so heavy. "Not if you continue in the manner in which you carried on last night," he agreed. He lifted a brow, casting a meaningful glance toward Alyss.

"'Tis true," Alyss interjected, "he *is* evil, m'lord."

Both Blaec and Graeham turned to face her. She met Blaec's eyes, her own entreating.

She came forward, wringing her hands. "'Tis for that very reason you should go after her, m'lord," she told him. Her eyes pleaded with him. "I swear to you that the lady Dominique is innocent of William's villainy."

Graeham motioned her forward, offering his hand. She came forward, yielding her own readily, and he told her gently, "No one has doubted the lady Dominique's honor. Your devotion to her is commendable, Alyss, yet can I not agree with your judgment—not this time. I must believe that William's threat is a lure for Blaec, and no more. I cannot see as he wouldst harm his own sister."

"You do not understand, m'lord." Alyss shook her head vehemently. "You see, I've proof . . ."

"What proof?" Blaec interjected at once, straightening within the chair.

Alyss lapped anxiously at her lips. "He swore he would kill me if ever I revealed this, but I must . . ." She glanced at Graeham, and then her gaze returned to Blaec, and she inhaled deeply, as though quelling her fear.

"Alyss," Blaec prompted, "I have already assured you my protection . . . If you know aught that would aid us, you must speak it at once."

She nodded jerkily. "Aye, m'lord, and I shall." She inhaled once more, deeply, closing her eyes, as she revealed, "Your sire did not murder Henry Beauchamp."

Blaec's brows collided. "What say you?"

She shook her hand free of Graeham's and

her face paled visibly. "'Tis God's truth, I tell you," she whispered. "I do not lie."

Blaec's head reeled with the disclosure. He cast a glance at Graeham, and found that Graeham's face mirrored his own stunned bewilderment. His narrowed eyes returned to Alyss. She stood before him, looking as though she would swoon, yet she did not withdraw her claim.

"Even were it so, Alyss," he allowed, "how could *you* have knowledge of such a thing? You scarcely seem old enough—"

"I am two and twenty years of age, m'lord—older than I appear—and I know because I witnessed the murder with my own eyes."

"How can that be so?" Graeham broke in incredulously. "How can you have? Henry Beauchamp and my father battled near nine years past . . ."

"We were there, lass," Blaec advised her. "We ourselves *saw* what transpired that day betwixt our sire and Beauchamp's—and nay, 'twas not murder, for the bastard rose up against my father mere moments after they had called a truce betwixt them. He meant to spear my father through the back. The truth is that my father merely defended himself—and that, only after I warned him with my own lips of Beauchamp's trickery."

Alyss's eyes began to shimmer. "Aye, m'lord . . . but there is more to the tale than that."

Blaec's brow lifted. "Then, by all means, tell it," he commanded her, casting another glance at Graeham. He found his brother's expression as disbelieving as his own.

Alyss nodded, glancing down at her feet. "Aye, well . . . Henry returned to Arndel, wounded, well enough . . . though in little danger of perishing from his injuries. I know . . ." She again met his gaze. "I know because 'twas I who was summoned to tend him. My lord Henry was well aware of the fact that I had learned the healing arts from my mother."

She paused an instant, swallowing, and then continued. "I was thirteen in that year, m'lord, and newly come to Arndel. Lord Beauchamp had requested I come, saying that his son, William, had taken a liking to me upon a recent visit to Kester, and that he wished I should come and be a companion to his daughter . . . and also that . . . when the time arrived, I should wed with William. As it was my father's wish that I go . . . I did . . . but none of it ever came to fruition."

"The bastard!" Graeham spat.

Blaec said nothing, merely listened with a sick feeling in his belly.

"I was so pleased when Lady Dominique received the news to be wed," Alyss continued, "and I followed gladly. I could not wait to be away from William . . . or to see the lady Dominique safely away. 'Tis my belief that he covets her for himself."

Blaec swallowed his bile. "You cannot mean . . ."

"Aye, m'lord, I do. You should have seen

the way he gazed at her when he thought no one could spy him. And more than once . . . he called her name whilst we . . ." She shook her head, shuddering, closing her eyes, unable to speak the obscenity.

She did not have to.

Blaec understood what she meant without her saying it. His gut wrenched, and he clenched his jaw. *God, she was there with him now.* He shuddered, and thought, irrationally, that he wished God had given him wings to fly, for he wanted madly to be there with her now, as well. Never had he felt more helpless in his life. "God damn the bastard!" he swore, feeling sickened.

"Why did you not send word to your father, Alyss?" Graeham asked her.

She lifted her chin proudly, straightening her spine, her dark eyes shimmering. "My father died that very year, m'lord. There was never an opportunity. Yet do I know that he would have come for me . . . and my mother . . ." She lowered her head. "Well, I wished not to distress her any more than my father's death already had. And then she, too, passed the following winter."

"Was there no one else?" Graeham persisted.

She shook her head sadly. "Only my brother, but he is loyal to Beauchamp."

Blaec inhaled sharply. "And the murder you spoke of . . ."

Alyss swallowed visibly. "I was there in the bedchamber, m'lord, tending William's father, when William came in . . . I could spy it in his eyes . . ."

"What in his eyes?" Blaec asked.

Alyss nodded jerkily. "His intent. Whilst his father slept, I watched him walk to his bedside, bestow upon his cheek the kiss of peace . . . and then proceed to asphyxiate him with a pillow . . . quite calmly and coldly . . . and then he lifted out his sword from his scabbard, and with it reopened the very wound his father had received by your sire's hands. Before my eyes he did murder his own father—that I swear to you, as God is my witness."

Blaec surged upward from the chair, to his feet, cursing profusely. "That whoreson allowed everyone to believe our father had dealt the killing blow."

Alyss flinched, moving warily away from him in his anger. "So you see, m'lord . . . that . . . that is how I know he would and will kill Dominique. It matters not what he feels for her. If he says he will do so, then he shall. 'Tis the truth that you may consider it done."

Dread raced down Blaec's spine, prickling his arms, his legs.

What if already they were too late? His stomach twisted.

"If you care anything for her at all, m'lord . . . then you *will* go after her and bring her back safely."

Graeham's face retained his shock. "If what you say is true . . ."

"Bastard!" Blaec exploded once more. "I *am* going after her," he said.

"Aye," Graeham agreed. "We must go after her."

"Nay," Blaec denied him at once. "You shall stay, I will go. We cannot both place ourselves at risk in this, and you are wounded, besides."

Graeham nodded, relenting, though reluctantly. "Mayhap you are right . . . though I wouldst bid you send word and assemble men enough to accompany you to Arndel. You've no way of knowing how many men Beauchamp has already amassed. As you know, I took with me nineteen to London, and thought myself well defended, yet did he have at least that many, and mayhap more."

"There is no time," Blaec told him, refusing. "I shall take as many as Drakewich can spare, and no more."

"Blaec," Graeham cautioned, "that can be no more than the nine I returned with me from London . . . mayhap ten, if Langford has not returned to his wife . . ."

"He is gone," Blaec told him. "No matter . . . the nine will have to serve."

A fateful silence filled the room.

"Go, then . . . if you must," Graeham relented. "I—" His voice broke. "I shall wish you Godspeed and a safe return, my brother."

"My *brother*," Blaec returned, coming forward, to Graeham's bedside, extending his arm. "God granted us the same womb," he said, "and I am grateful for it, for I am proud to share your blood."

"I was never persuaded by our father's ravings—I only wished he could have seen the truth . . . that we indeed share the same blood." They locked arms, and the two embraced in that fashion for an awkward moment. And then, unable to keep himself from it, Blaec knelt and embraced Graeham as they had done when they were children, a full-bodied clasp that bespoke their fierce allegiance.

"Do me a favor," Graeham said gruffly, throwing his own words back at him, "try not to die before your return . . ."

Blaec ceded a chuckle. "I wouldn't dream of it," he swore.

Chapter 31

Within the hour, Blaec rode out from Drakewich with a contingent of nine—Nial at his flank, bearing his banner high against the noonday sun, its golden threads glittering fiercely.

Yet no fiercer than Blaec's mood.

Though the distance from Drakewich was a mere three and a half hour's journey, it seemed to continue without end. His thoughts driving him like demon hounds, he pushed his men harder, faster, without mercy.

There would be no mercy for Dominique did he not arrive in time.

He tried not to think about her—reflected instead on the ways he would torture Beauchamp. Never had he taken so much pleasure in the prospect of one man's death, but he fully intended to make Beauchamp pay for *all* his treachery.

Before the sun set this day, he swore, *one of them would writhe in the flames of hell.*

"Lady Dominique . . . please . . . unlatch the door . . ."

Hearing Rufford's voice instead of William's, Dominique went to the door, speaking through the crack. "Why?" she asked him warily. "What is it you wish of me, Rufford?"

She'd locked herself within last eve, and had sworn to die of hunger rather than come out and face her brother again. And at the moment, she felt as though it were a possibility, for her belly had been grumbling for the last hour. Still, she refused . . .

"Lady Dominique . . ." He sounded as dispirited as Dominique felt, but she didn't care. She couldn't care. If he would serve her brother in his heinous dictums, she cared not a whit what punishment would come to him.

"I'll not open the door," she told him with certainty. "If you wouldst come within . . . 'twill be by force, for I'll not go willingly."

"But you cannot stay in there forever, m'lady . . . You must needs eat sometime . . ."

Dominique snorted. "I know not why!" she said with no small amount of hysteria. "He plans to kill me anyway, Rufford. What does it matter whether I eat, or nay?"

Silence met her proclamation. And then, "I do not believe he wouldst truly do so, m'lady . . . He is but angry, I think . . ."

Once again Dominique snorted. "Aye?" she snapped. "Well, I didst not believe him capable of what he has done to me, and yet he has. How can you know what William intends? Nay—I'll not come out. I would as lief—"

There was a sudden commotion on the other side of the door, and Dominique backed away from it, fully expecting to see it fly from its frame. When it did not, she returned to it, placing her ear to it. "Rufford?" she called out.

She could hear him speaking in low, frantic tones behind it, to whom, she could not tell, but he did not respond at once . . . and then he did. "M'lady," he said firmly now, rapping sharply upon the door. "I must insist you unlock the door. My lord William . . . he wouldst have you brought to the castle walls."

"Why?" she demanded to know.

"Blaec d'Lucy . . ."

Dominique's heart tumbled violently at hearing his name. God—*Blaec*. He was here. Her hands trembling, she unlatched the door at once.

"'Tis not good enough, Beauchamp!" Blaec called upward. His destrier pranced restlessly beneath him, snorting impatiently. He'd ridden in mere moments before, and had summoned William at once, issuing him a challenge he knew the bastard could not refuse. He waited now, negotiating the terms, whilst they brought Dominique before him. "I want her here below!" he exacted, pointing to the ground before him. "I want her here where I might see for myself that she is unharmed—not there upon your God-accursed walls, Beauchamp!"

A weighty silence drifted down from the walls.

"Come now, Beauchamp," Blaec taunted, removing his helm to peer up at William's silhouette standing arms akimbo upon the parapet above. *Arrogant bastard!* "You cannot be afeared to face me?" he mocked him. "Or can it be that the mighty Beauchamp has only the heart for deceit?"

"Afeared of you?" William snorted. "Hardly, d'Lucy! I merely wonder why I should give you any advantage at all. Look around you. I can do what I wish with a single command from my lips, lest you forget . . ."

"Aye, but then you must take Drakewich by force. A formidable task at best," he reminded him. "Murdering me outright will not get you within those gates, and 'twill gain you Stephen's wrath, besides."

"Hah! Stephen is a milksop!" William shouted down to him, laughing uproariously at the prospect of earning the king's wrath.

Blaec could not argue when he thought much the same of their vacillating king. Though he was no coward, by far, neither was Stephen a daunting force, and justice was never imminent. 'Twas said openly, in truth, that Christ and his saints slept whilst Stephen sat England's throne. "Nevertheless," he persisted, "accept my challenge and you gain yourself witnesses. What have you to lose? Unless you are afeared of me, Beauchamp?"

"Afeared of you?"

"Bring her down," Blaec insisted, "or I ride away now and you will lose your chance at *earning* Drakewich."

Again silence.

"Think on it, William . . . Do you best me in hand-to-hand combat, I will commit myself into your hands—myself in exchange for Dominique's freedom. 'Tis a small price to pay."

Blaec could tell by his stance that he was wavering. "And you say Graeham is dead?" William relented at last.

This time it was Blaec's turn for silence, though he did not hesitate long. One lie, for the good of all.

"Aye," Blaec answered tersely, "my brother is dead," he lied. If it would damn his soul to hell for eternity, then so be it. If William thought Blaec the last obstacle betwixt himself and Drakewich, then it would serve him all the better. He doubted William would come down elsewise, for he had nothing to gain, save to kill him—and that, he could do easily enough from whence he stood. As he'd pointed out, he need only give the signal for his men to rain their arrows down upon him.

Nay . . . this way if Beauchamp thought Graeham dead, and he believed himself, in his vainglory, able to defeat Blaec, then he would have the added incentive of securing witnesses to their bargain in order to carry his case before Stephen. Though it would do little more than facilitate his taking of Drakewich, it would save him much grief in the end—or so he would think.

Only Blaec didn't intend to lose.

If there wouldst be trickery here this day, then it would be his own, and he felt no dishonor in using it, for he'd never claimed to be the saintly one; that was Graeham's role. He only knew how to survive.

"Come down, Beauchamp . . . and should you succeed in killing me, as well," he challenged, "then Drakewich will be yours at long last. Isn't that what you wish?"

"'Tis my right to hold it," William called down to him, his tone bitter. "My right! Do you hear me? 'Twas stolen from my father!"

Blaec's jaw clenched. "Aye," he shouted back. "I hear you, Beauchamp! Come down now," he challenged once more. "Come down, or you shall be evidenced as the coward you—"

The words fled from his tongue as the figure of a woman appeared above upon the parapet, her hair a burning mass of ringlets, glinting red against the waning sun. She was dragged before William, only to be jerked about to face Blaec below.

Dominique.

Blaec flinched in the saddle, for his gut wrenched at the sight of her. Though he could not see her face from whence he sat, he saw her shoulders were drawn back proudly, and he wanted to do nothing more in that instant than wrap his fingers about Beauchamp's neck and squeeze until he breathed his last.

His own sister.

The very thought of it sickened him.

"You wished proof," William called down to him. "Well, here she is, d'Lucy . . . Feast your eyes upon her now, because today you die— as does she, for her faithlessness, when I am through with you."

Fury surged through him. "Nay!" he bellowed. "I want her here before me," he shouted, beginning to lose his patience. His knees clasped his mount with such ferocity that it protested, rearing, and nearly unseated him. "God damn you!" he said. "Bring her down, Beauchamp! Do it now! Or the deal is done," he swore.

William laughed from his perch above them. "Very well," he relented at last, seemingly pleased with Blaec's reaction to his words. "I think it would suit me well enough to have her see you die at that." With that, he shoved her before him, urging her to walk the parapet. Blaec could see that she resisted, stumbling, but William lifted her up and propelled her swiftly along before him. They disappeared from view as they started below.

Blaec waited for what seemed an eternity as the gates were unlocked, adrenaline surging through his veins. And then, at last, they flew wide, and he caught his breath at the sight of her. Beauchamp—the coward—appeared with half his garrison at his back, but he saw none of them, only her.

His eyes drank in the sight of her. Like some dirty waif, she wore the same blue bliaut he'd last seen her in, though it was wrinkled now and unkempt. Her hair was wild, her ringlets uncombed. And her face— he watched Beauchamp's approach with barely suppressed rage—it was swollen and bruised, her lips split and bloodied.

Cursing profusely, Blaec dismounted with a vengeance, unable to bear the sight of her, so abused, even an instant longer. *Christ, but he would kill the bastard!*

Without preamble, he replaced his helm upon his head, and then started toward them, scowling, uncaring that his anger was manifest within his eyes. "I'll kill you, you filthy whoreson!" he exclaimed, never hesitating in his stride. He unsheathed his sword as he stalked him.

Seeing his intent, Beauchamp shoved Dominique away, into the arms of his men, and then moved to his right, away from her, backing away from Blaec, his own eyes gleeful. "It does my heart such good to see you so enraged," he said, laughing, skipping backward as he retrieved his own sword from his scabbard.

"You bloody bastard!" Blaec exploded, and lunged at him, slicing the air between them with such force that the air sang. Yet in his blind fury, he missed.

Beauchamp laughed again, hideously. "Is she worth dying for, d'Lucy? Does my harlot sister lie so well beneath you?" He hooted hysterically.

Blaec snarled at him, once more slicing the air between them, his eyes glittering coldly, and this time he came too close for Beauchamp's comfort. Blaec discerned the instant William's mood changed, for he recognized the look of sudden apprehension in his eyes. With that knowledge, something inside him snapped, and he was propelled to protect that which he valued. *Loved.*

He loved Dominique—and he would protect her with his life!

"Tell me," Beauchamp gibed, daring to provoke him still, "who will be left to protect her when you are gone to feed the worms?"

Blaec felt the change come over him, felt himself transform with rage. With a hellish battle cry, he positioned himself and wheeled with his sword, placing the strength of his body into his swing, crying out as he moved with blinding speed. Beauchamp was not quick enough to avoid the slice of his blade. Blaec heard the shredding of his mail, and was spurred by the metallic smell of blood.

Beauchamp cried out, falling backward with the impact, dislodging his helm in the fall. He ripped it off in order to see as Blaec charged him again. He lifted himself up, barely avoiding another swipe of Blaec's sword. Standing again, he lifted his own sword and struck a blow.

Blaec met it with his own.

The clashing of metal rent the air.

Feinting and slicing, Blaec and William battled until both were perspiring with the exertion, and still Blaec continued, unrelenting.

Until he chanced to look up and spy the look of horror upon Dominique's face . . . It took him aback enough that he evaded the next strike much too slowly, taking a slice upon the shoulder. He felt the warmth of his own blood run down his arm. The smell of it, coupled with the image of Dominique's anguished expression, caused him to reel. With the next strike, he fell backward, staving off William's blows with a strength and fervor that came from desperation. His helm went flying, leaving him, like his opponent, without protection against a blow to the head.

But he had no intention of dying—or placing his head within reach of William's sword, for that matter.

If Dominique was repulsed of him for this, then so be it, but he could not allow her to remain in her brother's vile hands. If it meant she would despise him for all eternity, it couldn't be helped, he told himself. He intended to kill the bastard, once and for all—for he deemed Beauchamp's perfidy against Graeham and his father, as well as his offenses against Dominique.

With a ruthless war cry, he struck out, knocking William off balance with the impact, and then thrust his sword above his head, and rolled, surging to his feet with ease, despite the weight of his mail and his wounds. Nor could he feel the blood dripping down his arm any longer.

With renewed determination, he went after William, slicing and hacking at the air between them. Once again, he spun, crying out, and this time he caught William's sword, cleaving it in twain with the force of his blow. The tip of his own sword went flying at the impact.

Startled murmurs filled the air about them.

With both of their swords destroyed, and William empty-handed, Blaec cast aside his own broken blade and went after him barefisted. Bellowing in outrage, he dove at him, driving him backward with the impact onto the bare ground. With a snarl, Blaec locked his hands about Beauchamp's neck and began to squeeze.

Together they rolled upon the ground, each struggling to dominate the other. First Blaec gained the advantage, then William, yet Blaec's hold upon William's neck was so fierce that even when he prevailed on top, straddling Blaec, he could not retain the advantage. He tried to reach for his sword, but the effort lost him his balance.

Once again, Blaec rolled, jerking Beauchamp along with him, and then straddled him. His eyes burning with anger, he clutched Beauchamp's neck tighter, pressing his thumb into the soft spot of his throat, feeling the life pulse beat against his flesh.

God help him, it would be so easy to crush it.
So easy.

William coughed, spewing, urgently seeking air, and in that instant of hesitation Blaec came aware of Dominique's shrieks behind him. Yet he continued to squeeze until William's eyes bulged and his face turned scarlet, and then blue.

And still her screams pierced his ears, driving him to distraction.

"Stop!" she was crying out. "Please . . . please stop," she wailed at his back.

He tried but could not, so fierce was the hold his battle fury held upon his body and his mind. William reached up, groping, and in his desperation ripped the ventail from Blaec's face.

And still her screams and shrieks split the air.

With a savage cry, he released Beauchamp's throat, unable to finish the bastard off with

Dominique witnessing it and screaming so hysterically.

Damn, but he could not do it!

Cursing in disgust of himself, he seized hold of Beauchamp's head instead, slamming it repeatedly, fiercely, against the hard-packed ground until William's eyes rolled backward into his head and then closed, and then Blaec surged to his feet, cursing, panting.

He spun to face Dominique, his expression murderous, and found her brother's men restraining her as she struggled to free herself.

He spied her battered face again, and rage, black and potent, filled his veins. "Take your filthy hands from her!" he commanded them, and like a man possessed, he charged after them, vengeance burning in his eyes.

The two who held her released her at once, their expressions alarmed as they retreated.

Once again Dominique began to shriek, but he couldn't stop himself; he kept going. He lifted up his sword from the ground as he passed it, fully intending to slice the heart out of each and every man who had dared to touch her. Like a madwoman, she shook her head frantically, screaming and waving her arms, and he paused, staggered by her reaction to him. It seemed for an instant that she was screaming in fear of him, and he shook his head, unable to bear it.

Didn't she understand that he did it for her?

"Nay!" she shrieked, her face bloodless. "Nay! William! Nay!" she screamed, and waved her arms, racing toward him, and in that instant, Blaec understood.

He spun to face William Beauchamp.

William had revived, his face swelling already, and stood a staggered instant before coming at him, his sword upraised, cursing.

Blaec wasted not a breath in his decision. Clenching his jaw, he raised his own jagged sword and charged at William, driving his blade with a single thrust through William's chest. He heard the splintering of ribs, and still he was not appeased. With another savage cry, he drove William's body backward, skewering it through and pinning him, with the might of his drive, into the very ground.

For an instant he watched with morbid fascination as William's blood seeped into the unfertile ground, poisoning it again.

"*Like father like son*," he spat, hissing the charge. "Only this time I *will* see you die!" he swore. "Before my eyes I will watch you breathe your last, Beauchamp!" With that, he drove once more, putting the weight of his body into the final thrust, pinioning William's massive frame inescapably to the ground.

"By the by," he added with great satisfaction, "*I lied.*" He wanted Beauchamp to hear the truth before he died, wanted him to writhe in hell, knowing he had succeeded at nothing. "Graeham lives," he said with relish, and then he smiled fiercely.

William's eyes burned with a hatred that matched his own, though only for a moment, and then with a gurgling sound, his head fell backward to stare sightless at the heavens above. In that instant, Blaec felt only a grim satisfaction, for all that mattered was that the bastard was dead at long last.

In his savage state of mind, it took him another befuddled instant to recognize that Dominique's screams had ended at long last. He spun to face her and found her insensate within Nial's arms. Nial embraced her, facing him, staring in silence, his own face expressionless, as were those of the men surrounding him—his own and Beauchamp's alike.

As he stood there, realizing the full impact of his actions—that she had witnessed the murder of her own brother, by his own hands—his face drained of blood.

Why was it the unloved fought so hard to gain what could not be held? The old question came back to haunt him.

As yet there was no answer. He only knew that it had not mattered *what* his father had done to him; he had sought Gilbert's love to the bitter end, and then, upon his death, he had grieved—as hard as any other.

And with that bit of knowledge, another question burned: *Could Dominique forgive him?*

Chapter 32

Dominique couldn't recall when she'd wept so much.

Though she told herself that it was the only course that could have been taken, and that her brother had long before chosen it, still she grieved for him.

And the guilt—it tore at her like daggers.

When William's men had started after them, she'd known they would interfere, and so she'd fought them wildly, screaming and shouting to make Blaec aware of them.

Alerting Blaec to her brother's fatal advance was another thing entirely. It seemed the ultimate betrayal.

Yet had she to do it over again . . . *she wouldst do so again.* As difficult as it was to see her brother die so violently before her, it would have been thrice that to see Blaec succumb to her brother's treasonous sword. God's truth, but she could never have borne it.

They had returned to Drakewich straightaway, arriving in the dead hours of the night, and Dominique had ensconced herself at once within Blaec's chamber. She'd slept for most of the morning and then the afternoon, wearied by her emotions and just simple exhaustion. And then she eschewed the midday meal, for she had no appetite—every time she thought of yesterday's bloody battle, she felt only like flying to the garderobe.

She kept hoping that Blaec would come to her, for she had not the energy to seek him out. God's truth, but all she wished just now was for him to hold her . . . but he did not come. When a soft knock came upon the door shortly after the dispersement of the evening meal, she glanced up in anticipation, bidding the visitor to enter, hoping to see Blaec.

She was startled to find Graeham there instead. He came in, gazing at her with no small measure of concern, and it warmed her heart to have him look at her so.

"I've no wish to disturb you," he said.

"Nay," she cried, swiping the tears from her face at once. "Please come in . . ."

He did, closing the door behind him, and Dominique noted the way that he held his chest as he walked, the grimace upon his face as he came to the foot of her bed. Guilt plagued her once more, for though she'd not wounded him herself, her brother certainly had. She didn't know how he could bear to look at her.

"May I?" he asked, waving a hand at the bed as he sat upon it.

In this way both of these brothers were alike— both wouldst do as they pleased, only Graeham, at least, seemed inclined to ask his leave after- ward. Dominique choked on a weary giggle.

"Forgive me, my lord," she said, sitting to face him, "but it seems to me you already have."

Graeham chuckled softly. "God's teeth! but my brother is right . . . You *are* an impudent wench."

Dominique's brows drew together dejectedly. Her lashes lowered. "He said that, did he?"

"Among other things," Graeham relented, his eyes glimmering. He sighed, she thought, at her reaction. "I came, Lady Dominique, to speak my piece, and so I shall do so and then leave you be at last."

Dominique braced herself, knowing he had every right to scorn her for all that her family had done to his. Alyss had revealed to her everything, had cried with her, held her and caressed her face, telling her the fault was not her own . . . but Dominique knew otherwise. "What is it you came to say to me?" she asked guardedly.

"Two things . . . among them a simple little tale," he revealed cryptically.

Dominique met his gaze charily. "First, I wish to ask your pardon for the way in which I treated you when first you came to Drakewich . . ."

She could scarcely mask her shock. She inhaled sharply, her face twisting, and shook her head adamantly. "Oh, nay, my lord—nay! 'Tis I who must beg your forgiveness! I never meant to . . ." She averted her eyes suddenly, and again shook her head, unable to speak the words. "I never meant to betray you with Blaec," she finished lamely.

"God's truth . . . it was not your failing. That . . ." He shook his head, as though considering how best to proceed. "You see . . . that is precisely what I wished to tell you. Dominique . . . you must trust me when I say that nothing transpired beneath this roof that I was not wholly aware of."

Dominique frowned, uncomprehending.

"Truly," he assured her, "everything ensued as I intended it should. In truth, 'tis to you and to Blaec that I must offer my apologies—and this I do wholeheartedly—yet there was no other way to accomplish what I felt must be done." It was his turn to appear discomposed. He averted his gaze momentarily. "The bloody truth is that given the same circumstances, I wouldst do so again. Yet—" his gaze met and locked with hers "—it would all be for naught do you not love him . . ."

Dominique felt her tears begin anew. She opened her mouth to speak, but he held up a hand, bidding her not to do so as yet.

"Before you answer that . . . allow me to tell you the second thing I came to . . ."

Tears welling in her eyes, Dominique nodded, feeling the emotion rise like a lump in her throat. *Did he not know? Could he not see in her eyes what she felt for his brother? She was lost without him.*

He smiled wanly. "Once on a time," he began, the glimmer in his eyes dimming, "there was a man and a woman who fell deeply in love . . . but the woman was betrothed to another and they could not love each other openly. And then the woman's betrothed was killed at war, and the woman was free to love where she would . . . and so then she and her love were free to wed at last. This they did, and it was not long before the woman found herself with child . . ." His voice trailed, and then he continued, "Twin sons, they were. One fair as his father and his mother . . . the other one dark . . ." He swallowed visibly. "Dark as the woman's dead betrothed."

Dominique blinked back tears. "Blaec?" she asked hoarsely, beginning to comprehend the tale.

Graeham nodded, and Dominique could tell that the telling of this particular tale pained him considerably. "At any rate . . . the boys' sire at once began to recount the days since their espousals, and found them too few in number. He found, too, that the dates coincided with the final time the wife had last seen the dead betrothed, and though he loved her . . . he could not keep himself from wondering. Even as she denied it vehemently, it plagued him. Yet the one son, he could not deny, for he was too much like himself. Though the other . . ." His jaw tightened. "The other he shunned."

For an instant there was only silence between them, for Dominique knew not what to say. "Did he never accept him?"

"Do you know of the scar Blaec bears upon his cheek?" he asked her by way of response.

Dominique nodded.

"'Twas done by my father," Graeham revealed. "Blaec wanted so desperately that our father should be proud of him upon his knighting, and when my father stepped in to administer the *colee*, Blaec's eyes did shine." He breathed in deeply, closing his eyes with the memory, and when he reopened them, they were shimmering with pain. "If my own heart was fraught with joy and pride that my father would at last accept him, Blaec's was near to bursting. He knelt there, his shoulders straight, his head lifted proudly, waiting patiently, unable to conceal the pleasure in his eyes as my father removed his sword from his scabbard." Graeham's jaw worked with emotion as he relived the moment. "And then my father did rear his arm back, and he smote him with the hilt of it—with all the strength of his body. God's truth . . ." His voice broke. "I thought he did shatter every bone in Blaec's face. Blaec fell backward from the blow, and then recovered himself, jolted. Yet he did nothing but kneel again before our father, still reeling from the buffet. God . . . he knelt there, blood flowing from his wound, and his eyes shadowing with pain even as I watched, but he took that blow like a man."

Tears streamed down Dominique's face. She could not speak, imagining him so spiritually broken. "He lied to me," she said choking on the words. "He lied when I asked . . ." Her heart longed for the little boy he'd been—she wanted to reach back in time and hold him, tell him that *she* loved him.

Graeham nodded. "It surprises me not, for he would never speak of it after." He smiled sadly. "Until you came, my brother's emotions were scant. He showed them not at all, neither

anger nor joy. Yet since you arrived here at
Drakewich, I have seen them both aplenty . . .
beginning from the moment you rode into the
bailey. You should have seen his face . . . Aye,
he loves you, Dominique," he told her. "Now I
ask you . . . *do you love him?*"

She laughed nervously, shrugging. "He's such
a domineering brute."

Graeham chuckled at her response. "Funny
you say so, but I did not ask you what you
thought of him," he debated, "I asked what you
felt . . ."

Dominique sighed deeply. "Aye," she relented, her eyes shimmering with tears all over
again. "I do, Graeham . . . with every piece of
my heart and my soul. *I do.*"

His eyes crinkled. "Then you must go to him,
for he'll not come to you. 'Tis long now been
Blaec's philosophy that he not pursue what he
may not have. Lest a prize fall into his lap, he'll
not see it."

Dominique nodded, and Graeham stood to
go.

"He is in the hall below if you wouldst seek
him," he disclosed. "And now, alas, I am off
to bed once more." He winked at her, grinning
mischievously. "Lest Alyss spy me upon my
feet, and decide not to tend me any longer."

Dominique smiled. "Thank you, my lord."

He stood looking down upon her an instant
longer, and then said, "Go to my brother with
my blessings, Lady Dominique." His eyes sparkled once more. "Make my domineering brother
happy," he urged her, "tell him what is in your

heart. He will receive it well, I assure you." And with that he turned to go, leaving Dominique to consider his words.

She didn't consider them long. She rose from the bed determinedly, refusing to pity herself any longer. What was done was done, and naught would reverse it. And the last thing she intended was to lose the man she loved, as well.

Not wanting him to see her with her face stained with tears, she washed it quickly over the lavatory, and then brushed her hair loose, letting it flow over her shoulders as it would—there was little else she could do for the riotous mass. And then after finding and lighting a taper, she made her way down the stairs, halting abruptly at the foot of it.

She found him easily enough, though he sat in the dark, for the hall was deserted elsewise. The servants, having finished with their labors, had dispersed. Only one torch remained lit, braced upon the far wall; its light cast his shadow into twisted forms at his back. He sat dejectedly, his head within his hands, brooding.

Seeing him there, she felt her heart trip. Dominique didn't want him to feel the guilt, didn't want him to hurt. She wanted to put her arms about him and hold him, soothe him.

She wanted to run to him.

Chapter 33

He heard her before he saw her.

Seeking the sound, Blaec removed his hand from his face, raking it down over his whiskered jaw, and when he spied her coming into the hall, his breath caught within his throat. Like some faerie angel she drifted toward him, her ivory gown swirling about her feet with the draft, a lighted taper in hand. She held her hand about its flame, protecting it, lest it go out, and it reflected upon her face.

Like the night he'd made love to her by candlelight, she froze when their gazes met, looking as though she would run did he so much as open his mouth to speak. The wavering glow illumed her eyes, and caught the glints of copper in the hair that flowed over her shoulders. Like snow before the sun's heat, his heart melted within him.

He swallowed, for 'twas the first time he'd set eyes upon her since their return to Drakewich. God's truth, he'd feared to look within her eyes, only to spy the hatred and revulsion there.

He couldn't have borne it.

Yet as she neared—though he could spy the evidence of her tears in her red-rimmed eyes,

364

and her pink little nose—he saw none of those emotions, and his pulse began to hammer like that of an untried youth as she came to stand before the lord's table.

"Dominique," he began, but found his tongue too thick to continue, his mouth too dry.

They stood staring at each other an instant—though only an instant, for from somewhere above them came the most ungodly sounds. Dominique started visibly at the cacophony, her face twisting in startle, and then at once she seemed to regain her composure.

Her brows lifted, and her lips curved at the corners. "It seems as though Drakewich has been inhabited by spirits in my absence," she said saucily.

Blaec chuckled softly, glancing toward the ceiling, his own lips curving. "'Tis Graeham . . ."

"And Alyss . . . I know," she said, ducking her head and smiling.

By the light of the taper, he watched as her blush spread down her creamy throat to her bosom. "I recognize the sounds," she confessed, laughing softly, her blush deepening. She met his gaze once more. "In truth . . . I used to believe that she and William were fighting when I was younger."

Blaec cocked a brow. "I can see why," he said.

"And later . . . well, enough to say that it always amazed me someone so timid and so quiet as Alyss could be so boisterous . . . er . . . during that time . . ." She nodded abashedly. "Well, you know, my lord . . ."

He did, and he chuckled at her guarded phrasing. Yet he did not share her squeamishness. In fact, the very thought of the word aroused him. *She aroused him.* "It seems my brother is a noisy lover as well . . ." He inhaled sharply and grew sober suddenly, shaking his head and exhaling. He leaned back into his chair. "All those years . . . and I never knew . . ."

"Knew what?"

He shook his head, knowing Graeham would not have him share his private affairs, not even with Dominique. "'Tis naught," he yielded. "Naught of consequence."

And once again there was silence between them.

Dominique swallowed visibly and parted her lips to speak. He waited; nothing came.

"I . . ." She glanced away, and then back, staring at his shoulder, looking somewhat disconcerted. "I am sorry for your wound," she said at last, again meeting his gaze, her blue eyes sorrowful. "H-How does it fare?"

Blaec shrugged. "'Tis naught." His voice softened at her disheartened look, reassuring her, "Truly . . . Alyss tended it in less than five minutes' time."

She peered down at the candle in her hands, hiding her face from him—yet it only managed to reveal the shimmer of tears upon her lashes. His jaw clenched at seeing them. He wanted to spare her from tears the rest of her life.

"Aye . . . well, I suppose I should thank you for coming for me," she said, her voice faltering slightly. "Though I would not have blamed you had you left me." Her blue eyes returned to him. "I should never have gone at all," she yielded with self-contempt.

Blaec's heart wrenched for her. She deserved better. *Bastard!* he railed at William silently. God ... he wanted to make up for everything that whoreson had done to her. "I am sorry, too," he told her. "Though mostly I am sorry you were forced to witness his death," he said truthfully. "Can you forgive me, Dominique?"

"My lord ... there is nothing to forgive. I knew someone would meet death," she said. "I only prayed it would not be you."

Relief jolted through him. Yet as much as her words eased him, they aggrieved him as well, for what must she have suffered at his hands that she could absolve him so easily of her brother's murder? "Did he harm you?" he asked her.

She shook her head at once. "Only my heart," she admitted, looking grief-stricken. "He ... he ..." Her eyes closed, and Blaec thought he'd spare her the grief of recounting the tale just now. Some other time he would hear it ... when she was ready to speak it.

Providing she didn't leave him. She was by no means obligated to stay. Stephen would surely welcome her as his ward—would leap at the opportunity, in fact, to offer both Dominique and Arndel to some fortunate man.

And any man would gladly accept them.

Over his dead body.

He gritted his teeth. "I already know, Dominique," he said softly. "Alyss told me aught."

She nodded, and seemed to be battling her emotions. "Blaec," she began.

"You need not say it," he reassured her.

Her eyes gleamed with tears. "*I love you.*"

He stiffened. "What did you say?"

"*I . . . I said that I love you.*" She spoke the words like a child standing in the shadows, afeared of the dark.

Joy rolled through him like thunder. He swallowed convulsively. "You love me?" he asked, choking on the question.

Dominique nodded uncertainly, blinking back the tears from her eyes.

His voice was gruff with emotion. "*Come hither, Dominique.*"

She did as he bade her, hesitating only an instant before coming around the table to his side. Without a word, Blaec removed the candlestick from her grasp and set it down upon the table, sliding it down out of their way. He then lifted her up, and sat her, too, upon the table before him. She gasped in surprise, but remained, nevertheless, with nary a protest, though she appeared never more bewildered.

He gazed into her beautiful blue eyes, and bent to grasp her ankles dangling before him. Cradling them, he brushed at her flesh gently with his thumb, and then moved up to caress her calves beneath her gown, raising it slightly in the process. "Do you know how badly I wanted to do this the first time that I saw them exposed?" he asked her, caressing her legs. "Do you remember, Dominique . . . when you caught your gown dismounting?"

Dominique felt as though her heart would stop at his touch. His attentions never ceased to steal her breath away. She nodded mutely, her heart tripping as he moved his fingers slightly higher.

"Now repeat to me what you said mere moments ago," he demanded silkily, "lest I misunderstood you . . ."

Dominique caught her breath sharply. He was scandalous and domineering . . . and oh, so strong . . . yet possessing a gentle touch. "God's truth, but you are an arrogant brute," she told him.

"Am I?" he asked her, unrepenting. He lifted her gown to her thigh. "And . . ."

"*And I love you, even so,*" she relented at last, frowning down at him as she endeavored to lower her gown. She slapped his hand beneath her dress, laughing. "You are incorrigible," she swore vehemently.

He grinned, his teeth flashing white, and his eyes sparkling devilishly. "Since when?" he asked, spreading her legs suddenly, and settling himself between them.

"Blaec!" she gasped, and frowned down at him, scandalized that he would take such liberties here within the hall. "Not here!" she cried softly, and peered over her shoulder.

"No one is watching, Dominique. I only wish to hold you, at any rate," he assured her, his tone as innocent as that of a boy as he wrapped his arms about her waist. "Now tell me, when did you first know?"

She shivered within his arms, loving the feel of him so close. Wicked though it might be, there was something delicious about the way he was settled between her thighs. "Since the moment I fell in love with you, of course!" she answered flippantly, entwining her fingers within his silky hair.

He gazed up at her, persisting, "And when was that?"

Dominique sighed breathlessly, her heart racing with his nearness. "In the forest . . . I first knew it then," she confessed, her voice husky and slightly flustered. "You are a wicked, insatiable man," she accused him, but she wrapped her legs about him, nevertheless.

He inhaled sharply, and tugged her down to sit upon his lap. Dominique cried out, laughing. "And you are a tease," he returned huskily, leaning to touch the warmth of his mouth to hers. It seemed as though when their lips met, a chorus rang out in Dominique's head, a symphony of heavenly voices that deafened her and infused her heart with joy.

"Stay with me, Dominique," he rasped, "be my bride . . . 'Tis God's truth that I do love you, as well," he murmured against her mouth.

As she heard his profession of love, Dominique's heart flowered with a gladness unlike any she'd ever known. "I will," she said, wrapping her arms about his neck, embracing him, clinging to the promise of his words. "Only tell me, my lord," she ventured haughtily, "when did *you* first know?"

"Know what?" he answered soberly.

"That you loved me, of course!"

"Hmmmm . . . did I say that I did?" he teased her, peering into her eyes, mischief dancing in his own.

Dominique laughed and smacked the back of his head with her open palm—and none too softly. "Only just now!" she berated him.

"Aye! Only now do I recall it," he said, reaching back and rubbing his head. "Mind you, demoiselle, that I am a wounded man!" he added plaintively, chuckling richly.

Laughter bubbled up from the depths of her.

"When did I first know that I loved you?" He repeated the question to himself, sighing. "'Tis simple." He grinned, forgetting his head and holding her close once more. He tightened his arms about her, and lowered his head, nestling the scarred side of his cheek against the pulse at her throat, listening to the quickening beat that matched his own. And for an instant he merely held her thus, savoring the simple pleasure of holding the woman he loved within his arms. He sighed then, and relented at last, "There, too, in the forest you spoke of . . . once upon a kiss . . ."

Dominique pouted. "Are you certain 'twas not sooner?" she asked him, her brows knitting. "Graeham said 'twas when you first spied me."

He chuckled softly. "Ah . . . well, did he now? That, I fear, was but a healthy dose of lust."

She gasped indignantly, lowering her lip. "And how is it you know the difference now, my lord?" she asked him petulantly.

"Simple," he revealed, his voice husky. "Because I would be as content to hold you just so, Dominique . . . for the rest of my given days." And then he proceeded to prove his point, though he had designs in haunting his own keep this night. He held her fast, till even the torchlight exhausted and guttered, flickering out.

And still he held her in the soft light of the candle that burned at their side; two figures entwined, sharing the same heartbeat.

Farther up the stairwell, in the darkness, two indistinguishable figures watched unobserved. And then even the two wearied, and smiling, turned and mounted the tower steps.

"You did well, m'lord," whispered the one.

"Aye," agreed the other. "And now I deserve my reward . . ."

There was a smile in the soft feminine voice as she replied, "Again, m'lord? You will kill yourself as yet."

"And die a happy man," he returned.

Quiet laughter drifted down after them, even as their paces quickened upward, leaving the two below to follow their own amorous pursuits.

Avon Romantic Treasures

Unforgettable, enthralling love stories,
sparkling with passion and adventure
from Romance's bestselling authors

CAPTIVES OF THE NIGHT *by Loretta Chase*
76648-5/$4.99 US/$5.99 Can

CHEYENNE'S SHADOW *by Deborah Camp*
76739-2/$4.99 US/$5.99 Can

FORTUNE'S BRIDE *by Judith E. French*
76866-6/$4.99 US/$5.99 Can

GABRIEL'S BRIDE *by Samantha James*
77547-6/$4.99 US/$5.99 Can

COMANCHE FLAME *by Genell Dellin*
77524-7/ $4.99 US/ $5.99 Can

WITH ONE LOOK *by Jennifer Horsman*
77596-4/ $4.99 US/ $5.99 Can

LORD OF THUNDER *by Emma Merritt*
77290-6/ $4.99 US/ $5.99 Can

RUNAWAY BRIDE *by Deborah Gordon*
77758-4/$4.99 US/$5.99 Can

Avon Romances—
the best in exceptional authors and unforgettable novels!

MONTANA ANGEL **Kathleen Harrington**
77059-8/ $4.50 US/ $5.50 Can

EMBRACE THE WILD DAWN **Selina MacPherson**
77251-5/ $4.50 US/ $5.50 Can

MIDNIGHT RAIN **Elizabeth Turner**
77371-6/ $4.50 US/ $5.50 Can

SWEET SPANISH BRIDE **Donna Whitfield**
77626-X/ $4.50 US/ $5.50 Can

THE SAVAGE **Nicole Jordan**
77280-9/ $4.50 US/ $5.50 Can

NIGHT SONG **Beverly Jenkins**
77658-8/ $4.50 US/ $5.50 Can

MY LADY PIRATE **Danelle Harmon**
77228-0/ $4.50 US/ $5.50 Can

THE HEART AND THE HEATHER **Nancy Richards-Akers**
77519-0/ $4.50 US/ $5.50 Can

DEVIL'S ANGEL **Marlene Suson**
77613-8/ $4.50 US/ $5.50 Can

WILD FLOWER **Donna Stephens**
77577-8/ $4.50 US/ $5.50 Can

Avon Regency Romance

SWEET FANCY
by Sally Martin 77398-8/$3.99 US/$4.99 Can

LUCKY IN LOVE
by Rebecca Robbins 77485-2/$3.99 US/$4.99 Can

A SCANDALOUS COURTSHIP
by Barbara Reeves 72151-1/$3.99 US/$4.99 Can

THE DUTIFUL DUKE
by Joan Overfield 77400-3/$3.99 US/$4.99 Can

TOURNAMENT OF HEARTS
by Cathleen Clare 77432-1/$3.99 US/$4.99 Can

DEIRDRE AND DON JUAN
by Jo Beverley 77281-7/$3.99 US/$4.99 Can

THE UNMATCHABLE MISS MIRABELLA
by Gillian Grey 77399-6/$3.99 US/$4.99 Can

FAIR SCHEMER
by Sally Martin 77397-X/$3.99 US/$4.99 Can

THE MUCH MALIGNED LORD
by Barbara Reeves 77332-5/$3.99 US/$4.99 Can

THE MISCHIEVOUS MAID
by Rebecca Robbins 77336-8/$3.99 US/$4.99Can